Knot
YOUR
Business

JILLIAN RINK

For all the people who picture themselves between three hot men.
Hope you love living through Violet.

Playlist

Welcome to New York (Taylor's Version)
Taylor Swift

Eyes Open (Taylor's Version)
Taylor Swift

Still Into You
Paramore

Hold Back the River
James Bay

Happy
NF

Vulnerable
Selena Gomez

Put Your Money Where Your Mouth Is
Ella Red

I Like Me Better
Lauv

Mistake
NF

I Can Do It With a Broken Heart
Taylor Swift

Animals
Alex & Sierra

The Only Exception
Paramore

Broken Crown
Mumford & Sons

Carry You Home
Alex Warren

Before You Read

This is a work of fiction intended for adult audiences. While there is a happy ending for Violet, this book does include violence, explicit sexual content, and potentially triggering events including parental death, abusive parents, and sexual violence.

Please consult the trigger warnings in the back of the book before reading. Your mental health matters most.

One

JASPER

"Have so much fun." Liz practically bounces in front of me, her cello already put away and perched against the wall. "Take tons of photos. Oh my gosh, I'm so excited for you both! I'm sure whoever the Council chooses will be perfect for you!"

Mason laughs, snapping the lid closed on his own cello beside me. "It's their first one, Liz. Hardly anyone gets matched on their first gala."

I ignore my friends and work to get my cello put away, double checking the humidifier and my bow's tension before shutting the case. I cross the room, opening the long term-storage locker offered at a monthly rate by the philharmonic. I'd have rather just taken it home, but the flight schedule worked out to be too tight to make a trip out to the estate and then back to Van Nuys. LA traffic downright sucks on Fridays, even worse than normal. Rylan moves by me, stashing his double bass in the same storage locker, his arm brushing mine.

Butterflies twist in my stomach, and a smile plays across my lips before I can hold it back. Not that I need to. It's been over six months since my apartment flooded, forcing me to temporarily move in with him. Six months since we finally figured out how to tell each other we craved the other. I skip over the fact it took his best friend—who was my date at the time—getting into a fist fight with him for it all to come to light. They don't bring that part up, so neither do I.

Rylan leans into me once the padlock is on the door. Our noses brush, his couple inches of height hardly noticeable when he's this close to me. His eyes are serious, his narrow jaw more pronounced from the way he clenches his teeth for a heartbeat. A low growl rumbles through him before he forces it to stop, his throat rippling with his swallow.

"You ready?" I ask, keeping my voice light. "Dominic should be here any minute."

Dominic, his friend and my other lover. Alphas are naturally wired to thrive in group dynamics, with multiple Alphas often being involved with a single central Omega. Our dynamic isn't as common, since I'm an average Beta and not an Omega, but I'm learning to be more confident about it.

With a single nod, he pulls me into his arms, kissing me without a care in the world that our coworkers are watching. Rylan is like that. From the moment I agreed to see if this could work between us, his hands have been on me. Alphas are like that. They need to touch, to mark, to know that the people around them understand that their partner is *theirs*.

And, hell, am I Rylan's.

My breath hitches as he swipes his tongue along my lower lip. My dick presses into his hip, hard and aching already.

"Come on, Rylan," Liz pouts, breaking the moment, "you'll get him all weekend. Let us at least say bye to him. He was ours first."

Rylan sighs and steps away from me. I bite back the groan that wants to rip from me. Fuck, but my friends really know how to cock block.

"You have your pin?" Liz asks the moment I'm turned back toward my friends. "And your tux is ready to go?"

"Liz, he's 26," Mason says, voice dry. He clicks his cello case closed and slings it onto his back in one move. "I'm sure he can handle his own outfit just fine. Don't forget that his boyfriend has a freaking *private jet* that they're using to fly into New York tonight. I'm sure they have a whole slew of staff that will make sure they get there in one piece in the proper attire."

Huntley laughs and nods her agreement. Liz pouts, but the outburst I'm expecting is interrupted by her quick gasp. Before I can turn, she's sprinting across the room, launching herself into a man's arms.

Huntley shakes her head. "Eventful weekend all around. Didn't realize Zach was getting back today."

Zach is one of four Alphas that Liz matched with last summer at a matching gala nearly identical to the one I'll be attending tomorrow night. He's been on deployment for the last six months, leaving just before Halloween. Liz was a mess over the holidays despite the other Alphas of her pack—and us—doing their best to keep her spirits up.

"And then there were two, Mason," Huntley says with a sigh.

Mason shrugs. "You could always call Jonas and see if he wants to go out."

I shake my head and sidestep between them. "Don't egg her on right now, Mason. Please. She just settled down over all of that."

Huntley and one of Rylan's recording buddies have been an on-again, off-again duo since the new year. Currently, they're off, and Huntley hasn't been handling it the best. She catches my gaze and shakes her head once, rolling her lips into a thin line.

Hint taken.

"You want a ride home?" I ask her, forcing the conversation away from Jonas and whoever else might be occupying her time recently.

She waves me off. "I'm fine. The walks are faster now that I'm not waiting for you to drag that *thing* behind you." She winks, and I chuckle. My cello might be larger than her instruments, but I'm no slower for it, and she knows it.

Mason's sharp intake of breath is my only warning before there's a hand on my waist, and I'm being spun around. Dominic's as breathtaking as ever, his brown eyes shining in the artificial yellow light of the room. He's dressed in his signature black-on-black slacks and button-up, though the first two buttons are undone, showing a triangle of skin just below his collarbones.

"Hey, Dom, hope you have a good weekend," Huntley says as she passes by us, grabbing her bag before putting her instruments on opposite shoulders.

None of my friends react to his sudden arrival. Technically, this room isn't supposed to be accessible to anyone other than bonded Alphas of the Omega musicians. But being directly tied to the Italian mafia has its perks when Dominic wants to use them.

"*Grazie*," my lover murmurs, not taking his gaze off mine.

Mason claps me on my shoulder as he heads past me and out the side door, his own silent wish for a good weekend. To all of them, this is the trip of a lifetime: the first matching gala we'll be attending as a registered pack. From their perspective, the best thing that could happen is the Council finds us a good fit with one of the Omegas that will be attending the black tie event alongside us tomorrow night.

None of them knows that's not even remotely our goal.

I lean into Dominic, tilting my chin so I can take his mouth with mine, easing onto my tiptoes to erase the small height difference between us. I palm his waist, tracing his lips with my tongue before pulling away.

"Time to go," Dominic says, though his voice has dropped an octave. The barest hint of citrus surrounds us. Rylan grabs my hand and kisses my shoulder. "The sooner I have you on the plane, the sooner we can play."

Two hours later, Dominic has me spread out on the absolutely monstrous bed at the back of whatever version of private jet he's told me this thing is. All I remember is that it can hold up to twelve people aside from the crew and that it won't need to stop anywhere on our way to New York City. And even that drains out of my mind as Dominic's lips close around the head of my cock.

"Oh God," I mutter, flexing my hips.

He pulls away from me. Again. He runs his hands down my thighs and palms my knees. Again. He frowns as he sits back on his heels. Again.

We've been playing like this for the last half hour while Rylan takes a shower and preps for the evening flight. Dominic's lost his shirt, leaving his chest on display, while he's stripped me out of everything. My cock sits hard and heavy against my stomach, but I don't dare move. I twist my hands into the sheets to keep from reaching for him—or my dick.

"*Bellissimo*," he says. "*Sei perfetto, Tesoro.*"

I moan at the praise. A moment later, Dominic's mouth is on me again, working me like a goddamn magician, pulling pleasure from me so thoroughly, it's as if he was made for me. Fuck, but Alphas are something else. You'd think I'd be used to it by now, that I would have gotten acclimated to how thorough they both are in bed when pursuing my pleasure.

My dick touches the back of his throat, and his muscles contract down around it. I can't help it, I thrust up into him, groaning.

"Oh God." I moan, panting, trying to hold out, not wanting our play to end.

Dominic has other plans. He pulls off until just my head is in his mouth, his lips stretching in a way that has my knees going weak. He swallows, and my back arches. He hums his satisfaction, and the added sensation is enough to send me over the edge.

"*Dom.*" It's a gasped warning.

A second later, my dick twitches, and lightning shoots down my spine, making my back bow again. I moan through the release, my hands tightening in the sheets even as the last bits of it fade out. His tongue runs over me before he swallows again, another satisfied hum making me groan. His mouth leaves me, and I grunt at the last moment of sensation.

He runs his hands up my legs and stomach, wrapping them around my waist. He traces my hip bone with his tongue. Already, my body is trying to coax back to life.

"Why do you always insist on me missing the fun, Dominic?" Rylan asks from the doorway, his Tennessee accent touched with humor.

I turn my head so I can see him. His hair is still damp, falling in soft waves to his chin, and he's foregone a shirt, leaving the large lotus and vine tattoo along his chest and left arm in full view.

"You're not missing it if it's just an appetizer," Dominic mutters, pulling away from me and stripping out of his slacks. Rylan raises an eyebrow but pushes the new sweat pants down his hips, letting his own hard cock spring free. Dominic climbs off the bed and grabs a small black bottle of lube from his bag.

My tired dick springs back to life. Fuck, I love it when he knots me.

I'd tried to talk him out of it, the first time he wanted to buy the specialty lube that would trigger his knot even though I'm a Beta. It's stupid expensive, and there was no guarantee I'd even be able to take it.

I should have realized by then that Dominic is incredibly persuasive when he wants to be.

"We have six hours, *Tesoro*," Dominic says as I move to kneel on the bed. "Think we can manage to stay busy the whole time?"

Rylan laughs, cupping my face and tilting it back, setting a small bite in the hollow of my throat. Another bruise, another mark. He's feeling extra possessive tonight.

"Suppose there's only one way to find out," I say, breathless with desire and giddiness, tilting my head to give Rylan more room.

I *love* when they're in a playful mood like this. It doesn't happen often, but I revel in it every time.

"Suppose you're right," Rylan says, his Tennessee roots coming out more prominently for a heartbeat. He pushes me onto my elbows, his hands soft in my hair as my lips run down the underside of his cock.

We don't quite make it the entire flight, but it's a damn near thing.

Two

VIOLET

The screen of my phone flashes, and I scowl, flipping it over and ignoring the call before it starts vibrating across the hotel's dresser. My mother has already called me three times since lunch, and no amount of ignoring her seems to be getting the message across. Is me being in Manhattan for this damn thing not good enough?

Of course not. She won't be satisfied until I've matched with whatever senator's son she's set her eyes on this cycle. My fathers have been more understanding, Dad sending me a text early this morning while Papa and Father video called me together before Faedra and I went to lunch. Only Papa really understands my disinterest in matching. He's the only one I've explained why I've dragged my feet in allowing the Council to woo me in with their promises of glitz and fun and passion.

"Violet, I think the car's here." Faedra's voice is as frazzled as my nerves, though I'd never admit it.

I sigh, finishing my winged liner and putting on mascara

before touching up my highlighter. I tuck both lipsticks into my wristlet before stuffing my phone in there, too, ignoring the two new notifications from my mother. The strappy heels take a minute to finagle into, and I'm silently cursing myself for being so stubborn about my outfit by the time I'm buckling the thin bands around my ankles.

"Violet?"

"Coming," I say, my voice betraying the nerves sitting just under my skin. I curse, grabbing my wristlet and adjusting the hem of my dress around the heels as I walk into the shared living space of the hotel suite.

I *hate* that I'm nervous for this.

Faedra's eyes skate over me, her lips tipping into a sly grin even as her eyebrows rise. The blush is instantaneous, though I silently curse that response, too.

"It's probably too much, isn't it?" I ask, smoothing my hands over my stomach and down my hips, adjusting the metallic green fabric.

She's quick to shake her head, her voice soothing. "It's perfect."

Good.

I cross the room, grabbing one of the hotel keys from the small table beside the door and tucking it into my wristlet as I meet her at the door.

"Don't know how I'm going to survive wearing these," I joke, pulling up the hem of the green bodycon dress, showing off the three inch gold and black stiletto heels that match my jewelry. "But I guess the Council will just have to factor that into their decision."

She cocks an eyebrow before shaking her head and letting out a huff of a laugh.

"Of course you'd wear something that would jeopardize your safety."

She sighs, twisting the handle. The door swings open, and I follow her into the hallway.

"They're fucking perfect, and you know it," I say, regaining a bit of my normal confidence as we head down the long hallway to the elevator. Her phone sounds with a notification as we near the end, and she sends a quick text to someone before stopping in front of the elevators. I step around her since I can't see over her shoulder even with the added height of the heels.

"Besides," I say, glancing over my shoulder, "Alphas are almost ridiculously tall. The last thing I want is for them to think I'm some dainty, virginal eighteen-year-old. The idea of ending up with a pack that idealizes that makes me want to vomit."

I scrunch up my nose as I push the call button. Twice. Who honestly only presses it once?

Faedra glances away, her flinch subtle, and I keep my gaze on the patterned carpet just behind her. We've never talked about it —not since that night freshman year when her date went poorly. I had double checked she didn't need a Plan B. Best friends look out for each other, you know? Her cheeks had matched her red hair, her freckles nearly completely invisible when she'd admitted she'd never slept with anyone and certainly not deadbeat Tyler.

Maybe the virginal comment went too far. I didn't realize she hasn't been with anyone since then. I know she's nervous for tonight.

Faedra and I are opposites, my dark to her light. She's been quietly stressing about this for weeks, agonizing over her dress and hair and makeup until I thought she would make herself sick. She's normally the first one to rise to a challenge, to throw herself wholeheartedly into something new. But matching is different, I guess. It's certainly more permanent. I cringe at the thought.

My mom was practically *giddy* when my dad told her I'd officially agreed to go to this gala. And anything that makes my mom happy makes me want to vomit and then run in the opposite direction. The reality is, I wouldn't even be here if my last heat hadn't been the absolute clusterfuck from hell.

For an unmatched, single Omega, there aren't a ton of options for dealing with your heats. You can either suppress them like Faedra has done, consent to being sedated, or ride them out using toys. But even toys suck after a while. It's like… like your body knows that it's all fake and starts to reject it. Ridiculous, I know. And it's not like my vibrators don't do it for me. It's just the knotting toys. Maybe it's only become that way for me because I've started hooking up with Alphas the last couple years. I had adamantly refused anyone that wasn't a Beta until my twenty-first birthday. You can't miss something if you don't realize it exists, you know?

But having now been through eight heats on my own, the appeal of the knotting toys has seriously diminished. Last fall, I decided I was willing to try going to one of the havens the Council has set up in larger cities to help Omegas that are caught off guard and don't want to be suppressed or sedated. Hiding out in the dorm for a week while Faedra still went to classes just didn't sound appealing to me. The place was nice enough— soothing colors and comfortable, plush nests. But everything smelled *wrong*, especially the Alphas who worked there and helped me through the heat.

Well, one of them, at least. The other had smelled…

The elevator opens, and I cut off my daydreaming, once again grateful for whichever group of scientists invented the newest scent blocking technology. Not a single note of my honeysuckle scent permeates from me despite that lingering fantasy. It's certainly better than remembering my heat last month at the same facility. The Alpha I'd liked apparently chose to deactivate. And the two that were there? Definitely not the Alphas for me.

Faedra steps into the elevator, and I follow, forcing more confidence into my walk than I feel at the moment, channeling all that desperation I felt over spring break into something useful right now. The display flashes with each floor as we descend.

"The hotel is really nice," Faedra whispers. "The Council must be happy we finally relented and picked a date."

I nod, keeping the secret of my Papa paying for the room to myself. The Council typically picks one hotel—two, if it's an especially large gala—for the Omegas. They intentionally coordinate with the staff to make sure no Alphas are working that day. One less place for possible unintended meet cutes or something. No way was I going to crowd into that hotel, surrounded by Omegas who were mostly younger than me and certainly way more excited to be at this damn event. When I admitted as much to Papa, he came in clutch, booking the room under Faedra's name so my mother wouldn't realize we were staying somewhere else.

Faedra taps her fingers against her clutch, pressing it into her stomach like a protective shield.

"Deep breath, Faedra." I clasp her elbow as the elevator opens to the main lobby. "Alphas are going to be interested in you, I promise."

Who wouldn't be interested in her? She's gorgeous, her red hair falling in perfect combed-through curls over one shoulder, her freckles dotting her skin like kisses of sun, her green eyes reminding me of Seattle in the summer. She's vibrant and confident and sharp as a nail, her intellect downright *arousing*. Everyone knows just how beautiful she is. Except, it seems, her... which is the cruelest irony.

She doesn't say anything as we cross the hotel floor but offers a smile to the doorman who helps us out onto the busy sidewalk. There's a nondescript black car pulled to the curb, hazards flashing orange in the glow of the sunset, and she cuts a direct line for it, leaving me to catch up to her. Once we're both settled in the back seat, the driver gives a small nod and starts the twenty block trek across Manhattan, right into the heart of billionaire's row.

By the time we've reached the third red light, Faedra is rolled into herself, her shoulders nearly to her ears.

"You're even more quiet than normal," I say, trying to get her talking. If she clams up now, the night is going to be a nightmare. When she shrugs, I lace our fingers together. "Once the awkward first round of mingling fades, it'll be good. The first ten minutes are always uncomfortable at big events like this."

I intentionally don't think about all the private galas I've had to attend with my parents. I try to not resent my dad's wealth, his influence, but those parties are always dreadful.

Faedra doesn't seem convinced, messing with one of her piercings, looking out over the city.

"By the time the dancing starts, I'm sure you'll have found at least one Alpha that you like."

She shrugs before saying, "I had to switch to the big suppressant."

"Oh shit, Fae," I say before I can reel in my reaction.

How many does that make now? I can't remember. She glances at me, chewing at her bottom lip.

"Is this your..." I think back quickly, trying to track them over the last couple years. "Third?"

She nods once, and I grimace. I've heard horror stories of *one* suppressed heat. I can't even imagine how rough it must be suppressing three in a row. Faedra sighs.

"I just worry that I won't be..." She twirls her hand near her head. "Omega enough, Vi. I don't crave touch the way you do. I don't desire to be around people all the time or hear compliments, either."

Except she does. Every time someone mentions how her hair

looks or that they like her outfit, she lights up. And not craving touch is a common symptom of the suppressants. I keep my mouth shut, though, knowing she just needs to get it out. Faedra gets like this, stuck up in her head. If I get her talking, she tends to calm down—and tonight, she needs to be as calm and relaxed as possible.

"What happens if no pack wants me, and I have to go through a heat alone?"

My chest tightens. I grab her arm and squeeze her hand.

How long has she been worried that she'll go unmatched? I've been sitting here stewing over my mother's social climbing by proxy, and my best friend has been agonizing over the—completely unfounded and virtually unheard of—potential of not being matched with any active and available packs after tonight's gala.

"They'll want you, Fae. You're witty, smart, graceful. Not to mention a fucking bombshell." Her lip quirks up, and I mentally high five myself. "Don't worry. There'll be good packs there that you'll fit with."

The car slows, falling in behind several other nondescript vehicles stopping at the curb. I unbuckle and grab my clutch, watching a group of guys get out of the SUV in front of us and head toward the waiting throng of cameras on their way to the entrance of the event center.

"I know this is practically impossible for you," I say, "but try to turn off that analytic brain and just have fun tonight. That's what the Council wants to see—it's part of why they don't show up here in person."

That, and to keep prying outsiders from trying to bribe them into making certain matches. Universe knows, my mom would be all over them in a heartbeat if any of them actually showed up to one of these to witness it all.

The car edges forward and a valet rushes to open our door,

his blue polo matching the rest of the staff working the outside of the event. I take the hand he offers, using it to give myself an extra moment to get situated in the thin heels, twisting to make sure Faedra is managing all right. The golden hue of her clutch flashes against the black leather of the car, and I grab it before the valet can close the door.

I tuck it into her hands, interrupting her nervous fidgeting and smoothing of her dress.

"Clutch," I murmur.

I keep my eyes trained on the group of media workers, noting two reporters heading our direction. One has that look in their eye—the one that means they recognize who I am. Faedra mutters a curse, and I manage a small laugh. She doesn't seem to notice just how tense it is—a testament to her own nerves. I force myself to relax and remember the years of training my Papa paid for so I wouldn't start throwing punches at these types of things. Keeping my steps sure, I move past the red carpet entry, bypassing it for the more normal walk toward the entrance. Faedra's breathless laugh follows as she keeps a step behind me.

The news reporter from earlier, her brown eyes sharper than her winged liner, steps in front of me, her microphone held confidently toward us. Faedra steps around me, keeping her head ducked away from the woman. Can't blame her. She glances at me, and I wink before focusing on the woman again.

"Everyone's been waiting for you to match, Miss Fallon." It takes every well-trained muscle in my body to not scowl at the woman. "What's it like for you to finally be standing at the precipice of your Matching Gala?"

"Oh, I'm just excited to have a night of fun," I say, intentionally bright and upbeat. The woman nods and smiles in encouragement. I ham it up just for her benefit. "It's a once-in-a-lifetime experience, and I'm ready to make the most of it!"

The woman murmurs a thank you and turns for the next

Omega, my name and borrowed clout already forgotten now that she has me on film. Another reporter starts zeroing in. I turn away and navigate the others nearing the entrance, catching up to Faedra before she makes it inside.

Faking it for one camera is more than enough for me tonight.

Faedra relaxes the moment I catch up to her, and I elbow her in the side, smirking.

"You're welcome."

She laughs.

Good.

"Owe you for that one," she says as we navigate around a few groups taking their time getting into the ballroom. The moment an Omega bumps into her on the other side, she bites her lip and messes with her hair, scanning the space around us.

"Let's get you your one allowed drink," I say over the din, hooking her arm in mine, "and then find a spot to see the Alphas. I'm sure there will be someone that sticks out to you."

Her shoulders relax as she takes a deep breath, though she fidgets with her ear piercings as we head toward the open doors.

"What about you?" she asks.

Making the most of tonight by finding someone who smells delicious and fucking them senseless. If I can walk straight in the morning, this evening went to shit.

I give her a wink.

"Don't you worry about me, Fae. You know how I am."

She giggles as I steer her into the room full of Alphas.

May the Council have mercy on me.

Three

VIOLET

The moment we have our drinks, I make a beeline for the outermost cocktail tables arranged near the dance floor, sidestepping various catering staff as well as a few Alphas already starting to mingle. Everything is done up in *white* even though it has to be a nightmare to get everything clean afterward. Flowers sit in an elevated vase in the center of the tables, small jewels nestled in some of the larger blooms.

Most of the Alphas stand around the outer perimeter, drinks already in hand, their eyes just as shrewd as mine as they take in the Omegas entering the party. A few pick over the tables of food set up on the opposite side of the room from the dance floor.

"I'm honestly shocked so few Omegas are wearing black. Really expected to be more ostentatious," I muse. Most of the people around us are dressed in pretty pastels that coordinate with the season, pinks and blues and even a few purples. While the green of my dress doesn't fit in necessarily, it's not as outrageous as I'd hoped.

Faedra laughs and shakes her head. "The entire room looked when we came in. I don't think you'll have any problem with garnering attention tonight."

I wave off her comment and look over the room again.

Do I look fucking amazing in this dress? Absolutely. The green silk hugs my curves and shines in the light of the room. But did I pick the color knowing that my mother would choke on her morning coffee when she sees the pictures tomorrow? Of course, I did.

Making my mother squirm is one of my favorite pastimes.

Faedra stands beside me, dropping her clutch to the table and messing with it, her drink nestled between her arms. A metallic reflection of light catches my eye, and I look more closely at what she's pulling from her clutch.

Of course Faedra would bring her own snacks.

"An entire dessert bar, and you bring Rolos from the airport?" I ask, trying to gauge if she's calmed down enough to not completely clam up tonight. If I want my own plans to be successful, it means I need to be able to leave Faedra to her own devices.

She smiles, her cheeks reddening, but then takes a sip of her drink. "Emotional support airport Rolos."

I can't help but smile a bit and scan over the room again, trying to decide which way to go first: snacks or dancing. The small pins everyone that isn't an attending Omega are wearing become more pronounced with each pass over the place.

"There's more Betas here with packs than I expected," I admit after seeing the tenth blue lapel pin.

This one is tastefully placed at the gathered shoulder of a woman walking away from the snack bar, a small plate in her hands, her smile wide as she talks with a man with a red lapel pin. His arm snakes around her waist, and she laughs before resting her head against his shoulder.

Something not quite jealous twists in my gut, and I force my gaze away, looking at Faedra again. Her eyebrow is cocked, and I sigh.

"That's what the blue lapel pins mean. Alphas wear red, Betas wear blue, and they'll have the official pack name on it." I cock my hip. "Didn't you read the information they sent a couple weeks ago?"

With all the stress she's been under, it's about a 50/50 chance she actually did. It doesn't really surprise me when she shakes her head and explains she was too busy with school.

Fair enough. I'd be drowning, too, if I had to write the papers her senior level literature classes require. I scrunch my nose as I think about the nights she pored over her books in our living room.

"The people working have purple pins in case you need to make sure." I force a deep breath and take a sip of my drink. I ramble a bit to help settle my own nerves. "Betas being part of packs is pretty rare. They don't have the same need to be surrounded like we do or to take care of someone, like Alphas. And the bond doesn't quite work the same, either."

Betas can only bond with the help of an Alpha's claiming bite, setting their own bite over the top before the Omega has finished knotting and the wound has begun to heal. The thread is hazier than between an Omega and an Alpha, at least according to everything I've heard about it.

Mom would be mortified if I were to bond with a Beta. Part of me hopes I do just to see her horrified expression when the match is made public.

"Do you think you'll bond with your match?" Faedra pulls me from my thoughts.

I twist my necklace around my finger and scoff, shaking my head. "Absolutely not."

Bonding is permanent. No way am I letting someone have

that much power over me. Escape routes are necessary, even in relationships. Maybe especially in relationships. "I may be Omega, but I still need some space to myself, you know?"

Faedra nods, a small smile on her lips. "Totally get that."

She focuses on her candy again. I can't help but scan the room. Again.

I'm not entirely sure what I'm honestly waiting for. It's not like I'm going to be the first one to make a move tonight. Violet from four years ago probably would have. But now? If they're that interested in me, they can come to me. It helps weed out those that are intimidated by my father's notoriety.

The thought makes me chuckle, just a little. Notoriety has him sounding like a mob boss rather than the CEO of one of the largest financial conglomerates on the West Coast. Which, to be fair, is the legal version of a mob boss.

Maybe it's not all that ridiculous of a descriptor, really.

A flash of blond hair in the far corner catches my eye, and my chest tightens. I breathe through the instinctive panic. There's no way it's actually him. He's a Beta. If he wanted to end up with an Omega, he would have stayed with me. Right?

A person moves just enough that I can see the rest of him. I see the sharp cheekbones and round eyes that I know are blue even though he's too far for me to actually see them. I see the easy gait as he cuts through the growing crowd, two tumblers of alcohol in his hands, the fingers worn and callused from his playing. I see it all, and my heart fucking *stops*. I can't feel my hands for a heartbeat, and my pulse roars in my ears.

Breathe, Violet. You have to breathe.

What is he doing here? And why the *fuck* does he have a blue lapel pin signaling he's part of a fucking pack? I press my clutch into my belly, trying to keep from absolutely freaking out. I can't have a panic attack. Not here.

"What's up?" Faedra asks.

My breath shudders out of me, and I force my gaze away from Jasper's retreating form.

"Just didn't expect to recognize anyone, that's all," I admit. She cocks an eyebrow, and I huff a sigh. "Remember that Beta I dated? When I was in high school?"

Faedra looks around the room, though she doesn't seem to notice him. Of course she didn't. She never looked him up on socials. She wouldn't have any idea what he looked like. And certainly not those small things you learn about a person when you spend so much time with them, like the way they walk or hold their shoulders or look out across a crowd.

"Oh shit," she whispers. "Jasper is here? Is he part of the string quartet?" She stands on her tiptoes, craning her neck toward where the musicians sit in the corner.

I shake my head, and she frowns.

"He has a pin." I mess with an earring to keep from picking apart my fingernails. I glance at the main entrance.

Could I just walk out? Would the Council just pick some random pack without me even interacting with anyone?

"Do you want to go chat with him?"

I purse my lips and take a long drink from my Old Fashioned. "I don't know."

Absolutely not.

There's too much that's happened. And that fucking *letter* he left me? I'd be arrested for assault if he came up to me right now, especially if he thinks he'll end up matched with me.

Except four years is a long time. Maybe things are different. Maybe whatever he saw in me that he couldn't stand is different now. Maybe...

"Not yet."

I take a long, deep breath, recentering myself. He's one

person out of literally hundreds. I'm not going to let his presence ruin this night for me. I focus on Faedra.

"Did you notice anyone while you were looking?"

Four

RYLAN

"I swear to God, Dom, you need to calm down," I groan.

Dominic scowls from where he stands on the other side of Jasper. He messes with the black cuff links. They reflect the light in the room, the only part of his black-on-black suit that offers any kind of levity. Jasper is dressed more traditionally, tailored tuxedo and simple bowtie. But Dominic? He looks like he's at a damn funeral, not one of the quarterly matching galas put on by the Council in their longstanding matchmaking tradition.

The acidic edge of Dominic's scent grows stronger the more people filter into the large ballroom and the din of conversation grows louder. We're tucked into the farthest corner from the dance floor, Jasper standing casually between us, his shoulder pressed against mine. A man in his early twenties starts toward us, his cheeks flushed but his eyes sharp. A low, menacing growl from the other side of Jasper has him pausing before redirecting his path to several feet to our left.

"Dom, you need to calm down, or we're going to get kicked out," Jasper whispers, leaning away from me. The black tuxedo hugs his body as he does, moving over him like water, and it makes my mouth fucking water.

For all he looks like he's attending a memorial, Dominic's dressed well, too, wearing some Italian designer I don't know the name of that costs more than my entire guitar collection. In contrast, I've opted for a more standard suit, riding the bare minimum line of the dress code. I wear tuxedos every single week. My one weekend in New York City doesn't need to include them, *black tie required* be damned.

Jasper adjusts as he whispers something into Dominic's ear, and it makes the small pin on his lapel catch the light, the gold name emblazoned against the blue background.

Montegue.

As far as pack names go, it's not the worst. Certainly better than Jameson, and I know Dominic is happy to be rid of his family name. Maybe they'll want to keep it after we deactivate, too.

Dominic whispers something too low for me to understand.

"They'll just make us come back for another one," Jasper says, keeping his voice low, his body leaning toward Dominic. "What's your actual plan for the night?"

"Seduce you in the bathroom to avoid having to talk to anyone, *Tesoro*," Dominic murmurs.

I roll my eyes. "If you're going to be that awful, just go get your alcohol and hide in the corner."

Jasper elbows me in the side, but I don't apologize.

Dominic mutters a curse in Italian and shoves his hands into his pockets before looking back at the growing crowd. There's a rush of noise, and I sigh, turning toward the entrance, prepping to see the next wave of Omegas joining the party. Most enter in groups of two or three, laughing and smiling. Some are obviously nervous, messing with their hair and clutches and ties, their eyes darting around the large room.

Dominic says something else under his breath, but all I manage to hear is something about God saving him.

"Didn't realize you'd given Jasper a new nickname," I say, keeping my amusement off my face.

Jasper cocks his eyebrow and purses his lips. "You intentionally trying to get in a fight tonight? Because I don't really feel like trying to separate you guys in a full tuxedo. The first time was bad enough, and I didn't even have my jacket on that time."

I shrug and finish the scotch and soda I've been nursing for the last half hour. For all of Dominic's hatred of this, it's not nearly as unbearable as the mingling events we have to do every so often as part of the philharmonic. Are there pompous, rich assholes here? Sure, packs tend to breed wealth, especially the ones that have been established for multiple years. Combined household income goes a long fucking way. But here, they're the minority. The people here want to mingle, want to get to know others, especially the Omegas, since the hope is to be matched by the Council with one of them in the coming couple of weeks.

Well, for most of the packs, at least.

I chance a glance at Dominic again as I drop the empty tumbler onto a tray carried by one of the catering staff. His shoulders are stiff, his lips rolled until they're a thin line, the creases at his eyes more pronounced under the warm lighting of the large room.

"I don't feel like getting the shit beat out of me tonight, either, for what it's worth," I admit on a sigh.

Tucking my hands into the pockets of my slacks, I look around the room more intently. The Omegas are starting to congregate around the cocktail tables as the lines at the two separate bars dwindle. A flash of bright green silk catches my gaze, and I follow it across the room, oddly invested in figuring out who was bold enough to wear something like that to this. She twists away from one of the tall inner tables, a redheaded woman holding up a simple black clutch in some unspoken response.

There's no pin anywhere on her dress. An *Omega* was bold enough to pick that dress?

I let my gaze drift up to her face, and my breath catches.

It's been six months, and I'm happily paired off. Triplet-ed off. Whatever. But, *fuck*, I can still smell that honeysuckle sometimes in my dreams, I swear. I still catch myself thinking of her hazel eyes and black hair and golden, smooth as fuck skin.

And there's no fucking way she can end up paired with us. Dominic will kill us both if we somehow manage to end up shortlisted. I need to hear her laugh, though. I need to know what she sounds like when she's not in the depths of a heat and moaning because of my knot.

It's completely unrealistic and borderline insanity. There are no soulmates, no perfect matches. Nothing waiting in the wings to justify bringing her into our little triad. But I'm as captivated by her as I was with Jasper when he first joined the orchestra. Did that situation have a happy ending? Yes. Eventually.

I'm under no illusion that this one will. It's not like anything will even happen tonight, even if she wants it to. But the memory of her curves forming to my hands, of her writhing against me, is too strong and visceral to simply ignore. Not without making a giant fucking scene, and God knows Dominic will do that for the three of us without me helping him.

Bergamot bleeds out from me, my scent rising in response to my thoughts. Jasper leans into me and hums. Tearing my gaze away, I focus on my lover and best friend. Jasper's eyes are half-lidded, his lips tipped into a soft smile. Dominic's lips have turned fully into a frown, his gaze cold and sharp.

"Fuck it, Jas," I say, talking over whatever new curse Dominic has come up with. I elbow Jasper in the side, pushing him away from me and fully into Dominic. "Better go find a corner and suck him off. He's going to lose it if we stand here for much longer."

Dominic glares, but Jasper laughs, tossing his head back and pressing a hand to his chest. After a moment, Jasper leans into me, wrapping an arm around my waist and pulling me close to him. The kiss is as fast as it is deep, and I make sure my scent is all over him before he pulls away. And then I trace the line of his jaw with my lips and set a small love bite under his ear for good measure.

"We'll be back," Jasper whispers, breathless giddiness making his voice lighter and faster. He grabs Dominic's arm and runs his hand down his forearm before lacing their hands together. The soft intimacy of the touch has a bolt of heat racing through me. Jasper levels a half-hearted glare at me. "Don't have too much fun without us."

"I should be the one saying that to you," I mutter, grinning, and then laugh fully when his cheeks flush a gorgeous dark red. I shove his shoulder and push off the wall, starting into the throng of people before they've walked away from me. "I need some fucking food. I'll see you in a bit."

I scan the crowd, looking for the telltale green, and my pulse jumps as I lock onto it, following it through the sea of people until I'm no more than ten feet from her. She takes a deep breath and grabs a small plate before turning toward the large spread of finger foods the Council has had catered.

The soft cadence of the string quartet fades, and a DJ

announces himself over the impressive speaker setup. Heavy bass of a newer pop song fills the room more thoroughly than the instrumentation did. I run my hands through my hair and scratch at the snake tattoo tracing up the side of my neck.

What the fuck am I even doing?

Being irresponsible, I guess.

Five

RYLAN

I stand back as I watch Violet work her way through the finger foods, loading up her plate until there's not an empty spot remaining. She adjusts her hold on everything as she grabs a glass and tries to pour herself some of the water that has cucumbers and strawberries floating in it. I'm closing the distance before I can stop myself, intent on helping her keep from spilling the food or dropping the glass. Her hold juggles a bit, and she mutters a curse.

"Let me get that for you," I say, grabbing the full plate of food from her hands as she bobbles it again.

Her gaze whips to mine, her grip tightening on the plate, before her eyes widen and her shoulders relax.

"Oh," she whispers. She glances around us, like she's making sure no one is paying attention, and then relinquishes the plate into my hold.

Why is she so concerned if people notice us interacting?

I bite back the question. It's not like it really matters.

Nothing can happen between us, so her motivations aren't my problem.

"Bold dress," I say into the lengthening silence.

Her lip quirks, curling up at the corner, and a flash of amusement crosses her eyes before a careful neutrality settles back over her.

"You think so?" She turns around once, the draping skirt moving like water around her curves. My dick stirs, but I do my best to ignore it. "It felt like a pretty safe option, all things considered."

I raise an eyebrow, and she grins.

"I could have picked something with a plunging neckline or pieces cut out of it. Or maybe something sheer. My mother would freaking lose it if she saw photos surface of me in something sheer."

I toss my head back and laugh.

"I can't imagine what you'd do to the Alphas here if you showed up in a sheer dress," I say, still chuckling. "Guarantee half of them are sporting hard-ons just with this one." Me included.

Her cheeks bloom a gorgeous deep red, and I grin.

"So you're Rylan, right?" she asks, sidestepping my comment.

Nerves clench my stomach. Why am I suddenly so unsure how to interact? I've been going to stuffy functions like this for literal years as part of the philharmonic.

You didn't know how to interact with Jasper either, you idiot.

True. But, again, it's not like this can end similarly to how everything shook out with him. So why do I care if I make a wrong move now?

Clearing my throat, I hand her the plate of finger foods and take the still-empty cup from her hands, turning to fill it from the large pitchers unobtrusively guarded by two waitstaff.

"Wasn't aware Omegas worried about the names of the Alphas," I say, handing off the water.

She shrugs and glances away. "Maybe I'm not like other Omegas." She grimaces, her nose scrunching. "Oh, disgusting. That makes me sound like a freaking 'pick me' girl. Not what I meant."

Tucking my hands into my pockets, I gently lead her away from the food and toward the nearest table, pulling a chair and dropping into it. She leans against the edge, cocking her hip and messing up the tablecloth. The damn dress moves over her again, highlighting the very real fact that she's a goddamn bombshell and I want to fuck her into next week.

I glance around the ballroom, trying to tell if the guys are back from Jasper calming down Dominic.

Except thinking about the ways Jasper enjoys calming down Dominic the most just has my dick going from half-hard to fully aching. I spread my legs a bit and lean back in the seat, trying to take some of the pressure off without making it noticeable.

"I made sure to know your name so I could request you again," she admits in a fast rush of air. Before I can respond, she looks back toward the dance floor and then shoves a small pastry into her mouth. Whole.

Fuck, why does she have to be so fucking alluring? I shouldn't have sought her out. I should have just let Dominic stay in a bad mood and keep us sequestered in the far corner like his plan clearly had been. What the hell could even happen? Absolutely nothing but the sad state of my dick.

"Couldn't they just look up your file?" My voice has dropped an octave. I stretch my neck and clear my throat.

She shrugs and focuses back on me. Her throat ripples with her swallow. "Assuming I get there in time to still be reasonably with it. And then assuming they pull the right Alpha. I'm not one to leave that many variables to chance."

That's only two variables. They're significant, sure, but still... I bite back the question. The last thing I want is to sour this one final interaction with my own curiosity that ultimately will mean nothing.

She traces the edge of the plate and crosses her ankles. Her gaze flicks across the room, like she's looking for someone. The movement has the light catching on a long silver bar in her ear, simple and understated.

"You didn't have that piercing," I offer instead of calling out her nervous fidgeting.

Who was she looking for? Maybe that girl she'd been chatting with? Or was there someone else she was hoping to find?

Something very similar to jealousy lodges in my stomach.

She shakes her head. "I took them all out so I didn't risk them ripping out."

There's another long pause.

"I guess this explains why they said you weren't available last month."

My chest absolutely does *not* twist under the thread of melancholy weaving through her voice.

"It's a noncompete type thing," I say, trying to ease the sting of not being with her for a second heat. I'm *happy* with Jasper, damn it. Dominic is convinced we can make this work without an Omega. There's no way I'm going to jeopardize our dynamic now when we're so close to being on his father's good side. I offer a quick explanation. "Once you're registered as a pack, they don't allow you to work at the Haven."

She tilts her head, her lips pursing. "I suppose that makes sense."

Her eyes widen, her hands stilling. Before I can say anything, she's ducking away, her food forgotten on the table. I'm two seconds away from going after her when a hand lands on my shoulder. I twist around, finding myself nearly nose to nose with Jasper. His eyes are wide, his mouth set in a firm line.

"I thought you were getting food," he says.

I glance behind him, but Dominic's nowhere to be seen.

"I was," I say, shrugging off his hand and standing. "And then I got to chatting with someone I recognized. What's wrong?"

Jasper sucks in a breath, his countenance going from concerned to betrayed to damn near *wild* in the span of a heartbeat. He moves the chair from between us, taking up every single inch of space until our noses are almost touching. He's shorter than me by a couple inches, and he doesn't carry that *presence* that Alphas have, but it still takes my entire control to not concede any ground.

Goddamn, he's been taking lessons from Dominic.

"How the fuck do you know Violet?" His voice is low and dangerous.

I've never heard him like this. How in the hell does *he* know Violet?

"How do you know who she is?"

Jasper shakes his head. "Don't fucking deflect right now, Rylan. How do you know her?"

I shrug and force nonchalance. "Just ran into her once in LA."

Not technically a lie. I ran into her all right. And then fucked her into oblivion multiple times over the course of 48 hours. My dick pulses at the memory. Bergamot bleeds out from me. Jasper's breathing turns ragged.

"Shit, Rylan, did you fuck her?"

This time, I take a half-step away from him, using the small space to fix my jacket and bowtie.

"I love you, but it was before we started dating," I mutter, keeping my anger leashed. Enough, at least. An acrid note bleeds into the bergamot, but I ignore it. "It's not really your business, Jasper."

He snarls and closes the gap again.

"Stay the fuck away from her, Rylan. You know we can't match with anyone here."

I cock an eyebrow and shove my hands into my slacks.

As if we haven't been hashing out exactly how to approach this whole mess for the last six months. Register as a pack and attend a single gala so that Dominic can access his trust fund. The moment we're notified we weren't selected for an Omega, deactivate with the Council and move on as our little trio.

Dominic will kill me—literally, probably—if I end up being the reason we're matched with someone. Not even a male Omega would be enough to keep his rage from landing directly on my head. And Dominic's level of lethality is not something I want focused on me. He was trained by the goddamn Italian mafia, after all. He's the precision knife of his father when his enforcer brother fucks up too much. At least he is until we get back from this whole event.

Anger over nearly having Violet again and having her snatched from in front of me makes me shorter than I've ever been with my lover. The itch to smoke rises up. Fuck me, I haven't *wanted* to smoke in literal years at this point. Resentment festers low in my stomach.

"I'm well aware, Jasper," I whisper, letting that intrinsic part of me out to play just a bit.

His throat ripples with a swallow, but he doesn't back down.

"Matching with Violet is the absolute worst thing that can happen." He presses a finger into my chest with each word. "Stay. Away. From. Her."

I take his hand and lace our fingers together. "All right," I whisper, kissing the back of his hand. "I won't talk to her any more tonight."

And it's absolutely not regret that's twisting through my stomach at realizing I won't get to see her again. That I won't get to smell her honeysuckle.

Dominic comes up behind Jasper, his eyes shrewd.

"We've been here for the minimum requirement. Let's get out of here."

Yeah, definitely not regret. That weightless sensation has to be relief.

Fuck, I want a cigarette.

Six

VIOLET

I roll over and pick up my phone without checking who's calling.

First mistake.

Actually, the first mistake was thinking that Rylan might actually be a decent match for me at the gala last night. Or maybe it was circling back after I realized Jasper hadn't noticed me just in time to hear him tell Rylan to stay the fuck away from me. Though really just being at the goddamn gala at all was obviously a bad decision. And then having to have Faedra pull me out of the bathrooms once I'd gotten enough control over myself to not weep hysterically where someone might actually *see* was certainly on my list of experiences I didn't want to repeat. Ever.

So, really, answering my phone without making sure it isn't my fucking *mother* is so low on the problem list right now, I can't even manage to muster up the automatic defensive walls I wear around my heart any time we're interacting.

"What the hell was that dress, Violet Fallon?"

Her voice is shrill and borderline hysterical, which means whatever photo she has pulled up has been the center of her attention for longer than the last five minutes.

"Good morning," I say, ignoring her question.

What time even was it? Could I manage to drop back to sleep before having to grab our flight back to LA later this morning? And what the hell was my mother doing up so goddamn early?

She sucks in a breath before clicking her tongue against her teeth.

"When your father told me the cost of the dress you ordered, I assumed it would be *presentable* at the very least. You've lost all access to your trust until further notice, young woman."

I hold back a sigh and sit up.

Joke's on her. I haven't touched that damn trust since the day I moved out of the house and into my small freshman dorm room with Faedra. I had to nearly drain my savings account to pay for that dress. Or at least, I would have if Father hadn't stepped in and insisted on paying for it.

"You know these matches are incredibly important, Violet. It's the single most important thing you will accomplish in your life. Scarlett was fit for a damn *prince* when I was finished with her."

Where the hell were we, regency England? She acts like we're part of the ton and she gets one chance to marry us off or something.

Sure, Scarlett looked amazing. She always did, the perfect canvas for our mother's machinations. For all the good it did her.

I bite my tongue before I let slip my sister's secret. It'll be out soon enough, I suppose. Assuming the Council processes dissolutions as quickly as they do matches. Though I'm not holding my breath on that front.

"You will make a damn laughing stock, I swear. How dare

you do this to me? I expect a formal apology posted by the end of the week."

The line clicks dead, and I drop back onto my bed, keeping my eyes closed.

A few minutes later, there's two soft knocks on the closed bedroom door.

"Violet?" Faedra's soft voice soothes out the barbs left over from my mother. "The ride share is going to be here in about fifteen minutes. You good to go?"

I roll out of bed and throw on a set of leggings and my favorite UCLA hoodie, not bothering to actually brush my hair before pulling it into a claw clip. When I open the door, Faedra's dressed similarly, though her hoodie is cropped and sports the logo of the Minnesota Wild. Shout out to Papa that I even know what team it is.

I pull out my phone and send him a quick message.

> Headed back to school. Love you.

And then I send one to my father, too. My dads will know what it means.

> The dress was perfect. Thank you. 

> You were gorgeous, darling. So proud of you.

"Good to go," I say, not bothering to try for peppy. I shove my phone into the pocket of my hoodie.

Her lips twist into a frown, her eyes growing worried, but she nods. "You'll talk to me if you need to, right?"

I blow out a breath and smile, relaxing as she visibly does, too. "Of course, Fae. You're my best friend."

I've done my best to forget Rylan for the last six months. Well, six weeks, at least, since finding out he stopped working at the Haven. And I've tried especially hard the last several days since the gala on Saturday, when I was confronted with his beautiful green eyes and that damn snake tattoo that haunts my fucking dreams.

Have I been successful?

My body shudders out an orgasm as I bite my lip hard enough to bleed, the small vibrations of my favorite vibrator nearly identical to the soft aftershocks pulsing down my legs.

No. I absolutely have *not* been successful.

I pull the small device away as my body grows sensitized and turn it off, letting myself relax into the bed even as my scent stays reasonably controlled. Thank the gods we live in LA where I can actually open the windows in the spring. Just another reason I can't stand Seattle.

That and not having to interact with my mother more than absolutely necessary.

Thoughts of my mom drive away the lingering weightless feel induced by my vibrator and memories of Rylan's knot. Before I can do much more than sigh, there's two knocks on the door followed by Faedra's soft voice, just like always.

"Vi, I know you're in there. Can I come in, please?"

Shit.

I fly off the bed as I curse, cleaning the small pink bullet before tucking it into my nightstand and then throwing on a set of ripped jeans and the faded Florence + The Machine hoodie I've had since seeing them in concert when I was sixteen. My cheeks are still flushed when I open the door, but there's not much to be done for it.

Faedra's dressed in her typical floral skirt, her hair braided back and falling over one shoulder. Her eyebrow rises as she takes me in, and I scrunch my nose in a grimace.

"Don't act like you haven't been hot and bothered, too, Fae," I mumble.

She leans against the doorframe and messes with her waistband.

"Wasn't going to, Vi. Just didn't realize that you were busy. You could have told me to wait."

Not like I was actually in the middle of anything, though. And if I had just laid there for much longer, I would have ended up needing another round. And the amount of times I've needed to decompress with my vibrator over the last four days is honestly embarrassing. Especially since he didn't even want me to meet his pack.

Probably because his pack includes Jasper fucking Miller.

Montegue. That's what Rylan's badge said. Jasper Montegue has a stupid good ring to it, if I'm being honest.

Ignoring the stab in my gut, I wave off her concern and cross the room to my desk, grabbing the nondescript envelope that's been perched there since being handed to me early this morning.

"Did you get yours, too?" I ask, holding the blank envelope so she can see it. When she replies, my shoulders slump. "Finally. I've been staring at mine all morning." When I haven't been chasing the high I felt while knotted with Rylan, at least. My cheeks heat. "I didn't want to open it alone."

I drop onto my bed in an ungraceful lump, and Faedra settles next to me, her movements so fluid the bed doesn't even jostle with her weight. She balances her own notice on her knee and messes with her hair, undoing it and then pulling it back fully into a new braid.

"What is it?" she asks, her eyebrows furrowing. "I don't remember reading about this step."

Maybe talking it through will help my nerves.

"They've settled on a list of packs for us and want us to rank them."

I rip open the notice and pull both sheets of paper from it, ignoring the blank one that's waiting for my ranking the packs and focusing instead on the list of cities.

Annapolis. Albany. Seattle. Bozeman. Los Angeles.

My breath catches.

"These are *cities*," Faedra says, her voice a mixture of confusion and offense.

I can't help but laugh.

"The Council tries to keep outside influences from interfering with the matches."

I set my list next to hers. None of our cities match. It's not surprising, but my stomach still twists at the first permanent marker of our being separated in just a few weeks.

I keep my voice light. "By giving us cities, it decreases the chance of someone outside of the packs manipulating potential final pairings."

Faedra blows out a breath, almost like a breathless scoff. "Outside influences like your mom?"

Being with her is so easy. She lifts my spirits when she doesn't even realize I'm down for the count. It helps that she's met my mother and seen firsthand exactly the type of person she is.

I purse my lips and nod before grabbing my list again. My gaze catches on Los Angeles again.

What are the odds that it's Rylan? There must be at least a dozen registered packs that were at that gala that are registered with an address here. LA is absolutely gigantic. I drum my fingers on my knee.

Absolutely no way am I moving back to Seattle. It doesn't matter if it's the literal Prince of England in that pack. I'll ask for reassignment faster than my mother scoffs at the fashion choices of her peers.

"What's wrong, Vi?" Faedra's soft question snaps me out of my thoughts. "You've been a nervous mess since we left the party. Did something happen you didn't mention?"

She hadn't asked any questions when she'd found me in the bathroom and I told her I wanted to leave. She'd simply looped her arm in mine and found a side entrance so we could avoid whatever media presence was still at the front of the hotel. She even paid for the ride share even though I know her budget is tighter than mine.

I breathe out an almost laugh. "Yeah, I met an Alpha. Just like you."

She shoves me. "Why didn't you *tell* me? Did he make you cry?" Her mouth thins and her gaze hardens. "If he did, I'll make him regret it."

I shrug, and she snarls. It's pretty damn impressive given how freaking fragile she looks half the time. Not that I'd ever say that. I pin her with a look, running my hands over the list again, pressing it into the mattress like I can make the whole mess disappear completely.

"He didn't make me cry." Not right then, at least. "Jasper did."

She laces her fingers with mine and holds on tight. "I'm sorry."

I've told her about Jasper. Mostly. At least part of it. She knows I dated a Beta in high school and we broke it off. That his name was Jasper. She also knows that I had a nasty break up my senior year right before I committed to UCLA. That he broke up using a letter through my *mother* of all people, and that it had absolutely wrecked me. What she doesn't know is that both of those were Jasper.

"Did you like his pack?" she asks after a while.

Liked? I *loved* him at one point. A sharp stab in my heart accompanies the thought. Probably still do, if I'm being entirely honest. But that doesn't change what happened between us, how he left me when I was most vulnerable to start a new life somewhere else without me. How he abandoned me to my mother's insidious ways just because I'd designated.

"He didn't introduce them," I say at last. "I really liked him." And didn't that feel good to admit, at least to the two of us? "But I'm worried about why he didn't want me to meet the others."

Which is true. He probably doesn't even realize I saw the interaction between him and Jasper. Why didn't he want me to meet Jasper? And why was Jasper convinced matching with me would be so horrible?

Probably the same reason why he left you in the dust in Seattle.

Goddamn, that awful voice in my head is loud today. Faedra hums under her breath as she presses her lips to my temple, her hold tightening on my hand. The tension and worry slowly bleed from me.

"He told me where he lives." Not technically, but I do know that he lives here. He didn't mention moving when he explained why he wasn't working at the Haven anymore. "And it's on here."

"Do you want advice or support?"

To get advice, I'd have to come clean with the whole fucked up mess, and that's not something I want to uncover right now. My smile this time is more genuine.

"Just support." Time to turn this back on her. "Did your guys tell you where they live?"

She shakes her head, her gaze dropping to the list again. She messes with her orbital piercing.

"I suppose it'll be fate that pairs us together. I'm going to take the day to think about it and then rank them on where I'd like to live."

Shit. That's a really good plan. Maybe I should do that, too.

"Good plan, Fae," I admit.

Forget that Rylan lives here. That Jasper must live here, too, then. Forget that my mom is in Seattle. Rank them based on where seems most appealing to me right now. I glance down at the cities again.

I'm not entirely sure I have it in me to live out in the wilds of Montana. I love the conveniences of the big cities. The East Coast wouldn't be terrible. Though winters would be an absolute drag. And isn't Albany pretty small? It's upstate, I'm nearly positive. Nothing at all like New York City. Is it similar to Bozeman, then?

"Let's go get coffee," Faedra says, lacing her fingers with mine. "You need to get out of here before you drive yourself mad."

Seven

DOMINIC

The house is silent as I close the front door and step into the overstated foyer. Unease settles in my stomach, but I ignore it, pulling out my phone and scanning through the latest betting forecast for the underground fights happening next weekend.

The irony that I enjoy betting on sports when I've spent the last ten years enforcing my father's sportsbook isn't lost on me. Turns out, gambling comes with the same high that freediving does. And at least gambling doesn't inherently mean I might not come back. Victor and I have made something of a tradition of betting on Lorenzo's fights. Not that we'd ever actually tell him. He'd throw the fight just to fuck us over. So far, we have a perfect score.

You see this?

I send the screenshot of the current odds. Victor responds in under a minute.

Bit busy, D. But yeah. He's fucked.

Chuckling, I walk down the long hallway toward my father's study. Before I make it there, a man stumbles toward me, his sobs echoing off the tiles and walls. He clutches his bloody hand to his chest, his tears streaming fast enough they're leaving marks on his shirt. My first instinct is to help him, but I crush it before it can get me in trouble. Anyone sobbing in this home did something to earn my father's ire. That training rewards itself when Nico turns the corner, following behind the man, his hands shoved into his pockets, his lip pulled up in a sneer. He's my father's favorite bodyguard and has the bullet scars to prove it.

I step out of the way before the man can fuck up my suit. That explains why the house is so quiet. *Mamma* hates being here when Father is conducting this sort of business.

The bodyguard tips his chin toward me.

"*È pronto per te*," he says, his low voice gruff and a touch irritated.

"*Grazie*, Nico."

The blubbering idiot that decided to cross my father startles as his eyes land on me. The movement has splatters of blood dropping to the polished floor. Nico rolls his eyes.

"Walk," he orders the man, crowding him toward the foyer. He sighs as he passes me but offers a fast smile just before they disappear around the corner.

I wonder what he did to piss off Father.

I don't bother asking, continuing down the corridor and sliding into my father's study, dropping into one of the leather wingback chairs facing his desk. He glances up once I'm seated, his frown so ingrained, I'm half-convinced it's permanent. The small lines around his lips certainly suggest it is. His hair is more gray than when I saw him a few weeks ago. A thread of guilt weaves through my ribs, but I ignore it.

He could have told me there was no option to get out. He could have forced me to stay, and he didn't. Whatever has him looking this concerned is no longer any of my business.

"You managed to avoid every single camera on the premises," he says.

I nod. "I was trained by the best."

Him. No unwanted press happened unless I was incapacitated. If I didn't want photos floating around, they didn't happen in the first place.

"It would have been easier if you had allowed at least one photo, *Domenico*," he snaps.

I shrug. "Jasper and Rylan consented to photos. I'm sure theirs are searchable if you care enough to look."

He scowls but doesn't comment. He doesn't approve of my relationship with Jasper. He's not so bold as to say it to my face, but I know it's there in the set of his shoulders and his subtle iciness toward my lover when we are here for family brunch every Sunday.

Again, not my fucking problem unless he decides to make his dislike more noticeable.

Without a word, he pulls a small packet of papers from one of the desk drawers and slides them toward me.

"Here is the information on the trust. It's officially signed over to yours in perpetuity. You will be available for extreme circumstances with me and your brothers."

I nod and stand.

If *Mamma* isn't here, I don't want to be here for any longer than I have to.

"*Domenico*," my father growls, warning ringing through his tone. I pause, keeping my irritation from my face. "Do not make me regret it. You were a keystone of this business, and your absence is already felt. You will make me proud in this now, instead, understand?"

I ignore the tightening of my chest and the sinking sensation in my stomach.

"*Certo, padre.*"

Jasper's hold tightens on my wrists, his teeth biting into my neck, and I arch under him. He hums as I grunt, holding back the noise I know he's waiting for. He shakes his head and sighs. His mouth drifts lower down my chest and belly until he traces my hip bone with his tongue.

My dick aches, but I keep my mouth closed, my breathing unaffected.

This game that we play is one of my favorites, and I'm not about to let it end too quickly. Control is something I have in abundance.

"We have three perfectly good bedrooms," Rylan mutters.

Jasper looks up, his lips leaving my skin. The view the movement gives of his chest and thighs? That control slips through my fingertips, and I let the moan slip out. He squeezes my wrist even as his lips quirk into a knowing smirk.

"We're watching a movie," he says, completely serious.

I grunt and arch up into him, letting my dick press into his stomach. He wraps his free hand around my neck, pressing in with the slightest pressure. My dick jumps, and the pressing forward of his hips tells me he felt it, too.

"*Tesoro,*" I murmur.

Rylan laughs, the sound echoing off the high ceiling and wall of windows overlooking the ocean. "A movie. With the TV off and your shirt thrown halfway across the house. Sounds convincing." His voice is laced with dry amusement, and I smirk.

Jasper laughs and shrugs before pulling away from me, his hands running down my chest as he sits back on his knees. "I got distracted. You have a recording session tonight?"

It's Thursday, so not the typical schedule Rylan has with one of the local recording studios. Both of them already have double rehearsals with the philharmonic, so he tries to push things out to other evenings if possible.

"Duty calls," he murmurs.

Jasper pouts, his shoulders dropping. There's the soft tapping of Rylan setting down several items before the click of his shoes on the hardwood. His shadow falls over the large sectional before I can actually see him where I'm still laying across the cushions, held mostly immobile by Jasper straddling my thighs.

Rylan leans over the back of the couch, running his hand through Jasper's blond hair and pulling him closer until their lips just touch. Just like that, our game is forgotten, my lover seamlessly handing control of the play over to us. I palm Jasper's thighs, letting my fingers trace up the seam of his sweats until I can hook them in the waistband. His breath hitches, and I grin. Rylan's scent explodes from him, filling the space around us with its citrus undertones. Mine is much more subtle, the rut suppressor keeping it from being so all-consuming. I'll be the last to admit it, but the two scents complement each other, his lighter citrus to my darker. There's an irony there, I'm sure.

Jasper's chest shudders with his panting, a palm flat against each of us. He watches Rylan with a half-lidded gaze, his cheeks flush with color. He's gorgeous.

"*Cazzo, sei perfetto, Tesoro.*"

The praise falls from me before I even realize I'm going to say it.

Jasper groans, his hips lurching forward, his cock nudging against my hand. Rylan laughs again, deep in his throat, before claiming our lover's mouth and twisting a hand into his hair to force the kiss deeper. Nights like this? This is what I've longed for, what I went against my father and the blood-soaked legacy laid at my feet to achieve.

"Please," Jasper gasps between kisses. "Oh, fuck, *please.*" He writhes in my hold, and I move to cup him, letting his length fill my hand as I stroke him from tip to root and back. My own cock jumps at the strangled noise he makes.

"I'm going to be late," Rylan says, resigned acknowledgement threading through his voice. His grip tightens on Jasper's hair as he runs his lips over his jaw before biting into his neck. Jasper shudders.

It's enough permission for me.

I have Jasper's sweats halfway down his thighs when the doorbell rings and my phone buzzes with the camera notification.

Jasper's groan this time is full of frustration, and I echo it with my own.

"I'll grab it," Rylan says, already turning away from us before I can even let go of Jasper.

I sit up, kissing under Jasper's ear the moment I'm close enough. Rylan's voice is a low thrum through the room but too indistinct to hear exactly what's being said. The thread of surprise is easy enough to hear, though. Jasper frowns, lacing our fingers together as he adjusts to sit beside me. The door closes, and Rylan's steady stride eats away the distance. I glance over my shoulder.

"What the fuck is that?" I ask.

Rylan has a nondescript envelope in his hand, a shell-shocked look on his face. Like the person at the door delivered terrible news. My gaze narrows on the envelope as he holds it up for both of us to see.

"That was a Council intern," he says after a minute.

Accidenti.

"We were hardly even there," Jasper says, rounding the edge of the sofa and taking the envelope from Rylan's limp grasp. He has it torn open and the pages unfolded before I can even get across the room to them.

His face pales as he reads over whatever list of potential Omegas the Council has assigned us.

My stomach revolts at just the thought. And seeing it affect Jasper like this? A growl rumbles through my chest, the possessive rage easily burning to life under my sternum. Not even the rut suppressor is enough to snuff it out completely.

"You promised me," Jasper hisses.

I shove my hands into my pockets and lean against the back of the couch, letting them stay across the room. I have no desire to see the list, especially if whatever Jasper's seen has him this distraught. And as angry as his reaction is making me right now? Best I stay away from Rylan.

"And I followed through," Rylan snaps back. A muscle in his neck feathers as he clenches his jaw. "You left with us. When could I have possibly snuck off to talk with her again, Jasper?"

Jasper's hands tremble as he shoves the list into Rylan's chest. "And yet she's on the fucking list, Rylan. The list that we can't decline because it's our first gala."

Rylan's growl is even louder than mine, the violence in it barely restrained. He flexes his hands at his sides even as he snarls. I push off the couch and cross the space, wrapping my arm around Jasper's waist and pulling him against me. I kiss the spot where his jaw meets his neck, and he relaxes into me. His breathing is short and shallow, and the trembling moves to encompass his entire body. Like he's scared for his life.

But why? Logically, there's nothing terrible about shortlisting. Yeah, I'm pissed. It'll be a disgusting amount of paperwork to get the match annulled if the Council actually selects us for one of the faceless names on the sheet of paper. But no amount of bureaucratic nightmare warrants this level of reaction.

"Why is it such a bad thing?" Rylan asks after several long moments. "What happened to us following through in good faith if we're actually selected?"

Jasper shakes his head, and Rylan growls again.

"What the fuck happened between you?" he asks, spitting the question between clenched teeth.

"She's the fucking Omega," Jasper hisses, his voice breaking. The small omega symbol flashes in the light of the room as he pulls it away from his chest. "She ripped my heart out, and even now I still can't quite manage to get over her. There's no guarantee that Dominic's maneuvering will work fast enough to keep us from having to see her if this goes through."

Rylan takes a step back, his eyes wide.

"I'd rather fucking vomit on stage than do that," Jasper admits, nearly sobbing in my arms. "I don't know what I'll do if I come face-to-face with her again. She... she was everything to me."

The confession rings through the room. I tighten my hold on him, keeping him steady.

The Council better not make this permanent. Jasper in a mess like this? It has me ready to use all the lethal training at my disposal to avenge his torment. Killing Omegas is one of those things I absolutely detest. But whoever this woman is he's describing? It sounds like I won't feel all that sorry over this particular one.

"I'm sorry," Rylan says at last. He blows out a breath. "I…" He shakes his head. "I have to go."

Jasper collapses into me as the other part of our triad leaves the house, grabbing his guitar and other equipment without looking back.

"Dom…" His voice trails off.

I mess with the waistband of his sweats. "Let me distract you, *Tesoro*."

Eight

VIOLET

The moment I'm clocked out, I strip out of my work shirt, tossing it into my bag and pulling on a simple black cut off hoodie before anyone else comes back to the stockroom. I brush through my hair and adjust my necklace, twisting it around my fingers a few times as I stare at the packet sitting just under my purse.

Two weeks since the gala. Since I've seen Rylan and thought maybe matching wouldn't be completely awful. Since I heard Jasper tell him to stay away from me. Since he said I'd be the worst thing to ever happen to him. That fucking fourteen days was absolutely brutal. And the culmination sits in my bag.

Don't be a fucking coward, Violet.

Easier said than done tonight.

It was nearly impossible to focus on work the last few hours of my shift. Why the Council sent the woman *here* instead of the school is as baffling as it is frustrating. I was prepared to handle the questioning gazes and whispered interest on the campus. But here, at the Rowdy Seahorse where I've been both waitress and bartender for the last two years? Where no one knows me as Johnathan Fallon's daughter? Hell, half of them hadn't even noticed I was an Omega thanks to the scent blockers I wear religiously.

Getting caught making out in one of the music rooms at the community college in Seattle was less embarrassing than fielding the woman in between managing two ten-tops tonight.

I grab the packet along with my other things and head toward the front of the restaurant.

Most of the patrons are gone, but there's still a few tables occupied, and about half of the bar is full, the various televisions turned on to a few different baseball games. Someone cheers as I walk by the bar.

"You good?" Marcus asks as I near the host stand. He's clicking through something on the tablet while double checking the silverware is prepped. He glances up at me when I don't immediately answer, his frown deep.

I nod, hoping he doesn't expect a verbal response because there's no way I can offer one right now. My heart is so far into my throat, I'm practically choking on it.

I fucking *hate* feeling like this.

"You'll give me two weeks, right?" he asks after a minute.

I must look lost, because he points at the packet that feels as though it's bright orange rather than the sedate white. "Imagine you won't be working here now that you're matched. Promise you'll give me a full two weeks, yeah?"

Fuck me. I don't even want to think about having to leave here. It's not like it's a glamorous job or anything. It's just what it represents: freedom. My own path, uninhibited by my designation or my mother's need for perfection or my father's notoriety. Outside of the dorm, it's the place where I can be *me*.

I remind myself of March, of the aftermath of that heat, and it helps temper the desperate rage rising in me.

"Yeah, of course," I say. It's dangerously close to watery. "Have a good night."

I push open the door before he can say anything else, blinking furiously, keeping the tears back. I want to run to my car, but I force myself to take steady steps, emptying my mind as I take in the clear night around me. The warmth and safety of the small space envelops me the moment I have the door closed. My scent drowns the space, and I relax into it. Once I can breathe without feeling like my chest is shaking, I pull out my phone.

A single text from Faedra lights the screen.

Couple people got packets today. You get yours?

Yeah.

Oh no. You good?

Will be. Late night tonight.

See you tomorrow.

My movements are automatic, and I don't realize where I'm headed until I'm passing the outskirts of LA proper. By the time I've pulled into the empty parking lot of Faedra and my's favorite beach, the panic and nerves are gone, replaced by a strange numbness.

I stare at the packet. It sits on the passenger seat, unmarked, and for a moment I'm sitting on my bed, the official bloodwork of my designating as Omega sitting between me and Jasper.

Get yourself together.

With a sigh, I grab the packet and start down the cliffside, sticking to the staircase that tends to be least popular. Like most nights, the beach isn't empty. There's a couple walking the edge of the water and another sitting near the cliffs. A photographer stands knee deep in the water, their camera pointed toward the stars.

My hands tremble.

Everything I've been running from sits in a pile of paper on my lap. Every fight with my mom, every late night studying to graduate top of my class, every hitching breath when I thought I'd seen Jasper while shopping or walking or driving. Even every phone call with my dads and their careful words of comfort.

Blowing out a breath, I rip the seal of the envelope.

My phone lights up with an incoming call, Papa's face on the screen. It's like he can tell when I'm in distress.

"Hey, Papa," I answer. This time, I don't try to hide the watery feel of my voice, the tears that I want to cry but refuse. Not yet, anyway.

There's a moment of quiet, and then the sounds of shuffling.

"That Vi?" Father's voice is muffled, but Papa answers him. "Tell her I love her."

"Love you, too," I whisper. Papa passes on the message. There's more shuffling. A door closes.

"Hi, darling," Papa says. My chest aches. "Your answering tells me what I wanted to know."

I let out a half-chuckle, and that's full of tears, too.

"You open it?" he asks.

"Not yet." I trace the broken seal of the envelope.

He doesn't say anything, and I press the phone tighter to my ear like that will actually make me closer to him.

"I hate feeling like this," I whisper.

He makes a noise in his throat, something between a hum and a grunt that has always been a sound of comfort. My chest tightens, but I ignore it.

"Darling, any pack will be lucky and honored to have you." Papa's voice drops into a low croon.

It's embarrassing how much it soothes me. I'm twenty-two. Isn't that old enough to not need this kind of comfort from your dad?

There's the sound of a door closing, and Papa sighs. "Your mother is home."

"I'll call you after everything is confirmed," I say.

He murmurs a quick, "Love you," and then is gone.

I set my phone on the stairs beside me and run my hand along the open edge of the envelope again. Like pulling off a bandage. Or getting waxed. Quick count to three.

One.

Two.

I pull the packet before I can lose my nerve. Skipping the letter on top, I rifle through the papers until I find it: the photo of the pack. Even in the glow of the yellow streetlight, I recognize the golden hair.

My breath catches.

Matching with Violet is the absolute worst thing that can happen. Stay. Away. From. Her.

The memory is so fresh, it slices across my heart again. Tears blur the picture of them, Rylan's black hair messier than at the gala and Jasper's small smirk devious enough to make my knees weak even now. The third man is unfamiliar, his brown eyes conveying a dark and lethal countenance, though he's dressed impeccably in a black button-up and slacks that suit his olive skin.

I grab the letter, part of me hoping against all odds they put the wrong picture in the packet.

Dear Miss Violet Fallon,
It is with immense pleasure that we are able to inform you of matching with Pack Montegue of Los Angeles.

No.

Closing my eyes, I pull my knees to my chest, trapping the information before it can fly away. I rest my forehead against my knees.

Everything drains out of me. Every moment of running, of fighting, of hoping.

The night stands a solemn watchman over my weeping.

Nine

VIOLET

Faedra's normally sunny demeanor is dimmed tonight, and I can't help but feel guilty about it. She's landed her dream match, that pack that had absolutely enthralled her at the gala, and yet she's got a carefully neutral expression on her face as she maneuvers around the various groups between the bar and the small alcove I've sequestered myself to.

Two guys lean close together, their gazes flicking over toward me every few minutes. No doubt they recognize me and are coming up with ways to approach me.

The question is do they want to fuck me? Or use me to get in with my father?

Both options have bile rising in my throat. I flick my hair over my shoulder and turn back to my phone, scrolling aimlessly through Instagram while Faedra pulls the other chair out with her foot.

"You sure you want to stay here? We can go to the other one," she says as she sits down across from me. She hands off the

Old Fashioned without missing a beat, taking a large drink from her copper mug.

"As long as they stay over there, I'm fine with here," I say. The sooner I have alcohol in me, the sooner this might not feel like an absolute disaster of a situation. And then maybe I can text my fathers so they don't have to find out from my mother.

The elation I expected to feel at mortifying my mother over matching a pack with a Beta is overshadowed by the fact that it's Jasper. My mood sours even more, and I throw back the Old Fashioned in one fast swallow, grimacing at the intense burn.

Faedra's eyes are locked on me as I set the glass down. Her frown twists her lips, and her fingers tap against the copper mug of her Moscow Mule.

"I can't quite decide if you're simply disappointed or actively distraught over your match," she says after a minute. Even concerned, she's calm and collected. I envy her for it. "Or maybe you're more upset about where you're having to move."

I roll the glass in my hands, breathing through my nose to keep from dissolving into tears. Again.

At my continued silence, Faedra takes another drink. One of the guys gets up and starts walking toward us, but Faedra glares at him. He hesitates, glancing between us.

"Not tonight, man. It's match week." Faedra's voice is hard, carrying across the bar.

The man pales and takes a step back, twisting back toward the tall table where his friend is still perched, carefully scrolling on his phone instead of directly staring at us.

"I fucking told you," he says as his friend drops back into a chair. "Should've done it last week, man."

Faedra rolls her eyes and sighs. "I don't know how you don't break something with people doing crap like that all the time."

"The resting bitch face helps most of the time," I say with a shrug.

Faedra snorts and shakes her head. The amusement melts away a moment later, though, and she breathes out a heavy sigh.

"It's Jasper," I say, ripping the bandaid off without warning.

Faedra's eyebrow ticks higher, but she doesn't offer anything.

I roll the glass around some more. "And it's the Alpha I met. They're in the same pack."

"So you're upset over where they're located, then? Is he still in Seattle?"

I shake my head. LA is my fucking home. It's the only good thing I've been able to find in this whole situation since I saw their picture on the pier last night.

Faedra purses her lips. "There's something I'm missing, Vi. If it's Jasper, why are you on the verge of tears? And not the good kind."

"Remember how I told you about the Beta that broke my heart right before I graduated?"

She nods, her gaze hardening. "He broke up with you using a *letter*. Like it was 1980 or something."

"Right," I agree. I set the glass down. "It was Jasper."

"But you loved him." Faedra doesn't discredit me, her gaze searching my own. "He was your first. You... you thought he was *it* for you."

For the first time in weeks, I let her see all the turmoil and rage that's been festering just under the surface.

"I did," I admit, my voice cracking.

Faedra's the only one that gets to see me like this. She doesn't judge, doesn't force me to get over things, doesn't expect from me anything more than I can give in the moment. She's the best friend any woman could ask for. Being paired with her freshman year was better than winning the lottery.

"Fuck, and I asked if you wanted to go see him. I'm so sorry, Vi. Did he run into you? Is that what made you cry?" Her hands tremble. "I'll punch him for doing that to you. That night was supposed to be *fun*, and you definitely didn't have any."

Her instant, unconditional support warms that part of me I have to keep under lock and key so my mother can't ruin it, the part that's all empathy and humanity. I take her hand. "For what it's worth, I was having a good time."

She nods and squeezes my fingers. "Good. Now tell me what actually happened."

So I do. I tell her about grabbing food to keep myself busy while she chatted with her Alpha—Logan. His name was Logan. I tell her about my goal of finding an Alpha to hook up with so the night wasn't a complete waste of time. I tactfully ignore how bright her cheeks get at the comment. I tell her how I ran into Rylan and got to talking.

"Wait," she says, her fingers stilling on one of her piercings. "Who's Rylan?"

"The Alpha," I say.

She tilts her head. "Oh. You said his name like you'd met him before. Sorry. Continue."

I nod. "I did meet him before. He was one of the Alphas assigned to me at the Haven last fall."

Her eyes widen. "And you didn't die of embarrassment? I would have hidden in the bathroom all night if something like that happened to me."

Which was precisely why she had chosen the suppressants, and I had chosen to ride out my heats by whatever means necessary.

"It's not really any different than running into a one night stand. And it's way safer on my side of things."

Typically, at least. The Haven is really strict about birth control and testing. Accidents happen, but they're rare. I suppose that's another fun thing I can add to the *Only Happens to Violet* list.

I shove thoughts of March aside and spin the empty glass tumbler on the table.

"Anyway, we were having a good conversation. I was starting to relax. I thought he was going to ask about dancing or something. And then I saw Jasper crossing the room, and I panicked. So I ducked into a larger crowd of people just coming off the dance floor and heading toward the food."

My throat closes up as I remember seeing Jasper, his eyes wild and his hands shaking, as he confronted Rylan. Faedra grabs my hand, squeezing my fingers until my breathing slows down again.

"Turns out, Jasper's part of his pack."

Faedra grimaces. And then I tell her the worst part of it all, the part that's made the last day an absolute nightmare scenario.

"I didn't hear everything that was said. But what I did hear was... awful. It was awful, Fae."

She nods. "You don't have to repeat it."

But I think I do. Having someone else know... it helped being able to admit to her how much I liked Rylan. "He said that matching with me is the absolute worst thing that can happen."

Her concern drops away, her eyes flashing with a rarely seen hatred. "What the actual hell, Violet? And the Council thought you guys were a good idea?"

I have nothing to offer. I'm just as confused as she is over the whole thing. What could the Council possibly have seen that made them convinced this was the best course of action? Unless someone's trying to use me to get back at my mom? Doesn't the Council have safeguards against things like that?

I've been thinking in circles all fucking day, and my head aches. I drop my head onto my arm and close my eyes. I could really use a second drink. When I mutter as much, Faedra laughs and heads toward the bar. She's quiet when she returns and presses a second Old Fashioned into my limp grasp.

I throw back this one just as fast as the first and then drop my head again.

"That's your last one," Faedra murmurs. "You have your last final tomorrow, and you cannot be showing up late for it."

I laugh, though it's heavy with the same despair I've been feeling.

"Pretty sure I've done my best work in that damn chemistry class hungover," I mutter, glancing up at her. "Remind me why I thought a fucking biomedics degree was the best option?"

"Because you weren't sure you were going to ever consent to matching when you declared it, and when you realized you might actually decide to let the Council control your fate, you were too far invested to change it." Faedra's voice is dry. The effect is lost when she giggles a moment later, though. "And also because you saw the first essay I had to do for that Ancient Western Asia class and decided you'd rather make your eyes go crossed looking at numbers."

Eight pages of talking about Mesopotamia. Eight. Pages. How did anyone manage to have enough to say about fucking *Mesopotamia* to fill that much space? I'll take the numbers and headaches, thank you.

A microphone feeds back, cutting through the din of the bar, and I groan.

How did I forget Wednesdays were karaoke night? The first guy isn't too bad, all things considered. But the second person makes me want to hide out in the bathroom.

"Are you going to fight the match?" Faedra asks, talking over the woman's second attempt at timing the chorus even remotely right.

I should have. And yet...

I shake my head.

Faedra's pursing her lips when I muster up the courage to

actually look at her, rolling my forehead along my arm until she's in my line of sight. I cock one eyebrow, and she sighs.

"Trying to decide if it's you attempting to get back at your mother in some weird, delusional type of way, or if you're hoping there might be a way to find out what went wrong with Jasper and try to fix it."

Did I say she was the best friend a woman could have? I may have to change my tune. Because right now I just want to punch her.

She tilts her head and takes another drink from her mug, never looking away from me.

Eventually, I lose the will to try to wait her out. We'll blame it on the alcohol. I'm typically way more stubborn than her.

"Both, I think." I push myself back up, resting my elbows on the table so I can prop my chin on my hands. "My mom will be absolutely mortified when she finds out the pack has a Beta. And... well, I really want to fuck Rylan again." Faedra's cheeks darken, but she nods in support anyway. "And maybe there's a small part of me that hopes whatever made Jasper decide I wasn't enough can be... persuaded now. That I've changed enough for him to want me again."

"You want me there for your call?"

Absolutely. I've never been more terrified of a video meeting in my damn life.

I nod, and she sets her cup down. "All right. Now let's get you home before you punch the girl that has no sense of timing on this song. The added benefit will be that you don't show up late to your final exam in college."

Ten

JASPER

"You guys still coming to trivia tomorrow?" Huntley makes it to me in record time, both of her instruments already slung over one shoulder, her bag tossed over the other. Her hair is pulled back today, though a couple of the short brown pieces frame her face.

"Pretty sure, yeah," I say. She grabs my music binder and follows me into the storage room. Rylan's already there, setting his string bass against the wall the other two bassists store theirs. We lock eyes across the room, and my blood heats. His lips twist into a knowing smirk before he turns away, his focus stolen by our conductor. They disappear into his office, their heads close together, Rylan pulling out his phone and going through the notes I know he keeps there even though he's too far away for me to actually see them.

"Gross," Mason jokes behind me. "How are you still in the honeymoon phase? Hasn't it been, like, three years?"

Huntley and Liz both laugh, and I roll my eyes.

"Real funny, Mason," I mutter, grabbing my cello case and propping it open.

He shrugs as he moves around me to his own case. "Not our fault you were blind as a bat. Now we just finally get to joke about it."

It had taken nearly three years for Rylan and me to realize that we were into each other. Three years of stolen glances, a pipe breaking in my old apartment, a couple dates with Dominic, and one very nasty fist fight after one of our concerts last September.

The din of the philharmonic chatting around me dies away between one heartbeat and the next. Giles—our conductor—leans out of his office. Rylan does the same a moment later. His gaze flicks to me and then away right before the color drains away from his face and neck, the dual snakes twisting up his neck an even more stark black. We twist around to see what's happened, and my heart lodges in my throat.

A young woman crosses the room, her simple navy pantsuit pressed to within an inch of the fabric's life, her black hair pulled back and tied against the nape of her neck in some sort of sleek bun. Her eyes are shrewd, the small pin on her lapel signaling her as one of the employees of the Council.

Employee. Not intern.

Fuck. Me.

She makes an impressive line to where Rylan and Giles are still standing in the threshold of the office, her feet never faltering despite several instrument cases and other small items littering the ground from the post-rehearsal rush to get out of here. My lover's eyes light on me for a heartbeat before she blocks him, the direction in them clear.

I pull out my phone and send a quick text to Dominic.

Council employee is here.

Che palle.

English?

I'll be there in ten.

There's no way that's what he actually said, but I shove my phone into my pocket instead of harping on him for whatever vulgar phrase is his favorite this week.

"Mr. Montegue," the woman says, holding out her hand.

Huntley gasps. Liz gasps. Mason chuckles.

"Think that might be a record, Jasper," he murmurs. "Not only did you manage the paperwork in less than six months, you matched at your first gala. You sure you're not an Omega?"

I scowl at him, my heart thundering in my ears. How long had I wished to designate? How many months had I hoped to suddenly display the innate characteristics of either designation so I wouldn't have to give up Violet? Of course it would be now, when I'm content with my partners and settled in my skin as a Beta that something like this would happen. The irony is like ash on my tongue.

I ignore how my hands shake as I close the cello case and start across the room. Giles urges the woman into his office after Rylan. The sudden scene over, everyone else's attention slowly returns to their own business. Giles steps aside as I get to the office, his hands in his pockets. I knock once on the doorway, and the woman looks over her shoulder.

"Perfect. I trust that between the two of you, all pertinent information will be given to your pack's third member."

Rylan mutters an affirmative. His knuckles are white where he clutches the thick, unmarked envelope.

"The video call is scheduled for tomorrow evening."

I force my breathing to stay even, to keep the panic that's

welling inside me off my face until we're somewhere safe for that kind of freak out. If Rylan can hold it together, then, fuck, so can I.

"Congratulations, Pack Montegue," she says, nodding her head first toward Rylan and then to me.

Before we can say anything, she turns on her heel and leaves the office, crossing the storage room with the same precision as before.

"You texted him?" Rylan asks.

I nod and run my hands through my hair, trying to keep my stomach from climbing up my throat. Giles leans around the doorway.

"Want to hang out in here until everyone else clears out? Liz looks like she's about to start mowing people over to get to you."

Of course she does. She's probably ready to throw a fucking party to celebrate. She has no idea that this is actually the worst possible scenario. Dominic's going to be livid.

"That'd be great, Giles," Rylan says, his voice way calmer than I'd honestly expected.

I murmur my thanks, too. No way am I walking out of here while everyone is still milling about.

Dominic climbs out of the Alfa Romeo the moment he's slid it into park and killed the engine, walking across the garage and into our home without a glance back. Rylan opens my door and laces his hand with mine as I toss my bag over my shoulder. With a heavy sigh, I start toward the house, too.

Rylan tightens his hold on me, urging me to stillness and turning me toward him in one fluid move. My heart flutters, my dick stirring despite all the stress and tension sitting heavily in the air.

"I love you," he murmurs, his eyes intent on mine. It's the most solemn I've heard him be, and for a heartbeat, the packet in his bag drops away from my worry, and it's just the two of us, alone in this moment surrounded by the products of our commitment. In another life, it might even be our elopement. "No matter what this packet says, Jasper. I love you."

It's on the tip of my tongue to ask him again how he knows her, how he ran into her and probably had sex with her. But I keep the questions locked behind my lips, opting instead to palm the back of his neck and kiss him until we're both breathless, my dick digging into his hip and his scent surrounding us. There's no point in asking when she might not even be the Omega the Council's chosen. And if she is?

Panic swells in my chest, stealing my breath more completely than the kiss.

Rylan grunts, twisting us until I'm pressed between the car and his hard body. He breaks the kiss as I grab his hips. His lips are soft as they brush along my jaw and down my throat. His teeth aren't. I gasp as he bites the small hollow between my collarbone and neck. He runs his tongue over the stinging skin, and I groan, letting my head fall back and my eyes close.

"Jasper." Rylan's voice is low and hoarse, nearly desperate.

He palms me through my jeans, and my hips buck forward.

"Fuck, I need you so bad, Jas," he mutters. "I can't fucking breathe."

The feeling's mutual. Six months together, and the aching need for him is just as overwhelming as the day I sucked him off in his kitchen. My mouth waters at the memory.

Maybe it's time to recreate that moment.

"You have me," I whisper against his lips.

Before he can protest, I drop to my knees and manage his jeans. His cock springs into my hands, hard and long, a drop of pre-cum already beading at the tip. I lick it off, enjoying the salty tang on my tongue, before tracing the metal piercing. He grunts, letting one hand twist into my hair. His curse is low and fervent as I swallow him whole, letting him nudge the back of my throat without preamble.

His Adam's apple moves with his swallow. Heat settles low in my belly, my dick hard enough to ache, but I don't rush my movements. Fuck, he's gorgeous. The way his hand tightens in my hair with each long stroke of my tongue, the way his eyes dilate when I swallow as he hits the back of my throat again, the tightening of his stomach as he leans over me and rests his open hand on the roof of the car. I want to capture this moment, print it out so I can remind myself of the way he looks at me like I'm his entire fucking world.

"Shit, Jas," he mutters, thrusting deep enough that my throat tightens involuntarily.

He pulls away just long enough that I can suck in a breath. I grab his thighs, squeezing in silent permission, and he groans. His scent surrounds us, a cocoon that has my heart settling even as it races in my ears from my arousal. I tighten my hold on his legs and relax my jaw. His growl is low, his teeth clenched hard enough that a muscle ticks in his cheek.

I run my palms along his calves and then back up, keeping the touch light and teasing.

He breaks. He takes a half step into me, forcing my back against the car door, as he adjusts his grip on my hair. His thrusts turn brutal, hardly allowing me the chance to breathe, but I keep relaxed against him. My jaw aches, and my eyes water, but neither eclipse the deep satisfaction of knowing *I* am the one doing this with him. He could have anyone, and he's with *me*.

The thought is enough to pull a moan from my chest.

Rylan grunts and then curses, the warning coming nearly too late for me to prepare. The salty tang of his cum on my tongue triggers an involuntary swallow, pushing his dick deeper.

"Ah *fuck*," Rylan hisses.

Eleven

RYLAN

My knees are still fucking shaking as Jasper pops off my dick and tucks it back away, careful of the jeans' zipper. His rising from kneeling is just as graceful as his drop into it. My stomach tightens, desire shooting through my still-buzzing veins.

Hell, it's been six fucking months. Six months, and it still feels like the first time. Every time he touches me, kisses me, fucks me, it's like the first time all over again—new and thrilling and fulfilling in a way I've never experienced before. His lips are soft against mine, his smile radiant as I pull away from him. The purr starts, low in my chest, and I don't fight it as I wrap my arms around his waist and pull him against me.

"I love you," he murmurs, his lips brushing my ear before his tongue traces the snakes on my neck.

I grunt and pull away from him. "We can't have round two right now."

As much as I'd enjoy it. We've christened just about every

corner of this place—and the cars, too. Jasper in a car is my favorite, I think. The confined space makes him even more desperate. I clear my throat and lace my hand in his even as I take another step away.

His sigh is wistful, but his smirk tells me it's not actually disappointment he feels. I shake my head and laugh before pulling him across the garage and into the house. Dominic's leaning against the island in the kitchen, poring over his phone. His black suit sits in stark contrast to the white of the cabinets and near-white of the counters. His gaze flicks up as we approach.

His silence as we near is more disconcerting than if he started spouting off curses in Italian. Dominic swearing means he's still listening to reason. Dominic silent? He's moved from ideas to action.

I drop my bag to the ground at my feet, keeping the island between us. My wire is razor thin right now, and Dominic and me fighting stresses Jasper out. The envelope blends into the counter, but it still feels out of place, like there's a giant spotlight on it demanding all of us acknowledge it.

"You want to do it?" Jasper asks, resting his head on his palms, his elbows on the counter.

He's taken up the side of the island between Dominic and me, and all the carefree joy he'd coaxed out of us both only a few minutes ago is gone. His eyes are tired, his shoulders tense, his lips twisted in worry. Worry over who the Council picked? Or whether Dominic will honor what he said in the fall? It better not be worry over whether or not he'll still have a place with us. We've spent the last six months proving that he's *ours*. No Omega will ever change that.

"Rylan?"

I pull myself from my thoughts and grab the envelope, ripping open the seal and dropping the packet of information onto the table. A small picture falls free from the rest of the papers, sliding across the island toward Jasper and Dominic, twisting so perfectly I'm half-convinced there's a magnet in it somewhere that's forcing its movements.

The black hair and smirk of a smile hit me in the chest, as strong as one of Dominic's punches. My knees buckle again, and I grab the counter. She's in a graphic tee in the photo, the album logo one I immediately recognize—The Script is one of my favorite bands. Her skirt flares away from her, landing mid-thigh. She's fucking *gorgeous*. A sick sense of excitement floods me. My dick's instantly hard, the remembered honeysuckle scent flashing through me like a damn aphrodisiac.

I'm going to get to fuck her again.

Probably. I'm *probably* going to get to fuck her again.

Jasper's gone pale, his hands trembling where they trace the edges of the photograph. Emotion wells in his eyes, so strong and consuming, it feels like I've been hit with it, too. Longing. Fear. And maybe, just maybe, some hope.

She's the fucking Omega. The raw confession from last week lingers unspoken, but it's practically shouting in my mind.

He's never talked about her, no more than that first night when I asked about the necklace. I've never pushed. He's here with me now. If he doesn't want to divulge previous relationships, that's his choice. I close the distance between us, running my hand along his shoulder before palming his neck. He glances away from the picture of Violet, and my breath catches.

"You all right?" I ask.

His throat moves with his swallow as he thinks over whatever he wants to say.

"*Non importa*," Dominic mutters, gruff. He's rifling through the paperwork, not looking at either of us. And certainly not the photo of Violet.

Jasper scowls and turns away from me. "What do you mean it's not important?"

"I'm having it annulled." He says it like he's saying he's going to get steak for dinner. Emotionless, clinical. My stomach twists, but I bite back the growl wanting to form. I knew he'd fight it. I knew it, and yet there was a heartbeat's moment of excitement, a hairsbreadth span of space for hope to form in my chest. I force my face to stay impassive even as Jasper freezes.

"Why?" His voice is ragged. He runs a shaking hand through his hair before messing with the chain of his necklace. "She's..." He swallows and grabs the informational letter from the top of the pile of papers Dominic's no longer looking through. "She's already accepted it. There's no way for you to undo this without her knowing about being reassigned."

Dominic shakes his head and fills out one of the forms. "That's not my problem, *Tesoro*. *You* are my concern. I won't allow you to be hurt."

"You promised me." Jasper's whisper hangs in the air. Dominic pauses, halfway through his signature, and narrows his eyes on our lover. "They get one shot at this, Dominic. You promised me you wouldn't sabotage it."

"What does it matter what I said then?" Dominic's voice is low, deadly. "You don't want her, either. You said you'd rather throw up with the philharmonic than see her again."

"That doesn't mean I want her ridiculed," Jasper says, surprisingly calm. "The match will be made public before any of that paperwork has a hope of being processed. The entire country will know that we rejected her."

Not really. Only the most drama-obsessed pay attention to the Council's matching announcements. There will be hundreds listed over the next couple days as the paperwork is finalized with the Omegas that attended the April gala. They'd have to actively hunt for this one, and we simply aren't famous enough for that.

Dominic's growl fills the kitchen between one heartbeat and the next. "And she rejected *you*, *Tesoro*. Why do you defend her?"

Jasper shakes his head before covering his face, forcing a deep breath.

"Because no matter what happened in Seattle, her mom is a goddamn piece of work. I wouldn't wish her on my worst fucking enemy, Dom, and God only knows how much worse she's gotten in four fucking years. *She* will pay attention to the matches as they're publicly announced."

Dread settles like a stone, weighing down my chest until it's difficult to breathe. Jasper isn't prone to hyperbole. If he says she's awful, then she's awful.

The silence stretches between the three of us, the house quiet and cold despite all the small things Jasper's been doing the last couple months to make it feel like ours. Dominic picks up the form that's still halfway filled out, his face eerily blank.

"All right, *Tesoro*."

He pushes away from the island and heads deeper into the house, toward the wing with our bedrooms, the paper still held tightly in his grip. Jasper blows out a breath that's nearly a sob, and I twist back toward him, my friend forgotten for the more important concern of my lover. His head is in his hands, his shoulders hunched and tight as he leans over the counter.

"How do you know her?" Jasper's voice is hoarse, like he's been screaming for days. "Where did you run into her?"

The truth sits like ash on my tongue, but I say it anyway. "The Haven."

Jasper tenses, his fingers digging into his skin. "She lives here?"

"I don't know," I admit. I never hunted her down on socials. What was the point? Not to mention it would have been in violation of working at the Haven. Strictly no contact outside of the facility unless the Omega approaches you. "You're not allowed to attempt contact while working there. And once I stopped…" I shrug.

Jasper nods once, his body still tight.

"Tell me about her," I whisper. "About what happened."

He drops his hands, revealing dual tear tracks running down his face. I wipe them away, cupping his cheeks and kissing him. His breath shudders out of him.

"I met her while doing my first couple years of college at the community college. Funds were tight, and my auditions didn't pull any scholarships. She was there with her friend who was touring the place." He pulls away from me, and I let my hands fall to my sides. He traces her face and then body on the photograph. "She hadn't even designated yet."

Surprise lights through my veins.

"How old were you?"

"Just about to turn 21," he admits. "She was seventeen, finishing her junior year."

He swallows, and then the rest of the words come pouring out of him, like a dam breaking on a river.

"She designated that fall, almost exactly a year after we started dating. She was in a panic. Her mom is awful, concerned with social standing and what people think about her. She sees her kids as pawns in her own PR game of sorts. Most of the super rich are like that from what I've heard and seen. Her dads are cool though, especially Kurt. He's her biological father."

I rest a hand on his. "She grew up in a pack?"

Jasper nods. "She'd hoped she wouldn't designate. She wanted to be a Beta, wanted to be less under her mother's thumb. She was heartbroken when she perfumed the first time and the bloodwork confirmed it."

There's a level of irony in that that has me forcing down a laugh. Of all of us, I'm the only one that's ever actually been *happy* about my designation. It helps that it's the reason I'm still alive. She'll probably fit right in. Assuming Dominic can get his head pulled out of his ass. And whatever went wrong between Jasper and her is fixable.

"Her mom wanted her on suppressants to keep her heat from emerging, said it was to keep her safe while she was finishing high school, but V-Vi—" He trips over her name and clears his throat. "Violet thought it probably had more to do with controlling what Alphas she interacted with. You know how vulnerable they are when they're in heat."

I move to stand next to him, pressing my lips into the nape of his neck, soothing him with my touch when words would never be enough. The tension slowly ebbs from his body, his weight pressing back against me, his temple resting against mine.

"So tell me what went wrong, why you ended up here with us at the philharmonic instead of staying in Seattle with her."

He does, each word more heartbreaking than the last, until he's completely limp in my arms.

I need another cigarette, and then I need to bury myself in a bottle of whiskey even though I know getting blackout drunk is just asking for problems. Because this rift between them? I'm not sure it's fixable.

Twelve

Faedra sets the plate of chocolate covered fruit on the coffee table before handing me my favorite mug.

"You didn't have to do this," I say as she sits beside me on the sofa.

Her eyebrows are drawn low, her lips pulled down in her concern. "Of course I did. You're my best friend."

My smile is less forced than the others I've given today. She leans her head on my shoulder. "Did you unblock him?"

"This morning," I say. Jasper's not overly active on socials, mostly just reposting from other friends. It was still enough to get a crash course of the last six months of his life, though. "He plays for the philharmonic. And he's been with Rylan and the other Alpha since the fall."

Unless the dates on the photos are off, they hooked up shortly after my heat.

It shouldn't sting, and it certainly shouldn't make me jealous. The Haven was literally his job. He got paid to knot me until my heat subsided. Doesn't mean that I'm actually rational about it. The fact that *Jasper* has gotten Rylan these last months while I've been dreaming of his knot and whatever citrus scent he has just makes it burn more.

"Guess it's lucky we didn't end up seeing that candlelight performance last November then," Faedra murmurs. "That would've been a shitty way to end the night. And then we wouldn't have gone out for ice cream and seen that blood moon."

I can't help but laugh, glancing at the print of said moon that's hung on her door. "You nailed that photo, so I can't be upset either." And she did. She's won two different photo competitions with that print.

A notification sounds on my computer, and I pull it toward me. Faedra stands from the sofa and heads toward her room. "Text me if you need me."

"Of course, Fae," I murmur, clicking the provided link from the Council. It takes me to a meeting with only one person, the woman who's been assigned to my matching. "Hello, Mary."

"Good evening, Ms. Fallon." She offers me a quick smile that isn't quite warm. "The pack is just finalizing their set-up with my coworker. I'll get you connected to them as soon as possible. Do you have any questions for me?"

I look over my shoulder, making sure Faedra's door is closed. "About annulment..." I start.

The woman's eyes grow sharp as she answers my questions.

"You're sure?" I ask again, nerves making my throat tight.

She nods again. "Absolutely, Ms. Fallon."

I blow out a breath and nod. "All right. Thank you."

She looks at something else on her screen. "They're ready. Are you?"

"Yes, Mary. Thank you."

She does something on her end, and then there's suddenly

two new boxes, Mary's face nowhere to be seen. A young man stares at me out of one screen. I vaguely recognize him as the man Faedra's been talking to about her own match. The other screen contains *them*.

Dominic sits in the middle, a heavy scowl making his features seem nearly severe, his cheekbones sharp and his lips literal perfection. He's in an identical black button-up and pair of slacks that he had in the picture. Rylan's hair is messier than the photo and the gala, and maybe a little bit longer, too. The hoodie he wears has *Snow Patrol* scrawled along the chest. His gaze is guarded but not actively hostile.

It takes all my willpower to take in the third person. Jasper's hair is longer now, a couple strands dropping across his forehead. His blue eyes are just as striking, though. He's wearing a simple gray t-shirt. The metallic reflection of a necklace catches the light, but it's tucked under his collar, so I can't see what's at the end of it. I force my breathing to stay calm and my face into a blank, half-there smile. Something that takes little effort.

"Good evening, Ms. Fallon," the man says, ripping me from my quiet perusal of the men. When I confirm I have no additional questions, he says, "This call automatically ends in an hour. Don't panic when it cuts out. I'd start with exchanging numbers or socials or whatever other way you prefer to communicate."

I murmur a soft agreement, noticing that the men are silent. His box disappears off the screen a moment later, leaving only the three men I've matched with.

Pack Montegue.

Dominic stands up, his scowl still firmly in place. Jasper twists toward him, stopping him with a hand on his thigh. My chest tightens at the simple intimacy of the movement, at the way Dominic's gaze softens for a heartbeat of time, the way Jasper leans into him. I glance away as they kiss, that blade twisting in my chest until I feel like I can't breathe.

No wonder he left me. I'm the literal opposite of Dominic. Well, except maybe in personality. He's as much a black cat as I am from what I can tell. But I'm Omega, not Alpha. I crave comfort and routine and safety. I need touch and smells and a place I can create as my own without restrictions. Alphas don't. They're possessive and territorial, needing to stake their claim and mark their people as their own.

Rylan leans forward, ignoring the other two men. "What's your number, Violet?"

Right. We're supposed to actually be productive with this thing. Asking for my number is good. Normal. I rattle it off, and he's quick to send me a single text, only his name and a winking emoji. I save the number and then put my phone away, leaning forward and crossing my arms, trying to keep my fidgeting from being noticeable.

By the time I'm resettled, Dominic is gone, and Jasper is looking at me like he's attending someone's funeral. Is it so awful that we're matched that he feels like something has died? I force a swallow, trying to move the lump lodged there.

Fuck me. I'm better than this, right? I can face down a call with these men. I can handle it. I promised myself I would give myself the weekend. If everything is still fucked after the weekend, then...

I cut the thought off, already feeling the frustrated tears springing to life. I blink to clear them, hoping they're not obvious on the video call. Rylan moves a paper around, pulling something that looks like it might have come from the Council's packet of information and looking it over.

"You go to UCLA?" he asks, glancing up at me.

Jasper's still looking at me. It feels like that somber, tired gaze sees right through me to the scared girl I feel at the moment. In another life, he was that person. He saw the scared girl and, for a time, helped me believe I could be more than that, could coax her into becoming something other than what society demanded of my designation.

And then he was gone.

I clear my throat and focus on Rylan, trying to keep myself together. Only an hour. I only had to make it an hour, and then I could cry again.

"Yeah," I say, picking at my fishnets. "I'll be graduating next weekend."

"That's fantastic," Rylan says, setting down the paper, dropping his hand to Jasper's thigh. Jasper visibly relaxes under the touch, and the knife in my chest twists again. "Send us the information for the ceremony. We'll make sure to be there."

Jasper stiffens but doesn't say anything, and Rylan runs his hand down Jasper's thigh, soothing him so instinctually it fucking *hurts*. Every single instinct in me wants to beg him for his address and pay whatever hellacious rideshare fee so that he can comfort me, too.

God, I'm a mess this week. And I can't even blame it on my heat coming soon.

Jasper clears his throat, and Rylan takes a deep breath. "I need to go run through some pieces before dress rehearsal tomorrow."

Rylan's mouth twists before his expression smooths out. He nods, drawing Jasper to him and kissing him, too. It's different than with Dominic, but the intimacy is the same. It's something my parents have never had, that I've only ever seen in groups around me on campus or in movies. Never in my own life. Not since Jasper.

I clear my throat.

"You don't need to stay on for the full hour," I say as Rylan focuses back on me, Jasper's retreating form disappearing from the frame.

"I know," he says. He grabs that piece of paper again. "It's been a long time since I've been in school. What's your major?"

"Biomedics." His eyebrow ticks up. I offer up the explanation before he can ask. "I declared my second semester Freshman year. I wasn't planning on matching then. I'd planned on going into research around Omega designations."

"Specifically Omega? Or Alphas as well?"

I scrunch my nose. "Definitely not Alphas. They're overbearing to start with. Asking them to consent to research performed by an Omega? Half of them would laugh me out of the room."

"That's a shame," Rylan says, his voice dropping, gaining a rough edge.

My breath catches in my throat, and my scent strengthens around me. I clear my throat to keep my reaction from being quite so obvious. I don't rush to fill the silence, not really sure what to ask him or offer up about myself. I've never tried to backtrack a one-night stand into a relationship, much less an Alpha that knotted me through my heat. Desire flashes across my skin, and I can feel my chest heat with it.

"I imagine these are helpful when all of this is long distance," Rylan says after a few minutes. He scratches at the snake tattoo on his neck. "But they drive me up the wall. How about I come grab you after dress rehearsal tomorrow morning?"

A seed of hope blooms in my chest, swelling almost too fast for me to tamp down. "All right," I offer, keeping my voice calm. "I can send you my address."

"Great," he says. "Rehearsal ends at noon, so I should be there by one. I'll let you know when I'm on my way, all right?"

I nod and give him a hesitant smile. I don't quite manage to hide the tears this time, and his eyebrows furrow. I glance away, blinking until they're gone again.

"I'll see you tomorrow, Violet."

Like an idiot, I nod again and wave. "Yeah, okay. I'll see you then."

The video message goes dark, a small box notifying me that everyone has left the chat. I close my laptop and lean my head against the sofa, blowing out a long, heavy sigh, letting the minutes tick by until I don't feel quite so helpless anymore. Then I pop two of the chocolate covered banana slices into my mouth and chase them with the now cold black tea. I knock once on Faedra's door, but when she doesn't respond, I set about getting ready for the night, turning off the lights in the shared space and turning on the air purifier we keep tucked under the window to keep our scents from drowning out the living room.

The annulment request form sits on my nightstand. I force a swallow, wetting my dry mouth.

And then I slide it into the single drawer, tucking it out of sight. For now.

I'm just about to cuddle into my bed when there's two hard knocks on the main door of our dorm. Shit, I hope it's not something happening with the sorority party I know is happening but don't *know* is happening on floor two. It's my night of being the on-call R.A.

I swing the door open, prepping for the worst.

"Ms. Fallon?" A man maybe a couple years older than me stands in the hallway, looking awkward as all hell. His tie is perfectly placed, held by a small tie tack in the shape of the Council's insignia. My stomach twists even as my shoulders relax.

"That's me," I say.

He hands me a small envelope. "No response from you is required if you wish to ignore the motion. If you wish to accept the motion, have this returned by end of day tomorrow."

He turns on his heel and heads down the hallway the moment I nod my understanding. I rip open the envelope and pull out the form, confusion making my movements clumsy. I mutter a curse and throw the entire thing in the trash.

Of course my mom has already filed a motion to have me reassigned. Fuck, she moved fast. It's only been announced since noon. I shut off the lights and climb into bed, cocooning myself in my favorite blanket.

It takes a long time for me to remember how to sleep.

Thirteen

JASPER

Friday rehearsals are typically my favorite. The entire symphony playing through the program, listening to all our work coming together into something inspiring and touching and sometimes extraordinary is the push I often need by this point in the week. Typically. Today, I can't focus on fuck all except the image of Violet on the mandatory video call last night.

I swear, I saw tears in her eyes. And not just once, but multiple times. I'd been prepped for anger or hatred. Cold disdain, even, like she felt I was beneath her. I hadn't been prepared to see the flash of vulnerability when Rylan asked her about school.

Of course she made it into UCLA. It was her dream school. She'd worked her ass off junior and senior years to get a high enough SAT score to offset the four Cs she'd gotten as a sophomore. Not to mention the volunteer work she'd done to prove she was invested. She'd been here, in LA, the last four years. Not long after I left Seattle, really.

All those moments where I thought I saw her, could have sworn I recognized her in a crowd. What if I had truly seen her? What if she had gone to the symphony? Had she known I was here? Had she avoided me all this time?

Mason nudges me, interrupting my counting, but I look at him knowing I have a bit before the solo in the third piece.

"You good?" Mason mouths.

I nod, grabbing my bow and prepping for the solo, keeping my full attention on Giles where he stands at the front of the orchestra. This time, I can't quite slip into the music, my mind still spiraling around everything that's happened since Rylan opened the Council's packet Wednesday night.

Do I hate her for that, the loss of my sanctuary? Or is it really the Council I'm angry with?

My gut twists. Or maybe it's Dominic.

He left the house when he left the video call, slipping out without taking any of the cars, and hasn't been home since. I slept in his bed last night, hoping to catch him when he finally came back. I woke up to the same empty bed I fell asleep in, the other side of his bed untouched. Rylan waited as long as he could before forcing me into the car so we wouldn't be late to rehearsal. As it was, we arrived with barely enough time to get set.

Liz has been restless next to Mason all morning, her eyes darting to me at every break in the music. My throat dries out as I try to think about what I'll tell her. The final note of the program rings out, and I try to sink into it, try to appreciate it like I've tried all week. But I can't quite manage. Giles holds us in stillness longer than typical, his gaze sweeping over us all. When he finishes, he smiles and drops his arms, clapping his hands a couple times.

"Wonderful work," he says, flipping through the music on his stand. "Call tonight is seven."

He steps off the podium and heads toward his office, glancing at his watch and then his phone.

"Think he has some hot lunch date he needs to get to?" Mason murmurs, humor lacing his voice.

Liz laughs. "I've seen him with Natalie a couple times the last few weeks. Wouldn't they be adorable together?"

I tune them out. What Giles does on his own time with another consenting adult isn't any of my business. It takes me longer than usual to pack everything up, that sense of urgency that normally stirs me along nowhere to be found. Why rush when Rylan is already here and Dominic has been gone for nearly an entire day without even a text letting me know he's all right?

Huntley's eyes are too keen, like always, seeing more than I really want her to. She grabs my music and motions for Liz to head into the storage room, her lips set in a firm line.

"That bad?" she asks once our friends are out of ear shot. Not many people are left picking up their things in the concert hall, just a few of the violas that are chatting about plans for the weekend. "You look like you've been broken up with, Jas."

My laugh is humorless. "Well..."

Huntley drops into the seat beside me.

"What happened?" All humor is gone, her eyes serious where she watches me. The last of the other musicians leave the stage, and I lean my head back, staring at the stage lights that are mostly turned off right now.

"Dominic's pissed, and I haven't seen him since last night," I admit.

Huntley doesn't know that we weren't actually trying to get matched up with an Omega. No one does. It's the type of thing that could land us in some serious fucking hot water with the

Council. And you don't just go around pissing off the United Council of Alpha and Omega Designations, Inquiries, and Concerns—not even if you have more than passing ties to the Italian mafia.

"He doesn't like the Omega?" she asks when I don't offer anything more.

I shake my head and stand up. "No. He wants to force a reassignment."

Huntley raises an eyebrow and walks with me into the storage room. "That's... that's a big deal, Jas."

My laugh is humorless. It's also the only reply I can manage to muster at the moment as I get my cello put away and slung over my shoulders.

"Well, I was going to ask about meeting them if they're going to be around this weekend, but..." She trails off, waiting to see if I'll correct her. I don't. "Give it a few days, Jas. I'm sure it'll all work out. You figuring things out in the fall was pretty rocky, too. I can't imagine the finesse it takes to introduce another person into a pack. Trying to reorient your life around one person is difficult enough."

Fuck, I'd forgotten how nice it could be just to chat with another Beta, someone who didn't have all the innate drives and needs of the other designations, someone who was just... normal. That awful thing that's been clawing at my chest since Wednesday night pauses long enough for me to get a deep breath. Maybe this type of horrid awkwardness was normal at the beginning of being matched. It's not like we saw Liz during that thirty day window. By the time we all reconvened in August, she was happily settled in with the four Alphas, her stacked rings a beautiful, if flashy, addition to her other jewelry.

Would Violet expect those? She probably would. They were traditional gifts given to an Omega within a pack. One ring for each person in the pack, typically tailored to the Omega's taste and with enough variance to be easily distinguished within the set. Her mom had a trio that she'd wear at home and another, more ostentatious set she'd don when going to events, especially anything attached to Fallon Capital.

The necklace sits like a heavy weight against my sternum.

Or maybe she'd hand it back to me with another fucking note telling me I wasn't good enough for her.

A hand on my elbow pulls me from the morose thought. Rylan's eyes are full of concern, though his face stays blank. I lace my fingers with his, squeezing just enough to let him know I'll be all right. Probably. He leans into me, pressing his lips to mine for a fleeting heartbeat, and then whispers in my ear.

"I'm meeting up with her." My breath catches. He runs his nose along my jaw, a purr vibrating low in his chest. It's just enough to make me relax. He still wants me, even with her around. Even with everything now different, and Violet and my's ugly history on the table for him to examine, he still wants me. "I'll be back in time for call. You take the car."

I nod and kiss him, this time not caring when he deepens it, forcing it faster and messier than I typically am comfortable with at our workplace. Bergamot surrounds us, and another bit of that tight band around my chest eases away.

"I love you," he murmurs as he pulls away. His eyes are bright, his hold on my hand unrelenting.

"Love you more," I manage to whisper, trying for our old joke. Desire races across his face before he can hide it, and he takes another half-step into me, just enough that I can feel the line of his dick where it presses against his jeans. My stomach tightens, and a flash of heat shoots down my spine.

"Don't make me prove that you're wrong, Jas," he murmurs. "You in a car is my favorite."

His phone pings with a notification, and I hum, kissing him one more time. "I'll see you tonight."

Fourteen

RYLAN

The address Violet gave me ends up being one of the large dorm buildings on UCLA's campus, tucked away from most of the academic buildings. It's large and overbearing, though I imagine some find it more awe-inspiring. The orange brickwork contrasts with the green landscaping. Two young women sit on the steps leading to the main entrance, and they pause in their giggling over something on one of their phones as I pass by them.

They don't say anything until I'm back out of earshot. I roll my eyes and stretch my neck, trying to remember how to fucking do this. How did someone start a relationship?

It's not like I could really just expect her to suck me off the way Jasper did. And that still resulted in a nasty fight between me and Dominic. Though there wasn't really anything to stop another one of those from happening right now.

I shake my head, forcing a deep breath to clear my thoughts. The woman at the front desk waves as I pass by but doesn't ask any questions. There are benefits to being clearly older and appearing confident. As long as I didn't look like I was lost, I'd doubt anyone would have the courage to call me out for being here.

Her dorm is on the fourth floor, tucked into the farthest corner of the building. The door is decorated with photographs, mostly polaroids filled with sunsets and profiles and tons of different people laughing. I knock on one of the only open spots available and tuck my hands into my pockets, clutching the small box stashed there.

A redheaded woman answers the door, her hair pulled back into two long braids that track down her head and fall below her shoulders and out of sight. Her simple white crop top doesn't quite reach her floral knee length skirt, a thin patch of pale, freckled skin peaking out with each small movement she makes.

"Is Violet here?" I ask, clearing my throat.

The woman raises an eyebrow but opens the door.

"He's here, Vi," she calls out.

She moves deeper into the shared space, leaving me in the doorway without any kind of greeting at all. A door opens to the left, and Violet takes a single step into the living room. The woman walks up to her and takes her hand. A cell phone sits on the coffee table, forgotten by both girls until it starts vibrating with an incoming call. The redhead looks back at it and purses her lips.

"It's Samantha. They probably need me to deal with something downstairs. You good?" she asks.

Violet nods and drops the woman's hand. "I'll text you if I'm going to be late, Fae."

The other woman—*Fae*—nods as she answers the phone and settles into the lone chair tucked into the far corner of the room. Violet crosses the space, stopping in front of me, her eyes shrewd as she takes me in.

I hold out my hand without comment, trying to gauge how she's feeling after the video call devolved last night. It takes her a minute of indecision before she takes it. I lace our fingers together and pull her into me, running my nose along her neck and marking her with my scent without making a big deal of it.

Her breath hitches, but she doesn't scent.

Damn scent blockers.

She twists around me, grabbing a small purse hung beside the door without dropping my hand, guiding us out of the dorm and down to one of the side entrances of the building. Another group of girls congregate near this one, spread out on the grass.

"Are we waiting for a ride share?" she asks when we're about a dozen feet from the building.

"It's just a couple blocks," I say. "Shit, sorry. I can order one if you'd like?"

I'm so used to walking everywhere, even after six months of living in the large estate Dominic owns out in Brentwood, I didn't think to double check if she would be all right with the walk. She shakes her head, tucking her hair behind her ear.

"I'm fine," she says. "Just wanted to make sure I didn't need to get us to an easier place for someone to pick us up."

I squeeze her hand and start us toward the edge of campus. Everyone and their damn cat seems to be out today. Groups of people sit on low brick walls or play various games on the wide stretches of grass. All of them seem to be in a good mood, laughing and smiling.

"Finals finished today," Violet says without actually looking toward me. "Everyone's enjoying the time off before move out next weekend."

Fair enough. I guide her around a group of guys playing hacky sack in the center of the large circular pathway.

Violet grows steadily more tense beside me, and it sets those instincts on edge. I look around, taking in everything more thoroughly, trying to figure out what's made her anxious.

"Hey, Violet!" A guy comes toward us. His dark hair is parted down the center and falls to his ears. Combined with the polo and shorts and leather necklace, he's practically a walking neon sign for *fuckboys* everywhere. Violet freezes beside me, her hold on my hand now closer to a death grip. Her face is blank, but even I can tell that her eyes are wary.

The asshole doesn't seem to notice, though. Or care. His gaze takes me in, his lip curling for a minute, before he focuses on her again. He stops a few feet away and tucks his hand into his pocket. His voice is bright and about two levels too loud for the environment, and it attracts the attention of those closest to us.

"Saw your dad in the news," he says. "Seems like the new project is really taking off! Was wondering if—"

Tugging on Violet's hand, I step in front of her, hiding her from view. She doesn't resist me at all. The movement is so smooth, you'd think we'd rehearsed it before.

Sometimes I forget just how ingrained the instincts are.

She trusts you.

My stomach flips. The possessive growl builds in my chest, though I keep it from becoming as loud as the asshole is. The smile falls away from his infuriatingly pretty face. Why is it that the assholes are always the pretty ones? At least Jasper broke that mold.

A growl builds in his own throat, nearly as loud as mine. "You got something to prove, asshole?" he snarls, quiet enough now that no one else will hear him.

"Only have something to prove if you're not going to figure out she's uninterested," I say, the same deadly calm as him, letting my accent thicken to add to the effect. Here, in LA, sometimes sounding like an outsider can be helpful.

He takes the bait—hook, line, and sinker. "Like you would

fucking know what she wants," he snarls, closing the distance between us. "You think you can just show up here and decide she's yours? Did you convince her to fuck you already, too? You so desperate for an Omega that will tolerate you, you have to fish around the local campuses, asshole?"

The growl rips through my chest, louder than it's ever been.

Another guy comes up next to him, his face pale, and grabs his elbow, trying to pull him away from me. Violet's hold on my hand is a death grip, and it's the only thing keeping me from completely losing my shit on the asshole.

"Eric, man, it was match week, remember? Shut up before he lays you into the ground," the guy whispers, loud enough that I can hear him.

Eric snarls but takes a step away.

"It was announced Thursday. I *told* you to pay attention to the announcements," the other guy says. "Let's get out of here before campus security gets called. You know that won't look good for you."

It's like a switch flips. All at once, the lethal energy emanating from the other Alpha is gone, replaced instead by an easy-going feel I don't believe for a single fucking second.

"Hey, sorry, man," he says, raising his hands up in surrender, adopting that overly loud volume again. If I hadn't seen the feral gaze from before, I'd be half-convinced he was actually apologetic. "Didn't realize now was a bad time. I'll just…"

He trails off as the growl gets louder. I take a step toward him, snarling.

Didn't know it was a bad time? Does he think I'm a goddamn moron? He singled her out in a public place where he assumed she'd have no option but to talk with him. If I can tell that, then those around us can, too.

And then he decided he could take me, too, the fucking dumbass. I'm not Dominic, but I'm not fucking helpless. I'd have him in the ground before he could find anyone to help him out.

"Rylan," Violet whispers. "Let it go."

I force my body to relax, though the growl doesn't stop. A few people closest to us have their phones pulled out and pointed toward us. As I focus on more than the asshole in front of me, the charged silence of the crowd sinks in. There's a growing sense of anticipation in the group surrounding us.

Hell, the last thing I need is to get into a fucking fist fight when I'm trying to handle a skittish Omega. Switching my hold, I guide Violet around to my other side, keeping me between her and Fuckboy Extraordinaire. He tries to lean around me, and I growl again, curling my lips back. He blanches, his eyes widening to the point I can see white all the way around them, and takes a quick step back.

Everyone else gives us a wide berth, some even skittering out of our way despite not being in our path of travel at all.

"Sorry," I mutter as we cross the street and head toward the beach.

She shakes her head. "Don't be. Some of those people need to remember that there's more than just a label with designations. Especially Eric. He should know better than to try to approach an Omega very clearly with another Alpha."

She spits his name like it's bitter on her tongue, and that thing in my chest relaxes at her obvious dislike of him. The need to scent mark her again is strong, though. Breathing deep through my nose and out through my mouth takes the edge of it off as we cross the street.

"He's bothered you before?"

I switch us so I'm walking on the outside of the sidewalk.

She nods and sighs. "Has been trying for the last year to get on my good side so I'll put in a good word for him with my father," she explains after a minute. "Or at least... I assume that's why he's been pursuing me."

I guide her up the street a few blocks before stepping into one of the small local cafés in the area.

"Oh, I love this one," she whispers. It's so low, I don't think she expects me to hear her.

Good. Snooping through her Instagram last night like a fucking creep was useful, then.

"Why does Eric want a good word with your father? And why does he think you'll give it?"

She blows out a breath and cocks an eyebrow. "Starting out with easy questions, I see. Did the packet give you all the basics, so you figured you'd skip straight to the heavier topics?"

Her voice grows brittle, a thread of anger twisting through it. I frown, stopping her just inside the door, twisting her around so she faces me.

"What?" I ask her. "No. I was just trying to figure out if I need to make sure someone's around so I don't smash Fuckboy Extraordinaire's head into the pavement next time I show up to take you out somewhere."

Her eyes widen at my outburst.

After a long moment, she nods and squeezes my hand.

"Sorry," she murmurs.

I shake my head. Something clearly has her on the defense. Jasper, maybe? Though my asking about some random asshole of an Alpha that goes to the same school as her couldn't really be related. Jasper hasn't ever stepped on UCLA's campus as far as I know, and that asshole Alpha sure as fuck doesn't run in the same groups as my lover.

She clears her throat and gets into the short line.

Fifteen

RYLAN

"Fuckboy Extraordinaire?" she asks, her lips flicking up for a heartbeat, glancing over her shoulder.

I cock an eyebrow and purse my lips. She can't honestly think he looks like anything other than an absolute asshole.

She giggles. "Yeah, all right. I can see it. I've just never stopped to really label him as a fuckboy. Though now that I think about it..."

She trails off as the barista calls us forward. I tuck my hands into my pockets, watching as she orders a cortado. *Really?* I expected her to be more of an iced coffee drinker. She starts digging through her purse, and I grunt, urging her aside before she can get any weird ideas in her head.

The barista smiles at me.

"Flat white, please."

She nods, and I hand her cash to cover the tab and a small tip along with my name for the order.

"Pick a spot," I instruct Violet.

She takes in the room, her eyes moving carefully over each zone. Without a word, she crosses to the far bank of windows and drops into one of the low-back lounge chairs wedged into the corner. I take her in rather than following right after her, leaning against the counter as I wait for our drinks to be ready. She's in a set of ripped up jean shorts and a light blue shirt that complements her warm skin and dark hair. The light catches on that industrial piercing in her left ear, and as she turns back toward me, I can see a small gold hoop daith piercing in her right one, along with two more typical piercings mirrored in both.

"Rylan," a different barista calls out, setting two nondescript white mugs on the countertop.

Grabbing both, I cross the room and settle into the chair beside Violet, placing both cups on the small table between us. She's quick to take a large drink, not flinching at all at the heat of the coffee.

I adjust my legs, giving my half-hard dick a bit more room. That should not be so fucking arousing.

"So why does F.E. think he can use you to get a good word in with your dad? And why does he even care?" I ask again.

She sighs and rolls her eyes. "Because dumb guys like that think that being friends with me will get them easier access to my father's company. And there's a long-held belief that if you can get into Fallon Capital, you've got it made. At least in the finance industry."

I tense.

Wait.

Fallon Capital.

"Johnathan Fallon is your father?" I ask, suddenly cautious.

She scrunches her nose. It's fucking adorable.

"The one and only," she mutters.

This is going to be a fucking *mess* if we're not careful.

Johnathan Fallon is practically God on the West Coast, the CEO and owner of the largest financial conglomerate outside of the big tycoons out on Wall Street. The company funds the recording studio Mark owns, at least partially. Enough that he's often the one called to run the sound on fundraising events hosted by the company in LA.

I clear my throat and take a sip of the coffee.

"Not as glamorous as the world thinks?"

She sighs and sets the mug down, relaxing into the seat. "It never is, really. People always see what they want."

I take a longer pull of the drink, giving her time to decide if she wants to leave it at that.

After a moment, she continues.

"People see an Omega and think they're pushovers. Or they envy the fact that most Omegas end up in packs where it looks like they're doted on at every turn. And, sure, some packs are like that. But not all of them. Especially in the ultra-wealthy."

There's a long pause. I put the mug down and prop my chin on my hand. Her eyebrows are furrowed, and she taps her fingers, her nails clinking against the ceramic of her mug.

"People see my last name and assume I can give them whatever they want," she says. "Clout. Social media engagement. Some kind of in at my father's company that doesn't even exist. It's fucking exhausting."

She sighs. There's no evidence of the girl that left Jasper in cold blood, of the girl that wrote that letter and let someone act as messenger instead of being brave enough to talk to him face-to-face. She seems... fragile, almost. And not in the way Omegas often are. She seems almost like she's prepared for everything to fall apart, for everything to blow up in her face. Like everything happening around her is just a front that will be proven false at the first minor inconvenience. I recognize that look, the one that says you don't trust the good that's happening around you.

I lived it for almost a decade, after all. I'm well-acquainted with what that fear looks and feels like. And what causes it to exist in the first place.

"I'm sorry."

I keep my voice gentle and soft, and she relaxes further into her chair.

"You don't have to do that," she mutters, her eyes dropping until they're only half-open.

Shrugging, I take another sip of the coffee. "But you're not upset that I did."

The corner of her mouth tips up. "I guess I'm not. It's... not very common for me."

"Which part?" I ask.

Her look grows guarded. I think back over what I said and hold back a flinch. Shit, did she think I meant like... how often she hooks up with an Alpha? Because I definitely do not give a shit about her body count. I literally worked at the Haven for years to make ends meet.

"No insult meant," I say when she doesn't fill the silence between us. The café bustles with life around us, the speakers playing an indie piano track that sounds vaguely familiar. I'm pretty sure it's one of the ones Mark plays when the silence in the studio is too loud for him to focus. "Just trying to figure out what you need."

"What I need?" The question is skeptical.

"As an Omega. As a woman. As a partner." I stand and adjust my chair, turning it so I can sit normally and still see her. The barista manning the counter frowns but doesn't outright object to the move.

"Oh," she whispers, tracing the rim of her mug, her eyebrows drawn low. "I thought..." She shakes her head. "All right."

Curiosity and maybe something deeper has me wanting to pry her apart, make her tell me what she thought I meant when I asked what she needed. What other ways are there? I blow out a breath and take another drink of the coffee to keep from being a complete ass.

"Sorry that I'm really shit at this," she says after another long minute of silence.

I glance up at her. She's twisting her hair around her finger, her eyes on her own mug, her shoulders rolled in just a bit. None of the confident woman from the gala or all the photos littering her dorm room door. No, she looks like the unsure woman on the video chat yesterday.

"You're doing fine," I assure her, letting my voice go soft and calming again. Her eyelids flutter. "I suppose this is a good time to admit that I spent way too much time on your Instagram trying to figure out details about you because the little bit the Council gave was absolute shit."

She laughs and scrunches her nose again. It's definitely one of the cutest fucking things I've seen. It makes me want to kiss her. I spread my legs a bit wider and force myself to focus.

"I've spent the last day trying to figure out why you have one daith piercing but not both—so it's probably not for migraines. And why you have a scar on your nose from where you probably let a piercing close." I chug the last of the coffee and set the mug down beside my feet, keeping the table clear for her own use. "And don't get me started on that damn dress that's haunted my thoughts for the last two weeks."

There's a long stretch of silence, and she twirls the mug in her hands.

In for a penny, in for a pound. I continue, "I've also been trying to figure out why your first time using the Haven was in the fall despite you having lived here the last four years. Part of me wants to just straight up ask you if you had a boyfriend and broke it off, and that's why you ended up needing to use the facility. Is that completely tactless? Absolutely. But, fuck, the thought has haunted me. And why you work as an Ra and also at the Rowdy Seahorse when your dad is literally richer than God."

"You actually looked up where I work?" she asks softly.

It's almost like she's surprised by my interest in her. The implication that no one really *has* been interested in her outside of her name or designation twists my stomach.

"Well, yeah," I say, keeping the frustration out of my voice. "I wanted to know what drew you there, if it's somewhere you can still easily work if you want to now that we've been matched."

Her eyes snap to mine. "You're not going to make me quit?"

I frown and lean back in the chair to keep from reaching for her.

"Not if you really want to work there. I mean, the finances of the pack are stable, so you don't really have to." Not even factoring in Dominic. Jasper and I are more than capable of supporting her financially. "But, again, your dad is richer than God, so I doubt you're working there for the money."

She taps her fingers on the mug.

"You noticed my piercing scar?" Her voice is damn near *shy* now.

Hell yeah, I have. It's fucking hot. "Every time you scrunch your nose, it makes it more obvious."

"I don't think anyone has noticed it before," she admits after a moment. "I got it freshman year on a dare like a month after move-in. Faedra got her first orbital piercing done. She still has hers. She likes to put little charms dangling from it to match her mood."

Her lips tip up, and her shoulders relax. Faedra must be *Fae*, her roommate.

"Mom called the moment the first picture hit social media. It was the first time she'd really yelled at me over something I'd posted." She purses her lips and rolls her eyes. "Oh, she'd made *comments* before that. Rude little asides about this person's dress or that person's makeup not being just right. But it had never been directed toward me. I was a mess for the entire week and pulled the piercing the moment she hung up on me."

I hold back the growl by the skin of my teeth.

"I guess I should have realized she'd be awful about something like that, but..." She shakes her head. "She'd helped me through the worst event of my life that spring, so I thought maybe the nastier side of her had softened a bit, especially since Scarlett was gearing up for her matching gala. I was fucking *wrong*."

Worst event of her life?

"What happened?" I ask.

That guarded look is back in a heartbeat.

"My heart got broken, that's all," she whispers after a bit.

A breakup? Wait. The spring before she started school would have been her senior year. I count back the timeline Jasper gave me, a knot growing in my stomach and a lump forming in my throat. It had to be the same event. So why did she talk like he was the one that fucked her over? His heartbreaking story certainly wasn't something that he created himself.

I swallow back the questions. Now is not the time to insert myself into that.

She shakes her head and blows out a breath.

"Anyway, I used the facility last fall because my heat didn't fall during the school break. It's really difficult to get the work excused without an Alpha verifying that it was actually your heat. Or the Haven." She scrunches her nose again, and I lean forward. "And hiding out in my room while Faedra continued on like normal just... sounded awful."

"You didn't have any interest in using the Haven before then?" I ask.

She shakes her head. "I didn't even really want to match until after my heat in March."

She purses her lips and takes a quick sip of her drink. An alarm goes off on her phone that she's quick to silence.

"Everything all right?" I ask.

She nods. "I promised Faedra I'd be there when her call started tonight. I set a timer so I could make sure I'd be back in time."

"You're protective of her," I murmur, grabbing her mug and helping her stand.

She nods as I put my chair back the way it had been. "Faedra's amazing. Everyone needs someone in their corner that loves as fiercely and cares as deeply as she does. She's... she's my best friend."

The admission falls out of her mouth, and then she glances at me, that same distrusting panic from before flitting across her face. I keep my touch on her light as I guide her out of the café and back onto the sidewalk.

"I'm excited to meet her properly," I offer.

She's quiet the rest of the walk, though she lets me intertwine our fingers again. Campus is just as busy as before. She hums and leads me a different way across, avoiding the large open pathway where F.E. ambushed her earlier. By the time we're back in front of her door, I'm just about ready to ask her about the physical stuff. Not sex. I'm not an asshole. But kissing?

Fuck, I've wanted to kiss her for days.

I press her into the door and cup her face, watching her carefully. Her eyes dilate, her breath catching in her throat. Her eyes flutter closed as I close the space, and it's the little bit of encouragement I need. She tastes as sweet as I imagined, her lips soft against my own. The little whimper she makes in the back of her throat has me hard and aching in an instant, and I press into her, crowding her against the door. Her hands twist into my hair, pulling me down over her, her nails digging into my skin.

I'm a second from pulling her shirt over her head in this

hallway when the doorknob twists. I pull her off the door a moment before it opens, revealing the redheaded woman from earlier. Her hair is out of the braids, soft waves falling around her instead.

Her cheeks blaze bright red as she freezes.

"Oh shit, Vi, I'm so sorry. I was just going to grab a smoothie before my call."

I chuckle and pull away from Violet. "Don't worry about it. I'll chat with you later, Vi."

Her cheeks darken as she nods. I kiss her one more time and then head down the hall, not even bothering to adjust my boner.

Sixteen

RYLAN

I'm just tucking my double bass into its typical storage spot at the back of the prep room when Liz appears practically out of nowhere. I have to adjust my arm so I don't accidentally take her out with my elbow. Not that the almost collision isn't noticed. A low, menacing growl works its way across the room from one of the side entrances.

"It's fine, Zach," Liz says, not turning toward the Alpha. "It wasn't on purpose."

Zach doesn't much care, his eyes narrowing on me. I force a deep breath and scratch at my tattoo, giving myself a minute to collect myself before turning around and focusing on Liz. Jasper's just putting away his cello, slinging it over his shoulder, his gaze on the floor.

"What's up, Liz?" I ask, not bothering to hide the tired impatience.

"When do we get to meet her?" She's bouncing on her toes, still full of energy despite it being nearly eleven at night. "Jasper didn't have an answer, so we figured we'd check with you instead."

Huntley raises an eyebrow as she draws close enough to hear Liz. Though, honestly, most of the room can hear her. It's not like she's subtle. Jasper still isn't looking at me, his hands shoved into the pockets of his tux slacks. I haven't had a chance to check in with him, but it's clear enough the update on Dominic. He's still not come home. My stomach twists. I grab his hand and lace our fingers together, running my thumb over his in silent comfort. His breath is shaky, but then he leans against me, resting his head on my shoulder.

"So? Are we getting to meet her? Or is she just going to stay this imaginary person? You haven't told us anything, Jas," Huntley says, crossing her arms.

His tensing is subtle enough that I doubt the others notice. I press a kiss to his temple and pull out my phone, tightening my grip on his hand. I send off a quick text to Violet.

> Some of the coworkers would like to meet you. You up for that?

It takes a few minutes for her to respond.

> Sorry, just got off shift.

> No worries. Take your time.

The others start up a small conversation about where they're hoping to go out tonight.

"You want to go?" I ask Jasper, keeping my voice quiet.

He takes a deep breath before shaking his head. "Not tonight."

Sure. I work a double tomorrow but am off Monday. Is that ok?

That's fine. We're off Mondays.

"She can hang out Monday."

Liz and Huntley cheer. Jasper tenses again but doesn't say anything.

"Perfect," Huntley says. "Let's go to our normal bar. They're pretty quiet on Mondays."

Mason shakes his head. "They have a local band playing Monday. It'll be crowded. How about the Rowdy Seahorse?"

"Not there," I growl. I don't offer an explanation of my refusal, but they take it in decent stride, quickly pivoting to other options. I leave them to it.

I'll grab you at 8.

Alright. See you Monday.

Jasper blows out a breath and pushes off of me, but he doesn't drop my hand. I grab his chin and turn him toward me, kissing him before he can pull too far away.

Someone makes a gagging sound. Jasper laughs and kisses me again.

"You guys going out tonight?" Mason asks as I pull away from Jasper.

"Not tonight. It's been a long week," my lover says, not hiding his exhaustion.

The others fade out soon after that, murmuring goodnights and offering quick hugs. It's a bit anti-climactic since it's our second-to-last weekend, but Jasper and I just aren't feeling up to faking it for everyone else's sake tonight. The walk to the car is quiet. Jasper tucks his cello into the back seat of the Alfa Romeo before sliding into the passenger seat.

As we head onto the highway, I say, "You're with me tonight."

He snaps his eyes to me. "What if he's home?"

I shake my head. "I don't give a fuck. He can have you in the morning. You're with me tonight."

~

VIOLET

There's a hard knock at the door. Nerves flare in my belly, and I have to swallow twice to try to move the lump that's seemingly taken up permanent residence in my throat. I brush down the Lana Del Rey shirt and adjust the way my fishnets sit on my thighs. I've traded out my preferred shorts for a simple black skirt, part of me hopeful that Rylan might want to do something other than kiss tonight. And skirts are better for that if we're in tight quarters.

Also, my ass looks fucking amazing in this set-up, so that's a bonus.

"Violet, he's here," Faedra says from the shared living room of our dorm.

I run my hands through my hair, shaking it out a bit, and close my bedroom door, trying to lean into the same etiquette training that got me through the matching gala without punching any of the reporters. Faedra's leaning against the kitchenette counter, picking apart a salad she must have grabbed from one of the dining halls before they closed for the night. Her phone is perched just next to the bowl, the screen dark, and her fingers tap against her thigh in one of her subtle nervous habits.

Rylan leans against the closed front door, his hands in his

pockets, his dark hair several inches shorter than when I'd seen him on Friday. He's wearing the same Snow Patrol hoodie as he had been on the video call. His eyes skate over me, the slow perusal warming my chest, and I can feel the blush color my cheeks. As I approach, the citrus scent of him hits me, and my thighs clench. What's it like being able to walk wherever you want and not worry if you're scenting?

At least I get to enjoy the benefits of it.

He pushes off the door when I catch his gaze, holding one hand out to me. This time, when I take his hand, he doesn't pull me closer to mark me with his scent. Was that a bad sign? Alphas always wanted to mark what they viewed as theirs.

"You'll call me if that party downstairs gets out of hand, right?" I ask Faedra.

She raises an eyebrow and crosses her arms. "Absolutely not. I'm more than capable of doing my job. You're supposed to be having *fun* tonight."

Damn her for being so confident right now. She gives me one of her looks, the one that says she knows what I was trying to subtly imply, and that she isn't going to give me the benefit of her friendship at the moment. So what if I wanted an escape hatch for tonight?

I let Rylan guide me out of the dorm. This time, he cuts toward one of the parking lots. It's late enough that most people have moved off of the main pathways around campus, opting for going out or staying in for the night. The sun's dipped below the horizon, the last rays starting to disappear, and the street lights are already on around the campus.

"If you want to leave, just let me know. Grab my arm and squeeze twice if you don't want to make a big deal of it." Rylan's voice blends into the evening.

I glance over at him, trying to gauge how he's feeling tonight compared to Friday. He seems more tired today, though I'm not honestly sure how I can even tell. Maybe there's something subtle about his scent that I'm noticing without being able to actually *notice* it. Instincts are fucking weird sometimes.

"Didn't expect safe words for a night out at a bar with your friends," I say, opting for humor to see what he does.

He smirks, his hold tightening on mine for a moment. "First of all, they're Jasper's friends, not mine. They're simply my coworkers." I ignore the quick slice of pain over his easy, happy use of Jasper's name. He purses his lips. "Don't tell Huntley I said that."

"I have no idea who that is," I say.

He chuckles. "You will soon." He pulls a key fob from his pocket as we near the curb. One of the cars flashes its lights, though it doesn't make any noise. "Second, they're a lot. All the time. And fuck knows one of them will manage to say something that will piss you off. Secretly, my money is on Liz since she's been out of her mind since the paperwork was delivered after rehearsal Wednesday. But, really, it could be any of them. Just making sure you have a way to get out of it without making them realize they've overstepped."

I nod. Should I be happy he's thinking about this so much? That he's worried about how I'm going to respond to trying to integrate with his circle of people?

Probably. But in reality, it's just making the nerves grow worse in my belly.

I mess with my shirt, obsessing over how it's laying against my stomach. Rylan catches my hand.

"Stop," he says, more bite in his tone than before. "You're fucking gorgeous."

I pause, focusing on him instead of my fidgeting. "I know."

He nods. "Good." He blows out a breath. "Sorry, I just don't want you panicking over anything that I can help you avoid."

"I've worked really hard to love my body," I say, forcing

myself to stop messing with my shirt since it bothers him. "Especially since living in LA. I'm not sure there's another city that detests fat bodies more than this one. You don't have to worry about whether or not I'm obsessing about it. Messing with clothes is just one of my nervous habits."

"I don't want you to be nervous," he says, his voice dropping into a low croon. Fuck, that has my body reacting in all kinds of ways. I force a swallow to try and stay focused. "Just remember we'll leave at any point, all right?"

When I nod, he starts toward the car—something I can tell is expensive, though I don't recognize the brand emblem. I'm just about calmed down when I realize who's sitting behind the driver's seat. Jasper's gaze glances down me once, quick and impersonal, as Rylan guides me into the passenger seat.

He doesn't offer a word as Rylan closes the back door and we start toward the bar.

<h1 style="text-align:center">Seventeen</h1>

VIOLET

Jasper leads us into the bar as Rylan laces his fingers with mine, walking close enough to me that my shoulder brushes with his biceps every few steps. The place is dark and yet bright, neon lights from over twenty different pinball tables casting odd shadows on everything in the large room. The bar sits in the middle of the room, chairs lining three sides of it, and there are a few round tables tucked into one of the sides as well.

Jasper walks toward one of those, not saying a word to me or Rylan, his hands shoved into his pockets. It's frustrating how good he looks in the black t-shirt and light blue jeans. Rylan grunts beside me before taking my hand.

"Those jeans look good on his ass," he mutters after a moment. Citrus surrounds us, Rylan's attraction obvious to anyone who's paying attention.

The truth falls from me before I can pull it back. "Yeah, they do."

"Rylan, I swear to God, if you keep her sequestered at the bar, we will riot." A woman with brown hair calls from the group along the wall, her hands cupped over her mouth so her voice carries over the din of the games.

"That," Rylan says, voice dry, "is Huntley."

He doesn't make any move to encourage us toward the table of people. After a minute, the woman jumps up, climbing over another guy at the table, and closes the distance between us.

"Hi, I'm Huntley," she says, holding out her hand. When I take it, she smiles. "We've been trying to get the guys to bring you around all week. We were starting to think maybe we imagined the councilwoman dropping off the packet. Jasper hasn't shown us a picture or anything."

She's quick and to the point, her words almost running over top of each other without quite managing. Her gaze is shrewd as she looks over Rylan, her eyebrow slowly rising in offended question. Rylan's warning of not telling her what he said makes sense.

I already like her.

Hasn't shown us a picture.

I tense, not able to control the stab that sentence causes to my heart. He's still not interested in me. Whatever has happened over the last four years, his thinking I'm not enough for him still exists. Rylan growls, low in his throat, reacting to my sudden change in demeanor, but Huntley doesn't seem to hear it.

Another of the group closes the distance, his smile easy. He slings a hand over Huntley's shoulders.

"To be fair, you practically ripped Jasper's phone out of his hand in September when he hesitated in showing you a picture of Dominic," he says.

Huntley rolls her eyes. Something untangles just a fraction at that bit of information.

The man holds out his hand, and I take it the same way I did Huntley's.

"I'm Mason. You want something to drink?"

Rylan's growl this time is loud enough for both of the others to notice.

"Mason, honestly, you should know better than to say something like that to a claimed Omega." Yet another person joins us.

This woman is short, just an inch taller than me, though she's also sprightly. Her dark hair looks black in the light and falls to her hips, her brown eyes large. Her smile is wide as she approaches me. A bond scar reflects in the neon lights, highlighting where it sits in the crevice where her shoulder meets her neck.

I offer up my hand, prepped for the greeting this time, but she ignores it. Instead, she wraps her arms around my waist in a quick hug that feels both too intimate and too informal for someone I've just met. "Hi, I'm Liz. My shadow is Zach." The man behind her scowls and doesn't offer his hand. "He's in a bad mood tonight because he'd rather keep me at home. Just ignore him."

Liz leans toward me and puts a hand to her mouth, like what she's saying is a secret. The effect is lost, though, since I'm pretty sure everyone in the bar can hear her. It's not like with Eric on campus, where he was intentionally trying to draw attention so I couldn't just slip away. Liz just seems to be a loud person who doesn't quite realize it.

"He's feeling extra possessive since we just bonded," she says, still in that too-loud voice.

Rylan's growl chokes off. "That's not really something we need to know, Liz."

She shrugs before giggling. "It's not like the scars aren't obvious."

"Scars?" Huntley asks. Liz turns her neck, the scar I'd noticed becoming more obvious as she pulls her hair away. Mason gasps, and Huntley's eyes widen.

"Not the point," Rylan sighs. Liz rolls her eyes.

"Wait, you noticed it?" Mason turns back toward us. Zach's growl gets louder.

"It's something that we're wired to notice," I offer even as Rylan steps between me and the other Alpha, adjusting so that he holds my other hand, and I'm pressed against his opposite side. "I saw it as soon as she approached us."

Mason makes a surprised sound in his throat. "I wonder how many I've not noticed, then." He turns back toward the other Omega. "Can I touch it?"

Zach steps between him and Liz, his growl now practically a snarl. Mason and Huntley back off, their arms raised. After a moment, everyone heads back toward the tables.

"Let's go get drinks," Rylan murmurs.

Neither of us bring up the bond scar as I order my comfort Old Fashioned and he gets a soda. He pays with cash, declining change, and then guides me toward the tables where everyone else has been sitting. Liz is wedged between two men, their large frames dwarfing her, while Huntley and Mason sit on either side of Jasper. They're chatting, smiles on their faces, as Rylan pulls two chairs up to the edge of the table and signals for me to sit at one.

Huntley chugs the rest of her drink before turning toward me.

"So where are you from?" she asks, talking over the two conversations actively happening within the group. "How was your move?"

"I actually live here," I say after a minute, forcing myself to ignore where Jasper leans back against the booth, his arm sprawled out behind Huntley. "I'm graduating from UCLA this weekend."

Rylan grunts. "Don't sell yourself short, Violet."

"Hard to avoid when I already am," I say, trying humor again to see what he'll do.

His lips tip up, and he drapes his arm over my shoulders. I'll count that as a good reaction, then.

"She's graduating Summa Cum Laude," he says. "And top of her major."

A round of congratulations ensues.

"What's your major?" Mason asks, sipping on a drink that's bright pink and frozen.

When I tell him, Huntley's eyes widen, and I swear surprise flashes across Jasper's face. I steer the conversation away from me, trying to just settle into the background and figure out if I can fit into this group.

After a while, I murmur, "I'll be back."

Rylan nods, moving so I can more easily get up from my chair. I pull my skirt down, adjusting it as I turn around.

Jasper jumps up as I stand, "I'm going to grab a drink. Anyone want something?"

Huntley and Liz both take him up on the offer. Anxiety tightens my throat, but I breathe through it, keeping my face blank. Rylan grabs my hand, pulling me back toward him, his eyebrows lowered. It's clear what he's asking me, though I'm not sure why he knows that any kind of interaction with Jasper has my stomach in knots. I haven't told him about the break up. Did Jasper? Is that why Rylan has been so careful in his interactions since the video call?

Oh, fuck, Jasper probably did tell him.

No wonder he asked me all those questions about my family and history. He was probably trying to decide if petitioning for reassignment—or, worse, annulling the match—was worth the hassle. His demeanor completely changed when I confirmed that my dad is Johnathan Fallon.

Fuck. The last thing I ever wanted was a convenience match, something like what my parents have. I wasn't so naive to think that I'd end up being in a pack that completely loved me. But I *had* hoped that we could at least figure out some sort of middle ground or mutual respect.

I continue past the bar, trying to not run to the safety that the bathroom provides. The hall is dark, only a couple small wall sconces offering light. A hand closes around my elbow, and my heart freezes, my breath catching in my throat.

"Violet," Jasper murmurs, his voice low enough that it sends a fucking shiver through my body. "We need to talk."

I keep my face as neutral as I can manage as I turn around. His eyes are intent on me, his jaw clenched.

"What happened in Seattle—"

Oh God. He cannot be trying to bring up Seattle in a hallway where there's no other witnesses. Has he already signed the annulment request? Is that why he's back here with me? My stomach turns, and I can't hide the panic that must shoot across my face. I push the door to the bathroom open and flee inside. I stand at the counter, staring at my reflection, trying to figure out what to do, breathing through my nose to keep from being sick.

My hands shake as I pull out my phone.

> This is me squeezing your arm twice.

> Be there in a sec.

Rylan's knock is soft, and I keep my head down as we leave the back hallway. The group of friends wave, a chorus of goodbyes following us out the door. The blade twists again as I see Jasper take up the seat between his friends again, not even looking back toward me.

Eighteen

RYLAN

I walk down the hallway toward the bedrooms, trying to ignore the sinking of my stomach at the reality sitting in front of me. This match is falling apart, and it hasn't even been a week. She isn't even living here yet. Dominic's door is closed, but I know he's not inside. The small Maserati was gone when we got home from Sunday's performance. He'd timed coming back so that he wouldn't run into either of us.

I blow out a breath and shake the thought from my mind. Dominic isn't the biggest problem right now, and certainly not one that I have any hope of trying to fix. When Dominic and I disagree, we just end up fighting. And the last thing I feel like dealing with right now is a fucking split lip.

Jasper's door is ajar, but I still knock on the threshold, not wanting to intrude if he's intent on being alone today. He's dressed in just a pair of sweats that have me immediately distracted. His eyes are tired, though, dark circles under them. The urge to calm him overwhelms me, and I palm his neck. His breath hitches as I run my nose over his jaw and down his throat, biting the soft spot where his shoulder meets his neck. Right where Liz's bond mark was last night.

Fuck, thinking about bond marks is not a good idea right now.

Jasper's dick hardens against me, and it twitches as I bite him again.

"What happened?" I ask when I pull away.

He sighs and runs a shaking hand through his hair.

"I tried to bring up Seattle so we could at least... I don't know. Be on the same page, maybe? I was scared to do it privately. I thought asking her at the bar would be better."

His body trembles under my touch, and not in the good way. I run my lips over his collarbone, trying to distract him. After a minute, he sighs.

"She ran into the bathroom. Like when I tried to bring up that blowjob I gave you when you were angry in the fall."

I grunt. Not my best fucking moment. He'd been trying to gauge where we stood after he sucked me off, acting on instinct when I'd been so angry over the hickeys Dominic had left on his throat the night before. And instead of actually having a conversation like a 28-year-old man, I had hid in my room like a fucking terrified teenager.

"She looked..." His throat ripples with a swallow, and I urge him farther inside. "She was fucking terrified of me, Rylan. Why would she be scared of *me*? Unless she thought I was going to rip into her over how she left me?"

I take his hand, pulling my lips away from his skin. I guide him to his bed, sitting against his headboard, and bringing him to kneel between my bent legs. He rests his hands on my knees, his dick tenting his sweats, but I stay focused on his face. For now, at least.

"I think there's something wrong with what happened

between you," I say, trying to come up with a decent way to tell him my suspicions.

Jasper drops his hands and backs away from me. I grab his wrist before he can get all the way off the bed.

"I would never lie to you," he growls, trying to rip out of my hold.

"I didn't say you did, Jas," I murmur, trying to pull him toward me again. "I'm saying that I think there might be discrepancies between what you remember and what she remembers."

He pauses and swallows again. "What do you mean? Like she thinks something different happened between us?" When I nod, he grunts. "What did she say to you?"

Pulling him toward me, I shake my head. "Just nonverbal clues, mostly. Nothing I could really put into words."

I don't divulge what she said at the coffee house. For all I know, I'm reading too far between the lines and am fucking this up more than it already is.

"And I'm not saying that you have to fix it or anything. Just that maybe..." I blow out a breath. "Fuck, I don't know. Maybe see about just trying to be around her. Maybe she'll bring something up if you don't push her too hard."

That was something I'd definitely noticed. She got spooked real quick. Her hackles raised at the slightest mention of her potentially being the problem in any situation, even when it was clear that she *wasn't* at all what was wrong.

Jasper sighs, kissing me. "All right. I'll try again. But if it's bad..."

I nod and pull him over me, letting his body drape over mine. "I'll figure out where the fuck Dominic is hiding, and we can see about changing things."

～

JASPER

A redheaded woman opens the door of the unassuming dorm room. Her green eyes are bright and her cheeks are flushed, making her freckles blend into her skin just a bit. The radiant smile brightening her face drains away as she looks me over. I tighten my grip on the flowers Bianca had dropped by the house earlier today, fresh from her favorite florist at my request. Best to have an item to justify dropping by unannounced. She'd also brought along a confirmation that Dominic was still alive and had been helping his dad out with some things regarding the business.

My stomach twists again at the thought of him going back to his father and the mafia. Did that mean he meant to dissolve our standing as a pack with the Council?

"Oh," the woman murmurs, pulling me from the morose thought. She glances at her phone and says, "I have to go. I'm so sorry."

"No worries, Red." The warm male voice is practically a croon, the power of an Alpha's soothing washing over me without finding anywhere to really stick. The memory of the selfie on Violet's Instagram flashes through me, both her and this woman dressed for the matching gala. She must have been on the phone with one of her matched Alphas.

Shit, I should have sent a text or something instead of just showing up, even if it meant her cussing me out.

The woman locks the screen of her phone and purses her lips.

"I'm—"

"She's not here," she says without preamble, cutting me off as she crosses her arms.

Rylan had made sure she wasn't working today. Worry twists my stomach. I blow out a breath, reminding myself that I've handled scarier people with better composure than this. Of course, I hadn't been chest deep in unresolved heartache and one bad fight away from my relationship falling apart. Was it even considered a fight if the other party never bothered to show back up? A lump forms in my throat.

Even still. I could do better than this. I swallow down the lump.

"My pack mate told me she would be." I keep my voice level, not letting any of my confusion and anguish weave through it.

One brow rises as silence stretches between us, her face incredibly impassive compared to all the photos I've seen of her on Violet's social media. There's nothing of the carefree college student standing before me. She looks like she's ready to go to battle.

I try again. "I brought her these. May I at least be here to give them to her?"

She looks me over again, her eyes catching on the large bouquet in my hand. "You broke her heart, you know that?" The words are stark, and they hit me just as solidly as a punch. "Twice."

"N-no," I say, trying to figure out when I had hurt Violet. "I was under the long-standing impression that she broke mine, actually."

She frowns and cocks a hip. "So you didn't tell your pack mate that matching with her would be the absolute worst thing to happen?"

I flinch. She had heard that? She'd disappeared into the crowd before I ever got close to Rylan that night. How had she been able to hear what I said to him?

"I'd rather talk to her about it than use a messenger," I say.

A long moment passes, and I clutch the flowers tighter, willing myself to stay still under her scrutiny. Just as I'm about to give up and try again later, she nods once and moves away from the door. She doesn't say anything as I step over the threshold. I take in the space, trying to absorb as much of it as possible, try to see the Violet I knew in Seattle anywhere in its furnishings. There's a couple of small pillows on the simple gray couch and a basket full of throw blankets, most either pink or blue. The walls are filled with framed landscape photos. Sunsets and snow storms and even one of the last time it rained in LA, the droplets on the lens distorting the Santa Monica pier that's as famous as anything else in the city except maybe Hollywood itself. They're beautiful and nothing of what I would expect of somewhere Violet lives.

My gaze catches on a group of photos hanging behind the lounge chair in the corner beside the window.

Violet's roommate crosses the small living room and opens the door on the wall to the right.

I stride across the room so I can take the pictures in better. They're nearly identical, though small things change in each one, and I realize they're a timeline of sorts, each picture from a different year. I focus on the one I think is newest, the redhead's hair nearly as long as it is now. Each detail of it slices across my chest until I struggle to breathe around the pain. Violet stands with her arm around her roommate's waist, their heads pressed together as they laugh. Around them, people mill about, boxes and bags and furniture being carried. The focus of the picture is perfect, the edges blurring so that the women are the sole focus, as if it's a memory plucked from someone's mind and then printed on the page.

I drink in Violet. At first glance, there's nothing left of the girl I loved to the point of my own heart shattering. Her eyes are flinty despite her laughter, and her ears are pierced multiple times. She wears a necklace, multiple gold chains of varying widths and lengths without a pendant. The careful skirts and dresses she'd always worn to appease her mother are gone. Instead, she wears cut off jeans and fishnets, black boots, and a band tee of some kind, though I don't recognize the artwork of the album. It looks like something Rylan would enjoy, though. It's so similar to the picture the Council had given us, except in this one... she's happy.

She's stunning, like everything we had ever talked about had been able to come out and express itself away from Sienna's hawkish, grueling gaze. I can't help but trace this photo the way I traced the other one, keeping my finger a hairsbreadth above the glass.

"You can use this for the flowers." The woman's voice is softer this time.

I drop my hand and turn toward the roommate, keeping from flinching by the skin of my teeth. She holds out a small decorative vase. It's navy with a gold floral design painted around it. I swallow again, trying to wet my suddenly dry mouth, and take the small object from her.

There's an unassuming kitchenette tucked beside the front door, and I set the flowers on the counter so I can fill the vase. The woman doesn't say anything, and I'm not quite sure how to broach the silence, my mind still caught up on the four photographs.

"I'm Faedra," she says once I've gotten the flowers into the vase and out of my hands.

I turn toward her and grab the counter to keep my hands from trembling.

"I'm Jasper," I say, though it's obvious she knows who I am. Shit, I should probably know who she is, too.

She settles onto the couch, grabbing a small pile of fabric and a needle. "Feel free to sit."

I drop into the lounge chair and close my eyes, messing with the chain of the necklace to keep from fidgeting.

"You're different than I expected," she says after a while.

I can't even manage a quirk of my lips. "I'm sorry?" It comes out as a question.

"You're much more... I don't know, really. Not as shrewd, I suppose."

I glance over at her and raise an eyebrow. I'm not sure anyone has ever described me as shrewd. That's more Dominic's specialty.

"Shrewd?" I ask.

She nods, tilting her head as she keeps sewing the small pieces of fabric together.

"I suppose I should have realized that her viewpoint was probably pretty biased. But I'm her best friend. It's kind of my job to take offense for her, you know?"

I grunt, and she looks up at me, her cheeks pink.

"I just expected you to be a lot more cold and domineering. Something that would match a guy that just left her with no warning." She purses her lips. "Well, aside from a nasty letter left with her mother of all people."

Warning bells go off in my mind. Was this what Rylan had meant this morning? Had she mentioned something about the breakup from her perspective, and he noticed the story didn't match?

I lean forward, a knot of unease sitting heavy in my stomach.

"Hold on, she thinks I left her? That I broke up with her using a note left with Sienna?"

Faedra frowns and drops her hands to her lap as she straightens. "Well, yeah. She still had the letter when we moved in together as freshmen."

I stand up and cross the room, messing with the flowers to keep myself busy.

How was that possible when I'd burned a letter from Violet the day I moved into my little shoebox apartment here?

"I..." I trail off.

Should I really be saying any of this to Faedra instead of Violet? Doesn't she deserve to hear it first? Except...

Except I've tried to have this conversation with her once already, and she ran from the room the moment she could. I shake my head and try again, closing my eyes.

"I burned the letter I received from Sienna stating that she was breaking up with me. But I bet there's still a picture saved in my drive somewhere on my phone."

"She gave you a letter?" Violet asks. "From me?"

I turn around fast enough that my vision blurs, the sound of her voice nearly bringing me to my knees. She stands in the threshold of a different door set into the far side of the wall opposite where Faedra had gone to find a vase for the flowers. Her hair is down, falling around her face, and she's in the same shirt as the picture, though her shorts and fishnets have been traded for a set of leggings that hug her hips and make heat burn in my gut.

So much for not being here.

I purse my lips and glance between the two women. Violet narrows her eyes and crosses her arms, but I can see the hint of vulnerability in the way she twists her lips and taps her fingers against her arms. Just like the video call, she seems fragile. Like she's waiting for me to say something that will absolutely ruin her.

But why would she think that? I would have burned the world for her, would have destroyed myself, to make sure she was happy.

"She did," I say, though my voice has gone dry. I force a swallow and continue. "She gave it to me on the front porch when I stopped by. You... you hadn't texted me back all week. I knew you might be radio silent since it was your first heat, but I had gotten worried over how long it had been. Kurt said they typically last four or five days, and it had been closer to nine." I run my hands through my hair. "She handed me the letter along with the necklace I'd given you."

Violet's eyebrows furrow as she frowns. Her question rings through the room, hitting me in the chest like a damn gunshot, my knees crumpling under me.

"What necklace?"

Nineteen

JASPER

It's instinct that has me grabbing the counter before I actually collapse to the floor. She'd never gotten the necklace? Sienna had lied? But it had been Violet's handwriting, right?

"The necklace I'd brought you when I checked in the first time. Kurt had answered the door and explained what was going on. He'd promised to set it aside for you."

This time, I know I'm not imagining the tears in Violet's eyes. Faedra doesn't miss them, either. She stands from the couch and crosses to where Violet leans, whispering in her ear. Jealousy burns through me and flashes white hot as Violet relaxes, giving her friend a single nod as she blinks quickly. Faedra gathers a bag from beside the couch and leaves the dorm without another word or glance at either of us, her phone already out and dialing someone.

Silence descends hard and fast on the room. It's worse than that of Faedra's hatred. It carries years of unresolved hurt and misunderstanding. There's a chasm between Violet and me, stretching the last four years, and I have no idea how to patch it or cross it to get to her on the other side.

"When did you bring a necklace?" Violet's question is a shaky whisper, and her arms press harder into her chest.

"The day after you went radio silent," I murmur.

Her throat ripples with a swallow. I repeat what I said before, adding more details.

"Kurt answered the door when I swung by. He'd looked worried and stressed, so I asked what was going on. He said you'd gone into heat. So I left the necklace with him, and he promised to give it to you once you were coherent again. I... I waited all week, but you never texted to let me know you were all right."

Violet shakes her head. "I never got anything from Papa. When I came out of my heat, my mom was standing at my door with a note she said was from you."

She drops her arms and holds out a hand, a single piece of paper held between her fingers. It's identical to the one I'd burned when I moved to join the philharmonic. It takes every single ounce of willpower I possess to cross the room and take the worn scrap from her hands. I let my fingers graze hers. Her breath catches, but she doesn't pull away. I can smell her honeysuckle scent now that I'm near her, but it's probably just from her room.

My hands tremble as I unfold the paper, and bile rises in my throat as I read what's written in a scrawl nearly identical to my own.

Thanks for the ride.

"Mom said she had already blocked your number and socials because something like this was unacceptable for her daughter."

I tear my gaze away from the harsh words. Her eyes are wide

and glassy, and while her arms are still crossed, the tension has bled away from her. My chest aches. I want to wrap my arms around her, bridge this last bit of physical distance in the hope it will erase the years of heartache.

Even my romantic heart knows it isn't that simple, though.

"I told you that you were it for me, Vi," I whisper, dropping the forged note. "Until the end of time. I meant it."

Her breath is shaky, and a single tear runs down her cheek. I can't help but brush it away. I swear her scent gets stronger.

"I'd just gone through a heat. My first one. It was... it was so much more overwhelming than I'd expected. There were entire days that I didn't really remember." Her words grow quieter with each statement until they're little more than a whispered breath between us. "I trusted her to tell me the truth." She shakes her head. "I knew she was catty. I'd seen her be awful with Scarlett. I... I guess you would remember all of that, though. But I still thought maybe she was on my side."

Another tear falls, and I brush that one away, too, before pushing my luck and cupping her cheek. She doesn't push me away, her breath hitching for a moment.

"I'm sorry," I whisper. "I... I should have tried again. Kept coming back until one of your dads opened the door instead."

She nods, her gaze distant for a moment, then she sighs.

"I'm not sure she would have let them answer it," she whispers. "Not if she had used my heat as a way to force us apart."

She brushes away another tear, looking at the ground. It's like a bucket of water is thrown over us both. She steps back, out of my hesitant touch. I let my arm drop to my side.

"Why was matching with me the worst thing possible?" she asks, a bite in her voice again.

I swallow and run a hand through my hair.

Can I honestly tell her? Dominic is already pissed. Having Violet know the truth won't help anything.

Assuming he comes back at all, that small voice whispers. My stomach clenches at the thought of him leaving me.

Her eyes grow guarded as my hesitation grows. That little bit of distance we just regained is already slipping through my fingers.

Fuck it.

"It... it wasn't supposed to be a real pack," I say.

Her brows furrow, and I continue before she can ask anything.

"Dominic doesn't want to match. He despises that he's an Alpha—not that he'll ever actually admit it. But he takes the highest dose of suppressor they'll allow for extended use." I definitely should not be divulging this to her, these intimate things between Dominic and me. But I can't manage to stop my mouth. "He hardly scents and doesn't crave needing to mark the way Rylan does." I blow out a breath. "Anyway, Dominic's father kept his trust fund from being released until Dominic consented to registering with the Council and going to a gala. We'd just really figured out that we wanted to try being a triad. Except not really? I don't actually know the term for what we are. They both fuck me, but they don't fuck each other."

Her eyebrow rises, but her cheeks don't darken the way I expect them to. I should have realized she wouldn't be the same blushing virgin she was when we'd first met. Rylan already admitted to fucking her through a heat last fall. And it's not like I really care. I don't. It's just... it's one more thing that proves the time and distance between us. Almost the same as before, but not quite.

I clear my throat. "Rylan and I agreed to register with him. The plan was to go to one gala then deactivate and move on with our lives together."

I turn away from her before I can see whatever level of disgust is bound to be there. It's an awful thing to admit to. The Council does an inordinate amount of vetting to avoid precisely what we had planned.

"And then..." My voice grows haggard. "And then I saw you there and realized you hadn't matched yet, and I panicked. The idea of having to see you after the way you left things in Seattle..." I drop onto the sofa and bury my face in my hands, leaning over my knees. "I didn't think I had it in me to handle another round of you ripping my heart out. And I knew Dominic would try to annul any match that went through. The idea of being in that awkward limbo and you hating me through it was..."

I let my voice fade out.

There's a long beat of silence before she says anything. Her voice is closer than I expect it to be.

"So it wasn't because you hated me and couldn't stand the idea of being stuck with me?"

She thought I *hated* her? I just admitted I was scared of her being angry at me, of hating *me*.

I lift my head as I snarl, "Never."

Her eyes are unfocused, her hands held limply at her sides where she stands a few feet away from me. She collapses onto the coffee table, her hand covering her mouth as she tries to hide a sob.

"Violet," I say. I stretch toward her, forgetting everything sitting between us, and pull her into my arms. "Don't cry, Vi. Please don't cry."

"I thought you hated me," she whispers, her voice broken and vulnerable.

My laugh is humorless. "Even when I wanted to despise you, I couldn't manage. It took me years to be able to date again."

I don't mention I haven't touched a woman since her.

She nods, her cheek brushing against my sternum, and I

swear I almost feel my chest rumble with satisfaction. She doesn't rush to fill the quiet, and so I relax into it, too, feeling her chest move with each breath. I twist a strand of her hair around my finger. A flash of metal catches my eye, and I trace the industrial piercing she didn't have before.

"I'm probably crushing you," she mumbles after a while.

I tighten my hold on her. "Don't you dare start with that bullshit."

She nods but adjusts in my lap until her legs drape over the side of my thigh. I palm her knee and pull her tighter against me. This time the honeysuckle isn't from her room, and my breath hitches for a moment.

"I brought you flowers," I say against the crown of her head. "Sunflowers."

Violet sits up, and I let my arms fall. Her throat moves with a swallow, and then she grabs my hand and presses it against her waist. The honeysuckle grows stronger. That hollow feeling in my chest lessens. Maybe this chasm isn't insurmountable.

"But they're not in season," she says.

I shrug. "Bianca loves having fresh flowers around the estate, so she has some connections."

Her eyebrows draw tight.

"Who's Bianca?"

It's subtle, but I hear the jealousy in her voice. I squeeze her knee, trying to use all the nonverbal things I've noticed both of my lovers use often.

"Dominic's mom," I say. "You'll love her."

I have no doubt. They're both fiery, passionate women that know what they want but have been forced to adapt because of life railroading them.

She frowns and threads her fingers with mine. I run my thumb down her side, trying to calm her the way Rylan always does for me.

"You said he..." She swallows. "You said that Dominic would annul any match that happened?"

I nod and tighten my hold on her knee.

She tilts her head, her eyes narrowing. "So why hasn't he? I've gotten the notice that Mom filed to get it overturned, but nothing saying any of you have."

Rage burns in my gut. "She's tried to overturn it?"

She nods but waves away the look of concern I give.

"Of course she has. The worst thing in her mind that could happen is having one of her Omega children matched with a Beta."

My lip curls.

"I had to turn it back in for it to hold weight with the Council. I threw it out," she admits.

Something crowds my chest that I refuse to name. Not yet. Not while there's still so much standing between us. I can't help how ragged my voice is, though.

"You didn't even have them review your other options?" I ask.

She shakes her head, though she drops her eyes, looking unsure again.

"Why?" I drop my voice, trying to calm her down. It's not nearly as good as Rylan's soothing baritone, but her shoulders drop away from her ears. A moment later, she blows out a long breath.

"I tried to convince myself it was just because I wanted to knot with Rylan again," she says.

It's absolutely *not* jealousy burning in my stomach. And certainly not morbid curiosity over what she felt about the experience or if it matches my experience of him knotting me. I raise my eyebrow, but she doesn't look up from where she's messing with her leggings, picking at imaginary lint.

She takes a deep breath and glances up at me, her eyes glassy with unshed tears again. "I needed to know for myself if you really hated me. I told myself that if you did, if you were truly angry over being matched, I'd put in the paperwork for the match to be annulled."

Annulled, not reassigned.

Annulled meant she wouldn't consent to being paired up with someone else. It meant that she would lose her chance to find a pack that would cherish her.

I force myself to breathe slowly and keep my hold on her light.

I want that chance. To hold her, cherish her, prove to her that we're enough for her, that she doesn't have to dread being matched.

"I'm glad you waited," I admit.

The tears run over her lashes. She doesn't try to blink them away or wipe them off her cheeks. It's the least guarded I've seen her since the video call last week, and my heart twists.

"Kiss me, Jas," she whispers.

Twenty

JASPER

Her lips curling around my nickname breaks me. I pull her tighter to me and cup her cheek, tilting her head as I bring us together, trying to savor her feel and taste. She's just as soft as before, just as trusting, melting into me the moment our lips touch. For a moment, the years between us disappear, and it's just her and me against her mom, the Council, the world.

Honeysuckle explodes around us, and I groan, tightening my grip on her hip, letting a single finger trace under the waistband of her leggings. She whines low in her throat. It's my only warning before she's scrabbling at me, pushing my shirt up my chest even as she keeps her lips pressed against mine. My dick twitches, aching where it presses against the zipper of my jeans.

Reality slams back into me, the years of heartache and the very real problems sitting in front of us.

"Violet, listen to me," I whisper, covering her hands. Her nails bite into my skin. "Hold on."

I put enough bite into my words that she actually draws back, her eyes wide and her cheeks flushed.

Her chest heaves with her panting. All at once, I see her walls fly up as she mentally shakes off her embarrassment. She moves until her feet touch the ground, keeping her eyes off of me.

"You said you had flowers?" Her voice is clipped and distant.

"Don't do that," I growl. I shake my head and wrap my arm around her waist, forcing her to stay in my lap. "Don't completely disengage when I just needed you to pause for a minute."

She glances back at me, a moment of confusion flashing through her eyes. I wait until she nods to continue.

"I didn't come here to convince you to sleep with me," I say. It hadn't even crossed my mind that she might want to, if I'm being honest. She stills in my arms, and I tighten my hold on her. "First of all, I don't even have condoms with me. Second, there's more to fixing this distance than just fucking and hoping for the best."

She sucks in a deep breath, her eyes searching my face. I force myself to stay relaxed, though my hand tightens on her hip. It's not like I'm not into the idea of sleeping with her. My dick is hard and aching, pressing into her thigh even through my jeans. But I have one chance to fix this with her, to lay a foundation that can't be broken, no matter what might happen with Sienna. Or Dominic.

Hell, that's going to be a nightmare on its own. Both of them? No wonder I haven't been able to sleep since we got the news last week despite Rylan trying his absolute best.

"All right," she says, relaxing against me. "Can you show me the flowers now?"

I pull her closer into me for a heartbeat, breathing in her scent.

"Whatever shampoo you use blends beautifully with your scent," I admit as I exhale and let my arms fall away from her.

She giggles. I haven't heard her laugh in ages, and to hear this one? The one she hides from the public and only lets those closest to her hear? The one that shows her vulnerability instead of her sass?

Suddenly the distance doesn't feel as bad, those years lost between us not seeming as all-consuming.

She slides off my lap and holds out her hand. I lace our fingers together before leading her across the small space. It's even smaller than my shoebox of a place before I moved in with Rylan. Her stuttered gasp makes my stomach clench. I force tension into my limbs, willing my hand not to shake as I reach for the flowers and impromptu vase and then hold them out to Violet.

"Faedra gave me the vase. I didn't think to ask Bianca for one."

Her hands shake, the small tremors making the petals rustle as she carefully takes the gift from me. Her eyes are glassy again as she looks up, her lips trembling even as they curve into an intimate smile.

"You remembered," she whispers.

Not quite a question, though the curiosity is burning just under the surface.

Of course I fucking remembered. Everything about her is burned into me, a permanent mark on my soul. Sunflowers, honeysuckle, Lana Del Rey. Even fucking *rain storms*.

"Couldn't look at them for months," I admit, running a hand through my hair. I blow out a breath. "Still makes my stomach clench sometimes when I see them."

"Sorry."

The single word is filled with so much angry bitterness, it breaks my heart. I tilt her chin, forcing her gaze back to me. A soft response is on the tip of my tongue, ready to calm her, convince her that Sienna hasn't completely fucked this up between us, but I can't quite manage to get the words out. My gaze catches on where she licks her lips, the fast swipe of her tongue making my skin heat. I tighten my grip on her jaw and pull her into me, slanting my mouth over hers.

There's a soft clink of glass against the counter, and then her arms wrap around my neck, her body molding to mine, all her soft curves against my hard lines, and I groan. She hums, her scent overwhelming the space so quickly, it's almost like it was always there, enveloping us in a cocoon of safety. My focus narrows to this moment, the sensations bleeding into one another until I can't hope to tell them all apart. The prick of her nails digging into my skin, the silken sensation of her hair where I twist my hand into it, the taste of her on my tongue.

I groan again, deep in my throat, and drop my hands to her thighs, picking her up before she can protest.

"I still don't have any condoms," I mutter against her lips.

"I'm tested and negative. And I have an IUD."

This is not something we should be negotiating while her legs are twined around my hips and her hands are scraping down the nape of my neck. But hell if I can find it in myself to care at the moment. I've ached for her for four years, and I am not the type of man to have the control needed to slow us down right now.

She kicks the door to her room closed as I pass over the threshold, dropping the room into near darkness, only the light of a walkway lamp outside her window offering any kind of illumination. It gilds her skin, coaxing out the beautiful warm tones of it, and sets her eyes aglow. My chest swells as I kneel beside the bed, cushioning her as she drops onto it in front of me. Her thighs bracket my shoulders, and suddenly I'm twenty-one and in a completely different bedroom.

I force a swallow and breathe through my nose to keep my

reaction in check. Reliving those moments won't help us now, won't change what's happened, won't allow us to move forward with whatever might develop between us at this moment in time. Her eyes narrow and her lips purse, a thoughtful look flashing across her features. I palm her thighs, running my hands along them, feeling her soft curves through the fabric of her leggings. She cups my cheeks before I can reach for the waistband and tips my face toward her, pulling me into her embrace as she kisses me.

This kiss is slow and searching, none of the white-hot demand of just a minute ago. Like she knows where my mind went. The thought soothes me. Even after all these years, she knows me—knows how much regret and turmoil I still carry over what happened, knows how visceral those memories are for me. Her tongue dances with mine, exploring and inquisitive, and I offer her everything I have. When our breathing is ragged and I'm drowning in honeysuckle, she pulls away and presses her forehead to mine, her eyes still closed.

"I'm sorry," she whispers. "I'm so sorry, Jas."

I push her back onto the bed and grab the waistband of her leggings.

Twenty-One

VIOLET

He still uses the same breath mints.

The cool tang of them makes my lips tingle as I drop back onto the bed and Jasper peels my underwear down my legs. My body burns with need, my nipples tight and slick coating my thighs. The moment he's dropped my panties to the ground beside him, I press up onto my elbows, not wanting to miss a moment of this—and find his eyes focused on my core. The floral feel of my scent surrounds us, seeping into every part of the room. His hands run up my thighs again, his calluses catching on the sensitive skin. I suck in a breath to keep from gasping, but I can't quite manage to keep my hips from pushing up toward his touch. His lips twitch into a near-invisible smirk.

"Jas, please," I whisper.

Now that I've let the nickname slip from between my lips, I can't seem to keep it in. Not that I'm honestly trying right now. The need for him burns hot as an open flame in my core, and I can feel another rush of slick coat me. His touch is soft, delicate, along the sensitive line where my hips meet my thighs, and I squirm, trying to move him where I want him—where I need him.

I haven't craved someone so intensely without the added force of my heat in years. Since the last time I was with Jasper, if I'm being honest. How can he work me so thoroughly, make my body sing like this, without being an Alpha?

I press my hips into his hands harder, whining.

"Yeah, okay," he mumbles, blowing out a breath. He runs a thumb over my core, barely brushing my clit. This time, I can't hold back the gasp. "Just trying to not fucking come in my pants like I'm seventeen again."

My belly clenches, desire ratcheting even higher at the admission. Nothing quite compares to knowing you affect a lover so intensely. If I'm at the mercy of his touch and body and voice, then he's just as equally affected by me. What a beautiful thing to share.

He pushes forward, planting his arms on the outside of my thighs and pinning my hips in place. My head falls back on a moan with the first swipe of his tongue.

"Violet," he groans. He traces me again, his tongue soft and searching, almost mirroring the kiss. Like he's reacquainting himself with this part, too, trying to find the ways I've changed and all the ways I haven't.

I press up into him, trying to urge him faster, but he brackets my hips and forces me still.

"Let me enjoy it," he growls, lifting his head just enough that I can see my slick coating his chin.

I flush but nod, and he smirks.

Enjoy it, he does.

I lose track of time, my body going boneless under him even as it tightens with need, the arousal so strong it's damn near painful. My moans devolve into whines and then half-voiced whimpers. All at once, he spears into me with two fingers, curling them with a timing that would make a god weep.

I arch and cry out, my orgasm lashing like lightning, shooting down my spine and through my legs until I'm a shaking mess.

"Oh fuck, oh fuck, oh fuck," I mutter, my chest heaving. He softens his touch before pulling away entirely. His face is soaked with my slick and his eyes dance with pride.

"I missed that," he murmurs before wiping his arm across his mouth.

I reach for him, pulling him over me.

"I need you," I gasp, biting at the skin of his throat.

He shudders out a breath, his hands twisting into my hair. "You'll have me, love."

He freezes as the endearment falls from his lips, but I clutch him closer. My heart's in my throat, the ache of having him with me after thinking he hated me for so long still pressing against my chest. But my body burns, slick coating my legs again as his hard body presses into my soft one. I arch into him, twisting my tongue with his as I lift his shirt up his chest. His chest is harder, more defined, a certain amount of youth I hadn't realized he'd still had now burned away completely. There's scars that I don't recognize, too.

My nails dig into his back as he thrusts against me, dragging his covered dick across my clit. The friction of the fabric against my sensitized flesh is enough to make me moan and drop my head back against the pillow. His teeth nip at my throat, my collarbone, before he pulls my shirt over my head and tosses it across the small room. My bra is gone before I can even try to help him, his body still hovering over mine, the front closure falling open like he's done it a million times.

Maybe he has.

Jealousy burns through me, swift and fierce, but I don't let it linger. It's not like I've been celibate, either.

His hands are soft as they cup my breasts, his thumbs playing across my nipples. I arch into him, forcing his hands into his chest in silent demand that he ignores. He bites down my sternum, letting his teeth mix with soft kisses until I'm moaning and trembling under him, the odd mix of pain and pleasure making my body sing. His tongue traces my nipple with the barest pressure.

I break.

"Now, Jas," I whisper, pleading with him.

I'm drowning in need, my scent so strong it reminds me of my heats, and my slick coats the sheets. He nods, pulling away from me and sitting back on his knees. He uses one hand to pull off his shirt, and my fucking core clenches around nothing. I thought that was something guys only did in movies.

He's gorgeous, all golden skin and lean muscles. The light from the lamp outside the dorm makes him nearly glow, the blue of his eyes seeming unnaturally bright. He blinks quickly, and my stomach clenches. I don't know why I'm caught frozen, but I can't manage to move to catch the single tear that tracks down his cheek. He doesn't bother to wipe it away as he undoes his jeans and kicks them off, his boxers quickly following. His cock juts forward, and my mouth waters. I want to taste him again, make sure that hasn't changed, either. I reach for him, pushing up on one elbow, but he shakes his head.

"Not yet," he murmurs.

His body covers mine, his hands twisting into my hair and his dick nudging at my entrance. He locks his eyes on mine, our noses nearly touching, his breathing just as ragged as mine. Without a word, he pushes into me, one steady, long stroke that fills me so completely, I cry out and arch into him, letting my head fall back.

It's almost like muscle memory, like part of me has remembered all this time how this is with him. It remembers the feel of his skin against mine, the weight of his body over me, the press of his hips against my thighs. It remembers, and I bask in the feeling, letting it erase for the moment the years and heartache that sit between us, the resentment and anger that I can still feel lingering in my chest from everything left unsaid between us those final months he was in Seattle.

I rock my hips. I need him to move, to take me hard and fast to drive out the unwanted memories. When he doesn't respond to my urging, I wrap my legs around his hips and use the hold as leverage to fuel my own movements beneath him. His hands tighten where they're fisted in my hair, and he bites my shoulder, his body trembling above me.

"Vi," he whispers, his lips tracing the shell of my ear. "Holy hell, I need a goddamn minute, or I'm going to come. And I need to feel you come again first."

I clench around him, and he groans. It's so deep in his throat, it sounds as if it's been forcefully pulled from him. The whine is slipping from between my lips before I can stop it. He drops his head into the cradle of my shoulder, his forehead pressing on the aching skin where his teeth just were. His breathless chuckle is more than a little desperate.

"There'll be more times, Jas. *Please*."

He groans into my skin, the sound of a dying man, and then begins to move.

He doesn't take me hard or fast, but it's consuming nonetheless. He strokes my clit with each thrust as his lips explore my body more, taking their time around my breasts until I'm shaking under him. I'm not even sure what noises I'm making, my mind halfway gone to the pleasure coursing through me.

His thumb presses against my clit, drawing tight, fast circles around it, and I shatter, clenching down around him as I scream, tossing my head and clawing at his back.

His rhythm breaks, his hips stuttering, and he breathes out a ragged moan into my hair, his lips pressing into my temple as he drops to his elbows above me. His arms shake, his body trembles, and he grunts as I roll my hips under him, the last of the aftershocks still washing through me.

"Love," he murmurs. My hold tightens around him.

He pulls out of me and adjusts us until I'm cuddled into his side, my head resting on his shoulder.

"You're magnificent," he whispers.

I preen under the praise, the last bit of me worried over what happened in Seattle dislodging at last. I wrap my arms around his waist, pulling him closer into me, breathing deep until all I can smell is him: his cologne, his aftershave, *him*. No Alpha scent needed. He's perfect the way he is.

His hands run down my back, goosebumps following in their wake. I shiver against him, and he reaches to the end of the bed, pulling the soft blanket over us both.

"You'll stay?" I ask, trying to fight against my body, trying to stay awake and enjoy this moment with him.

He nods, brushing my hair off my face. "Always, love."

Twenty-Two

VIOLET

Two soft knocks pull me from sleep.

"Violet, you okay?" Faedra's soft voice filters through the door.

An arm tightens around my waist and a body tenses against my back.

Last night washes over me, one long memory that has my body singing with arousal and yet aching in all the right places at the same time. Jasper's lips press into my neck, his quiet chuckle a vibration against my skin.

"I'm fine," I call out, not wanting to figure out how to get enough clothing on before it becomes suspiciously awkward for my best friend.

There's a long pause. "Does this mean we're not getting breakfast together?"

Oh shit. I'd forgotten in the midst of figuring out all the baggage with Jasper last night that I'd promised to go out this morning with Faedra. I sit up, cursing, and Jasper fucking *laughs,*

"

not even trying for subtlety. I smack his arm, leveling him with a glare, but he doesn't even look embarrassed, his grin wide and his posture relaxed as he rolls onto his back.

I can hear Faedra laughing through the door now, too. "I'll see you later, Vi. Have fun."

"Sounds good," I say, trying for at least a modicum of dignity.

I've never once brought a hook-up back to our place. The fact that it's happening now, only a few days before final move out, is incredibly ironic. At least it was with one of my matched pack and not a random stranger, right?

The front door closes a minute later, and then I'm turning toward Jasper, tossing my pillow at him as he laughs again, the sound so bright and full it pulls a smile from me, too.

"You didn't have to make it so obvious," I say.

He shrugs and sits up, the blanket dropping dangerously low on his hips.

"Faedra's not oblivious," he murmurs. "When you weren't awake and ready to go, I'm sure she figured out I stayed."

I tilt my head. "How do you know that would be what clued her in?"

He rolls his eyes. "Because you are the most punctual person I've ever met. If you're the one running late, then there's something wrong, either with the situation or your outfit." He tilts his head toward the door. "And if I know that after not seeing you for four years, then I guarantee your best friend does, too."

My cheeks heat, and he laughs again, reaching for me. His lips are soft, and I sink into him, letting him distract me from, well, everything else. The blanket falls lower, and *holy crap* I want to suck his dick. It lays hard and long against his hip, large enough that my fingers struggle to close around it. He stutters a gasp as I touch him, licking my lips in that universally understood question.

He groans and nods.

The moment I have my lips around the head, my tongue flicking across the top, his hands bury in my hair, tight enough I know his unspoken question. I pop off, letting my lips smack, and his hips thrust up.

"Let me enjoy it," I say, smirking, and he groans.

He drops his head back, letting his hands fall from my hair. "Fuck, I knew I'd regret that last night."

It takes another half an hour before we're dressed and figuring out breakfast in the living room. He taps something into his phone.

"You have a kitchenette but not a private bathroom?" he asks, running his hands through his hair as he drops onto the couch. I scoff and grab a mug from the cabinet before turning on the electric kettle.

"It's literally two doors down," I say, pulling out my French Press.

Jasper laughs. "Not the point. How are we supposed to have hot morning-after sex if the bathroom isn't private?"

My blood heats at the casual question, and I spin around, grabbing the counter to keep from getting dizzy. That small smirk is back, a relaxed feel about him I haven't seen since the video call last week. Something soft and foreign bubbles in my chest at his trusting me enough to let down his defenses.

"Well, it's not something I've had to worry about up to this point," I say, rolling my eyes. "It's something you just adapt to. And this one is the least busy of them in the building. It's not really any worse than sharing a bathroom with roommates."

His gaze flicks up to mine, surprise lighting them.

"What?" I glance down at the simple set of leggings and hoodie I threw on after we finally managed to drag ourselves out of my room half an hour ago. "Is there something wrong with my clothes?"

"Your outfit is fine, love," Jasper says. When I glance back up at him, my brows furrowed, he's halfway across the small room, his hands shoved into the pockets of his jeans. "What do you mean you haven't had to worry about a date of yours needing to use the shared bathroom?"

"That's not what I said," I mutter, my cheeks flaring with heat.

I turn away from him and mess with the coffee, pouring the water even though it's not quite boiling. His hand is soft but unrelenting as he cups my chin and forces me to look over at him, his body a wall of heat at my side. His eyes are intense, the easy laughter gone from them, their blue depths searching me so thoroughly I'm nearly positive he can see all the way to my fucking soul.

"You never brought someone back here?" The question is quiet but fervent.

I blow out my breath and try to break his hold. We might have found common ground last night, but this is too much for me to reveal in a single twenty-four hour period, no matter who he might be to me. His hold tightens, his hand slipping from my chin to my throat, his thumb and finger finding the small spots where my blood heats faster than I can control. His eyebrow rises as my scent explodes around us, betraying my arousal, but I force myself to remain impassive.

When the silence stretches between us, he crowds me into the counter, seamlessly moving us until his hips press into my belly.

"I'll give you a truth for a truth," he murmurs. Lightning shoots down my fucking spine, my knees weakening at the rasp of arousal in his voice and his dick pressing into me.

"You first, then," I whisper.

He nods. "I haven't touched a woman. Not since you."

My surprise is even stronger than my arousal, rushing through me in one great wave.

"What?" I can't keep the question from falling from my lips.

He raises an eyebrow, his fingers tightening the smallest bit on my pulse points. Fuck me. Honeysuckle grows stronger around us both, and he smiles, his eyes lighting with a mischievousness I've never seen before. When the hell did he learn to do things like *this*?

"Tell me, Violet," he murmurs, dropping until our lips barely brush. "You never brought someone here?"

I shake my head, my body trembling under his touch. "N-no."

Fuck me. Even my voice shakes.

He breathes deeply for a heartbeat, his eyes fluttering closed. "Why?"

"You first," I mutter.

"Because every time I tried, all I could think and feel and hear was you, and it was too painful." His response is immediate. Pain weaves through his voice, so strong, it's nearly palpable. "You were the last woman I touched. And will be the last one I ever touch again."

I force myself to swallow, trying to clear the lump in my throat, trying to remember how to talk. Something that feels terrifyingly close to *love* spreads through my chest until I'm struggling to breathe past it. He drops his hand, running his fingers along my arm until he takes my hand in his confident grasp.

He doesn't say anything, the silence stretching between us.

"It was never worth someone seeing them with me and then having to deal with my mom," I admit softly. His mouth brackets with tension, but he doesn't interrupt me. "There wasn't ever a person that I felt was *it* for me. And letting them into my nest was too intimate."

He groans, low and nearly mournful, and then his lips are on mine and he's lifting me onto the counter. He steps between my legs, letting his free hand bury in my hair as he runs his tongue along my bottom lip.

"Move in," he whispers as he pulls away, palming my knees, his chest shuddering with his breathing.

I force another swallow and glance away from him. Logically, I know it's the best idea. Move out is this weekend, and I *really* don't want to have to make that stupid apology that my mom will require for me to access enough money to live on my own in this city. But moving in means giving up a certain amount of control, of having a harder time accessing an escape route if Dominic decides to fight the match.

Will he fight the match? With Jasper and Rylan both approving of it?

Jasper's gaze grows worried, his lips twisting into a frown. "What's wrong?"

"Just that voice," I manage to whisper. He nods and kisses my forehead, his lips soft and warm.

My eyes catch on the silver chain of his necklace. I trace it before I can think better of it. The pendant pulls free of his shirt collar, falling onto the fabric, and my breath catches in my throat.

It's a small silver Omega symbol, simple and elegant. No flashy stones, no over-the-top secondary pendants to detract from it. I twist it in my fingers, and a small engraving catches the light. I lean forward, trying to read what it says. Jasper's hand tightens on me as he runs one palm down my thigh and around my hip. His heart beats so fast, I can see it in his throat.

Until the end of time.

"This was it?" I ask.

He nods, his throat rippling with a swallow. "I don't really know why I kept it. Or why I wore it."

"I get that," I say. I tuck the necklace under his shirt again before running my hands up his neck and twisting my fingers into his hair. "I don't know why I kept the letter, either. Or your sweatshirt."

"That's where it fucking was," he mutters, a corner of his lips flicking up. "I thought I'd lost my mind when I moved and couldn't freaking find it."

My laugh is small, but at least it's there. "All right."

He tightens his hold on my hip.

"Move out is this weekend. I can't do it any time before Friday because of being an R.A."

His kiss is softer this time, more exploratory, but my blood heats just the same. "I'll work it out with Rylan. You don't have to worry about any of it, all right?"

Before I can nod, there's a hard knock at the door.

I mutter a curse and drop from the counter, adjusting my shirt and my hair before opening the door. The same Council intern from last week stands in the threshold, a small envelope in his hand, the same tie tack keeping his tie in place. He doesn't look quite as uncomfortable this time.

"Miss Fallon," he says, handing me the envelope. "Same as the last time. If you'd like to file a counter motion to prevent this from happening again, I've included my number and can walk you through the steps."

I murmur a thanks and close the door, trying to ignore Jasper's strong body behind me.

"What's that?" he asks, his voice going low and dangerous in a way I've never heard from him before.

I rip open the envelope and sigh, holding out the motion without a word of explanation. His frown is deep, his snarl nearly as violent as an Alpha's.

"What the fuck is wrong with her? How did she even find out?"

I shrug. "I told you how she feels about Betas being in packs."

He shakes his head. "It's not me this time." He holds up the paper so I can read the official reason listed on her motion to have me reassigned again.

Concerns over the safety of the family regarding Dominic Montegue neé Gallo.

My eyebrow ticks up. "What's so concerning over his family? Are they drug dealers or something?"

It wasn't the vibe I'd gotten from him, neither in the packet of information or the video call. If anything, he reminded me of the Old Money families my mother practically kissed ass to. Jasper shakes his head.

"He's part of the mafia," he says.

Well, that's certainly not what I expected.

Twenty-Three

DOMINIC

Alessia texts me again before I can tuck my phone into my pocket, and I have to force myself to not get irritated. This is what happened when I went home for more than a couple hours during family brunch on Sundays.

> You sure you can't come tonight? Mom is being a bore.

> Yes, sorellina.

> Cazzo.

> Don't let Mamma hear you say that.

I can't help the small smile that curves my lips at her sass. Alessia has always been a firecracker, and her designating a few years ago hasn't changed that. Her and *Mamma* have been at each other's throats the last several months, though, since I officially registered with Rylan and Jasper. Nothing puts my *Mamma* into a frenzy like the idea of one of her children getting married. Or matched. And don't even bring up the idea of *bonding* with her unless you're prepared for a thirty minute tirade about how she wishes she could have had the experience.

The patio door clicks closed, and my stomach clenches.

Jasper's flash of blond hair shines in the midday sun as he perches on the seat next to me, his elbows braced on his knees and his chin resting on his clasped hands. He doesn't look over at me, keeping his gaze firmly on the ocean. Like he instinctively knows that I need a chance to look him over before we discuss the last week.

How is a Beta so in tune with what an Alpha needs?

Because he is perfect for you, that voice whispers inside me.

The thought sours as I think of the Omega's picture in the packet and his unwillingness to send her off to someone else. Why are we not enough? Why am *I* not enough?

I force myself away from the thought.

My gaze catches on a small bruise just under his ear, hidden enough that most people wouldn't notice it, especially since his hair has grown out over the last few months. Something suspiciously similar to jealousy slinks through me, and I have to breathe through the instinctive possessiveness that wants to claw out of my chest. It might just be from Rylan.

Except that Rylan was here when I came home this morning, and he was not. He was with the Omega.

Rylan didn't have any more information about what they were discussing than a simple, "Trying to find common ground."

It's clear they spent the night fucking. I swallow down the growl that wants to climb up my throat.

Cazzo.

"I'm not sure if I should start by asking why you decided to leave for nearly an entire week without even texting me or by telling you she's moving in," Jasper says after a while, his gaze still on the water. His shoulders are rolled forward, and his knuckles are white where his chin rests on them. His heartbeat races in his neck, so fast I can see it from here.

The urge to comfort him rides me hard, to alleviate from him the worry and stress of what he fears is happening between us.

I don't let the words escape my lips.

"I do not get the courtesy of being included in such plans?" I ask instead.

His jaw clenches, and he breathes through his nose.

"I guess we'll start with the first one, then," he mutters. "I wanted to talk with you all fucking week, Dom. You came back while you knew we would be gone. How am I supposed to have a conversation with you if you're intentionally avoiding me?"

The words come out more hurt than angry, a layer of bitterness I've not heard between us before. My chest tightens, but I breathe through it.

"You know I don't want to match," I say.

He sighs. "But we have, and you promised me when I agreed in the fall that we would do our best to make it work. They get one chance, Dominic."

The words taste like ash on my tongue, and I despise it. "And yet the Council gives ample chances to have them reassigned. It's not their only chance."

Jasper stretches his neck, his eyes fluttering closed. "Is it her that you don't like? Or would you have gone back on your word regardless of who the Omega was?"

Would I be fighting this so intensely if she didn't have such a history with my lover? The sensations from the last time I was around a scenting Omega roar to the surface, my dick jumping behind my zipper and my scent bleeding out from me despite the suppressors. Fuck, I hate being so out of control, my body responding when I'd rather not—responding even when I have no true interest in the person causing the reactions.

I don't offer a response, but that proves to be answer enough. His shoulders drop, and he shakes his head. When he finally looks over at me, it's distrust written on his face rather than anything else I've ever seen him wield.

"You know that I love you," he says after a long silence, his gaze still caught between sorrow and anger. "And that I wasn't sure this would even work between us. But I took the leap. I *trusted* you. Now I'm asking that you do the same for me."

The insulated bubble I've created over the last week cracks under his attention and his words. I lean forward, twisting so that I'm facing him entirely. He doesn't back away from me, though his gaze grows more wary as I close the gap between us.

"You are so quick to forgive her trespasses?" I ask, leaning over until there's barely a gap between us at all.

His throat ripples again, and he shakes his head. "It isn't that simple."

I palm his throat, smirking as his breath catches. "She left you. And yet after one night of fucking her, you're ready to pretend it didn't happen?"

I trace the small bruise she left behind. He shudders in a breath, his eyes dilating under my touch. "We're both very aware that it happened," he whispers even as he tilts his head, letting me see the bruise in its entirety. The need to mark over it, to mark *him* is a rising wave in me.

I resent it. Fuck, do I resent it. But I don't fight it. I bite over the spot, my dick leaping at the low, strangled sound my lover makes.

"But a lot can change in four years," he whispers, palming my hip as I ease onto my knees in front of him.

I bite a second mark I find tucked just under his collar,

making sure it's enough to bruise over before running my lips over his jaw. I leave my own bruise just under where it meets his neck, that possessive part of me easing at the sudden intake of his breath, at the way he tucks his hands under my shirt and into the waistband of my slacks.

"I don't need you to fuck her, Dom," he says after a moment. I pause where I'm running my lips across his collarbone over his shirt. His blue eyes pierce me, his lips set in a thin line I've rarely seen from him. "I'm not asking you to be involved with her at all. If you don't want to be, then don't. I'm asking that you give Rylan and me the space to pursue her."

I've never paused long enough to really consider that I might be polyamorous. It must seem so obvious to those looking in, since Rylan and I both fuck Jasper. But bringing in another person forces me to pause. Can I handle knowing that sometimes he fucks her the way he does me?

A growl rises in my throat, but I force it back.

When I nod, tension releases from his body, like a marionette dropping the strings. He falls into my arms, his head pressed against my shoulder. I wrap my arms around his waist and pull him completely against me, guiding his legs until he straddles me even as I continue to kneel on the concrete patio. His cock pushes into my stomach, and I grunt. His lips are on mine a moment later, his tongue fighting with mine over control of the kiss—and of our coupling this time. When he doesn't immediately let me lead, I back off. He grunts, and then his hands are working through the buttons of my shirt, his lips tracing down my neck and across the hollow of my throat.

The bare hint of grapefruit surrounds us, the most that the suppressors will allow me to scent, and he groans.

"When is she coming?" I ask.

He pulls away from me, hands pressed tight against my chest, our noses nearly touching. The afternoon sun reflecting off the ocean gilds him in perfect lighting, highlighting his hair and brightening his eyes.

"*Sei bello, Tesoro*," I murmur.

A corner of his lips turn up, and he eases another button open. He eases the fabric off my shoulders and drapes it over the seat behind me.

"Friday," he says. Before I can say anything, he asks, "What were you doing for your dad this weekend?"

I frown. He's never asked about the business before.

"Bianca said you were helping your dad out," he murmurs when I don't answer. He leans back, letting his hands fall to his sides. "What were you doing?"

"Enforcing the books," I say, nearly a growl.

Why did he want to know?

His throat moves with his swallow, worry moving across his face.

"I needed to blow off steam," I explain, leaning into him until our lips brush again. He doesn't fight me, his hands soft where he buries them into my hair. "And it helped Victor get caught up."

"Isn't that Lorenzo's job?" he asks, his breath catching as I mark him again, just under his other ear.

"Lorenzo is too busy fucking an Omega to keep track of his obligations," I growl. Goosebumps rise across his arms as the wind picks up, blowing off of the ocean. I chase some with my tongue, and his hips flex. "I will not stop you from being with her, *Tesoro*. But I do not wish to know her like you do. Is this enough words between us right now?"

With a sigh, he nods. He pulls a small bottle of lube from his pocket and then eases me onto my back. My dick jumps, and I breathe in his cologne, letting it wash away the stress of the last week.

Twenty-Four

VIOLET

"I feel completely useless right now," Faedra whispers, leaning in close enough that her hair blocks her mouth from prying eyes. "What are we supposed to be doing?"

The movers work around us, emptying out the things in the dorm that are mine without a word to us. One guy looks up as he comes out of my bedroom, a set of boxes propped on a dolly, and smiles. He seems vaguely familiar, but I can't quite place him.

Faedra waves. "Hey, Sam. Didn't realize you started a second job."

Well, that explains it. Sam is one of the guys in her major. They've taken nearly every class together and are often in the same study groups.

He shrugs. "Just something to tide me over until grad school starts in the fall. Keeps me busy. When do you move out?"

"My family's coming out tomorrow to help me finish packing, and then the movers will be here Saturday."

He nods, and one of the other men ducks around him, my nightstand in his arms.

"Denver, right?" Sam asks.

Faedra nods and leans her head against mine.

"Yep." She pops the "p" in the way she does when she's tired of the conversation. Sam seems to notice it, too. His cheeks grow pink and he tilts the dolly back into his hands.

"Well, I don't think I'm scheduled for your move on Saturday. I hope it goes well."

My best friend leans against the counter and smiles, offering a warm thanks.

I glance out the door as Sam leaves. Rylan and Jasper lean against the hallway just outside the dorm, mirror images of each other in their dark jeans and light shirts, their hands shoved into their pockets and their jaws clenched. Despite them being nearly identical, Jasper seems merely broody while Rylan feels like leashed violence.

Hell, the differences between designations are so subtle sometimes.

"Think it's still okay for me to go with you?" Faedra whispers, her eyes trained on Rylan. She fidgets with one of her orbital piercings. I grab her hand and lead her out of the apartment, stopping in front of the guys.

Rylan notices her anxiety right away, even with her so suppressed, and relaxes his shoulders, letting a small smile curve his lips.

"You girls want to stop for some lunch first or head straight out to the house?" he asks, his voice low and smooth. It shouldn't send a thrill down my spine, but I can't quite manage to keep from shivering. Faedra relaxes beside me. Jasper takes my hand and kisses the crown of my head, and I relax into him.

"I'm up for either," I say. "What do you want to do, Fae?"

She shrugs and messes with her piercing again. "Could we get something delivered to the house? That way we don't have to try to manage both."

Rylan nods, and Jasper pulls out his phone. "Any preferences?"

When we answer in the negative, he nods. One of the movers approaches, standing back a few feet, his eyes wary as he takes in the four of us. It feels a little over-the-top, but then I hear Rylan's low growl, and I take a deep breath. Sidestepping, I lean into Rylan.

"We're just about finished, sir," the man says, clearing his throat. "Last load is heading down now. We'll stop for our lunch break and then be on our way to the address given. Anything else you need from us here?"

I shake my head. "Thank you," I murmur.

He nods once before following the other men down the hall and toward the truck.

Jasper tucks his phone into his pocket. "Bianca's on her way to the house, and she's bringing food, so we should get headed over there. And it sounds like Liz and Huntley want to stop by, too. You all right with that?"

Faedra shrugs, and I nod. "Sounds good to me."

"Holy shit," Faedra breathes, her hand clenched around mine.

We're tucked deep into Brentwood, high enough on the cliffs that I'd bet money there's at least partial ocean views from the backyard of the house. Though, honestly, *house* is too blasé of a word. Estate works better. I refuse to use mansion, though it fits, too. Mansion just reminds me too much of my mother, and her hands are already too involved in this whole damn mess as it is.

"I didn't realize the philharmonic paid this well," Faedra says.

Jasper laughs behind us, wrapping an arm around my waist and kissing the crown of my head.

"It doesn't," Rylan says, voice dry, as he gets out of the car. "This is all Dominic."

My stomach clenches.

Italian mafia.

I don't say the words out loud, Jasper's rushed warning of discretion a couple days ago still ringing in my ears.

It feels a bit anticlimactic, honestly. I'd expected a gate and subtle security and maybe even a valet of some kind. Not quite like the books always make it sound—coming from money tempers expectations a bit—but certainly more opulent than this.

The house is huge, yes, and clearly worth a metric fuck ton. But it's understated, modern rather than traditional with its square lines and large walls of glass. The landscaping leans on the natural vegetation of the cliff sides rather than forcing a manicured lawn. There's small pathways built throughout the yard and a small set of garden boxes that don't seem to be in use set off to the side of the house, positioned perfectly to see both the cliffs and the ocean when working in them.

It's nothing like my parents' place, and for that I mumble a small prayer of thanks to whatever god might be listening. A woman with olive skin and long black hair curled and pinned back walks down the front steps. Her simple jewel purple wrap dress is as understated as the house, though the large diamond ring and coordinating necklace belie her wealth.

"Lunch is just about finished. Perfect timing," she says, hugging Rylan before turning to me and Jasper. Faedra tightens her hold on my hand.

"Bianca." Jasper's voice is warm as he drops his arm and steps around me, hugging the woman and letting her kiss his cheek. She's the same height as Faedra, so he doesn't have to move far.

When she pulls away from him, he holds his hand out to me. "This is Violet and Faedra."

The woman smiles, and it lights up her entire face. "Wonderful to meet you both. I've heard so much from Jasper about you, Violet. *Sei bellissima.*"

The compliment falls from her between one breath and the next, but it feels genuine. Warmth fills my chest. She closes the distance between us, hugging first me and then Faedra, her movements quick but warm, like she greets everyone with a hug rather than a handshake.

"You are Violet's friend, yes?" Faedra nods, and she smiles again, even wider than before. "Welcome to the family, both of you. I'm sure my son has done a terrible job of making you feel welcome, so let me do the work for him. Let's go eat. I brought lasagna."

When she pulls away, she takes my hand and Jasper's, leading us both inside. Faedra keeps hold of my other hand, following close behind me.

The foyer opens into a large open concept, the living room larger than my entire dorm and then some. A formal dining room is tucked off the doorway to the right and a study is immediately to the left, its frosted doors open, revealing a bright room with at least half a dozen guitars scattered throughout it— and no actual desk. Everything is done up in white and dark wood tones, the floor nearly the perfect match for the sand of my favorite beach. A literal wall of glass overlooks the backyard.

And it has more than passing ocean views: the entire back wall is filled with the midmorning sun reflecting off the water. Faedra's breath catches in her throat.

"Holy hell, Vi," she murmurs, leaning into me.

"*Quando arriveranno gli altri?*" Bianca asks, crossing the main living room to the kitchen tucked against the back corner. It's also done in shades of white, though the backsplash is a warm gray that reminds me of sandstone. She flips her hair over her shoulder and rolls her eyes as she looks back at us. "*Domenico* tells me nothing. But you already know that."

"Bianca, you know I'm not good enough with my Italian to know what you asked," Rylan says as he closes the door behind us, his voice warm. Almost... happy? I glance over my shoulder and find him leaning against the door, his hands in his pockets again, a half-smile on his lips. His head is tilted just enough that I can see the double snake tattoo crawling up his neck. He looks like a fucking album cover model for some alternative rock band.

Holy sex appeal. My thighs clench, and I can't quite manage to keep my breath from catching. Faedra looks between me and Rylan before laughing.

She leans in, covering her mouth with a hand, and whispers, "Violet and Rylan sitting in a tree—"

I elbow her in the stomach before she can continue, the blush darkening my cheeks despite my best intentions.

Bianca sighs even as she pulls a large dish from the lower wall oven and sets it on the stove. "One day, you will understand. You will not learn if I do not speak it, though, *monello*."

Jasper laughs as he follows Bianca across the room, grabbing a set of plates from one of the upper cabinets. The two of them work seamlessly around each other, like they cook together often. Something twists in my stomach, an odd combination of jealousy and excitement.

"The movers should be here in another hour or so," Jasper says. He holds out a plate for Bianca, and she spoons some of the lasagna onto it. There's a sharp knock on the door. "And that," he says dryly, "would be the girls."

I turn just in time to see Rylan open the door, revealing Liz and Huntley.

"Holy crap, I forgot how long of a drive it is out here," Liz says, her voice just as loud as the last time I saw her. Two of her matched Alphas follow, their heads close together and their hands in the pockets of their shorts. I recognize both from the bar, but neither of them are Zach. "I hope traffic doesn't suck going back down later today. It's only Thursday, so it shouldn't be completely awful—Oh, hi, Violet!"

Huntley rolls her eyes and steps into the foyer. "These are for you," she says. She holds out a large bouquet of sunflowers in a simple gray vase.

"Thank you," I say, trying to keep my surprise off my face.

Had Jasper told them my preferences? We'd only just reconnected a couple days ago.

She turns the moment I have a solid hold on the glass, introducing herself and Liz to Faedra. The three of them settle into an easy conversation, migrating across the room toward the kitchen. Bianca waves them off.

"Go sit, *ragazze*," she says, pointing toward the large dining table. It's large enough to sit at least ten, though there's only six chairs placed around it.

"The things you ordered are here, by the way," Rylan says, easing past me, letting his hand run along my waist as he passes. "I've put them in the room I thought you'd like most, but we can adjust things after we eat if you're not in love with the set up."

He kisses Jasper's cheek and takes the plate from his hands.

"Oh! Is she getting the purple room? Because holy crap, that one is so pretty, and the views are to die for," Liz says, giggling. "I love living downtown, but man, the views you guys get up here are stunning, I swear."

One of the men leans in and kisses her shoulder, and she blushes.

"We'll figure all that out after food," Bianca says, carrying a pitcher of something that looks like lemonade.

Huntley smiles. "Bianca, you make the best limoncello."

The other woman beams as she sits across from me. Rylan

settles on my left, Faedra already sitting on my right. Jasper sits next to him, his hand high on Rylan's upper thigh. The others settle in around us, one of Liz's Alphas grabbing a couple extra chairs from where they're sitting in the corners of the room beside the large front windows.

"*Grazie*, Huntley," Bianca says. "Now let's eat before the men get here."

Twenty-Five

RYLAN

I rap my knuckles on the doorframe of Violet's new room, not wanting to intrude. Jasper just left to take Faedra back to the dorms, and I'm not sure if Violet is the type of Omega who needs downtime after so many people being around her.

She disappeared quickly after dinner, intent on getting as much of her stuff sorted before helping Faedra get packed up tomorrow. Bianca, Huntley, and Liz stuck around for a while, helping her get situated more thoroughly than Jasper and I could have ever managed. Between the four of them, not only is her room nearly completely unpacked, but her nest is complete, too, with the last couple items on order. Women are fucking terrifying.

The large couch that took up most of this room is now pressed up against the far wall of glass, a large bed sitting against the wall to my right, the metal frame feeling nearly delicate in the space. The setting sun reflects off the water, illuminating the room in an orange glow that highlights her skin and black hair.

Goddamn, she's beautiful.

She glances up from where she's sorting through a pile of pictures on the bed, the last couple boxes surrounding her.

"Everything all right?" I ask, leaning against the threshold, crossing my arms.

She's taken off her scent blockers. Honeysuckle permeates the room, and I breathe deeply, trying to enjoy it without coming across as an absolute creep. It's different than when she was at the Haven, an edge to it missing that keeps me from being a mindless, possessive asshole. It's not something I could even really name, just a piece inherently present in an Omega's scent when they go into heat.

A growl rumbles through my chest before I can reign it in.

"Oh, sorry," she murmurs. "I can turn on the purifier."

She stands in one fluid motion, sliding off the edge of the bed, her slip of a dress falling to mid-thigh, the black silk moving like water over her body. My half-interested dick is fully invested in the span of a heartbeat, pushing against my gray sweats without a hint of shame. She's halfway across the room before I remember how to speak.

"Don't you dare," I say, though it comes out low and rough and dangerously close to a growl. She glances over at me, an eyebrow cocked. "It's your room. You don't need to change anything about it for me."

She tilts her head and messes with her dress, smoothing it over her stomach and down her hips. After a few moments, she clears her throat and grabs the pictures. The dress rides up her thighs, and I can't help but groan. When she glances over her shoulder, her cheeks dark, I adjust my dick so it's not quite so painful.

"Do you want to come in?" she asks, suddenly shy.

Shutting the door softly behind me, I cross the room and drop onto the couch. "How can I help you out?"

She shrugs. "Not really much to do at the moment. The movers did all the heavy work. I haven't decided which pictures to put up yet, so there's not even frames you could hang right now."

I nod as she puts the pictures in one of the boxes and then moves both to the bench sitting at the foot of her bed. "How are you feeling?"

She glances up at me, tucking a strand of hair behind her ear. The light reflects off her industrial piercing. "Feeling about what?"

"Everything," I say, leaning forward, resting my elbows on my knees. "The match. The move. The graduation ceremony. The motions filed by your mom."

Surprise flashes across her face, and her mouth drops open for a moment before she recovers and clears her throat.

"I didn't realize Jasper told you," she says, messing with the top of one of the boxes, keeping her eyes away from me.

"He wanted to know if there was anything we could do about it," I say, gentling my voice.

She feels cornered again.

After a minute, she nods. "Unless I sign the motion, it won't go anywhere. You don't need to worry about it."

"Do you want me to worry about it, though? You don't have to deal with it alone."

Her gaze snaps to me, confusion lowering her eyebrows. "Why would you?"

I shrug and lean back, forcing myself to relax. "We're matched, aren't we? Isn't this part of the relationship process?"

She grimaces and tucks her hair behind her ear again. "I guess so. It just feels..." She makes a sound in the back of her throat, a cross between a gag and a groan. "Awkward as hell, I guess. But maybe I'm reading too much into everything."

"To be fair, I'm absolute shit at it. Relationships, I mean. Especially this beginning part," I say, trying to keep my voice light. "Jasper can attest to it. It took a damn fist fight with Dominic to figure everything out between the three of us last fall, and it hasn't been smooth sailing since then. To be honest, I'm not really sure how to handle this without asking you to get on your knees in front of me."

She laughs. Full-on belly laughs, her nose all scrunched up in that fucking cute way and her smile wide.

"Why is it assumed I'd be the one on my knees?" she asks between gasps. "Why can't the Omega ever be the dominant one?"

My half-forgotten dick roars to life.

"Come here." My voice is low, commanding, and her throat ripples with her swallow. She closes the gap between us faster than I expect. She arches an eyebrow and cocks a hip. I grin up at her, though she's so short it's not much of a gap. Humor fills my voice as I say, "Probably because of things like that."

She scoffs and rolls her eyes. I grab her hand before she can turn back toward her bed and pull her into me, palming her hip as she props her knee on my thigh to keep her balance. The move puts her breasts directly in front of me. She's not wearing a bra. The dress rides up her thighs as she adjusts her weight to keep her balance, revealing a set of black lace panties.

"And I can do this just fine without getting on my knees," I whisper, glancing up at her.

She nods once, and it's all the permission I need.

I palm her breast, flicking my thumb across her nipple, watching her for every little sign of arousal. Her breath hitches in her throat, and honeysuckle bleeds out from her, though not as strong as her heat. I follow my thumb with my tongue, tracing the same path, and her scent grows stronger. She runs her hands along my shoulders, her nails biting into my skin as I pull her nipple between my teeth.

"Holy—" She bites her lip as she whines. A second later, her scent explodes around us.

I release her nipple with a low groan, smirking at the wet circle I've left on her dress. I take my time giving her other nipple the same treatment, not stopping until she's pressing up against me, her head thrown back and small, near constant whimpers falling from her lips.

That's not just something she does in her heat, then. I fucking love it. I run my lips down her body, enjoying the way the silk feels under them. *Silk.* Not satin. Not whatever weird knockoff the affordable slips like this are made out of that they kept available at the Haven. It's freaking silk. And she doesn't give a flying fuck that I just ruined it.

"Why do you work at that bar when you're as rich as Dom?" I ask, not really meaning for it to be said out loud.

She shudders. "Orgasms now. Answers later."

I chuckle and push up the hem of the dress, gathering it around her hips until I can see her in full.

Before I can even get my mouth on her over her panties, she's whining. With the first swipe of my tongue over her clit, even blocked by the thin fabric, she cries out and twists her hands into my hair.

"Oh God," she gasps. I repeat the motion, and she shakes in my hold. With the third, she's begging for more. "Knot me. Please, Rylan. Oh God, fucking *knot me.*"

Shit. We haven't had any of the needed conversations about sex and protection and pregnancy. Nothing like letting my dick put the cart in front of the horse. I force myself to still. Before I can pull away, she's scraping her nails down my neck and pressing her hips into my mouth.

"I think I still have condoms if you want one. It might take me a minute to figure out where they are. I have an IUD. Jasper and I were bare together."

Each sentence is more rushed than the last, the words falling over each other on breathless pleas. Her scent grows even stronger, my own bergamot mixing with it. The idea of her fucking Jasper makes my cock twitch. When I don't move, she pushes her hips into me again, her clit running over my lips.

Even a gentleman would be unable to resist her like this. And I am anything *but* a gentleman, especially with only a few days left of the philharmonic season where I have to keep myself on a tighter leash.

I groan.

She takes the sound as the surrender it is, scrabbling at my sweats until my cock springs free. She doesn't even bother taking off her dress, just pushes her panties to the side and lowers herself onto me. Her knees slide forward, bracketing my hips. Her body trembles as she takes all of me, forcing myself all the way to the goddamn hilt.

"Shit, pretty Omega."

It's a goddamn moan. I clench my teeth, breathing through the need to fucking come right now, the pressure already sitting at the base of my spine.

She doesn't fuck around, chasing her orgasm like her damn life depends on it. It's fucking beautiful. The last rays of the sun catch on her piercings, reflecting off of them. They kiss her hair, making it shine as I run my hand through it and twist it around my palm. They highlight her curves that I trace with my other hand, running it down her side and over her hip.

Her whines and whimpers get faster as she speeds up, and my stomach clenches, that pressure growing more insistent. I run my lips over her neck, trying to keep from coming before she does, feeling my knot already trying to swell and lock us together. The moment the pressure starts to peak, I run my thumb over her clit, pulling away so I can watch in rapt attention as she falls apart above me. Her body shakes, and her legs give out. She tips her head back on a strangled moan. I bite the hollow of her throat, keeping the urge to break her skin and rut up into her at bay by a fucking hairsbreadth. Her scent explodes again, doubling in strength, and I'm fucking *gone*.

I push up into her, snapping my hips a handful of times before my orgasm rockets through me. I grab her hips and pull her down into me, forcing my knot deep into her as it swells.

"Holy hell," I mutter, tipping my head until it rests against the back of the couch.

She screams as my knot locks fully into place, her body trembling as another orgasm rips through her. I'm drowning in her scent.

I fucking love it.

Before I can lift my head, she collapses against me, her forehead tucked into the crook of my shoulder, her chest moving with her quick pants. I wrap my arms around her, threading my hand into her hair and tracing random symbols on her back.

"Freedom," she murmurs after a while.

I pause my movements, pulling on her hair until she looks at me.

"What?" I ask.

She swallows, her gaze searching mine. "I work there for freedom. It's not money tied up with my mom or her shitty rules or any of the other things that come along with being her daughter."

I tighten my hold on her hair, pulling her tighter against me.

Fuck, did I understand the need to separate yourself from

your family. So would Dominic, not that he'll get within ten fucking feet of her.

"The Audi is yours," I say as my knot releases her. "Keys are on the third hook from the right next to the main door. Text me your schedule."

She adjusts in my lap, tucking her nose into my throat. "Thank you."

Twenty-Six

VIOLET

"I really thought most of the stuff here was yours," Faedra says, dropping onto the sofa in the living room of our dorm. "But, damn, do I have a lot."

I toss my head back and laugh. "To be fair, some of it is joint property that neither of us are taking." Like the sofa, though she's bringing the lounge chair in the corner with her to Denver. "Did they mention if they're bringing lunch? Or should I get some ordered?"

Faedra grabs her phone off the coffee table and taps through it. "Mom texted a bit ago to say they're grabbing Chinese and that she ordered our usual. They should be here any minute."

Two hard knocks on the door fill the immediate silence with the timing of a damn 90s sitcom. We glance at each other before laughing. Faedra wipes at her bottom lashes as she crosses the room and opens the door.

"All right, Faedra Rose." Her mom's voice carries across the room, fast and efficient and maybe a bit manic, though it's not lacking warmth, either. "Put the guys to work and then tell me about these Alphas. All I've gotten is the picture the Council gave you!"

I pull out my phone, giving them the privacy of the moment, ignoring the jealous stab in my chest that happens every time Faedra's with her family. What I wouldn't give to have a mom that genuinely cared about *me* and not how I fit into her own public persona.

"Let's start with some lunch," Jay—Faedra's dad—says, his voice warm and happy, as he guides Faedra back into the dorm. "We came straight from the airport, and Aiden has been cranky since we left Boston."

I glance up as the door closes, sending off a quick text to Rylan.

> I'll let you know when I'm finished.

> Sounds good.

> I have to record after the concert tonight, so Jasper will pick you up.

He might have offered me one of their cars last night, but driving in LA sucks in the best of conditions. Add to it that they're down here already for the philharmonic and that we won't be done at the dorm until late tonight, it was a no brainer to ask if one of them would be willing to pick me up.

"There she is!" Jay crosses the room, holding out a hand to help me up from the couch. He hugs me the moment he can. "I was wondering if we'd get to see you or if you'd be out of here already."

I can't help but laugh, the extended touch relaxing me. "I thought I told you a couple years ago that you're stuck with me for life."

He grins, humming as he starts pulling food from the takeout containers. I follow him into the small kitchenette, grabbing two plates and filling them with the Kung Pao Faedra's family detests but we adore while she chats with her brother. Her dad and brother are already settled in the living room when her mom starts in on her questions. It's a record for her, I'm pretty sure. In patience, not prudence.

"So who are these men my daughter is going to be living with? They live in Denver, right? And you said they're really into camping. What are their names? What do they do for a living? What—"

"Elizabeth." Jay cuts her off, his voice humor-filled despite his exasperation. She huffs, her eyebrow raised, but stops asking questions.

These are all questions my mom should have asked me. Instead, I've gotten one passive aggressive voicemail and two notices from the Council of her trying to force reassignment. Papa and Dad have called twice, at least, and I've cried significantly less each time. I haven't managed to broach the subject of Mom's meddling with Jasper and me, though. That's bound to start a fight that I just don't want to mess with while trying to figure out the next couple weeks.

I pull myself out of the train of thought and focus on my best friend.

"The pack name is Bennett," she says, a glint of challenge in her eye.

I laugh, elbowing her as I shake my head. She breaks after a few moments, pointing her fork at her mom.

"How do you know I've gotten a chance to really get to know them?"

Elizabeth rolls her eyes. "Because you're *you*, Faedra Rose. Curiosity might as well be your middle name. Though Rose still sounds better."

Faedra's blush is dark and quick, hiding her freckles from one breath to the next.

She's been glued to her phone the last two weeks. One of them is almost always chatting with her, and she spends the evenings laughing. Another stab of jealousy sours my stomach, and I force myself to take another bite so I don't lose my appetite while she relays the basics of their professions. None of them seem too concerned until she mentions that Jude's tenured at one of the local universities.

"He's old enough to be tenured?" Aiden's voice is a mix of shock and worry. Faedra blushes again. "I thought the Council paired everyone up so there weren't huge age gaps."

I can't help but snort. Age is one of the last factors the Council considers when selecting matches. Sure, maybe a decade or two ago, it was easier to find packs of similar age to the Omegas in attendance. But now?

"Every year the Council pushes Omegas into matching younger," I say. "We were some of the oldest ones there this time."

Elizabeth frowns. "Just how old are they?"

Faedra's blush darkens, spreading onto her chest, and she stabs at her food for a few minutes. Guilt pricks at my stomach. Maybe I should have found a better way to say that.

"Faedra," Jay says, a clear warning.

Faedra takes a deep breath but doesn't look up from her food. "Logan is 35. Carter turns 40 in August, and Jude turned 40 in February. His birthday is one week after mine."

All three of them fidget, doing various things to hide the level of their surprise. A not-so-nice part of me rejoices over her family struggling over the match, too. They're fucking perfect for her from what I've been able to tell, but it's refreshing to see her have a less-than-stellar moment with her parents.

I wonder what they'd think of the ages of my match. Jasper's 26, so not that much older, but Dominic and Rylan are both nearly thirty, their birthdays only a month apart from each other.

Jay's the first one to break the silence.

"Well, the Council has been doing this for a long time," he says. "I'm sure they had a reason for selecting this pack for you. We'll reserve any judgment until we meet them tomorrow."

There's a long silence where Elizabeth glares at Jay, clearly unhappy with his answer. Eventually, she turns to me.

"So tell us about your match, Vi. Where are you moving?"

I lean against Faedra. "I'm actually staying here."

Elizabeth brightens, her excitement practically contagious. "That's fantastic! Have you gotten to spend a lot of time with them?"

Her happiness for me is like a balm to my soul, and the next words aren't forced at all.

"It's been great." I elbow Faedra, smirking. "Way less stressful than Faedra's current setup."

On cue, she scoffs and shakes her head.

"Liar," she says. "You're nervous every time you go to meet up with them."

True. The next words fall from me before I can pull them back.

"You would be too if the Beta you had a fling with in high school was part of the pack you've been matched with," I mutter.

Aiden chokes, and Faedra giggles. I elbow her again.

"Betas aren't that common in packs, though," he sputters after a moment, his eyes wide. "How the hell did you manage to draw that match?"

Fuck. If. I. Know.

Though I'm not as bitter about it as I was. Good sex will do that to a woman.

"The Council works in mysterious ways," I say in a sing-song voice. Faedra laughs. After another minute, I push my cleared plate away. "Reconnecting with Jasper has been the easiest part of it, actually." And that's fucking saying something. "It's one of the Alphas that's making me question the match."

Shit. I didn't mean to admit that out loud. Did I sound vulnerable? Or just irritated? I glance at Faedra, and her lips turn down.

"They're flying in tonight," she says, pulling the conversation back to her in a moment of undying friendship that I fucking owe her for. "They're supposed to get in sometime around seven, and then they're staying at one of the hotels near the airport."

Elizabeth perks up, but Jay is quick to cut her off.

"We're excited to meet them *tomorrow*."

Show me someone who says that man doesn't understand his daughter, and I'll show you a liar. Faedra's shoulders relax, her nervous fidgeting with her orbital piercing stopping despite her mom being clearly frustrated. My phone vibrates in my pocket. I tune Elizabeth out while I check it.

See you tonight, Love.

My chest flushes at Jasper's using the nickname again, but I breathe through it, trying to keep attention off of me. Faedra leans against me, pulling me back into the conversation.

"They only had a slot left for tomorrow afternoon," she says.

Jay nods, hugging her before surveying the room. "Sounds like tomorrow's going to be hectic. Let's get this done so your mom has enough time to actually breathe tomorrow instead of just bombarding your pack with questions, yeah?"

I laugh even as Elizabeth rolls her eyes. She points at me.

"Don't you dare hop sides, Violet. We're supposed to be buddies."

I shrug and smile. "Bestie privileges mean I don't have to pick a side. Let's get this done so you can go eat on the boardwalk before it closes."

Twenty-Seven

JASPER

Dominic's room is still dark as I slip into it. He's sprawled out on his stomach, his arms tucked under his pillow, his phone on the far nightstand and not plugged in. Worry gnaws at me, but I ignore it as I close the door.

"*Tesoro*," Dominic mumbles, not turning toward me. "*Cosa fai?*"

I don't offer a response. Instead, I cross the room and pull back the sheet, laying beside him in the large bed. He slits one eye open, and that worry digs deeper. It's bloodshot, like he hasn't slept for a week. Or he drank too much last night.

"This isn't sustainable," I murmur, resting my head on my arm.

He sighs and closes his eye.

"I know," he says after a moment.

"Dom..." I let my voice trail off, swallowing to soothe my suddenly dry mouth. I finally let the admission slip into the space between us, already tensed for his refusal and rejection. "I need this to work."

He moves faster than I expect given his hangover, twisting us both around until I'm pinned under him, one hand holding both my wrists pinned above my head and the other spread at the bottom of my throat.

He says something in Italian that I don't understand, his voice too low and too slurred for me to parse out a word to give me context. "Slower," I whisper.

He blows out a breath and closes his eyes. "Am I not enough?"

That worry drops like a stone. Of course he's enough. He was enough in September, too. What about Violet makes him question whether I love him? Why is it with Violet but not with Rylan? Or has he been feeling this way about Rylan, too?

I push against his hold, sitting up and palming his neck, kissing him with everything that I can't manage to put into words yet. He still tastes like whiskey. His scent bleeds out from him, the grapefruit not as controlled as it normally is.

Did he lower his suppressor dosage? Fuck, that would explain why he's so volatile right now.

"Why wouldn't you be enough?" I ask, pulling away just far enough to see his eyes. "*Ti amo.*"

"Good," he growls. He runs his hand up my chest until it settles at the base of my throat again. "You need her."

I nod and grab his other hand, lacing our fingers together. "But I need you, too. Just like I need Rylan. Some people aren't built for monogamy. It took me a long time to become comfortable in the reality that I'm one of them."

He stares at me, fear and nerves in his eyes. I force myself to stay relaxed under his gaze. When he doesn't say something, I lean forward and kiss him again. I let my lips track over his jaw and throat, biting the sensitive spot just behind his ear. His scent grows stronger, the grapefruit distinct from his cologne that's left over from last night.

"I need to make you breakfast," he murmurs as I trace the line of his collarbone.

"Shower first."

He grunts and tightens his hold on my throat. "You're coming with me."

I pull away, cocking an eyebrow as I smirk. "I'd hope so. Otherwise it would be a boring ass shower."

His lips curl into an almost-there smile, and that band around my chest loosens.

"*Tesoro*," Dominic growls.

I flip the pancakes, playing innocent, and he laughs low in his throat. He steps up behind me, his chest pressed to my back, his arms bracketing me in. His lips are soft where they trace my ear.

"You're going to regret that," he whispers.

Goosebumps race down my throat, but I ignore them. Just like I ignore how my dick jumps at the unspoken promise. He marks the skin just below my ear, forcing my head to the side, a purr rumbling through him. I relax into his body, letting him mark me, trying to ease away his fears over the whole match.

Tension slowly eases away from him, his hold on the counter lessening until his knuckles are no longer white.

"*Ti amo*," he whispers.

I turn and kiss his cheek. "Love you, too."

Footsteps echo down the hall, but I ignore them, focusing on Dominic behind me.

"I'll grab it as soon as we get you dropped off," Rylan's voice is low and soothing. "You won't be late, and you won't be missing your robes. I promise."

I glance over my shoulder—and Dom's. Rylan holds Violet's hand, keeping her from grabbing a set of keys thrown on the kitchen island. Anxiety is written all over her face, her lips turned down and her hands trembling.

"What's wrong?" I ask, flipping the last pancake onto the plate beside the stove.

Dominic tenses behind me, the small intimacy from a moment ago nowhere to be found. He pulls away, his hands dropping to his sides.

"I forgot my robes at the dorm," Violet says after an extended silence.

Rylan guides her into one of the chairs on the other side of the island, tucking her hair behind her ear. She's already done it into waves and pinned part of it back, and her makeup is flawless, black mascara and copper eyeshadow making the hazel of her eyes pop.

"The ceremony's on campus, right?" I ask.

Dominic pulls away from me, plating a few of the pancakes and leaning against the counter. He's left as much room as possible between him and Violet. She glances at him before nodding, picking at the gold necklace she wears.

"I'll drop you both and then swing by her dorm and grab them," Rylan says.

I set the pancakes on the island before grabbing some fruit from the fridge. I pick out a few strawberries and put them on the same plate Rylan's making for Violet. Her eyes flick to me, surprise flashing across them. I add another one just to make my point clear. Her cheeks darken. I palm her cheek, leaning across the island until I can just press my lips to hers.

A growl boils out from Dominic, and she ducks her head, suddenly focused on her food.

I breathe through my nose, trying to keep from saying something to either of them I'll end up regretting. Rylan sits beside her, blocking her view of Dominic. I lean over the island, dropping my head into my hands. Before I can manage to attempt eating my own breakfast, Dominic has his plate in the sink, and he's disappearing out the back door, dropping into one of the outdoor lounges that overlook the ocean.

~

Violet clutches her phone to her chest, blinking back tears.

"I knew she would do this. Why am I fucking upset when I knew she would do this?"

I spin her into me, keeping myself between her and the growing crowd heading toward the event center on UCLA's campus. She shudders in a breath. I don't offer any words, not entirely sure what to say that isn't just encouraging her to cut all ties to Sienna. It's not like I'm unbiased in the whole situation, after all.

"Are your dads still here?" I ask instead, running my hand down her spine.

She nods once, dropping her arms around my waist, tucking her phone into the back pocket of my slacks. "They said they're working on parking, and that they'll meet us for lunch afterwards. We need to find Faedra."

My own phone buzzes with a notification, and I dig it out, keeping one arm around her shoulders. A text from Rylan brightens the screen.

Finally found parking. Be there soon.

"Oh, well, here's Violet at least. Maybe she'll be able to help us figure out where Faedra is."

A woman materializes from the crowd about twenty feet in front of me, her blonde hair falling stick-straight to her shoulders. Her charcoal pantsuit is well-tailored, and her jewelry simple. She has the same eyes as Faedra, though the men with her are nearly carbon copies of Violet's best friend. The woman's voice is bright with an edge of frustration. Violet takes a deep breath and pushes off of me, none of her worry or hurt anywhere to be seen.

"Hey, Jay, Elizabeth," she says, waving. I wrap my arm around her shoulders and pull her into me, keeping her from crossing through the crowd. The others navigate the people well enough without her getting separated from me. "This is Jasper."

Both of them smile as they close the distance between us, the man holding out his hand. I take it easily enough. The third man looks out over the crowd before waving, trying to get someone's attention. Elizabeth follows his gaze and mutters a relieved gratitude.

"There you are, Faedra Rose," she says, exasperated. She starts across the crowd, and the rest of us follow. I drop my arm and lace my fingers with Violet's. Elizabeth raises her voice. "Faedra Rose! There you are!"

This time, a redheaded woman looks around three older men clad in expertly tailored suits they wear like second skins. They don't immediately follow the woman, taking a moment to chat between themselves. The one to the right, whose hair and beard lean more gray than brown, frowns before breathing deep and nodding. Faedra hugs her mom and dad, her movements growing more awkward as the minutes pass. Violet squeezes my hand, and I glance down at her, an eyebrow raised in silent question.

She shakes her head once.

Point taken.

I keep us half a step back from the others, letting Faedra navigate her family on her own.

"All right, all right, enough with the greeting," her mom says. "Introduce us."

Oh shit. This must be the pack Faedra matched with while at the gala. She swallows and then introduces each of them, each man smiling.

"This is Logan." She points to the man in the middle with short blonde hair similarly styled to my own before indicating the tallest man, his black hair minimally styled and his brown eyes sharp. He looks like fucking John Mayer if John Mayer spent significant time in the gym. "This is Carter." She points to the older man with the scowl. "And this is Jude."

He nods once, closing the gap between him and Faedra as she introduces her family. They all do the customary exchanges, her father relaxing as conversation slowly eases into the first bits of small talk. After a minute, Violet clears her throat, pulling away from me just enough to step up beside Aiden.

"Shit, sorry, Vi," Faedra says, grabbing her open hand. She turns back toward the men. "Everyone, this is Violet. She's my best friend and has been my roommate for the last four years. And this is Jasper." She holds out a hand toward me, and I offer a small nod. "He's part of Pack Montegue." Fuck, that felt weird to hear. "Which Violet matched with at the same gala we did."

Logan offers his hand, and I take it.

"Betas aren't that common among packs. I'd love to hear your story if it's something you're comfortable sharing."

I can't help but laugh, reliving how Rylan, Dominic, and I even managed to become a thing in the first place.

"It starts with me being bi," I say with a grin.

Carter laughs, and Faedra's lips curl into a smirk.

"Where do you need to be? Last thing we want is you girls to be late," Jay says, clearing his throat.

I glance over my shoulder, trying to figure out where Rylan might be. Some of my tension bleeds away as he steps up beside Violet, just behind Faedra, his suit unblemished from what must have been a pretty significant walk.

"Hey, Vi," he murmurs, holding up the robes he has tossed over his shoulder. "Here they are. Sorry it took me a bit to find parking."

She nods and reaches for the robes, but Rylan shakes his head, helping her into them himself. He centers both honors cords before helping her into the medal, adjusting it until it lays flat against her chest. When he's satisfied, I help her into the cap, trying to keep all the emotion roaring through me in check. This should have been the second time I got to help with her graduation.

She takes my hand, her eyes keen. "Thank you," she murmurs.

I nod, and Rylan kisses her temple.

A moment later, she's managed to wedge herself between Faedra and her Alphas, locking their elbows together.

"All right," she says. "We'll see you after."

Twenty-Eight

VIOLET

"We're getting lunch together, right?" Faedra pushes through the throng of other students until she's in front of me, her question managing to cut over the din of the crowd. She messes with her earrings, her diploma holder tucked under one arm.

I nod and grab her hand, doing my best to work toward the far entrance since it isn't as busy.

Crowds are not my happy place, and today is definitely not the exception. One good thing about Faedra being so suppressed is the people don't seem to bother her, and she helps cut a path through the gathering groups of families seeking out graduates.

Faedra pulls out her phone and sends a text.

"I left my phone with Jasper," I admit as she tucks it away in her dress's pocket. She nods.

"Logan said to meet them at the east entrance. They said it's not as crowded and there's a nice spot for photos. Mom's adamant we get some done."

Not surprising. I try to look around the arena for any sign of my dads, but there's too many people taller than me to see much more than five feet in any given direction. Damn me for choosing sensible shoes instead of heels that would have given me a few extra inches.

Faedra's strides get longer the closer to the doors we get, her fingers picking away the ends of her hair in her nervous tick. I'm not much better. By the time we make it back out into the California sun, I'm ready to peel my skin off of me and hide in a damn corner.

"Fuck me, I hate crowds," I mutter. "You'd think they'd have some option for Omegas given how many were fucking there."

Faedra nods and shakes out her hands before running her fingers through her hair. "I guess we could have waited until everyone dissipated a bit."

We look at each other, a moment of shared understanding extending between us, and then laugh, leaning into each other.

"Could you imagine the look on your mom's face if we just sat there?" I ask.

She shakes her head. "The only reason why yours didn't come extract us is because she decided there was something more important going on."

I scrunch my nose and push her playfully.

"Hey! Too far, Fae." I keep my voice light so she knows I'm joking. "I haven't once mentioned how awkward your brother has been all weekend. No way are you allowed to bring up Mom."

She grabs my hand. "You okay?" she asks, all levity gone.

I breathe carefully through my nose before nodding. "My dads are here somewhere, so that helps."

"Faedra Rose!" Elizabeth's call cuts over the white noise of the people.

Faedra and I turn together, our hands still interlaced.

Elizabeth stands at the front of an impressive group, all things considered. I'd forgotten just how many are involved when you factor in matched packs. Jasper and Rylan stand just off to the side with Faedra's Alphas, Rylan murmuring in Jasper's ear, his arms around Jasper's waist. Elizabeth and Jay step up to Faedra, hugging her again.

Just behind them, a flash of familiar gray hair has my heart in my fucking throat, and I blink quickly to keep tears from forming in my eyes.

Papa's grinning, his hand intertwined with Father's, as Dad makes a joke of some kind, low enough I can't hear it, though all three of them laugh. The moment Father catches my gaze, he drops Papa's hand and closes the space between us, sweeping me into his arms.

"There she is!" he says, the smile clear in his voice even though I can't see it. "So sorry we ran too late to see you beforehand. Today has been a mess."

It's the meanest I've ever heard my father be, even when Mom has been absolutely awful.

"All right, stop hogging her," Papa says, his deep voice a balm to my soul.

Father sighs as he sets me back on my feet, holding my elbows until he knows I'm steady. Papa doesn't lift me up, simply wrapping me into his arms and kissing the crown of my head. I close my eyes, focusing on the way his cologne mixes with his scent, letting it calm me like it has since I was first adjusting to being Omega.

"How are you holding up?" he whispers, keeping his voice low enough that only Dad and Father can hear him.

"Somewhere in the middle, I think." I shrug and hold him tighter for a heartbeat before forcing myself to let go.

Dad's eyes are worried, his lean frame held stiff, his hands shoved in his pockets as he takes me in.

"You're all right?" he asks in his soft-spoken way, cupping my cheek in his careful hold.

When I nod, I realize I'm not even really lying. This morning was awkward as fuck but not completely terrible. He blows out a breath and grabs my hand, kissing the back of it before taking a step back, removing himself from the bulk of our small crowd. I frown, trying to figure out what has him concerned, when an arm snakes around my waist and pulls me against a hard chest. Bergamot surrounds me despite the open air.

"Shit, sorry," I mutter, twisting so that I can see both Rylan and my fathers.

Dad's gaze grows sharp as he takes in someone other than Rylan. His jaw clenches, a muscle in his cheek feathering, and my stomach tightens.

I should have warned him at least about Jasper. Papa sucks in a harsh breath, and Father's growl rumbles through the crowd. Rylan tenses, his own growl starting, his grasp on my elbow firm as he pulls me closer to him.

Fuck. My. Life.

"Father, please," I whisper, turning away from Rylan completely. "Don't make a scene here."

"At least I understand why your mother has been fighting it so much," Dad says, his voice now cold and slicing.

Papa nods. "First time in a long time that she was actually right."

Father stands beside Papa, their shoulders brushing, his scowl the most menacing of the three.

It's Dad that says something, though. "I'll happily put in my own complaint with the Council to speed things up."

I pull away from Rylan, moving until I'm within easy reach of all three of my dads. Rylan's growl fades away. I glance over my shoulder. Jasper's whispering into Rylan's ear, his body carefully neutral and his gaze on the ground, like he knows how volatile my dads are right now.

Softness wells in me.

"I know reassignment isn't glamorous," Papa says, his hand warm on my cheek, forcing my attention back to him. "But there's no reason for you to settle for something like this."

"I don't want reassignment," I whisper. His eyes narrow, the look nearly identical to one I give all the time. I might take my coloring from my mom, but my features are all my dad. "Not right now, at least."

Father leans closer, blocking Rylan's view of me in one subtle twist of his shoulders. "You have nothing to lose by leaving, darling. Not like us."

My chest clenches. Me. They would lose their kids if they left. Not really anymore since we're all adults, but when we were younger... I swallow the lump in my throat.

"I need you to trust me." My voice trembles, a wealth of emotion carried in the plea.

Dad is silent, his breathing deep and controlled, his gaze calculating. After a long minute, he nods.

"What's changed?" Papa's question is quiet but warm. He runs his hand down my arm, circling my wrist.

"We figured out what went wrong," I say, trying to decide if I want to add fuel to their fire while Mom's not even here to justify herself. Jasper's face when he realized I'd never gotten the necklace has rage boiling in my stomach. Dad raises one eyebrow in silent question.

"Mom."

All three of them freeze.

"All right, darling. Let's meet them." Papa squeezes my wrist and then drops his hold.

I wave Rylan over. His gaze is hard though his body is

relaxed. "Rylan, these are my dads." I point to Father first. "This is Phillip."

Rylan shakes his hand while wrapping an arm around my shoulders and pulling me into his side.

I point to Papa. "This is Kurt." I point to Dad last since Rylan probably recognizes him already. "This is Johnathan."

Jasper keeps a step behind, his hand on the small of Rylan's back as I look over at him. Before any of my dads break the silence, Elizabeth calls me over.

"Violet, you too, sweetheart. Let's get some photos of you both. And then we'll get some with your dads and your pack."

I duck out of Rylan's hold, adjusting my cap and diploma holder. Leaving Jasper alone with my dads so soon after finding solid ground between us isn't a good idea, but I do my best to stay focused on all the pictures. The guys take it in better stride than I expect, and by the time Elizabeth is ushering my dads into the photo along with Rylan and Jasper, the tension is nearly gone, only a lingering stiffness in Dad's shoulders.

"Thank you," I murmur as Faedra convinces her mom to relent and we start heading toward the various parking lots.

"Love you," my dads say in unison.

Twenty-Nine

RYLAN

"You look fine, Vi."

Jasper's low words are barely audible from where I'm perched against the wall beside her cracked open bedroom door. I shove my hands in my pockets and lean my head back, trying to remember how to breathe without my heart getting in the fucking way. I thought I'd gotten past all of this weird reactionary crap when Jasper and I figured out our shit last fall.

Dominic doesn't look up from his phone as he closes his own door and stalks past me, his steps nearly silent despite the shiny black Hermes shoes he wears.

Fuck. That means this is going to be even worse than Jasper and I figured it would be. Dominic only ever gets this bad when he's especially angry. Though, in reality, he's been a festering cesspit of rage since the woman from the Council brought the official packet of paperwork informing us of the match. He's a fucking keg of gunpowder just waiting for a match to get within ten feet of him.

With any luck, neither of his brothers will manage to be that damn match today.

"Fine? Just fine?" Violet's not trying to be quiet the way Jasper had been. I can hear the nervous thread of her voice, and I clench my hands to keep from stalking in there. "Jasper, it's his entire freaking family. I can't be just fine."

"Fine means good," Jasper says, exasperated.

I sigh and knock once on the ajar door before leaning inside the room.

Violet stands in the doorway to her closet, her arms wrapped around her middle. She frowns as she turns away from where Jasper sprawls across the sofa.

"Is this okay?" she asks me.

She turns once to her right and then again to her left.

The dress is a goddamn masterpiece. A soft blue that makes her skin practically glow in a draping fabric that accentuates every single gorgeous curve of hers. It gathers on her left hip, a small smattering of jewels holding the fabric together. Is it a pin of some kind? It looks intentional, so I don't ask. She's done her hair similar to the gala, though more pieces frame her face this time. Her makeup is softer, the bold red lipstick traded for something nearly identical to the natural light brown of her lips.

My dick jumps, and I don't downplay having to adjust myself.

Her gaze drops to the movement before flicking to Jasper and then back to me. The telltale blush of her embarrassment darkens her cheeks, and I smirk. She's so damn bold in everything she does. But show her just how thoroughly she affects my body? Instantly shy and blushing like a damn maiden. It's endearing.

"You're gorgeous, Violet." My voice is husky, but I don't do anything to change it. "Honestly a bit overdone for Sunday brunch."

Not actually true, but I want to see how she responds to my own humor. She pouts her lips, her gaze taking in my attire twice before she rolls her eyes.

"You're nearly as dressed as the gala. Certainly just as formal as you were yesterday, where it was business casual," she says, waving her hand toward me. "No way am I overdressed if you're not."

"He could just enjoy wearing suits," Jasper says, sitting up and spreading his arms along the back of the couch. I smirk as his gaze catches mine.

Violet snorts, her nose scrunching.

"Absolutely not. He barely wore a suit to the gala that the Council demands everyone wear black tie for. He'd much rather be in a set of jeans and a hoodie. Though May really isn't the best time for wearing hoodies. Not in LA, at least."

An odd sense of pride flashes through me at her noticing my preferences.

Jasper nods. "Fair enough. Though we both play the part of well-dressed often enough that sometimes it feels like a second skin."

He crosses the room, brushing his hands over his slacks before running his hand through his hair. He pulls Violet into his hold and kisses the top of her head.

"Do you believe me now? You're beautiful, love." He takes her hand and pulls her farther into the room and away from her clothes. He mutters, "Bianca's going to have fresh pasta, and if we're late, Victor and Lorenzo will eat it all."

"They're really that bad?" Violet tilts her head as she lets Jasper drag her closer to me.

"*Sono golosi*," Dominic growls from behind me. "*Cibo e donne entrambi.*"

I twist and take a step back, keeping both him and Violet in my line of sight. To her credit, she doesn't balk, her spine straight and her hands steady where she has them pressed into her stomach. Jasper laces his fingers with hers as the silence stretches on, his worried gaze flicking between them. I swear I can smell fucking *grapefruit*.

Before it grows strong enough for me to be sure of it, Dominic nods once and says, "*È ora di andare.*"

Jasper drops Violet's hand and closes the space between him and Dominic, crowding into him and grabbing his hips.

"English, love," he murmurs.

"*Accidenti,*" Dominic mutters, cupping Jasper's face. "*Mi dispiace.*"

While I normally enjoy watching Jasper soothe and settle Dominic—who knew that would be such a turn on for me—I focus on Violet instead, stepping between her and the others and cradling her face in my hands. Her eyes are wide, but her lips are bracketed in tension and her shoulders are stiff.

Impressive that I hadn't been able to tell any of her unease until getting this close to her.

Running my nose along her neck, I hum the newest guitar solo Mark has me working on for the studio. The tension slowly leaves her body, and I bite the small, sensitive spot where her shoulder meets her neck. She gasps.

"Remind me to hide your scent blockers," I mutter. "It's criminal I can't smell you right now."

"My scent's all over the room," she whispers.

"You know that's not what I mean," I say, biting her earlobe. She shivers. I run my hand down her throat, chasing the goosebumps. My own scent dominates the space immediately around us. "It smells better when it's yours and not mine."

She hums and tilts her head, giving me more room. "I don't

think you'd appreciate everyone else being able to smell me, though. Aren't Victor and Lorenzo both Alphas?"

The growl is swift and vicious, but she laughs rather than tenses.

"Yeah, that's what I thought. Scent blockers it is."

Thirty

JASPER

The kitchen is bright and happy as the four of us pause in the threshold of the room, Dominic's hand on the small of my back, his fingers hooking into the waistband of my slacks under my jacket. It always strikes me just how beautiful the room is, like his parents took a picture from the Italian countryside and recreated it to the smallest detail. Warm stone surrounds the large stove set against the far wall, and the warm gray cabinets contrast against the dark butcher block counter of the island. The large sliding doors that lead to the patio and pool are closed, but the large table is set for at least ten people. I do a quick count in my head.

Who's the extra place setting for?

"*Domenico*, there you are. You had me thinking you weren't going to show up."

Bianca looks up for a second from where she's chopping tomatoes, her hands never faltering. Alessia, Dominic's sister, stands next to her, working through her own pile of tomatoes and dropping them into a large bowl set between them. She gives me a quick smile.

Lorenzo and Victor glance up from where they're leaning against the back door and messing around on their phones, their heads close together as they discuss something.

Lorenzo smirks. "It's his own event, *Mamma*. Not even Dom is that bad."

She huffs and rolls her eyes, her slicing speeding up.

"I'm excited to meet her," a voice I don't immediately recognize says, echoing down the hallway. "It'll be nice to not be the newest person here."

A woman about Alessia's age steps into the large room, a tray of bread in her hands. Her blonde hair is pulled back, small braids running along the sides, and her eyes are done up in heavy black mascara that makes the brown color pop. Her dress is a simple a-line and the deep purple compliments her fair skin. She glances at Lorenzo across the room before focusing on Bianca at the island. She seems vaguely familiar, though I can't really place it.

"Isn't Jasper the newest?" Rylan asks, coming up beside me. He has Violet tucked into his side, subtly keeping her as far from Dominic as he can manage without giving away how tense our dynamic is at the moment.

"Oh, right," she says, biting her lip as she looks at me. "Sorry, it's just... I meant newest to designate."

I shrug and shake my head. "No offense meant."

Rylan chuckles, kissing my cheek.

Alessia rolls her eyes and points her knife at Rylan.

"Give her a break. Her brain has been a mess since December."

The blonde woman blushes and ducks her head. "Alessia, that's private."

Dominic's sister levels a look on the woman that's identical to one Bianca gives when she thinks one of her children is being unreasonable. The woman isn't apologetic the way Dominic often is, though. Her cheeks are still a deep scarlet, but her eyes are flinty.

"There's nothing wrong with them knowing about your heat," Alessia says, returning to her chopping. "It's like them knowing about your period. It happens. We manage. We move on."

"But these are your *brothers*, Ale."

Victor laughs but covers it with a cough when Alessia turns on him, her glare as impressive as the blade in her hand.

"Don't you even start, Victor," she says. "You have no idea what it's like."

Victor raises an eyebrow. "Of course, *sorellina*," he says, completely deadpan. Only a quick smirk gives away his humor. "I know nothing of being at the mercy of instincts."

Alessia scoffs. "No, you don't. Not like this. You can smell any old scent and it gets you off. But us? One day we're completely normal and the next we're obsessed with *peppermint* like our life depends on it. *Cavolo, è un disastro.*"

Violet steps up to the island, the pan of brownies she made last night in her hands. "You enjoy peppermint? I've always been partial to citrus."

The other woman looks up, interest clear on her face. She runs a finger along the rim of the pan in front of her. Alessia grimaces. "Citrus? Definitely not. Dominic's is grapefruit. I can't stand the association."

Rylan chuckles and crosses the room, tucking his hands into his pockets as he flanks Violet, a few inches separating them. "Yeah, that's fair. Not sure I'd want to think about my brother while trying to fuck someone."

Bianca looks up, an eyebrow raised, her own knife pointing at Rylan. "*Linguaggio, monello.*"

"*Mi dispiace,*" Rylan murmurs, though it doesn't sound genuine. A corner of her mouth tips up as she blows out an exasperated huff.

"Doesn't understand Italian until it's convenient," she mutters. "*Un tale monello.*"

Rylan chuckles.

"Peppermint's not bad," Violet says. She twists toward Rylan, leaning into him. "Though, really, anything is better than floral. Maybe it's because mine is floral? But I can't stand it. It reminds me of my mother's bathroom."

Alessia and the other woman laugh. The blonde woman nods and holds out a hand toward Violet.

"Yes! That's exactly it! It smells like my grandmother's home. I couldn't figure out why it made my skin crawl. The Council makes it sound like we'll like any scent ever presented, but there's this Alpha at work who smells like roses, and it makes me want to gag every time he comes near me."

Suddenly I recognize the woman who's clearly friends with Dominic's little sister. Her hair is longer than it was last year when I saw her while on a date with Dominic, and there's a confidence in the way she holds herself that wasn't there before.

I lean into Dominic, tucking my lips against his ear so his family can't see what I'm whispering.

"I didn't realize Sarah was going to be here," I say.

He shrugs and turns into me, his voice even quieter than mine. "Lorenzo."

Surprise jolts through me. "Really?" I ask.

Dominic nods even as he frowns. "*Un segreto, Tesoro.*"

"What's a secret, *Domenico*?" Bianca asks, looking past Violet toward Dominic. "What are you chatting about over there in the corner like some cartoon villain? At least be helpful and get the wine from the cellar. *Tu e i tuoi fratelli.*"

Victor sighs, but Lorenzo is silent as he slips his phone into his pocket and joins Dominic and me.

"Your pick," Bianca says to Violet. "Since it is you we celebrate. Tell the men what you would like to drink."

Violet tucks her hair behind her ear and looks over her shoulder, focusing on me rather than Dominic.

"Mimosas?" It comes out as a question.

Sarah moans, low in her throat, her head tipping back. "Oh, yes, please. Those sound amazing."

Bianca nods and motions her sons toward the hallway that leads to the large butler's pantry and wine cellar. Once they're out of ear shot, Alessia sighs.

"You brought brownies?" Sarah asks, and Violet nods, grabbing the pan again. "Let's put them back here."

She takes the pan and sets it on the back counter near the stove, moving around Alessia with ease.

"Now that the boys are gone and won't growl over all of us," Bianca says, dumping the tomatoes into the bowl and wiping her hands on a small towel on the island, "let us introduce everyone. Violet, this is my daughter Alessia and her best friend Sarah."

The girls offer small greetings, Sarah and Violet dropping into an easy-seeming conversation about waitressing of all things. I cross the room, palming Violet's hip, still enjoying the absolute fuck out of being able to touch her again. She leans back against me, though her head is tilted just enough that she can scent Rylan.

Just as Bianca points to two large, covered pans on the stove, another man walks in from deeper in the house, his black suit impeccably cut, his brown eyes shrewd.

"Hello, Dante," I say quietly. He nods once in silent greeting. It's the warmest Dominic's father has ever managed to be with me.

"*Mi dispiace, amore,*" he murmurs, crossing the room and kissing the top of Bianca's head.

She bats him away. "You can apologize later. The food is getting cold, and we have not even gotten a chance to celebrate Violet." She looks up, pointing her knife at me and then Rylan. "Boys, grab those pans, *per favore.* Alessia will finish this and we'll head outside. You," she points at Dante, "go extract your sons before they get drunk in the wine cellar because of some stupid bet they made."

Sarah and Violet walk onto the patio, laughing, as Rylan and I do as instructed.

The rest of the family settles in after a few minutes, Dominic on my right and Rylan on my left, Violet tucked in next to him. Some of my nerves ease away at seeing her blend in so seamlessly with Alessia and Sarah. I reach across Rylan and grab her elbow. She glances up at me, her eyebrows furrowed, before she relaxes and offers a small smile.

Conversations start between small groups. Lorenzo shoves Dominic, some joke I missed making them both laugh. I'm filled with contentment, especially as Dominic palms my thigh, his hand warm and strong. Bianca holds up her glass of wine, and the table quiets.

"Congratulations, Violet," she says with a smile, her eyes crinkling at the corners with her happiness. "Welcome to the family."

Thirty-One

VIOLET

"You good?" Jasper asks. When I say that I'm fine, he nods and reaches behind him without looking. Dominic laces their hands together, his gaze neutral. I tighten my hold on the bag Rylan handed to me and ignore the gnawing in my stomach of his clear disinterest in me. He hasn't outright glared or sneered at me, so I'm refusing to worry about it right now. If anyone is aware that most matches aren't actually love matches, it's me.

Rylan opens the door of the restaurant and guides us inside. He nods once toward the hostess, and she points toward the back corner where several people are already sitting around a large table. I smooth the front of my shirt where I have it tucked into the same black skirt I wore the last time we went out like this. Rylan raises an eyebrow, and I scrunch my nose.

No way is he about to call me out for being nervous. It's been a long ass day already with navigating Dominic's family this morning and the concert this afternoon. Not to mention the absolute marathon yesterday was.

At least my dads aren't angry with the match anymore. Will Mom survive their ire? I'm not sure. And I don't honestly think I care at this point.

"Don't you dare," I whisper, and Rylan laughs, shaking his head once before taking my hand and starting across the restaurant.

"Same as before," he whispers, low enough I'm not sure even Jasper can hear him. "Squeeze my arm twice if you need a break or want to go."

I murmur a soft agreement and then pick a seat at the large table. There's a ton of us here. I fucking hate working large tables like this. I make sure to smile at both waitresses as they take our drink and first round of food orders.

Liz sits wedged between two of her Alphas, her eyes glassy no matter how many times she blinks. Huntley sits across from Jasper, a man I recognize from the concert next to her though I don't know his name. He nods once and holds out his hand.

"I'm Owen," he says, his voice a warm baritone. "Nice to finally meet you."

Everyone dissolves into smaller conversations as the first round of food is brought out. Liz still seems on the verge of tears, but no one seems overly concerned, so I do my best to treat this like any other dinner event.

"All right," Huntley says, just loud enough that the rest of the table quiets. "Let's get to it."

It's like everyone was waiting for the phrase. Jasper grabs the bag I brought in from under his seat, pulling out two smaller wrapped presents and handing one to Rylan.

"We do a gift exchange at the end of every season," Liz explains. Her voice doesn't betray any of the tears, though her hands shake as she takes a small present from Zach. "We draw names at Christmas."

Mason nods. "Gifts should be sweet and functional, though there's always room for pranks. Huntley currently holds the title of Best Gifter."

Huntley nods. "Damn right I do. Speaking of which, we got this for you." She leans down and grabs a second present from under her seat, holding it out to me. "We wanted to make sure you felt welcomed since this time of year can be really overwhelming with us going on summer hiatus, especially with this being Liz's last season with us."

My hands tremble as I take the small package, though I can't quite manage to keep the confusion off my face. Fuck, should I have gotten them something, too? I definitely should have. Why didn't Rylan warn me? I'm sure my dads would have made sure I had enough to cover all of them even if Mom's still got my trust locked down.

"No, don't give me that look," she says, shaking her head. "We all pooled together. It's not a big deal."

The package is small, fitting in the palm of my hands. It's wrapped in a simple metallic blue paper that reflects the light with each small movement. It reminds me of the ocean, of all things. The table quiets as I slowly peel back the paper to reveal an unassuming jewelry box.

The necklace is small and simple where it sits cushioned against black velvet, a gold chain with a single pendant hanging from it. It's a hollow heart made of small vines, four gemstones inside. I recognize my birthstone as well as Jasper's. The other two must be for Rylan and Dominic.

A warmth spreads through my chest.

I blink away the tears that try to form. If Liz can keep it together, then goddamn it, so can I.

"Thank you," I say, trying to get all the emotion into the small phrase. "It's beautiful."

Huntley nods, her gaze intense. Liz grins.

"You were right. Yellow gold is gorgeous against her skin."

Rylan runs his hand down my arm. "You want to put it on? It'll blend well with your other necklaces."

The others start exchanging gifts as he helps set the hook, and I smooth my hair, messing with the heavy pendant as I adjust to its presence against my skin. Jasper's laugh distracts me, and I focus on him. He holds up a large tote bag, the bottom and straps black while the main body a simple natural canvas. On the front, there's a drawing of a cello made from a lemon, the word *lemoncello* next to it along with a social media handle.

Huntley smirks. "Looks like I've still got it."

"Of course you do," Mason jokes. "Where did you even find that?"

"An artist on Instagram. She posted it one night. I think it started as a joke, but I fell in love with it. It's perfect for Jasper. So I reached out to her to see if she'd sell me a tote or the license to print my own. Totally worth the cost, by the way."

Dominic smiles, just a quick curve of his lips, and my heart fucking stops. I shove the jealousy down until I can't feel it, focusing on Rylan and Jasper's warm bodies on either side of me.

"*È perfetto*, Huntley," Dominic murmurs.

She smirks and nods. Before anyone else can say anything, the food comes, and we all grow quiet as we focus on eating. I see flashes of the other gifts, small items that seem to hold some kind of emotional sentiment, like the lemon cello joke.

I realize with a bit of a start that I actually *understood* the cello joke. That insidious voice in my head grows quieter, and the thought I've been twisting over all weekend doesn't seem quite so wild to me anymore.

"Let's go get drinks," Rylan murmurs, leaning down until his lips brush the shell of my ear. What little bit that didn't do to my body, his voice does, the baritone, raspy feel of it sending heat straight down my spine and making my core clench. Holy hell, praise the scientists who made scent blockers a thing. Jasper reaches across the table, grabbing something out of Huntley's hands.

"But I already have one, and this is dinner, not a bar." I'm not quite sure why I'm fighting. If he wants to disappear into the bathroom and knot me, it's not like I'm going to say no. I wore the damn skirt for a reason, after all. And especially with Dominic on the other side of Jasper, a wall of heat and coiled, restrained anger just waiting to strike.

"Just say yes," he says, chuckling.

When I nod, he stands from the table. "I realized I left Liz's gift in the car. We'll be right back."

He holds out his hand and helps me stand. Jasper raises an eyebrow but doesn't disagree.

"You didn't have to get me anything," Liz says, but Rylan and Jasper both shake their heads.

Once Rylan has me outside, he pauses, pressing me against the Alfa Romeo and running his lips across my jaw.

"What has you looking like you've just seen God?"

I laugh, but it's brittle. "I did not look that shell-shocked."

He grunts and bites the small spot just under my ear. My knees buckle, and he pushes more insistently into me, keeping me from collapsing. It also lets me feel just how interested he is in me right now, his cock a hard line against my belly.

"Tell me," he whispers. "Before I rip off your scent blockers."

I force a deep breath. "You say that like I'll be irritated by it."

His chuckle is dark and breathless. "You will when you realize you won't be able to go back inside."

Fair enough.

"I was thinking that I feel like maybe I fit in here with you."

He pulls away like I've struck him, his eyes wide as he focuses on me.

"You didn't before?" he asks.

I shrug. "I wasn't sure with Dominic."

His lips tighten as he nods, palming my waist.

"So why the surprised look?" His voice is so low, it brushes over me.

"I think I want to quit and apply for grad school," I admit in a whisper. The last week of not being at the restaurant has been amazing. And maybe my desire to study Omega designations isn't out of reach even matched. "Even though I'm scared of being dependent."

He nods and then his lips are on mine, and he's guiding my legs around his waist.

The house is quiet as I pad down the hallway into the main room, intent on getting some kind of caffeine fix before brunch with Faedra's family. It's late for me, already past eight, but none of the guys seem to be awake. Rylan certainly wasn't where he was stretched on the other side of my bed, his hair an unruly mess and his body beautiful enough to make me perfume.

Two hard knocks on the door pull me from the fridge before I can grab the cold brew I'd stashed the morning before. I adjust my hair and dress, making sure I look mostly presentable.

The man from the Council greets me, another unmarked envelope in his hands.

"Again?" I ask.

When he nods, I sigh. His voice is carefully neutral, his gaze growing worried. "Would you like to file a counter motion?"

A hand on my waist has me practically jumping out of my skin. I bite my lip to keep from actually shrieking. Bergamot surrounds me in a few heartbeats, and I relax into Rylan's shirtless chest.

"Yes, I'd like to go ahead and do that," I say to the councilman. He nods, handing me the envelope with instructions on how to fill out the motion. Rylan disappears from behind me, returning a moment later with a pen.

I sign the paperwork and hand it to the man.

"You shouldn't hear any more from me," he says as he takes it and tucks it into a new envelope. "But you still have Mary's phone number in case something comes up, right?"

When I nod, he smiles and heads toward his car pulled in front of the house, his hands tucked into the pockets of his slacks.

Rylan kisses the sensitive spot where my shoulder meets my neck.

"Do I even want to know?" he asks.

I shake my head as I scan the new motion my mom has filed. It's the same reason as before, though this time she's added a bit about Dominic being linked to a place I've never heard of.

"The Tabernacle?" I ask. "What's that?"

"How the fuck did she learn about that?" Rylan pulls away from me. "It's a club. Mostly. But there's a shit ton of other stuff that happens there that is definitely illegal. It's Lorenzo's favorite spot to hang out."

I raise an eyebrow. "So on top of being the literal Italian mafia, Dominic's involved with underground fighting?"

Rylan shrugs and takes the paper from me. "He's not. His brothers are. Most Dom does is bet on the fights. I don't think he's even gone to one of them."

"Oh," I mutter.

Rylan chuckles and kisses my shoulder again. "I guess we

should get ready and then extract Jasper from Dominic's room. Don't you have a hot brunch date in an hour?"

I glance at the clock and curse. "We're going to be late."

His smirk turns devious as he pulls me against him, his cock hard and heavy where it presses against my belly.

"Better make it worth it, then," he says.

Thirty-Two

VIOLET

Rylan pulls me closer as the little café comes into view, tightening his arm around my waist even as he kisses Jasper's temple.

"I didn't get much of a read at the ceremony Saturday. Do we like her family?" Jasper asks, looking across Rylan to me.

I nod, smiling, though it takes a lot of work and honestly feels fucking forced. Rylan hums and kisses the crown of my head.

"They're great," I say. "Elizabeth can be a bit much sometimes, but it's not malicious or anything. And Jay is great. He loves Faedra. And for being a Beta, he has a really good sense of what she needs."

Jasper nods. "That was the vibe I got from him Saturday."

"That's impressive," Rylan says. "Didn't you say she's suppressed? I wonder if he took a few of the optional courses from the Council when she designated to help fill in some of the gaps."

I shrug. "Yeah, she's been suppressed since her bloodwork was confirmed in high school."

Rylan tenses. "That's at least four years," he says, glancing down at me, incredulity in his voice.

"Yep." I pop the "p" the way Faedra does sometimes.

"How many heats?" he asks.

I elbow him in the side. "Personal information, Rylan. You're not matched with her, so it doesn't matter."

Jasper looks between us both. "Aren't they worse the more you suppress?"

I nod, walking quicker as I see Faedra and her family at one of the outdoor tables of the café.

"Fuck, I hope they've gotten an Omega through a heat before," Rylan mutters, scratching at the double snake tattoo on his neck. "Because that's going to be fucking *wild*."

I smack his arm again.

"What? It is. I was assigned an Omega that had suppressed one heat, and that was..." He trails off, shaking his head. "Not sure there's much else that's that level of intense. Maybe a forced heat, but I never had to help with one of those."

I scrunch my nose and flinch.

Forced heats sound fucking miserable. There's medication you can take to trigger a heat if you're close to when you'd normally drop into one. Lots of Omegas use them as a way to help plan around their heats. Scheduling childcare and time off is easier when you're not fighting through the haze of the heat. Forcing one is taking those drugs and using them nowhere near when you're supposed to be going into heat. The farther off the timing, the higher dosage it requires.

I force myself away from that train of thought, focusing on Rylan's arm around me and his subtle scent blending with Jasper's cologne. They smell delicious together.

We're close enough now to hear Faedra, though her back is turned toward us at the moment.

"I'm on my period. Now stop asking, Mom. It's none of your business anyway."

Rylan laughs. "First time you've seen them in a month, and you're on your period? Tough break."

Faedra glances over her shoulder, her cheeks slowly staining red.

"Whatever, man," Jasper says, laughing even as he shoves away from Rylan. "Periods don't bother me."

Faedra drops her head into her hands as she groans. I elbow Rylan again without really meaning it. When my best friend glances up, an eyebrow cocked, I snicker.

"It's not like it'll be a problem for long. You're only getting them because you're suppressed."

Incredulity flashes across her face, and I'm suddenly sure she's moments away from punching me out of frustrated embarrassment. Rylan tenses beside me, noticing it, too.

Jay intervenes before it gets dicey, though. Thank the gods.

"You bring that project you started?" he asks Faedra.

Rylan helps me into the seat across from Faedra, Jasper on my left and Rylan taking up the seat on my right. The moment Rylan's settled next to me, he's running his hand along my thigh, first the outside and then the inside. His face is impassive, a polite half-smile tipping his lips as Faedra pulls out the new quilting project she's been working on since the gala.

My breath hitches as his finger brushes over my clit. Jasper glances at us, his eyebrow raised, but doesn't say anything. Rylan's next touch is more insistent, and I roll my hips, trying to keep from making a noise. He leans over and kisses my shoulder before pressing his grin into my skin.

Bastard fucking knows how hard it is for me to be quiet.

Who the hell thought he'd have a fucking exhibitionist streak? His hand is featherlight where he runs it back down my leg.

Fuck, am I trembling?

Faedra's mom takes a few of the finished pieces of the quilt and turns them over in her hands, tracing the sewn seams.

Rylan runs two fingers over my clit, and even with my clothing between us, it sends a rush of heat through me. Holy hell. I clench my thighs and force a swallow, trying to focus on whatever Elizabeth is saying right now.

"Interesting choice of colors," Jasper says.

Rylan's fingers move faster. Jasper grabs a menu from the table and smacks his wrist, angling the hit so he doesn't manage to strike me at all.

Rylan grunts. "Fuck off," he mutters before lacing his hand with mine and resting them on the table.

I adjust in my seat, trying to calm my heart. I can feel my pulse in my fucking pussy right now, and he barely touched me. My heat in September is going to be—to use his word—wild. I mentally shake myself and force myself to focus on my best friend, trying to fill in the gaps of the conversation that I've missed.

"So I'm just going to quilt these onto one large white background and then quilt it all together," she says, moving a few of the pieces around.

Her mom's voice lowers, losing a bit of the manic edge she typically has, as she sets the pieces down. "It's going to look great, Faedra."

Faedra's cheeks are warm as she looks up, her eyes misty with new tears. The waiter appears literally a second later like it's a freaking scripted scene in a movie, and it gives Faedra a chance to blink quickly and tuck her project back into her bag. The man is nice enough as we all put in our orders.

The moment he's gone, I lean forward and adjust my skirt.

"So have you looked up where they live yet? I can't believe you've managed to not look."

Honestly, it's shocking at this point. Faedra's so incredibly curious about *everything*. And yet she's managed to not even run a simple search of the guys' address to get a sense of what she's walking—flying, I guess—into tomorrow.

"I don't know Denver," she says with a shrug.

Yeah, that's not the reason.

It occurs to me that all the fears I had to work through last week are still circling for her. Where she's going to be living, if she's going to fit in with their group of friends, what she's going to do regarding suppressors and career and everything else that comes after graduating college. Well, what are best friends for if not holding your hands during terrifying moments? I arch an eyebrow, and she sighs, digging through her bag and grabbing her phone.

"Aiden, switch," I say, standing up and moving around the table.

Her brother takes it well enough, dropping into my old seat and striking up a conversation with Jasper. Rylan grabs my other hand and adjusts his seat to be closer to me while Faedra types in the address and pulls up the first listing offered on the search results page.

The moment the site loads, I'm tipping my head back and laughing, nearly missing Faedra's jaw dropping in complete shock.

"Holy shit, Fae," I manage to say despite my laughing growing borderline unhinged.

Jay looks over her shoulder while Rylan looks over mine. They give nearly identical surprised grunts. Must be a guy thing.

"Eight million dollars?" Rylan asks, voice warm and happy. "Damn. Does one of them have a black Amex, too?"

Faedra ducks her head, trying to hide her blush, and digs

something out of her bag. The golden soldier flashes in the sunlight, practically glowing like neon against the all black card.

Jasper leans forward, grinning. "No fucking way."

Dad has one, so it's not really that shocking to me. What is surprising is that they still fly commercial. You have to have literal millions to be offered a black Amex. And yet her guys definitely didn't act like Old Money. Or New Money, either, flashing it everywhere they could. It makes me wonder how newly into the money they are. Or maybe it's different because they're so much older? My dads don't flash the wealth, either. That's all my mom.

Aiden leans back in his chair, an eyebrow raised, and Jasper laughs.

"I need to find me an Alpha with that kind of connection."

Rylan scowls and reaches across the table to shove Jasper in the shoulder. "You did," he grunts. "He just has a stick the size of Texas shoved up his ass right now."

My stomach drops, but I keep it off my face.

Jasper grabs Rylan's hand and kisses his palm. "He still doesn't have a Centurion." He tilts his head and then shrugs. "And to be fair, Sienna has that effect on most people."

I clear my throat, glaring at them both.

The last thing I want right now is to have to discuss the shit show that is my mom's bullshit.

"Wait." Faedra puts down the card, covering it with her palm. "What has your mom done this time?"

I turn my look on my best friend, flipping my hair and twisting my industrial piercing to keep from answering right away.

Rylan says, "What *hasn't* she done at this point?"

I cover his mouth. "I don't want to talk about it," I say, giving Faedra a desperate look.

Rylan bites my palm, his teeth grazing the skin, and lightning shoots down my spine. My nipples tighten, and he smirks against my hand, noticing the sudden change in my breathing. I can't help the giggle that falls from me.

Jasper clears his throat and rests his elbows on the table, his chin on his palm. "Sienna has decided that Dominic's *pedigree* is not nearly as perfect as she would like." His lips curl back from his teeth as he says it. "She's filed three motions with the Council to have Violet reassigned."

I push away from Rylan and shake my head as Faedra's gaze turns worried.

When no one rushes to say something, Jasper drops his arms and stretches his neck.

"Please tell me you're going to buy something ridiculous with that card, Faedra," he jokes.

Faedra rolls her eyes even as she laughs and then tucks the card away.

"I'm not built to spend that kind of money all at once. Maybe I'll have Violet do it for me, send her a list and everything."

Rylan laughs and nods. "Perfect."

Thirty-Three

VIOLET

The house is empty as I wander through it, trying to appreciate it for the first time since moving in last week. There's small touches throughout that I recognize as Jasper's. The picture of the three of them on several of the walls, the warm color palette in the large main room, the simple but comfy sectional that fits into the modern feel of the home while not being modern at all.

A door closes, and Dominic walks in from the garage, his eyes glued to his phone. He glances up at me, his lips tightening, and then disappears down the hallway toward our bedrooms.

Anxiety tightens my chest.

I'd thought he would be starting to at least warm up by now. Not necessarily to being involved with me, but at least to the idea of me being around and involved with the others.

Before the worry can fester, I pull out my phone and dial Faedra's number. There's no guarantee she'll be able to answer.

Isn't Denver an hour ahead? It's worth a try, though, if only to distract me from my own thoughts right now.

She picks up on the second ring, and I release the breath I'm holding.

"Your timing is unreal, Vi," she says.

The tension immediately eases. "It's a gift, I swear."

There's the sounds of her moving things around and then her walking. Her steps echo like mine do, and I wonder if the condo is loud and empty, too.

After a couple minutes, I ask, "How is it out there?"

"It's great so far," she says. I can hear the smile in her voice. "They intentionally left my room a blank slate, so I'm working on getting it personalized. I was thinking a soft yellow for the walls."

I hum, trying to envision it. I've looked up that condo more than I'd care to admit, trying to keep this connection between us alive despite the new physical distance. She laughs.

"Would you like a tour?"

I feign innocence, brightening my voice. "I thought you'd never ask."

I pull my phone from my ear so I can see the video as she adjusts the call. The condo is even brighter than the photos on the real estate website. And there's definitely double the rooms as what was listed. She guides me through the place, pointing out small features she likes throughout. I can't help but gasp as she walks into the living room. The view is fucking *stunning*. It's different from the view here, where the ocean stretches for miles. Hers is a fascinating mix of city skyscrapers and towering mountains. It's a lot like her, actually.

She climbs a separate set of stairs, and I get the impression of a damn library. Two different walls are full of bookcases that are crammed full, books shoved in every single possible cranny of open space. There's a kind of organized chaos to it all that makes me think someone uses those books often.

"This is Jude's," Faedra says when she realizes how invested I am. "He doesn't have an office here since he has one on campus. But this is where he keeps all his books."

She walks through one more door and then blushes, hard and fierce.

"I need your help with this room," she admits. She spins in a slow circle so I can see the entire space. It's large and mostly empty aside from a gigantic bed pushed against one wall and a nondescript dresser nearby. It's clearly her nest, though there's no personalization yet. "I'm not really sure where to start with it. I thought maybe you could help me narrow down what kind of items will be useful."

"Of course, Fae. Send me links to what you're thinking."

She slides down the wall of glass this room has, showing off the balcony and undisturbed mountain view in the process. I whistle.

"Are they as stacked as their finances?" I ask, grinning.

Her damn blush is even darker this time, and I fucking lose it. My laugh is so ridiculous, it sounds like a cackle, but I don't even feel bad. Fuck, I miss her already.

"That's a 'Faedra Yes' if I've ever seen one," I say, and she rolls her eyes. I walk onto the patio and sink into one of the large chaise lounges that overlook the ocean. "Have they mentioned anything else about you thinking about photography?"

Her smile is bright and wide. "We talked about it yesterday. They all took the day off to help me settle in. They're supportive of whichever avenue I take."

I manage to smile even though my stomach twists on itself. I'm so grateful Faedra seems to have found a really good, supportive match. She fucking deserves it. But part of me is so incredibly jealous, and it's hard to breathe past it.

"Seems like you really hit the lottery with them," I say. I don't quite manage to keep the frustration out of my voice, though. Her smile falls away, and she focuses more completely on me.

"Has it gotten better?"

Translation: has Dominic managed to come around to the idea of me being integrated into the pack? Absolutely not. I'm nearly positive he'd rather walk into the ocean with a fucking rock tied around his neck than be within thirty feet of me.

I shrug, trying to downplay it so I don't worry her.

"Maybe," I say. "It's hard to tell since he's never really around." And thank fuck for that. The small moments where I've seen him have made me seriously contemplate the annulment paperwork still tucked into my nightstand. "Even Rylan and Jasper are getting fed up with him at this point. But they can't separate from him since there wouldn't be the minimum number for a pack."

Not to mention it would break Jasper's heart. He might like me, but he fucking *loves* Dominic with a devotion I've never seen outside of movies. I prop the phone against the arm of the chaise and pull back my hair, trying to distract myself. Even still, tears line my lashes as I look back at my best friend.

"Losing Jasper a second time will break me, Fae," I admit, the truth both gutting and freeing.

It's the thing that keeps me from actually pulling the paperwork from the drawer.

"I'm so sorry," she says. "If you need me, I'll make it happen, okay?"

I manage a half-decent smile and wipe my eyes.

Time to get the attention off of me.

"Fuck me, I'm not a crier." Faedra laughs. "My heat must be coming soon." The lie slips out before I can stop it, but she doesn't seem to notice the timing discrepancy. My heat isn't due until September.

"If you disappear for a few days, I'll know not to panic," she jokes.

I laugh. It's thin and way too watery, but it's still there.

She checks something on her phone before glancing back toward the rest of the condo.

"You need to go?" I ask.

She shrugs. "Carter's back."

I smile and mess with my hair some more. "Definitely should go, then. Text me with what you pick for your room. It's going to look so cute, especially the polaroid wall." She nods. "And send me what you're thinking for your nest, too. Happy to help you figure out where to start with all of that."

"Of course." She waves bye and then ends the call, my screen dropping back to my wallpaper.

I tip my head back and close my eyes.

The jealousy gets worse with each minute that passes, but I breathe through it. I have Jasper. I have Rylan. That has to be enough.

$$\mathcal{Thirty-Four}$$

DOMINIC

My bed is cold when I wake up, the sheets mussed from where Jasper slept next to me. I blow out a breath and duck my head back into the pillow, trying to remember how to breathe without him plastered to my side. The ache is getting worse even with the suppressor. The longer she's here, the more thoroughly my body pines for hers, the need to feel her skin and taste her lips and smell her perfuming for *me* instead of Rylan and my lover.

I cut the thought short and push up from the bed, kneeling as I run my hands down my face.

Over two weeks since she moved in. Two weeks of catching small moments of her scent, of having Jasper marked by her mouth, of having him split time between three beds instead of two.

Not as much of me hates it as I want, and that pisses me the fuck off.

I grab my phone from the nightstand, reading the quick text from Jasper as I head into the bathroom and get ready for the day.

> Gone for a run. Be back in time for our brunch date.

> Ti amo.

I manage to get myself mostly together, my black slacks and button-up feeling like my own personal armor more so than they ever were in my parents' estate. I resent the fuck out of her for making me feel like I need it at all in my own damn house.

My feet freeze the moment I'm in the main room, the desire to just keep walking right out the front door sitting on my chest like a damn freight train. And yet I can't manage to move, my body caught up in the faint honeysuckle scent of *her*.

She leans over the counter, her hair draping over one shoulder, revealing a black hoodie with a band logo I don't recognize. Even from here, I can smell the tang of Rylan's scent all over it. She sets down the pen in her hand as I pause in the hallway, her hand covering a piece of paper I hadn't noticed before. Her gaze is wary though not overtly hostile. I ignore the part of me that feels remorse over her being unsure around me.

I don't want to deal with an Omega, the way they solicit for attention and touch and smell, how nothing you ever give them is good enough, how they crave babies like they need them to fucking breathe. And I absolutely don't want to deal with the fact that my body is happy to be strung along on their little leash, regardless of if I'm even interested in them at all.

Cavolo.

I edge around her, forcing tension into my limbs as I grab a simple breakfast so I don't respond to her nearness. Her breath hitches as I brush behind her, grabbing one of the pans hung above the stove and lighting a burner.

The honeysuckle grows stronger. Heat flashes down my spine and into my dick.

I eye the air purifier she tucked into the far corner of the large room when she first moved in, trying to decide if it'll actually help when she's less than three feet away from me. Probably not.

"The final paperwork is due to the Council in a few days," she says. Her voice is quiet but not timid, no inflection at all in the simple statement. "Jasper asked me to wait until he was here to talk about it with you."

I grab an egg and crack it into the pan. My voice is too low and angry, but I don't apologize. "So why didn't you?"

There's a long pause, and I grab a second egg.

I'm reaching for the third when she says, even quieter, "Because I'm not a fucking coward."

Tipping my head back, I let my eyes close, the carton of eggs forgotten on the counter. Jasper probably asked to be present because he's worried over *my* reaction, not hers. Omegas are sensitive like that.

"So are you going to sign it?" she asks, a thread of steel in her voice now. "Rylan and Jasper already have. And I've been applying for graduate programs assuming I'll be here."

Graduate programs?

Curiosity gets the better of me.

"Why are you applying for graduate school? Aren't Omegas more concerned with babies?"

She scoffs. I go back to breaking eggs into the pan and then stirring before they can burn.

"At the risk of sounding like a 'pick me' girl, absolutely not. I'm not built like that." Her voice is louder now, more fire in it. I've seen her use that tone with Rylan before, seen the way her eyes flash and her lips curve into a smirk. And then seen how Rylan pushes her into whatever piece of furniture is closest and fucks her. If I'm being honest, there's been a couple times I've wanted to join.

Another flash of heat shoots down my spine.

Porca puttana, I cannot do this right now.

"Why should I?" I ask, letting my voice drop into a growl. "I don't want you here. I've only tolerated you for the sake of my lover."

There's a long stretch of silence. "You're not the first person to only have me around for ulterior motives. If you think that'll be enough to send me crying to my room, adjust your expectations."

Those instincts in me perk up, the hurt in her voice pulling on that intrinsic need to protect. I set down the spoon and grab the counter so I don't reach for her.

"Who?" This time my voice is threaded with lethal intent.

"I'm not asking for you to like me or fuck me," she says, ignoring my question. "I'm well aware that most matches are without love. I'm asking that you sign the paperwork that lets me stay here permanently instead of throwing me to the wolves at the Council a second time."

The growl rumbles through my chest, that *need* too great to ignore now. Who in the fuck taught an Omega that her pack would hate her? Certainly not the Council, though I can't help but agree with her terming them wolves. The Council fawns all over Omegas, stuffing the information down their throats so they'll consent to matching younger and younger.

"Tell me who, *Sirena*," I say, turning.

Her eyes are steady, her palms flat on the counter.

"Why do you care?" she asks.

I close the distance between us. She doesn't shrink away. She doesn't even focus on me as I move, dropping her gaze to the paperwork and reorganizing it all into a single stack. When she continues to ignore me, I grab her chin, forcing her to look up at me. Her throat ripples with her swallow, but her eyes are wary rather than scared.

I give the command again in a whisper.

She shakes her head as much as my grip will allow.

"No," she says.

My grip tightens, the rage starting to overtake my common sense. Someone *hurt* her. Hurt her enough she won't easily divulge the information to someone she's naturally wired to want to make happy. Even if I were still on the highest dose suppressor, the information would be enough to override it. The fact I was forced to step down the dosage a couple weeks ago just makes the reaction worse.

I swear her honeysuckle scent grows stronger.

The last bit of common sense, of resenting my body's reaction to her bleeds out from me.

Her words cut through the thundering of my pulse.

"You've done nothing to warrant that type of trust or intimacy. I am not a buffet for you to take what you want while avoiding the rest," she says, that steel back in her voice. Like I'm not holding her within an inch of me, half ready to fuck some sense into her. Like we can't both tell that she's scenting for me and that she's probably wet with her slick. The flint in her gaze has my dick straining at my slacks, the need to feel her so strong my hands are practically shaking.

Cazzo.

Kissing her is the last thing I should do. It's hard enough to resist her, to remember why I resent her being here, with just her scent around me and her marks all over my lover. If I know what her cunt feels like around me? If I know I'm the one making her whimper as I fuck up into her?

I'll be fucked for keeping this icy distance between us.

She runs her tongue over her lips, her gaze dropping to my mouth before her scent increases again.

"Fuck it," I mutter, low and lethal.

And then I slam my lips to hers.

Thirty-Five

DOMINIC

The kiss is angry, full of teeth and bites, and she doesn't just let me lead. She fights every moment our lips touch, every twist of our tongues. It makes my dick ache where it's pushing against the zipper of my slacks.

Her scent explodes around us between one heartbeat and the next, the floral undertone of it becoming so strong, it feels like it's always been here. The kiss swallows her whimper as I drop my hand from her chin, letting it rest against the base of her throat.

"Tell me to stop," I mutter against her lips, my hands dropping down her body to the hem of her sweatshirt. I pull it off before she can respond, drinking in her body, her brown nipples peaked, goosebumps running down her sternum. Small love bites dot her collarbones and shoulders, and the need to cover them with my own is so strong, it's impossible to think around.

"Tell me to stop, *Sirena*, or I'll have you over the counter and my knot inside you."

She shakes her head, reaching up until she just manages to grab the hair at the nape of my neck and twists her fingers into it. Fuck, the grapefruit of my own scent smells half-decent mixed with hers.

"Knot me," she whispers, her lips whispers of movement against mine.

All common sense is gone, the control I pride myself for so foreign now it's like it never existed. I pull away from her, dropping my hands to her hips and spinning her toward the counter. Her knuckles are white as she grabs the edge of it and presses onto the tips of her feet, trying to alleviate some of the height difference between us. I don't bother to strip her out of the simple gray shorts, ripping them down the side seams and letting them drop to the floor at our feet before repeating the action with her hip hugging panties.

Her breath hitches, and her fingers curl as if she can actually dig them into the stone under her palms. Slick drips down her thighs, and my mouth fucking waters at the idea of tasting it. That rage festers under my sternum again, nearly enough to snap me out of the moment, but then she perfumes again, so strong I wonder what it feels like when she's in heat. She cants her hips back toward me, pressing up even higher.

I palm the nape of her neck, gathering her hair around my fingers as I work to undo my belt and push my slacks low enough they won't be ruined by her slick.

If she's expecting a slow seduction, she doesn't say it. She glances over her shoulder as I nudge the head of my cock into her entrance, testing to make sure I won't hurt her. Her eyes are glazed over, her cheeks dark with her blush, her lips swollen from my teeth. I slowly push into her in one single, unrelenting thrust, and she moans, tipping her head back as much as my grip will allow.

There's still too much of a height difference for me to have a decent angle. Or maybe I've just gotten used to fucking Jasper, where he's only a couple inches shorter than I am. Either way, she presses back into me anyway, a mewl rising up her throat as she drops her head onto her arm.

The pressure is already there at the base of my spine, my body happily racing to the point where my knot will lock us together. I run my palm down her spine and around her hip, smirking as she shivers under the touch. Her mewls turn to whimpers as I circle her clit, and she pushes back against me with each forward push of my hips, that awkward moment where your partner's motions don't match yours not happening at all between us.

Her breath catches, her muscles locking, and then she moans, low in her chest. Her scent grows around us, one last wave as she climaxes from my touch. I lean over her, grabbing the counter edge as I fuck her faster, chasing the feeling rushing down my spine. Her curves are soft against me, her breathing ragged even as she keeps pushing back against me with each thrust. Her slick sticks to my thighs, each push into her making a wet sound that reverberates through the large room. She clenches around me, and my orgasm rockets through me.

I push into her until I'm buried completely, my knot swelling as I come.

Her voice breaks around another moan as another orgasm causes her muscles to clench.

The room is quiet as we catch our breaths, her body trembling under mine.

Satisfaction roars through me, the sight of her shaking beneath me, impaled on my cock and locked with me because of my knot feeding all those pieces of me I've kept suppressed for a decade. I drop my forehead to her shoulder, biting over one of the love marks left by one of the other guys.

My chest rumbles, the purr low and soothing, and she relaxes under me.

Bile rises in my throat, and I freeze.

VIOLET

Dominic's body stiffens where he leans over mine, his lips pulling away from my bare shoulder, the sting of his bite still aching. The sudden change dampens the aftershocks of the orgasm, the bliss of his knot fading. The low purr cuts off all at once as he pushes away from me.

"*Cazzo.*"

Dominic's low growl raises the hair on my neck, and I suck in a quick breath, bracing my hands under my stomach. He starts to pull away from me, but his knot is still swollen, and I can't help but whimper at its movement. He stills, the silence between us gaining a charged edge that has anxiety racing through me. Something instinctual within me forces me to be still and quiet.

He mutters something else in Italian, too low and quick for me to parse out individual words. It doesn't sound like a compliment, though. There's too much violence in the words, in the way his voice curls around them.

Whatever he said, my silence is the wrong response.

A growl rips through him, bouncing off the kitchen and making me shiver. The moment we'd had as his knot locked us in place—however small—is gone, replaced by a stark terror at realizing how incredibly vulnerable I am right now. My mind, ever the helpful bitch, brings back memories of my heat in March, and that terror triples. I press my cheek to the counter, trying to keep myself calm.

He's on rut suppressors, and I'm not in heat. The odds of my panic setting him off are low. And he purred. That lowers the chances, too. I manage to breathe through the fear, in through my nose and out through my mouth. Just as I'm relaxing against the counter, hissing at the cool stone pressing against my nipples, his hands tighten on my hips.

Before I can brace for it, he pulls away from me completely, another muttered curse falling from him. His knot isn't gone, though, and pain lances through me as he forces it out anyway. I can't hold back my cry. Tears fall over my lashes before I can even process the extent of the pain.

"*Cazzo*, I even fucking purred," he mutters, though I can barely hear him over the roaring of my heart in my ears. A moment later, the front door slams shut.

Realization swamps me, and my knees buckle. I drop to the floor, pain lancing through my knees as I land on them in an undignified heap. My core throbs, each heartbeat filled with pain from him forcing his knot out.

It had felt fucking phenomenal, letting myself surrender to him, letting our designations out to play and feeling him take such efficient control. I should have realized it would make him angry, that his body responding to mine on such an intimate level would infuriate him. That whatever I did, if it ended up forcing or highlighting this natural dynamic between us, it would never be enough.

Another door clicks closed and steps echo off the walls, though I'm not entirely sure how I manage to hear them. My chest heaves as I sob, my tears falling hard and fast enough that I can't see anything.

"Violet?" Rylan's voice is low and filled with worry. "What happened?"

His arms wrap around me, pulling me toward him. God, just kill me now. Embarrassment races through me, and I push away from him. Or at least try to. The moment I'm nearly upright, I scream, the pain from Dominic's knot getting worse. Rylan freezes, his hands gentle where they barely skim my sides. An odd haze I've never felt before settles over me, dulling the pain along with my other senses.

A hand brushes across my face before disappearing.

"Violet, you need to tell me what happened," Rylan whispers. "I know you're hurting. You need to tell me why."

Fuck, how long was I out of it? I shake my head and wipe at my cheeks, horrified to realize just how hard I've been crying.

"Shit," I mutter. I push away from Rylan, forcing myself to stand despite how shaky and unstable I feel. My pussy aches worse than it ever has—and that's saying something considering I've had two heats with multiple Alphas. I keep my gaze on the ground, not willing to see what kind of horror is in Rylan's gaze. He mirrors my movement, grabbing my wrist as I turn toward my bedroom.

"Omega," Rylan says, his voice low. It sluices over me, stealing the shred of ability to walk away from him I still have. "I can smell Dominic."

I force a swallow, my mouth dry and my throat aching. At my silence, he curses.

"Come here, pretty Omega," he says, gathering me in his arms again, lifting me like I'm nothing more than a sack of flour. The moment I let my cheek rest against his shoulder, his chest rumbles to life, the purr as soothing as Dominic's had been.

My breath catches, and he rubs circles on my thigh with his thumb as he heads toward the bedrooms.

"I thought you were waiting until Jasper was back," he murmurs once we're in his room.

He kicks the door closed before crossing the space, ignoring both the couch and the bed and walking into the bathroom instead. He presses a few buttons near the faucet and sits on the edge of the large tub with me, my legs draped over one side, my feet in the warm water.

He presses soft kisses into my temple and finger combs my hair, his purr still vibrating through his chest.

"You're braver than me," he says after a while.

The water's now up to my ankles, even deeper for him, but he doesn't flinch. I shrug.

He sighs and eases me into the water, adjusting us until I'm leaning against the back of the tub, and he's brushing out my hair. "I'm sorry. Let me get you cleaned up."

Thirty-Six

VIOLET

The paperwork taunts me from the small end table in the living room, an invisible spotlight continuing to draw my attention to it from where I sit perched at the island. I can't decide if it's the form itself or my signature that keeps drawing me back toward it. Or maybe it's the location. I'm used to seeing it in my nightstand the last few weeks. Sighing, I push around the pasta on my plate, not really even hungry but not sure what else to do with my time.

Rylan left early this morning for a marathon recording session, something he said is common during the summer when the symphony is on hiatus. His gaze had been sad, his hands gentle on mine. His kiss had been even more soft, so full of emotion it made me want to collapse on the floor and scream at the entire situation. He hadn't looked at the paperwork as he'd left, but he knew it was there. I'd cried on his chest all fucking night, after all.

Jasper's out on his daily run, though he nearly didn't go

267

when he saw the mood I was in. It took everything in me to get him out the door. I needed the time. My eyes settle on the paperwork again, and I can feel my heart shatter. Again.

There's a lot I can handle. But yesterday with Dominic was a line I can't come back from. I can't live my life terrified of my own home and my place within it. I spent so much of my childhood walking on eggshells. Designating as Omega made it hundreds of times worse. And watching what it did to my dads? For all my dread of having to go on suppressors or end up completely alone, I'd rather face those realities than live in the suffocating panic that was my childhood home.

I just need to figure out how to tell Jasper so he doesn't think I fucked him over again. How do you tell someone you love with your whole fucking heart that you're leaving?

I hadn't had to tell Rylan. He just knew. Once he'd managed to coax out of me what happened with Dominic, he connected the dots on his own. He'd spent the night worshiping my body, never letting me get so deep in my sorrow that it overtook me completely. There will be plenty of time later for that.

Bile burns my throat, and I drop my head into my hands, trying to breathe through the wave of nausea the thought of leaving brings. My phone rings before I can really get it to go away. For a moment, relief floods me. Talking with Faedra is exactly what I need right now, even if seeing her happy makes me want to sob. Except isn't she doing that hiking event with her guys this weekend? Or was that next weekend? I can't remember.

My stomach drops as I see who it is.

Of course *she* would call now. It's like she has a fucking radar that tells her when I'm at my most vulnerable. I swallow around the lump in my throat and blow out a deep breath, building up those walls to keep her from disintegrating me right now.

"Oh, Violet, so nice to finally get to chat," my mom says once

I've answered the phone. "The last month has been just so hectic."

I roll my eyes and push away the uneaten lunch.

"What's up?" I ask, doing my best to keep my voice neutral.

"Well, I hadn't heard back from you about the event tonight, and I wanted to make sure we didn't accidentally coordinate. I mean, I know the men will. It's impossible for them not to when there's only three options, but still."

Confusion races through me, and I cut her off. "Event tonight? You didn't tell me you were in town at all."

She scoffs and then sighs, the sounds of her ruffling through something filling the background of the call. "Johnathan has his annual fundraiser tonight for that charity. I'm sure I sent you the information about it."

No, she hadn't.

Dad hosts a large fundraising gala once a year for two LA nonprofits that help underserved and marginalized youth. Mom has never invited me to it before. I would remember if that had changed this year, especially since I'm nearly positive Dad would have called to give me a heads up about it since the match has been so messy.

"Anyway, you absolutely must be there," Mom continues, sighing like all of this is one giant inconvenience for her. "Can you imagine what the press will say if my daughter that lives in LA isn't in attendance at our LA function? Absolutely not. You'll be there. On time. And not in that disaster of a green dress."

She hangs up the moment I offer a small agreement, too engrossed in whatever prep work she's doing to notice I'm not even faking it well at the moment. I leave my phone on the island and step onto the front porch, resting my head against the door as I sit. I try to take in the landscape, the house, the way this part of the land shades out because of the positioning of the house on the cliff. But my head is too much of a mess to really enjoy any of it.

Do I have a dress that will work? It's not like I can just order one and have it ready to go in three hours. I love my body, but finding clothes that work off the rack is hard, especially in this city that worships at the altar of unrealistic beauty standards.

I mentally go through the options I have, trying to decide which one will keep her from being angry at me. I can't come up with a single one. They're all either too bland, too underdressed, or too "improper." My heart races as the panic starts to set in.

How the fuck am I going to face my mother tonight with the annulment paperwork sitting finalized in the living room just waiting for the Council member to process it?

"Love?" Jasper's soft voice breaks me out of my panicked haze. His finger is gentle under my chin as he urges me to look at him. He's crouched in front of me, his shirt sweat-soaked and his hair a spiky mess. "What's wrong?"

Everything.

Shrugging, I get to my feet and walk into the house, grabbing my phone from the island. Jasper keeps a hand laced with mine. A single text waits for me, the invitation mom swore she sent me earlier. I open it and show it to Jasper, blinking back tears.

I do not have what it takes to tell him about the annulment and also face my mother tonight.

He mutters a curse but nods. "Wear the blue dress you wore to brunch the other week. I'll give Rylan and Dom a call to see if they'll be able to make it, too. We'll need to be leaving in an hour to get there on time. Don't worry, love. We won't make you face that woman alone, all right?"

My heart is in my throat.

I can only manage to nod, the tears coming too fast to blink away now, pouring down my face. He curses again and wraps me in his arms.

"Don't cry, love. It'll be all right."

He guides me into his room, turning on his shower and stripping us both. His phone sounds with multiple notifications before we manage to get under the spray. He looks them over as I step into the hot water and close my eyes, trying to find that odd haze I'd had on the porch. At least I hadn't been crying then.

"All right. Rylan is going to head in as soon as he can get away from the recording session."

I nod and take a deep breath. His hands are efficient yet gentle at getting us both clean, though he doesn't get my hair wet to save us time. How he remembers that hack, I'm not even sure at this point. His look grows more worried as the minutes pass, and I can feel the question coming, the one that's going to ruin this entire night before I can even manage to put on a decent front for my mother.

It's when we're dressed and I'm finishing my makeup that he finally asks it. He comes up behind me, palming my waist, his eyes locked on mine in the mirror.

"What happened between you and Dom yesterday?"

My chest tightens, and his lips turn down as he sees the pain flash across my face.

His voice is nearly a whisper as he says, "Tell me, love."

So I do.

By the time he's helping me into the passenger seat of the Maserati I've never actually seen him drive, his jaw is tight and his shoulders are stiff, an unmistakable anger riding him. I don't manage to break the silence on our trek down into the city. What can I say to appease his anger? *Nothing.*

As he pulls up to the valet of the hotel, he blows out a breath.

"He promised me he'd make it work," he whispers, so low I'm not sure I was supposed to hear him.

I mutter an apology, focusing on my clutch. I still haven't

told him about the annulment. Will it make it worse if I admit it now? Or wait until the morning?

Mom's smug look at realizing my match has failed and she'll have a chance to pawn me off to whatever asshole whose parents have struck her fancy sets steel in my spine. She'll get to see me struggle when Hell freezes over. Jasper runs his hands through his hair, messing up the gel styling he'd put in at the house, and then steps out of the car. He adjusts his suit jacket as he opens my door, offering me a hand even while handing off the key to the valet.

He's calm and collected as we head into the hotel, following the sign to the rooftop deck.

"I love you," he murmurs, kissing my temple and tucking my arm around his. "I've got you. All night."

That lump blocks my throat again.

"Thank you, Jas."

Thirty-Seven

VIOLET

Jasper's hand is tight where it's laced with mine as we take the first step out of the hallway and onto the rooftop. We pause just on the edge of the event proper, Jasper's breath just as unsteady as mine.

For all my mom's bullshit, she knows how to decorate to make a statement. Strands of large globe lights criss-cross above the space, complimenting the orange glow of the setting sun over the water just visible over the other downtown buildings. Large floral displays sit at the center of each of the tables, lavender and white roses and hydrangea forming a beautiful aroma that helps overlay the scents of the attending Alphas. It's almost as impressive as the set up the Council used at the matching gala. A bar sits tucked into the far corner, the line for it decently long. On the opposite side of the rooftop, a string quartet plays and a simple music system sits unobtrusively nearby. It's not set up for dancing, more so a speaker and probably a presentation of some kind once the sun is completely below the horizon.

"Are all your dads here?" he asks.

I shake my head. "Just Dad, I think. They haven't done an event of this scale all together in a really long time."

"Damn," Jasper mutters. I manage a laugh, elbowing him. He looks down and smirks. "Kurt is fun at these things."

I breathe through the ache in my chest at him remembering something from so long ago. His gaze softens on mine, and I manage a small smile. He rests his finger under my chin and tilts my face toward him, letting his lips brush across mine. Not enough to mess up the lipstick I've put on, but I can just barely taste the tang of his breath mint.

"There you are!"

My mom's voice cuts over the quiet music of the quartet. It's not the happy exasperation Faedra's mom used at the graduation. Instead, it's angry and a little disapproving. It reminds me of that asshole Alpha that cornered me the first time Rylan took me out. Jasper stiffens and pulls away from me.

Mom purses her lips as she takes me in. "Well, the color is perfect for the season, so I suppose it'll do," she mutters. She hands me a large glass of white wine. "Here's this for you so you don't have to stand in line."

Jasper's shoulders tighten, his grip firming around my hand. I lean into him, trying to keep him from saying something he'll regret in the first ten minutes of us being here. I take the wine without comment, hiding my irritation at her taking the opportunity for me to get my own drink. I fucking *hate* white wine. Her gaze coasts over Jasper, an unfeeling once over that ends with her frowning.

"And where is your pack? You didn't come unchaperoned, did you? That's hardly safe."

I'm wearing scent blockers and am nowhere near my heat starting. It's more than safe for me to be here alone. She's just making a point. I breathe through my nose, holding onto my control by a hair.

Jasper clears his throat. "The others are on their way and should be here soon. They had other prior commitments."

I squeeze his hand. "Mom, you remember Jasper, right? He's part of Pack Montegue."

She doesn't react to my question, her lips pursed. A man I don't recognize comes up to my right, standing too close for my comfort. I lean into Jasper.

It's like a switch flips in my mom. Gone is the cynical, critical judge, and in her place is Elle fucking Woods or some shit. She smiles brightly, her eyes crinkling as she turns to the man.

"Jack, how lovely to see you," she says, her voice warming and softening. She angles her body until she essentially leaves Jasper out of the conversation. "I hope everything has been going well."

The man smiles, though it doesn't touch his eyes. I take a couple sips of the wine to keep my expression blank. I've mostly tuned out the conversation, staring at the fading sun over the ocean, when another man joins the conversation, his dark brown hair trimmed shorter than when I last saw him. My stomach clenches, and I have to breathe carefully to keep from panicking.

What the *fuck* is Eric doing here?

Jack rests a hand on his shoulder. "You've met my son, haven't you?"

Oh no.

He's already part of this fucking network of assholes? I force a swallow and try to calm my racing heart. Then he wasn't pestering me to get in with my dad. He was pestering to get in *me.* I feel sick at just the thought, not to mention the memory of his floral scent. I take a larger gulp of the wine and squeeze Jasper's hand. He murmurs something and then pulls me away from the trio, his gaze focused on the far corner of the roof.

"How upset will your dad be if we interrupt whatever conversation is happening right now?" he asks, dropping his lips until they brush my ear. A shiver races down my spine.

I follow his gaze. The person Dad's chatting with is vaguely familiar. It takes me too long to realize it's the president of one of the charities. I shake my head.

"He won't." Is my voice breathless? I can't tell.

Fuck, it's hot up here.

Jasper leads us over to him, a saccharine smile plastered to his face. I take another drink of the wine, though I'm not entirely sure why.

Dad smiles as we approach, holding out his hand until I set my palm against his. He pulls me into his side and kisses the top of my head.

"Lena, let me introduce you to my daughter, Violet."

The woman smiles. Her black hair is pulled back in a low, decorative ponytail, and her brown eyes are warm. Her pale skin glows against the charcoal gray of her pencil skirt.

"Lovely to meet you," she says. "I've heard wonderful things from Johnathan."

I smile, not trusting my voice. My body is hot, and not in the way that means the room is too warm. It's the way my body feels when I'm going into heat.

But that's not possible.

Dad squeezes my hand as the woman walks away.

"You all right, Vi?" he asks, kissing the crown of my head again.

A shiver runs down my spine, and Jasper palms my waist.

"Let me take the wine," he says, extracting the glass from my clenched hand. The small brush of his fingers against mine has my legs fucking clenching. "We should get you something to eat. We didn't manage to have time to grab something on our way here."

"I think I just need a second in the restroom," I mutter. Both men look at me with worry in their eyes, identical frowns on their lips. It'd be hilarious if I weren't *freaking the fuck out* right now.

How the hell am I feeling like I'm on the verge of my heat when it's not supposed to happen for another three months? I offer a small smile and cross the space, opening one of the doors that leads back into the hotel hallway, cutting a quick line to the bathroom.

I drop my clutch on the counter before running my hands under the cold water, trying to get my body temperature lower. My heart races, my breath sawing out of me.

There's no way. There's absolutely no way this is fucking happening right now.

The door closes behind me before a lock clicks into place.

I force a swallow and glance up into the mirror, dread curling in my stomach as my mother's hazel eyes—identical to mine—stare back at me. A cruel smirk graces her lips, and she crosses her arms, one eyebrow raised in silent, condescending question.

"You feeling all right, *love*?" She twists the nickname into an insult. "You look like you're a bit uncomfortable. Flushed, even."

My mind spins, that telltale haze starting to settle over me. I force the faucet even colder and press my wrists to my chest, not worrying about the water ruining the silk neckline. I lick my lips, trying to calm my breathing, but it's no use. My body is on fucking *fire* even with the ice cold water.

"It was a pain in the ass getting enough of that damn medication into the wine without Johnathan noticing. He's been breathing down my neck since your graduation." Her lips twist into a frown. "What lies did you tell them when they went to your little event? They've been absolutely abysmal to live with the last couple weeks. You always did make everything about *you*."

It's not the first tirade she's had about how my dads dote on us—Scarlett, Cole, and me. She's always hated that they love us and only tolerate her. My mind catches on her first comment, though.

"You drugged me?" My voice is breathy. There's none of the outrage I feel. The force of the heat is overriding it. The pulses through my body worsen, a sharp stab in my belly with each one, and I grab the edge of the counter to keep from doubling over.

"I wouldn't have had to do this at all if you hadn't behaved like such a whore, going to the Haven," she says with a scoff. She glances down my body, pursing her lips. "Be grateful I'm willing to clean up your mess, young woman."

I'm too far gone to even keep track of what she's going on about.

My mess? What mess? The Council matched me. It's not like I had a hand in it. I spent an entire week agonizing over the pack that was selected before Jasper and I realized what she'd done to us.

Another wave of desire races through my body, and I whimper, tightening my grip.

"Oh, one more thing," she says, completely calm and collected, like she does this every day of the week. Before I can even track what she's doing, she grabs my hips, ripping the scent blockers at the seams without ripping the delicate silk of my dress. I gasp as my scent floods the small space. She smirks. "Handy trick to know when you want attention and they just won't entertain you. Now be a good Omega and *stay here* while I fix your mistake."

She unlocks the latch and walks out, leaving the door propped open.

It's less than a minute before someone grunts in the hallway and footsteps pound toward me. Part of me hopes it's Jasper, even though I realize it's not likely. My heart drops as someone fills the doorway.

Oh no.

<h1 style="text-align:center">Thirty-Eight</h1>

DOMINIC

Rylan's quiet in the passenger seat, his typical antsy movement gone. In its place is a somber mourning I can't quite figure out. I pull out from the music studio, heading into the Saturday evening traffic.

"Thanks for picking me up," he murmurs as he pulls out his phone and sets it on the dash of the Alfa Romeo, bypassing the built-in map for the one on his phone.

A message pops onto the screen, and Rylan curses, swiping the notification away after reading it.

"*Cosa c'è che non va?*" I ask.

He glances up at me, his scowl deep enough that a line appears between his brows. "You know I'm shit at Italian, man."

"Sorry," I grunt. "Habit when I've been with my brothers all day."

He doesn't ask why I spent the last twelve hours incognito with Victor and Lorenzo, and I don't offer any specifics. The fact that my father already had to call in the bargain between us and use me to clean up Lorenzo's mess is infuriating in the extreme. Add to it that the mess only happened because his mind is fuck all gone due to that Omega he's fucking around with?

Fury doesn't begin to cover my feelings over the whole situation.

The memory of Violet bent over the counter, her perfume surrounding me, dampens the thought. Fuck me, I can't manage to get the feel of her out of my head. I thought maybe fucking her once would be enough. It always has been before. But the longer I'm away from her, the more I *crave* her the way I do Jasper.

If my brother feels anything near what I feel about my lover, maybe he's justified in his idiocy.

And Violet? Maybe I've been wrong about her, too.

"What's wrong?" I ask.

Rylan blows out a breath. "Jasper says Violet's feeling sick. He thinks it's maybe because they didn't have time to grab food before getting to the event."

"She get nervous at these types of things?" I make the final turn toward the address, surprise lighting through me at it being in one of the newer upscale hotels whose only event space is outdoors.

Rylan snarls. "You'd fucking know that if you hadn't spent the last four weeks avoiding her."

I shrug, and he shakes his head.

"And then when you *did* finally interact with her, you fucked her and left her before your knot was even gone. You do realize that shit fucking hurts them, right?" His voice is low and dangerous, lethality woven through it. The threat is clear enough, and part of me wants to rise to the bait just to burn off the frustration of the last thirty-six hours.

I breathe slowly, counting to ten.

Was it my best moment? No. Definitely not. But I'm not

about to waste my time trying to explain it to Rylan when he's never struggled with being Alpha.

The moment I've pulled the car into the line for the valet, Rylan's opening his door and heading toward the entrance. I hand off the keys, adjusting my suit jacket and tie before following after him, making sure to outpace him without actually running. There's a small sign at the back of the lobby, indicating the event's name and rooftop location.

The silence is tense between us and only grows worse once we're in the elevator and the floors are passing by us. By the time we're opening the glass door and stepping onto the rooftop, the need to punch something is so strong in me that my hands tremble.

"She's signing the annulment," Rylan whispers as we pause to look for Jasper and Violet.

She's leaving. I should be fucking ecstatic. It's what I've wanted this entire time.

No more hearing her snark with Rylan, hearing her giggle with Jasper, hearing her talk with her friend that moved to Denver. No more finding her things scattered around the house because Omegas need to make every little space their own safe haven. No more seeing her cold brew in the fridge or seeing her eyes light up when she realizes Rylan or Jasper made it for her. No more waiting for her to announce Rylan or Jasper knocked her up.

I should have relief flooding me. And yet...

My stomach twists.

Fuck. Me.

I do actually like her, don't I? And not just because her body sings to mine. I want to see her eyes light up when *I* walk into the room. I want to see her shoulders drop away when *I* kiss her temple when she's had a stressful day. I want to hear the noises she makes when it's *my* knot that's setting off her orgasm.

"I expected celebrating," Rylan says, voice dry, his Tennessee accent heavier than normal. "Don't tell me you've actually decided to like her after I had to spend last night saying goodbye. Let's hope she hasn't told Jasper yet, or he'll probably throw you over the side of the building."

"Has she filed it yet?" I ask, ignoring the jab. Jasper probably *will* throw me off the building. Out of his life at the very least. He begged me to make this work, to find a balance so he could have us all.

Rylan shakes his head and shoves his hands into his pockets. "Council isn't open until Monday. Final paperwork is due Wednesday. She'll probably wait for Faedra to get back from her trip."

Cazzo. Her friend isn't even home right now? How had I never noticed before just how fucking brave she is?

Because you only saw what you expected, that voice whispers to me. I shove it away along with my feelings over the whole mess and scan the rooftop, trying to find Jasper. He's easy enough to spot despite the moderate crowd. His blond hair is a bit too ruffled to match everyone else's perfectly polished appearance. Rylan blows out a breath and starts toward him. I follow half a step back, scanning the space for Violet, something dark twisting in my chest when I realize she's not here.

Jasper swallows as we approach, a wariness in his gaze I haven't seen before. The man next to him is older, his light brown hair fading into gray along the sides. His green eyes are sharp, though. I recognize him at once. Johnathan Fallon is incredibly well-known, after all. Even in the mafia.

"Johnathan, you've met Rylan," Jasper says as we stop in front of them.

The man nods and shakes Rylan's hand easily. His gaze grows cold as he looks me over.

"This is Dominic," Jasper says. His gaze is full of warning that's unneeded right now.

I offer my hand and the man takes it, tighter than necessary.

"I'm Johnathan Fallon," he says quietly. His voice is calm, but his eyes flash with the threat of violence. "Violet is my daughter."

Cazzo.

"Nice to meet you," I say, letting my hand drop.

He nods once before turning as his name is called across the space. He claps Jasper on the shoulder in wordless apology and then heads toward whoever needs him.

The moment he's out of earshot, Jasper says, "You had better not be here to make a scene, Dom. The literal worst thing that could happen right now is you doubling down on refusing to make this permanent."

His voice is cool. Not quite cold with hurt or anger, but the careful neutral used between strangers. Even on our first date, he never sounded like this. Regret slices through my chest, and an apology sits perched on my tongue.

But it's not him I owe it to, is it? Not really. It's Violet.

I shake my head. "*Devo scusarmi, Tesoro.*"

"You're here to apologize?" Jasper asks slowly. He shoves his hands into his pockets, but it doesn't hide their trembling. "During a large public event like it's some third act moment in a romance book? Who are you and what have you done with Dominic?"

I shrug.

"Where is she?" Rylan asks.

"Bathroom. She left a couple minutes ago to see if she could figure out why she was feeling sick."

I nod and start back across the roof. Jasper grabs me, his grip digging into my elbow.

"You *cannot* make a scene here," he says, his voice biting.

The unspoken command is clear.

I force my feet to still as I focus on my lover.

"It's not just her dad that's here," he whispers, leaning closer to me. "Her mom is a goddamn piece of work. Even worse than she was when we lived in Seattle. She'll use every single thing we do against Violet if she thinks it'll serve her best."

Rylan frowns, his throat rippling with a swallow.

Jasper squeezes my elbow. "*Tread carefully.*"

I palm his face, running my thumb across his cheek. "All right, *Tesoro. Starò attento.*"

He nods and leads us across the space, letting his hand slide down my forearm before lacing his fingers with mine. Some of the weight in my chest lessens.

Rylan pulls the door open.

Honeysuckle slams into me so fast and completely that my knees buckle and a growl rips up my throat. I barely manage to bite it back, but the telltale haze starts settling over me.

"What the fuck?" Rylan whispers. He closes the door behind us, the glass muffling the noise of the event. "Why is she perfuming like she's in heat?"

Jasper glances between us. "What?" His voice fills with dread. "How can you tell? It just smells like her out here."

Rylan shakes his head. "There's a... Fuck, I don't know how to explain it."

I start down the hallway, noticing the sign for the women's restroom, the door standing open. Was that normal here?

"We need to find her," I say, my voice low enough it rumbles through the space. "She's not safe if she's had a breakthrough heat."

"We shouldn't even be able to smell her," Rylan mutters, shoulder brushing mine. "She would have worn scent blockers when she left the house. She doesn't go anywhere without them."

That weight settles heavier on my chest.

Jasper stands in front of the event's entrance, his hands shoved in his pockets, worry etched on his face.

Rylan knocks on the threshold of the bathroom, leaning against the wall. "Violet?"

There's nothing from inside. He glances at me, frowning. His hand is poised to knock again when I hear it: the soft rustling of fabric.

It's not coming from the bathroom.

I turn, trying to figure out where it's coming from when there's a muffled cry from several feet down the hall.

"*Tesoro*," I call.

The moment Jasper has my hand, I start down the hall, trying to figure out which door the noise is coming from. As we pass the third, the rustling of fabric turns into blatant tearing, though I can't tell if it's out of excitement or something worse.

A man's irritated voice carries over the din of ripping fabric.

"Why are you fighting? Omegas need knots when they're in heat."

There's another muffled cry. Rylan's eyes go wild, and he grabs the handle. He swings the door open, forcing light into the dim room, just as the man speaks again.

"I'm just helping you. You could be grateful."

I get a look at Violet. Rage burns through me, emptying my mind of everything but the trained lethality instilled by my father.

Thirty-Nine

DOMINIC

A young guy has Violet pinned against the only open wall, his arm pressed against the base of her throat. The blue dress hangs off her body in tatters, her breasts on full display from the ripped out neckline. Rough bruises are already darkening her skin, and her hair is falling out of her styled updo. Her eyes are glassy, her breath coming in short pants, even as her hands shake against the man's shoulders. She looks like an extra for a horror film, not an attendee at the black tie optional fundraising event for the upper crust of LA.

The man pinning her looks over his shoulder, his lips pulling back in a snarl.

Violet's honeysuckle scent is so strong, it's only the rut suppressor that keeps me from leaping on her, too. She pushes against the man, but he doesn't even flinch. There's no sour scent caused by her unwillingness. Her heat has already reached the point of no return.

"Fuckboy Extraordinaire?" Rylan sounds dazed, like he just took a punch to the face.

The man's hand stills on his belt. His eyes are glazed over. His scent is tangy with his rage and nearly overbearing with the hallmark *feel* of an Alpha in rut. Alphas like this are dangerous. Rutting means bonding.

My rage grows hotter.

"Alpha?" Violet whispers, her voice as distant as her eyes. "Oh my god. Alpha, please." She drops her hand, holding it out toward me. No, toward—

Rylan lurches forward, taking her hand in his and pulling her away from the asshole. The other man leaps on him and takes him to the ground. Fueled by his rage and emerging rut and mixed with Rylan being caught off guard, he manages to do decent damage despite his shit form, Rylan's lip splitting on the second hit. Violet cries out and reaches for him before realizing her dress is fucked. She scrambles at the scraps, trying to pull them over herself, not so far gone yet that she's lost her unwillingness to be vulnerable around me.

"*Tesoro*," I murmur, stepping out of the room to try and get a breath that doesn't have Violet's siren call of a scent in it.

Dropping my hand, he says, "I've got her."

The moment he has her in his arms, his body blocking her from anyone who might happen upon this, I take out my rage on the asshole who touched her. *My* form isn't shit. It only takes two well-placed hits to have him off Rylan and held against me, my forearm pressing into his throat hard enough that he thrashes, his feet kicking out and trying to get enough purchase to push up and break my hold.

I press harder against his neck, enjoying the fuck out of his desperate little grunts.

"You can't kill him," Jasper whispers.

I look over my shoulder, and he's staring at me, his jaw set.

His arm is wrapped around Violet, and her head is buried in his arm. She rubs her face against the fabric of his suit jacket before whining.

"Alpha," she whispers. It's nearly inaudible over the din of the asshole still trying to get free of my hold. Rylan rolls onto his knees and grabs her hand, running a hand over her knuckles. She shudders in a breath, the distant look clearing from her eyes for a heartbeat. "I... Oh fuck, Jasper. It... it happened so fast. I thought I could get it under control by cooling down my body. But then she..."

Her voice fades away as she whines again. Her eyes flutter closed as her body trembles in Jasper's hold. The honeysuckle of her scent grows stronger, and the man thrashes against me even harder, snarling in his rut-induced rage.

"She's *mine*," he snarls. "I found her. She's unbonded. It's my right."

I couldn't control the growl that rips through me if I tried. And I don't. I adjust my hold on the asshole until I'm kneeling over him, my knee in his chest. The feeling of his ribs starting to give way feeds that insidious *thing* inside me hardwired to protect.

"*Sbagliato, stronzo,*" I mutter. "She's no one's but her own."

He was going to rape an Omega.

My Omega.

The thought races through me so fast, it momentarily stuns me. A moment later, the rut slams into me, only marginally dampened by the suppressor. She's *mine*, not his. He doesn't get to know the little noise she makes when a knot locks into her cunt. He doesn't get to feel the way her slick drenches her thighs when her nipples are played with.

But I do. I *have*. And I need to fucking feel her come on my knot to prove it to the bastard.

"*Dominic,*" Jasper's urgent voice cuts through the haze.

I blink, trying to clear it, but the scent is too fucking strong. Jasper kneels in front of me, cupping my face and running a thumb over my cheekbone.

Where the fuck is my Omega?

"Listen to me." His voice rushes over me, softening the edges of the haze. It's instinct to breathe deeply, but he shakes his head as my nostrils flare. "No, don't breathe yet. You have to listen first."

There's weeping somewhere nearby. I twist, trying to find my Omega, but Jasper tightens his hold.

"I can't hold you if you fight me, Dom, and you *have* to listen to me right now."

I pant through the desire to punch him, trying to rationalize it's just the smell of an Omega's heat pushing me to be so out of control. I'm not the brother that's known for unrestrained violence. That's Lorenzo. He's the fighter. I'm simply the one that goes in and cleans up messes with the precision of a goddamn surgeon.

"I've got you, Omega," Rylan murmurs. Violet's sobs grow louder. "We'll get you to your nest soon, all right? Give us long enough to sort through getting you out of here."

Rylan's voice, miraculously, pushes the haze back enough that I can fucking *think*.

Cazzo. This is exactly what I hate about being an Alpha.

I close my eyes for a moment, counting back from ten.

When I open them again, Jasper's blue gaze is right in front of me, his hands brushing across my face and down my neck. He takes my hand and threads his fingers through mine, forcing them off the man's throat.

"Sienna won't just let this be buried. Not if she thinks there's a way to boost her own image with it," Jasper murmurs. "We have to let the authorities handle it."

I nod once.

"I heard yelling," a woman says, her voice growing closer. "Someone go get Lena. And maybe Margie?"

Jasper's hand tightens around mine. "Rylan?"

"Got her," he says with grim determination.

More voices come from the hallway.

Jasper takes a deep breath and stretches his neck. "I need you to let him up. Before whoever is out there sees you pinning him like this. The sooner we get out of here, the sooner we can make sure Violet is safe."

Violet. That sickening lurch happens in my stomach again. I twist to see her, but she's hidden completely by Rylan. His gaze locks with mine, one eyebrow rising as he takes in my haggard appearance.

"Come on, *amico,*" he mutters. "God only knows how long Jasper will be able to keep you calm enough. I can't have you waiting for your father to bail your ass out tonight. She's going to need us both. At least in the beginning."

As if on cue, Violet whimpers, and the force of her scent slams into me again.

I ease off the asshole. His eyes are livid, his breath sawing out of him in short, ragged pants. There's a bruise forming under his left eye, and he snarls at me as I brush off my trousers, though he doesn't attempt to get up and fight me anymore.

I'm just finishing adjusting the suit jacket, Jasper's hand still tightly laced with mine and his other flat against my chest, when the doorway darkens.

"What is going on here?" a man asks, his voice low and gruff, his short frame blocking most of the doorway.

Jasper tenses for a heartbeat, his eyes urging me to caution. I give him a subtle nod and squeeze his hand.

Violet drops into another round of crying, her whimpers morphing into sobs between one heartbeat and the next, her breathing ragged from where she's stashed behind Rylan in the far corner. It's dark enough that the man has no hope of seeing her in her ruined dress. Another man rushes in behind him before any of us manage to say anything. The lights from the hallway cast shadows on his face, leaving only a general impression, but it's enough.

Forty

DOMINIC

"Jasper, where is she?" Johnathan asks, pushing the shorter man out of his way and taking a single step into the small room. "And why the hell did you guys come if she was on the cusp of her heat? My event isn't that important."

"She wasn't." Rylan's words are a snarl, and Johnathan pauses just inside the room.

There's too many people in here, the scents of the Alphas responding to Violet's siren song overwhelming the small space. Jasper tightens his grip on me as my body coils tighter.

Fuck me, I need to get out of here before I actually start killing people, beginning with the asshole still on the ground.

The man behind Johnathan chokes on his breath, his eyes widening as he messes with the collar of his uniform. "I can't have an Omega in heat here. Not in the open."

"How do we get out of here?" I ask. "One of us needs to get the car."

Jasper squeezes my hand and frowns. Violet's father looks at me, his eyebrows low.

"Rylan, can you get the car?" I ask, frustrated at everyone's lack of response.

"For the love of God, Dominic, please use English," Rylan mutters.

I grind out a curse and sigh.

Johnathan takes another step into the room, reaching for Violet where she's hidden behind Rylan's form. "Come on, sweetheart. I'll help you get out of here while your Alphas get everything ready downstairs."

Violet sobs, pulling her hand away from her father. Even my heart clenches at the heartbreak in the sound and the shattered look that crosses Johnathan's face.

"How long has she been on the cusp? She shouldn't be this lost to it if it just surfaced." He tucks his hands into his pockets, glancing over his shoulder like he's perfectly calm, even as his words are full of devastation. A woman runs up beside the hotel employee, her brown eyes worried. Johnathan shakes his head once, and she nods, turning and walking back toward the event, motioning for another woman to do the same.

"Johnathan has it in hand," she says, loud enough that we can hear her over Violet's noises. "Let's start the presentation. Margie will present instead of him."

Violet whines, and her scent thickens. The man on the ground growls as his body coils tighter. I pin his leg with my foot to keep him from trying to stand, putting more pressure when the asshole inevitably fights me.

Johnathan looks down at the man and scowls. "What the hell is going on?"

Jasper shakes his head. "I'm not sure. But Rylan needs to get her home before we attract even more unwanted attention."

Both men share a look that says a thousand words. Johnathan nods and turns to the hotel employee.

"I need a valet to grab Jasper Montegue's car."

Jasper voices a quick disagreement. "I drove the Maserati. There's not enough room."

Johnathan closes his eyes for a minute. "Right. I forgot..." He shakes his head, letting the thought trail off. "I need Dominic Montegue's car. Is there any way it can be pulled around to the side entrance? The sooner we get her out of here, the sooner it's no longer your concern."

The man nods and pulls out his phone, sending off a text. "What else do you need, sir?"

While he sorts through how to get Violet out of here in one piece, I step over the asshole. Rylan moves in sync, guiding Violet out from behind him. Before she can protest, I pull her into my arms bridal style, one arm under her knees and the other tight across her back, breathing through the rush of possessive rage at her scent being so near to me. She shudders, another round of whimpers moving up her throat.

Rylan murmurs something too low for me to understand, the feel of his voice soothing even to me, as he strips out of his suit jacket. Violet relaxes as he drapes it over her, covering the worst of the torn dress.

"I'm having one of our security guards escort you," the employee says as we step out of the small room. I scowl, and he swallows. "He's a Beta, so he's of no risk to your Omega."

"Thank you," Johnathan says, stepping between me and the other man.

Bold fucking move.

Rylan runs his hand over Violet's cheek and then down her neck and shoulder, never once letting his touch stop.

"Jasper, I'll need you to stay for a bit," Johnathan murmurs as the hotel employee walks away, his head bent over his phone.

"The officer will need a statement from someone who isn't influenced by her perfuming."

My lover nods once and shoves his hands into his pockets. "Whatever you need."

They stand in the middle of the hallway, Jasper's attention split between eyeing the event and the three of us. The elevator opens, and a formidable man in a black security uniform steps out, his blue eyes cold and calculating.

I start across the hotel, Rylan keeping pace. Jasper grabs my elbow before I can pass him, his eyes sad as he looks at me and then Violet. He palms her cheek, and she writhes under the touch.

"*Please*," she begs in a broken whisper. "It *hurts*."

Johnathan's look is shattered again as we pass him, his hands clenched at his sides.

"I know, pretty Omega," Rylan murmurs. "Give us just a few more minutes, and we'll make it better."

The elevator is even more tense than on the way to the event, but I have to admit the man has a spine of steel. His hands don't shake, his mouth doesn't quiver, his eyes don't betray any fear at all. It helps keep all the possessive, territorial bullshit festering because of her perfuming from becoming unmanageable.

"This way," he says the moment the doors open. "They have the hallway blocked off to keep others from crossing your path."

The night is warm as we step onto the sidewalk outside the side entrance of the hotel. The blast of fresh air helps dull the ache in my body from Violet's heat-soaked scent. The car is pulled to the curb, the engine already running and the keys tucked into the middle console. The security guard doesn't utter a word before ducking back into the building.

Rylan opens the back door. Before I can slide into the seat, Violet writhes against me, dropping the jacket to the ground.

"I... I can't hold it back anymore," she says, her voice breaking. "It fucking *burns*."

Her eyes glaze over as she shivers. Her scent doubles in strength, the core of it calling to me, and I force a swallow to keep from pouncing on her. My hands spasm and dig into her skin, and she whines.

"You... you don't want this," she mutters, trying to twist out of my hold.

Rylan runs his arms parallel to my own. "I've got you, Omega," he murmurs.

She leans into him, her body shaking with a sob. I don't lessen my grip, the need to have her too great. Not that I'm really fighting it. Rylan looks across her to me, his question burning hot between us, and I offer a single, small nod.

"You sure?" he asks.

I give him the look that question deserves. He's not usually quite so dense. But then I notice the sweat on his forehead, the tight line of his jaw as he clenches his teeth, the careful stillness of his body that is almost never actually calm.

He's holding it together by a fucking thread.

"*Mi dispiace*," I murmur. "*Sí, sono sicuro, amico.*"

"I'm assuming that's you doubling down that you're sure. Pretty sure I heard a yes in there somewhere," he mutters, letting his arms drop to his sides.

Violet cries out, trying to follow him. I palm her cheek, forcing her to look at me as I settle into the back seat of the Alfa Romeo. Rylan closes the door and then slips into the driver seat, letting his hand brush across her cheek before throwing the car into gear and guiding it onto the streets.

"*Va tutto bene, Omega.*"

I push so much comfort into the words, she collapses against me with a gasp, her eyes fluttering shut. Not even a full heartbeat later, she's moving to straddle my hips as her hands scrabble at my belt and slacks. I shrug off my suit jacket and undo the top couple buttons of my shirt before rolling up the sleeves.

By the time the lights of the skyscrapers start to fade into the background, Violet's whining, her hands slipping with her growing desperation.

"*Please*," she begs. "*Make it stop.*"

I ease her hands away, undoing my zipper and dropping my slacks low enough that my cock slips free into the small space between our bodies. She whines again, the sound full of an excitement that feels foreign to me, my entire focus on not losing my fucking control and accidentally dropping into a rut. She signed the annulment. She's leaving. The last thing that can happen is I bond with her during this mess of a heat and force her into staying.

She pushes up on her knees. She palms my dick, lining the head up with her cunt, and slams down on me, not easing into it or going slowly in case she's sore from me being an asshole yesterday.

Her head falls back on a desperate moan, her muscles clenching around my cock. I grunt, grabbing her thighs to keep from fucking up into her quite yet.

Suppose she's ready enough, then.

Slick drenches her thighs. It occurs to me she hadn't had to move her panties so she could fuck me. Rylan's comment from earlier pushes through the building haze.

She would have worn scent blockers when she left the house. She doesn't go anywhere without them.

Fury builds in my stomach, festering under my skin, the strength of her heat making it even worse. I want to fucking pummel that asshole we found her with until he realizes just exactly who he pissed off.

Violet trembles in my arms, her hips rocking against my own, and it steals my attention away from the ideas of violence. Her nipples are peaked and right at mouth level. She shakes as I pull the first one into my mouth, rolling it with my tongue before biting the tip of it.

"*Alpha*," she moans as I move to the other and do the same thing.

Her thighs tremble, and her rhythm starts to break. I palm her knees and kiss under her ear, right where an Alpha would place a bond mark, letting my teeth graze her skin even though I know it's fucking playing with fire. Her hips falter and her knees squeeze my hips as she orgasms with a soft cry.

"*Cazzo, sei bella.*" I whisper the admission into the bruise I've left on her skin, low enough I'm nearly positive Rylan can't hear me. Not that he would know what I'm saying. Probably.

Wouldn't it be ironic if it's the one thing he manages to understand after all these years?

"Alpha," Violet moans again, writhing on my lap. "Knot me. Please."

The car eases into the garage as I wrap my arms around her, my palms on her shoulders forcing her lower onto my cock as I fuck up into her, the deep strokes taking me closer to the edge with each passing moment. Even under the artificial yellow light, she's fucking gorgeous, her cheeks rosy and her chest flushed. Rylan climbs into the backseat, shedding his shirt as he does and letting it fall to the floor.

As he settles in beside me, he runs his hands down her neck and across her collarbones, the touch soft and delicate. It reminds me of the way we fuck Jasper together sometimes. The thought has me racing for the edge, my dick pulsing. My knot swells as I come, and I pull her down harder as I surge into her, forcing my knot entirely inside. She screams, her head falling back and baring her throat. I clench my jaw, breathing through the blinding *need* to bite her truly and bond her so I can feel her within my chest the way she can feel my knot in her cunt.

"Good job, pretty Omega," Rylan murmurs. She tilts to the side, falling into his hold. The movement pulls a low moan from my chest, and Violet shivers. "I'm so proud of you. Rest now."

She nods, her eyes drifting closed. Her weight is oddly comforting as she settles against my chest, her cheek against my collarbone. Her breathing evens out into the cadence of sleep before my knot even releases. I grimace as it does, my cum and her slick mixing into a mess that ruins the suit pants before I have a chance to avoid it.

Rylan laughs.

"Just buy a new pair, Dom," he says. "Not like you don't have the funds."

I roll my eyes but offer a small half-smile.

"We should probably get her inside while she's out of it," I say after a few minutes.

Rylan nods. "She'll need to get out of this dress at the very least."

He tucks Violet's hair behind her ear before pulling out the remaining pins from her ruined updo, his gaze equal parts guarded and soft. Her breath hitches, and a corner of his mouth lifts for a heartbeat.

I've never been attracted to Rylan. But in this moment? I see exactly what Jasper must see. My chest tightens, my breath ragged.

"Let's go," I say, wrapping Violet into my arms and easing out of the car.

Forty-One

RYLAN

Violet whimpers in her sleep as Dominic lays her on the plush bed I ordered for her nest the day before she moved in. He moves away from her like his skin burns, crossing the space and turning on the air purifier tucked into the corner.

"I can't fucking think with her scent so strong," he says as he crosses back toward me.

I shrug and ease away the ruined silk of her dress. Goosebumps race down her arms, but she doesn't move, lost to the deep sleep a sated heat induces. At least until it roars up again and she needs one of us.

Me. Until she needs me.

The reality of having to get her through a heat entirely alone is daunting enough. Knowing it had to be forced by someone and that it'll make it exponentially worse? Dread coils in my stomach.

Dominic and Jasper didn't bring up the fact that she wasn't

due for a heat, and no one seemed to notice me commenting that the timing was off. Had she not told the others of her heat in March?

I keep my suspicion of her being drugged behind my lips as I ease the last piece of fabric out from under her and drop it into the large trash can tucked just inside the bathroom. While I wet a washcloth, I grab my phone and send a text to Mark. Tomorrow's recording session will have to happen without me.

The washcloth is new. So is the mouthwash and the toothbrush and the hairbrush. Everything in here is brand new. She wasn't supposed to need it for three more fucking months.

I shove the thought away and head back into the nest, grabbing the hairbrush on my way out.

Dominic sits in the chair in the corner, his gaze focused out the window.

What the fuck is he still doing here? I expected him to bail the moment she was safely in the bed. He's made it abundantly clear he doesn't want to be involved with an Omega and that she is no exception. Fuck if I know what goes on in his head, though. And Jasper's still cleaning up the shit show at the hotel.

I set the hairbrush on the nightstand and run my hand down her leg. She lets them fall open with a whimper. Keeping my touch as light as possible, I clean up the mess left from her knotting with Dominic, letting it settle the ache in my chest induced by her heat. She shifts, rolling toward me, and I run a hand down her arm to soothe her. She's only been out for half an hour at most. She needs more sleep before the next wave starts.

I toss the washcloth in the general direction of the bathroom and grab the hairbrush. Dropping into a crouch, I ease it through her hair. Her eyes flutter open just as I'm finishing. Her gaze is unfocused, and for a moment, I'm back in the Haven, watching her rise to her knees as she begs for my knot.

"You need to sleep, pretty Omega," I murmur, running my thumb over her lips.

She perfumes as she bites my thumb and pulls it into her mouth. My dick's hard in an instant.

"Omega," I groan.

She pushes up onto her forearm and grabs the waistband of my slacks, pulling me toward her until I'm forced to rest a knee on the bed near her hips. She perfumes again, so intensely the air purifier can't manage to touch the intensity of it. Her breaths saw out of her as she sits up and digs her hands into my stomach. She whimpers deep in her throat, and I'm gone, giving in without much of a fight at all.

Omegas in heat get what they want. Especially *my* Omega during a fucking forced heat.

"All right, Violet," I murmur.

I try to pull my hand away, but she tightens her bite on my thumb. Her hands shake as she undoes the belt and zipper of my slacks and pushes them as far as she can manage. I shove them the rest of the way and then straddle her, easing her back onto the bed. And all the while, she keeps my thumb in her fucking mouth, running her tongue along it and sucking on it.

My dick fucking aches, a bead of precum dripping onto her belly as I lean down and kiss her nose.

"You want to suck me, pretty little Omega?"

She nods her head, her eyes wide and glassy. She runs her tongue along my thumb again as if I need another demonstration of what she wants to do to my dick.

"You can't do that if you're biting my thumb," I murmur, smiling.

She releases my thumb with a whine, her lips pouting. I laugh and shake my head even as I move to kneel next to her, giving her room to sit up. She follows me, like a string attaches our chests, and reaches for my dick, her fingers shaking from the force of her heat.

Again, it's like I'm back in the Haven last year. Everything fades away as her lips part and her tongue traces over the cool metal of my piercing. She groans, an excited little squeal in the back of her throat, and then closes her lips around the head of my cock, pulling me inexorably farther into her mouth, her cheeks hollowing out as she glances up at me through her lashes.

"Fuck me, you can't look at me like that," I mutter. I gather her hair into my hand, keeping it away from her stretched lips. "I'll give you whatever you want, you already know that."

She smirks. How she manages with my dick stuffing her mouth, I have no idea. My blood heats. I tighten my hold on her hair, urging her faster, and she hums, the sound full of happiness.

Did I think fucking her in September was hot?

It's nothing on this. She's no longer *just* an Omega. She's *my* Omega. At least for right now.

I know what kind of coffee she likes, which blankets are her favorite, which bands she loves and which ones she only tolerates because Jasper likes them. I know *so much* and yet not enough. Never enough.

I blink back the sudden tears, focusing on the feel of her tongue as she traces it over me and the tightening of her throat as she swallows just as my dick touches the back of her throat.

My dick twitches, and I mutter a curse. I pull her away from me, ignoring her whine, and press her onto the bed, spreading her knees and wrapping them around my waist. I don't lean over her as I push into her, the muscles of her cunt gripping me like a too-tight fist.

If I get anywhere near her skin right now, I'm going to be fucked for control.

She's leaving, I remind myself as she throws her head back and exposes the column of her throat. I clench my jaw, moving faster as I ignore the bone deep need to mark her and make her mine in truth.

She's leaving.

It becomes my mantra as I force my pace faster, watching her skin flush darker and her hands twist into the sheets of the bed. That telltale pressure builds behind my hips. I drop one hand and flick my thumb over her clit. She might be in heat, but I need her to come around me first. This time. Every time. For as many times as I might have left with her.

"Come for me, pretty Omega. Let me feel it one more time," I murmur.

Her muscles ripple around me. I press harder against her clit. Her back bows as her cry of ecstasy rips through the room. Not a second later, lightning rushes through me, a pulse of all-consuming sensation that has my hips stuttering and my legs giving out. My dick twitches as I shudder out my release, my knot swelling and locking us together. I drop over her as the last waves leave my body, my fucking fingers still tingling.

She moans, the sound hoarse, as my knot sends her over the edge again. Her nails scratch down my back as I drop my forehead to her shoulder, breathing in her scent, ignoring the ache in my chest that has nothing to do with the haze of her heat and everything to do with understanding this is all temporary.

It was easier to stomach when it was my job, when I knew I would never see her outside the walls of her temporary nest inside the Council's facility. Here? In my own house where she built a nest that was supposed to be permanent?

Fuck, it aches worse than when I got the call about my mom. I never thought anything would come near the pain of being told she'd been too intoxicated to get out of the tornado's path. Yet here we are.

Violet hums into my ear, her hands slowly stilling until they fall away completely, her breathing evening out. I press a kiss to her collarbone and then her temple as my knot releases.

I don't immediately pull away from her, closing my eyes and focusing on the feel of her under me, the smell of her honeysuckle mixing with the fragrance of Jasper's body wash.

"Go eat, *amico*," Dominic says, resting a hand on my shoulder. "I can get her cleaned up and safe."

I don't even fight him. Why he's suddenly wanting to be involved is beyond me, but I'll take the offer. It's on the tip of my tongue to ask what he wants, but he beats me to it.

"I'll be down as soon as she's clean. And then we'll talk."

JASPER

The house is silent when I finally close the door to the garage. My feet are leaden, and there's a headache pounding just behind my eyes and down my neck. My phone rings before I can dump it on the kitchen counter.

I answer without looking. "Jasper."

My voice is as tired as the rest of me, but I don't apologize for it.

"Mr. Montegue? This is Detective Forrest."

My exhaustion fades between one breath and the next.

"I didn't expect a call so soon," I admit.

His laugh is nearly as tired as I feel. "Omegas being abused isn't something we wait to handle during normal business hours."

"I suppose I should be grateful for that," I mutter.

Difficult to feel grateful when I don't want to be dealing with this nightmare at all. My stomach is still tight with anxiety, my throat still raw from the bile I'd had to keep from surfacing while recounting everything that had happened with the officers that arrested Eric.

What had Rylan called him? Fuckboy Extraordinaire? I need to find out why he recognized the asshole.

The detective clears his throat. "I want you to know that I'm not a stranger to working high profile cases, Mr. Montegue." His voice has gained a careful edge that has warning bells going off in my mind. "The notoriety and scrutiny that comes with them is within my wheelhouse to handle."

"I feel like there's a 'but' coming."

"Isn't there always?" He sighs. "The Fallon family is asking for this to stay as quiet as possible."

Johnathan had told me as much. The less in the spotlight it was, the less likely Sienna would use it as some kind of ammunition for her own gain. His eyes had flashed when he'd said it, the anger so extreme I almost felt bad for the woman.

Until I thought about Violet's shattered face as she realized we'd both been played by her.

The detective clears his throat, and I force myself to focus.

"The man's official statement is that he stumbled upon her while she was trying to clean up in the bathroom. Another woman left the bathroom, and the smell of her heat was strong enough that he responded on instinct. She didn't fight him until they were in the utility room. According to the hotel staff, there were no witnesses to any of this."

Of fucking course not.

What if Dominic and Rylan hadn't shown up when they did? I had no idea she was in trouble, didn't even realize she was in heat when I could smell her in that hallway.

"The Fallons are content with this explanation." The detective is neutral, but I can almost swear there's a thread of frustration underlying the comment.

I lean against the counter and tip my head back.

"All right. It's a decent explanation. I saw the way my own partners changed in the span of a heartbeat when they smelled her perfuming." I close my eyes, remembering the shock cross Rylan's face as we entered the hallway.

The man murmurs an agreement, and the line drops to an uneasy quiet. After a moment, he says, "I've done some looking into Ms. Fallon's past since you were unsure of her previous heat cycling. It turns out she had a heat in March. She used the Haven. According to their records, she stayed for six days and was helped by two Alphas."

March.

I count back the months, and my stomach drops. "That's not long enough. It should have been in January at the earliest."

The detective makes a noncommittal grunt.

Horror settles in my gut. "It was triggered?"

"It appears so." The detective sighs, and the sound of rustling papers cuts through the phone.

"And her parents are content with not pushing for further information?" I ask.

It doesn't make sense. Johnathan was beside himself. It was only the understanding that Violet had made it out of the hotel mostly unharmed and with Rylan that kept him from completely losing it. And when Kurt and Phillip find out?

Fuck, Kurt's going to be *livid*.

"As they are not her immediate kin at this juncture, they have not been informed of the update."

Oh God. Right. We're matched. *We're* her immediate kin now.

I clear my throat. "Sorry. It's still an adjustment."

"I've been told those thirty days are a whirlwind," he says, his voice filling with wry humor. He drops back to the important information. "The Alpha has been charged with assault and attempted forced bonding. He's not fighting the charges, though I believe he expects to manage some kind of plea deal with the court given his cooperation with the investigation and it being his first offense."

I grimace. "There's no way in hell that dipshit is the one that drugged her."

I don't mean to say it, but it's too fucking late for me to manage any kind of filter right now.

There's a long, heavy pause.

"I'm inclined to agree with you, Mr. Montegue," he says. "We are willing to keep the investigation open if it's what you're wanting."

It's on the tip of my tongue to say that of course we want to get to the bottom of who set the *love of my life* up for being raped at a public event.

Detective Forrest continues before I can manage to say it, though, and his words cut through me with the precision of a blade and the iciness of the fucking Puget Sound.

"I want to warn you, though, that while we may be able to piece together what transpired, it's quite likely that we will not be able to do so with enough substantive proof to lead to any sort of conviction in court." A tapping cuts through the phone, like he's messing with a pen. "Ms. Fallon's testimony is likely our best information, but it will hold little weight in a trial given that she was already in the throes of the heat cycle, induced or not. She, for all intents and purposes, was impaired. Her information will be considered tainted."

Fuck. Me.

"Did the asshole mention if he recognized the other woman leaving the bathroom?" I ask unable to keep the question to myself.

Violet had been feeling uneasy but was still cognizant when

she left for the bathroom. What had happened while she was in there to push her over into the depths of the heat? And why had no one noticed her being followed into the bathroom? The rooftop was event access only. Someone would have noticed if a random dipshit had followed her in.

My chest tightens, a damning realization settling on me. My mind races, putting together pieces I'd rather not notice.

Sienna's strangely indifferent demeanor toward me when I'd expected outright hostility or disdain, her comment about Violet being unchaperoned when I'd literally been holding her hand, her giving Violet a glass of white wine when even I knew it was one of her least favorite drinks.

"The description matches that of Mrs. Fallon."

God *fucking* damn it.

It didn't matter that Johnathan was doing what he could to keep all of this out of the spotlight. Sienna was already knee deep in the entire fucking mess of it.

Rage burns through me, though not nearly hot enough given my exhaustion.

I should talk with the others about what to do, about if they want any of this to be on open record. Violet's word might not hold up in court, but it might end up being important later on that it was documented anyway. And keeping it on record means that Dominic will be less likely to turn around and involve his family if he feels so inclined.

Not that he will.

My stomach sours again.

I glance at the illuminated numbers on the microwave. Nearly two in the morning.

Realistically, they're probably sleeping. And if they aren't? There's no way we'd be capable of having a conversation right now.

I clear my throat. "On record, we're content to close the investigation if you feel that asshole will be convicted."

Silence stretches on the other end of the line, and I have the sudden thought that maybe he knows who Dominic is and what his family is.

"I understand, Mr. Montegue," he says, back to the careful neutral. "I'll submit my report to the chief. As he's confessed on record, he'll absolutely face the justice system. I'll be in contact regarding the trial."

I drop my phone to the counter after a quick goodbye.

What kind of self-righteous asshole drugs their own daughter to force a bond with another Alpha?

No amount of twisting the question over in my mind gives a better answer than *an asshole*, so I give it up, leaving my phone in the kitchen as I head to my room and change out of the suit. The shirt I grab smells like Violet, and I breathe in her scent. No matter what the guys say, I can't tell anything different between this scent and the one that greeted us in the hotel. Maybe it's strength? But that could just be because it's been a couple days since Violet wore this shirt.

Another stab of guilt hits me that I would've been helpless to keep her safe if Rylan and Dominic hadn't gotten there in time. And there was no guarantee they were going to show up at all.

Damn. I really thought I'd gotten past my resentment of being a Beta at this point.

My bed is large and inviting, but I don't drop into it, rubbing my eyes to keep the exhaustion from dropping me to my knees. The need to make sure the three of them are safe rides me hard, and I know I won't be able to sleep until I've seen the three of them tucked away where Sienna can't fucking reach them. When I see that Dominic's door is open and his bed empty, I cross the house toward where her nest is tucked away.

The unassuming single piece of paperwork sits on the coffee table, but it might as well have a fucking spotlight on it. The single black signature stops me dead, my heart racing even as my stomach drops out.

No.

Forty-Three

JASPER

Why had she signed the annulment? *When* had she signed the annulment? It must have been while I was out for a run this morning. She hadn't been gone from my side since the moment I came back and found her sitting on the porch. Had she seemed more resigned than just the bullshit with her mom would have caused? And even more important: did Rylan and Dominic know?

My mind races, and my breath is ragged. I close my eyes, forcing the questions back until I can think around them, locking them down. There's no time to ask any of them now. It'll be days before I can get any kind of answer to most of them, anyway. I climb the staircase to Violet's nest on wooden legs.

Dominic leans against the wall just beside the door, his head tipped back and his hands held limp at his sides. His shirt is gone, the dark gray sweats hanging low on his hips. There's a smattering of bruises across his throat and collarbone, light enough they nearly blend in with his skin. His hair is still damp, falling on his forehead in small black waves. He looks tired and worn, more than I've ever seen him.

Rylan closes the door, letting the latch catch as quietly as possible. He's also changed into a set of sweats, his hair damp, too, and sticking to his neck. The black shirt he wears clings to his skin, small droplets of water darkening it further from where he didn't towel dry his hair quite enough.

Desire flashes through me.

Is it bad that I want them to fuck me so I can forget how awful tonight was? Probably. Heats are no fucking joke and asking them to put out again when Violet will need them both within a matter of hours is incredibly selfish.

Doesn't change the ache in my bones or the pulse of heat through my dick, though.

"She all right?" I ask, closing the distance between us and taking Dominic's hand in mine.

Nothing of Violet's scent clings to either of them.

Dominic nods once without opening his eyes. His hand pulses around mine, a low purr vibrating through his throat.

"She'll be fine. Just going to be a long several days," Rylan says, leaning his forehead against the closed door. Acid leaches into his voice, and his hand tightens around the doorknob until his knuckles are white. "She had a heat in March. There's no fucking way this wasn't forced by someone."

Dominic raises an eyebrow. "How do you know she had a heat in March?"

Rylan tenses, a growl ripping through him.

"*Mi dispiace*," Dominic says, grabbing his friend's forearm. Rylan relaxes and lets go of the doorknob. The smallest bit of hope blooms in the pit of my stomach at the small gesture. Maybe something good might come from this whole fucking mess. Maybe Rylan and Dominic's friendship surviving will be enough to dull the ache of the rest of it.

I clear my throat, but Rylan talks over me. "She told me the first day I took her out."

Surprise flashes through me. They'd talked about it so soon after reconnecting?

Dominic grunts.

"Something about it went wrong, though," Rylan says after a minute. "It's what pushed her to consent to matching. She's never said what it was, just that it was bad enough to risk a bad match made by the Council."

My stomach clenches. Not many things would push Violet into risking her mother's attention. And matching? It was the single biggest way to do just that.

Dominic mutters a curse before opening his eyes. His voice is nothing more than gravel as he says, "Please tell me you figured out who the fuck drugged her."

Nerves close my throat, and I force a swallow. When it doesn't help, I nod once. Dominic squeezes my hand.

"Yeah, I figured it out," I manage to say. My voice cracks, my mind still struggling to accept the damning truth.

Rylan palms my neck, pulling me nearer to him, kissing my temple. Dominic leans in, too, like I'm an Omega that needs comforting. They both must be absolutely exhausted. They need to sleep before Violet's needing them again. Instead of pushing them away, though, I lean harder into them both, letting their strength hold me up as my knees collapse under me.

Dominic wraps an arm around my waist before I can actually fall.

"Shit, Jas," Rylan says, twisting his hand into my hair. "We've got you. It's going to be all right."

I let my head fall onto his shoulder, and Dominic kisses the nape of my neck. My breath shudders out of me before hitching on a sob. Both men step closer, crowding me until their bodies are solid and warm and holding me up when everything in me wants to collapse. Dominic murmurs in Italian, soft things that I can't manage to hear enough to pick out exact phrases.

"You did good, Jasper," Rylan murmurs, his thumb tracing my ear.

"I didn't even know she was in trouble," I bite out. "I wouldn't have known what her scent meant without you there. I... I still can't tell the difference, and she's sitting in the room next to me in the depths of a heat."

Dominic tightens his arm around my waist but doesn't stop his soft murmurings.

"You kept Dom level when he would have killed the asshole," Rylan says, his touch never faltering. Goosebumps race down my spine. "And then we would have been in an entirely different mess. Don't hold this on you. This isn't your fault."

His words are soft but firm, the thread of power through them strong enough that even my shoulders relax under it. Eventually, the soft fall of tears slows, and I blow out a breath. Rylan's eyebrows are furrowed and concern brackets his mouth as I lift my head and take him in.

"You can't do anything until she's out of her heat," I whisper. "It's... it's not something that the police are going to investigate. And Violet deserves to know before either of you run off and do something impulsive."

Rylan's inhale is sharp, his eyes searching mine as the realization settles on him.

"*É sua madre?*" Dominic's voice is a growl that has the hair rising on my neck. "*O uno dei suoi padri?*"

I force another swallow and close my eyes. Dominic runs his lips across my neck and shoulder before biting the soft junction where they meet just hard enough that I groan.

"*Tesoro?*" he asks.

My stomach drops out at the nickname, the warm feel of it sliding over my skin and skating down my bones. Longing mixes with bitterness until I'm choking on it. I'd begged with him to make this work, to find a way to tolerate her. He'd promised me that he would.

I push the thoughts away and focus on this moment.

"Sienna," I whisper her name, refusing to call her Violet's mother. Not right now. "I... I don't know if she did it alone. I think she did. Vi... her dads love her. You saw how upset he was over everything that happened."

Dominic's growl rumbles through his chest, vibrating against me. Even exhausted, I tense under the sound, the feral lethality of it. Rylan runs his lips down my throat, humming, and I settle into him. His cock lays hard and heavy against my hip. My pulse thrums, my blood heating, but I force my body to remain unresponsive.

"You need to sleep," I mutter into his shoulder.

Dominic grunts and closes the last bit of distance between us, his own interest pressing against my ass. My knees weaken, and his arm tightens around me.

Fuck, I've missed him.

Reality slams back into me so hard, I lose my breath and flinch. Dominic freezes, his lips stilling on my shoulder, his open hand pausing where it had been working to undo my belt. Rylan's growl starts again, and I push away from them both, not wanting to be in the middle of whatever I just accidentally triggered. Not tonight. I have nothing left in me right now.

"*Tesoro*," Dominic growls.

Fuck. All I want is to sink into his warmth and strength. But I can't. Not when I'm days away from having to watch Violet walk out of my life. Again.

Will we survive it? I think so. But I don't want to have to survive it. I'd begged and pleaded so that I *wouldn't* have to survive it.

I shake my head. "I can't do this right now. Not with her in heat and the annulment sitting in our fucking living room."

Both men freeze. A long silence stretches between us.

"Jasper," Rylan whispers, his voice soothing. It sluices over me but doesn't find anywhere to latch onto. Another reminder of me being a goddamn Beta.

I frown and take another step away before cracking open the door to Violet's nest. She's curled into herself, her back toward the door, a light pink throw blanket covering most of her body. Her shoulders move with her steady breathing. A single lamp in the far corner illuminates the room, gilding her in light so perfect it makes my knees weak.

I resist the urge to touch her by the skin of my teeth. I shove my hands into the pockets of my sweats, clenching them against the force of the need to feel that she's really all right. If I touch her right now, it'll probably wake her up. And there's nothing I can do to help her through this.

As angry as I am with the men, I won't take away the few hours of rest they're going to have while she sleeps.

Closing the door, I blink back the sudden tears, the exhaustion of the night compounding everything else that sits on my chest like a stone. Movement behind me has me blowing out a breath.

"Jasper," Dominic says.

I shake my head again before twisting away from the door. My lovers stand in front of me, shoulder to shoulder, their mouths identical thin lines. I dodge around both men, avoiding touching them, and start down the stairs.

"Not tonight," I say. "I need one more night where I don't have to actually acknowledge that she's not mine. Again."

Forty-Four

RYLAN

I close the door to the nest, keeping the latch from making any noise. I double check the sound monitor is on before heading toward the main living space of the house. The smells of breakfast filter through to me, and I hold back a groan. My stomach rumbles, and I try to remember when I last ate.

Probably last night while Dominic admitted to me that he'd been wrong about Violet while waiting for Jasper to get home.

Never in a million fucking years had I expected him to look me dead in the eye the moment he'd reheated some pizza and set it on the island and then spill so much about his own internalized hatred of his designation and the limitation he sees it being. By the time he confessed that he not only felt awful over how he'd treated Violet but that he wanted to try and mend things between them before letting her file the annulment?

Part of me is still convinced I dreamt the entire fucking sequence.

Jasper looks up from where he's mixing something at the

stove, his eyes red with fatigue. Dominic stands beside him, a hand on his hip, and he looks just as wrung out. Both wear nearly identical white shirts and gray sweats. It makes me smile for a heartbeat, and Jasper's shoulders ease away from his ears.

"Yours is over here," Jasper says, motioning to a smaller pan that's already off the heat. "It doesn't have any of the jalapeño in it."

I grab a tortilla and then the egg mix, rolling it all into a simple—if ugly—burrito.

Thank God for Jasper and his phenomenal cooking. This is leagues better than the food provided by the Haven.

"How is she?" Jasper asks, not looking up from the eggs he's still stirring.

"Definitely into the thick of it," I say, setting the burrito down and hopping onto the counter on the other side of the stove. "I had to force her to use mouthwash, and her hair is a mess right now, but I think it'll wait until after her next wave. She cried over it being too bright, so all the blackout curtains are shut now."

Jasper nods. "I can work through her hair after the next wave while you rest." He turns off the burner's flame and spoons eggs into two tortillas already arranged beside him. He blows out a breath as he sets the pan on the back burner, dropping his head, not looking at either of us. "Paperwork is due Wednesday. What are the chances she'll be lucid by then?"

I shake my head. "Her heat in September lasted five days. That was without any kind of augmentation. There's no way she'll be out of it by Wednesday."

Jasper sighs and swallows. Dominic runs a hand up his side before kissing his shoulder.

"I guess I'll file the annulment on her behalf tomorrow. I..." He swallows again. His voice is so full of sorrow, my chest aches.

"I think I'm allowed to do that if I can provide proof she's in heat."

I glance at Dominic just in time to see his jaw tighten, a muscle feathering in his neck.

"Come eat, *Tesoro*," he says, grabbing Jasper's hand and guiding him to the dining table we hardly ever use. I set the sound monitor on the counter before grabbing his forgotten plate and following them both, settling into the other seat beside Jasper.

"I'm sorry, Jasper," Dominic says, his voice low and grave. "I made you a promise, and I broke it."

Jasper tilts his head back, his hands slack in his lap. I leave Dominic to his explanation, keeping my eyes off my lover. I'm exhausted, and Dominic and I already dance around each other when the dynamics between the three of us are testy.

My lip aches where the asshat split it open last night. God knows Dominic'd be able to do that much and worse with a single fucking hit. And, realistically, I don't have time for him to lay me out right now. Violet's only been averaging three hours between waves, and we're already at hour two. Though maybe me making her wake up just enough to maintain baseline hygiene will be enough to extend the gap this round.

My phone vibrates, and I pull it from my sweats.

A text from Huntley is not what I'm expecting.

> Hey, heard from Liz that Violet's in heat. You guys need anything?

How in the fuck does *Liz* know that Violet's gone into heat?

A new series of messages from Liz light up my screen, and I swear to God these women are telepathic or some shit.

> Jasper told me Violet went into heat last night. Said it wasn't expected?

You guys need anything? She have everything she needs in her nest?

Riley says he can help if you guys need a last minute extension from the Council in case you didn't get a chance to sign the paperwork.

The guys made it a whole day for me, so totally get if you hadn't gotten to it yet.

I text Huntley back first.

Aren't you supposed to be soaking up the sun in Colorado right now doing that backpack thing?

Doesn't mean I can't check in with my friends. It's 2024. I even get service in the backwoods of the Rocky Mountains now.

We're good. Don't fall off the mountain.

Wouldn't dream of it. I'd never leave you to the whims of George.

I shake my head and blow out a breath. George isn't all that bad, all things considered. He's just newly graduated and still needs to figure out how to blend with the rest of the orchestra. I'm sure next year, he'll be great.

I send a single text to Liz. Anything more, and she'll end up calling me. I glance at the time.

And there's absolutely no way I have time to field one of her calls right now.

> We're good so far. I'll have Jasper text you if it changes.

"Rylan?" Jasper's whisper grabs my attention. "What do you think?"

His eyes are on me, the tears lining his lashes making them glassy and emphasizing how tired he seems. His hands tremble on the table, his burrito all but forgotten on his plate. I grab a piece of egg and offer it to him, not answering him until he's taken it from me.

"What do I think about what?" I ask. "The girls were texting. Sorry."

"You think she'll actually entertain Dominic apologizing?"

I look between them both.

"I'm not sure," I admit. Jasper nods, a tear spilling over. I wipe it away. "Before yesterday? Absolutely not. But with everything that happened..."

I shrug, wishing I was more sure of everything.

"I don't feel comfortable filing it while she's not lucid. If it were a request for reassignment, I might feel differently. But annulment is irreversible," Dominic says. "We should get an extension at the very least so that she can make the choice herself when she surfaces from her heat."

Jasper blows out a breath and blinks away the tears.

It fucking kills me to see him like this. I pull him into me, taking his mouth with mine until his breath catches and the tension eases away from him. I run my hands under the hem of his shirt, enjoying the fuck out of the way goosebumps race up his stomach.

There's a noise from the monitor still perched in the kitchen, a soft whine followed by the rustling of fabric. Fuck. That's even shorter than the last one. She's needing more. I eye Dominic and scratch at my tattoo.

"Alpha?" Violet's tired voice is clear but tired, like when I first met her in the fall.

Jasper pulls away from me, looking over my shoulder back toward the kitchen. "She needs you."

I take his hand and lace our fingers together.

Dominic stands from the table and gathers all three plates. "I'll get in touch with Victor's contact at the local Council office and officially get an extension figured out. And then I'm going to be gone until tomorrow morning. I'll take over her care as soon as I'm back."

Jasper freezes. "You said you'd wait until she resurfaced." Accusation and betrayal war in his voice, but he keeps his eyes on me.

Dominic nods. "I am not *doing* anything, *Tesoro*. I simply wish to meet her fathers and understand the dynamic of her family. They were happy to oblige."

Jasper blows out a breath and turns toward him. "All right. Be safe."

"Always, *Tesoro*," he says, smirking. He kisses Jasper before disappearing down the hall toward his bedroom.

I lead Jasper back to Violet's nest before he can protest, urging him inside before me. Violet's sitting up in bed, the blanket gathered around her hips, her hair even messier than when I left her an hour ago. Her eyes are glassy, and her scent drowns the room even with the purifier running.

Her gaze catches on Jasper, and she whines, crawling across the bed toward where he's stopped near the nightstand. I shrug off my shirt as she pulls him onto the bed, her lips already roaming over his neck and shoulders.

"Love, I can't help you," he murmurs, grabbing her hands as she pushes down his sweats.

She whines, fighting his hold, her lips pushing into a pout. "Please," she whispers. "I need you."

He glances over at me, panic in his eyes. I shrug and shove off my pants, dropping them with the shirt at the threshold of the bathroom.

"Pretty Omega," I say, crossing the room and running my hand through her hair. "Do you need Jasper?"

She nods, pushing into my touch. She pushes his sweats as low as she can and then reaches for his dick. Jasper's gasp has my own dick jumping.

"How do you need him?" I ask.

I climb on the bed behind her, already pretty confident in what she'll say. Or signal, at least. She might be too lost for words right now. She leans toward Jasper, and he runs his hands up her arms and across her shoulders.

"He's worried that you won't like him," I murmur, leaning over her and kissing the center of her back. "That you'll decide he isn't enough for you."

She shakes her head, and her scent grows thicker, redoubling again. "Need."

She's fallen into one word sentences. Her heat is getting even stronger. "Show him, pretty Omega. Show him how you need him."

"Yes, Alpha," she says. Jasper lets her drop his sweats until his dick springs free.

I watch Jasper's face as she sucks him off, her moans as much a sign she likes it as the slick dripping down her thighs. I run my hands up her thighs, and she pushes back into me, spreading her knees apart. I don't make her beg any more than that. I line my cock up with her entrance and push into her, sinking deep in one steady thrust. Her toes curl into the bed as she groans around Jasper's cock. She's already halfway gone.

Jasper tips his head back, his throat rippling with a swallow.

"I'm not going to last," he mutters.

I speed up my movements, running one hand over her hip until I can play with her clit.

"Good," I say, my voice rough. "Neither is she."

Jasper's ragged gasp is the only warning he manages, but Violet isn't bothered at all, her throat moving as she swallows. Jasper shakes, his hands trembling as he works them through her hair and across her cheeks. The moment he pulls away, she smiles and tilts her head to him.

"You're perfect, love," Jasper mutters, urging her to kneel with a finger under her chin.

He claims her lips, the kiss messy, and I increase my tempo, holding Violet's hips so she doesn't move. I run my lips across her shoulder and up her neck before following the same line with my tongue. She clenches around me, moaning into Jasper's kiss.

The orgasm hits me out of nowhere, plowing into me with the strength of a freight train. My vision goes hazy and my fingers tingle.

"Fuck," I groan as my knot locks us together.

Violet screams, shaking in our arms as her release washes through her. She collapses back against me, her head resting against my shoulder. I kiss her temple as her eyes drift shut and reach for Jasper's hand, lacing our fingers together. His eyes are just as soft as he focuses on me, the love in them so pure and strong it steals my breath for a moment.

"Love you," I murmur.

He nods and squeezes my hand. "I know."

Fuck, I hope she can forgive Dominic.

Because this? I want this for the rest of my life.

Forty-Five

DOMINIC

My phone vibrates just as the car pulls up to the curb in front of a mansion that could seriously rival my parents'. It sprawls out in both directions, the traditional architecture nearly overbearing in the bright green landscape that's typical to the Pacific Northwest. It strikes me as ironic, actually. Violet's the opposite of this in every way I can imagine.

What's odd to me is that I never once suspected that she came from this amount of wealth. She doesn't flaunt it with large, gaudy purchases. And she doesn't wear subtle designers, either. Nothing that would indicate the amount of cash she must have access to. Not to mention that she worked on campus at UCLA and maintained a second job as a waitress.

For some reason, I never thought to connect the dots between her last name and Fallon Capital. It seems obvious now that all the pieces have been laid out on a single map.

I take a deep breath and step out of the car, giving a single wave to let the driver know he's welcome to leave. I take my time heading toward the mansion, observing as much of it as I can—the windows, the doors, the streamline security system tucked every thirty feet or so across the front façade of the house. It feels like overkill considering they're already in a gated community and the nearest house is over an acre away, but perhaps growing up in a pack is different than growing up as part of the Italian mafia.

The front door opens before I make it up the steps and onto the porch.

All three of her fathers stand in the entry, dressed in variations of dark jeans and simple polo shirts. Johnathan's eyes are softer than the others, a concerned wariness about him rather than overt hostility like what bleeds from Kurt and Phillip.

It's easy enough to figure out which one is Kurt. His expression is nearly a carbon copy of the one I saw Violet use on Friday. Her coloring must come from her mother, though, because his pale skin and blue eyes are nothing like Violet's gorgeous tan and hazel.

"Dominic," Johnathan says as I close the distance to the door. "You really didn't need to discuss this in person. We are not strangers to the demands of an Omega's heat."

"It's only one night," I say as I shake his hand. "Rylan will manage well enough. He used to work at the Haven in LA until we registered last fall."

Kurt's eyebrow raises, but he doesn't say anything. He holds out his hand, and I take it as easily as Johnathan's, intent on making sure I don't cross them until it's necessary. I'm hoping it's not necessary, that what Jasper had said last night about her fathers being devoted to Violet is the truth.

Phillip and I exchange a small greeting, and then Johnathan guides me inside the lavish home. We don't go far, only a couple doors down the main hallway. The French doors open into a large sitting room, the sectional a clean blue velvet that coordinates with the other classic furnishings. Johnathan motions toward the sectional, and I settle into one corner of it, crossing my legs and messing with my watch while I wait for the others to choose spots and get comfortable.

Phillip stands near the door, his hands clasped behind his back, while Kurt sits on the opposite corner of the sectional. Johnathan opts for the chair across from me, leaning forward on his elbows and resting his chin on his folded hands.

I start in on the small talk before they can ask direct questions about yesterday.

"She's applying to graduate programs," I offer. "I'm not sure if she's heard back from any of them yet. I know that the parameters for newly matched Omegas vary."

Or at least I do now. I gave myself a crash course last night when I couldn't sleep after Jasper came home.

Phillip lets his hands drop to his sides, the tension easing away from his shoulders.

"Good," he says, his voice full of relief. "We were worried she'd shelve her dream of research once she matched. It's part of why we never pushed her to do it."

"Not that she needed much convincing to wait," Kurt murmurs with a dry sort of humor. The exasperated look he gives is identical to the one Violet uses. "It's not like she had an example that had her tripping over herself to set a date with the Council."

Johnathan sighs and rubs his eyes. "We did our best to shield her from the worst of it."

"Didn't stop her, though," Phillip says with a resigned sadness. "She was always the most curious."

I clear my throat and lean forward. *This* was the information I came for.

"Your match has always been tense?" I ask.

Kurt nods. "The process was different thirty years ago. Not the galas themselves, but the follow up. There wasn't really the trial run they give now. You got handed a match and were told to make the best of it. So we did. It was... fair."

Phillip snorts in derision, and Kurt pins him a look. He shrugs before crossing the room, sitting next to Kurt and taking his hand. Kurt's mouth opens, his gaze snapping back to me.

"By the time we realized we'd rather be just a trio," Johnathan says, interrupting whatever Kurt was about to say, "Sienna was pregnant with Scarlett. It was an accident. We thought we'd taken precautions during her heat. In dissolutions, the Council almost always sides with the Omega when children are involved. If we left, we'd lose Scarlett."

Pain flashes across all three of their faces. Phillip shakes his head.

"So we stayed," he says. "We're not oblivious to Sienna's..."

He trails off, clearly trying to figure out what word to use.

"Bullshit," Kurt supplies.

Phillip nods and laces his fingers with Kurt's, his knuckles whitening from his grip.

"But we've tried to balance it out," Johnathan says. "Tried to make sure all three of our children know that we love and adore them."

The others murmur their agreement, and then the conversation lulls into silence. I adjust my cuff links. Johnathan crosses the room, pouring a single knuckle's worth of amber liquor from a cart tucked in the corner. He glances at me and holds up the decanter. I shake my head.

I don't want to be drinking during this.

Once Johnathan is resettled, tension grows between us, buzzing through the room so intensely I'm surprised I'm not electrocuted by it.

"Is Violet all right?" Kurt asks, his body tight, his gaze hard. "That son of a bitch didn't touch her, right?"

"No permanent harm done," I murmur. I'm not willing to outright lie to him, and I don't want him to carry the weight of knowing just how close his daughter came to being hurt. "To be honest, I'm not sure how much of it all she'll remember."

Hopefully very little.

Phillip frowns. "It doesn't matter if she remembers it. It's inexcusable either way."

I nod.

Their devotion for Violet eases some of my coiled anger. My voice is gruff as I say, "The problem is that she had a heat in March."

Johnathan freezes, a low growl rumbling through his chest. I breathe slowly, reminding myself that he's angry *for* Violet and not *at* her. He's on my side of this entire clusterfuck.

Kurt frowns, but it's Phillip that asks the question that'll set us past the point of no return tonight.

"Then how could she have possibly dropped into heat while at the event?"

Kurt says it before I can, his voice ice cold. "She was drugged. And it would have had to be an incredibly high dosage if she was three months out from her heat."

"She hardly interacted with anyone," Johnathan says slowly, like he's terrified of reaching the inevitable conclusion of this train of thought. I don't blame him. "And the only drink she had was given to her by Sienna."

Phillip pales. The reality washes through them in one swift wave, their expressions moving from horror to despair to anger in the span of a few seconds.

"I'm going to kill her," Kurt says, pushing up from where he sits beside Phillip, dropping his hand in favor of clenching them both. He starts toward the door, his own growl loud enough to drown out Johnathan's.

I relax at the display. Jasper had been right. They hadn't been involved. Which makes this much easier... and potentially even more heartbreaking for them. Johnathan stops Kurt with a single hand on his chest.

"Hold on," he says, his voice firm. "The last thing we need is to alert Sienna that one of Violet's Alphas is here."

Kurt shakes his head, his body trembling.

"She set Violet up," Kurt snarls. "Her perfume would have been enough to set off an unsuspecting Alpha's rut. She meant for Violet to end up bonded."

That explains the sorry excuse of an Alpha we found all over her, then.

Johnathan's eyes flash to mine, the hatred in them palpable.

"Does Violet know?" he asks.

"We aren't sure." I shake my head. "She isn't lucid enough to talk about it."

"And she won't be for days," Phillip says. "Probably not until the end of the week."

Kurt's growl slowly fades, the leashed aggression in his body bleeding away the longer Johnathan touches him. Johnathan guides him to the chair he'd been occupying, urging Kurt to sit and then taking his hand as he perches on the chair's arm.

"We intend to discuss it with her once she surfaces," I offer.

"And then what's your plan?" Johnathan asks, tucking his open hand into the pocket of his jeans, his thumb tapping an unheard rhythm. "Do you intend to bring in your family?"

I don't even worry about him knowing my family's reputation. Jasper had mentioned Sienna knew. It's not a stretch that she brought it to his attention as well.

"That's entirely up to you," I say. "Let's discuss the options."

Forty-Six

VIOLET

My body's on fire. Need tightens in my core, pulsing through me in waves that leave me whimpering. I roll over, trying to find something to take away the pain. My hand lands on something warm and solid. I move toward it. It smells delicious, and I take a deeper breath.

"I'm here, *Sirena*," a deep voice whispers.

My head vibrates with the sound, and the citrus smell grows stronger, though not nearly as strong as the floral one. Another wave rushes through me, and I whimper. The warm body next to me moves, taking its heat with it, and I cry out, trying to follow it. I open my eyes, needing to know where it went, but there's only a dim light.

I don't know how I know that the body will fix the pain, that it'll make the pulsing waves stop. I just do, like I know my heart beats and my lungs breathe.

"*Please*," I gasp, my eyes blurring with tears. "Alpha, *please*."

A hand cups my cheek, and I turn into it, biting down on the flesh. The voice laughs, and then the heat is back, covering me so completely that I breathe a sigh of relief. It'll stop soon, the heat will make the waves stop.

My body coils tighter with each driving movement of the heat, each point of contact with... with... *my Alpha.*

Yes, my Alpha. He makes the pain go away. He runs his lips down my throat and then again with his tongue, his movements growing faster.

"*Sei perfetto,*" he murmurs against my skin, and I flush.

He says the words like they're his salvation, and I preen under the praise.

"*Cazzo,*" he grunts, the sound breathless. The movement stops, holding me just on the precipice of relief. I whimper, desperate to be thrown over the edge. He kisses my shoulder before biting my skin.

His knot locks into place, and I fall off the ledge, tumbling into the blissful relief on a breathless cry.

"Sleep, *Sirena,*" he says. "You're safe here."

He feels warm. He feels safe. He feels... like home.

And so I do.

I awake all at once, sucking in a hard gasp as reality crashes back into me. Memories flood me, too fast for me to do more than see flashes of them. Arriving at the fundraising event, Jasper's worried gaze as I told him I wasn't feeling well, my mom cornering me until I was helpless to fight her, the awful floral scent of the Alpha that found me in the bathroom. And then Rylan's careful touch. My dad's devastation as Dominic carried me through the hotel.

Dominic... the flash of heat through my body accompanies

the memory of him pressing up into me, forcing his knot into me in the back of the car as the heat overwhelmed me entirely.

Dominic, who hates being an Alpha.

Hates heats.

Hates *me*.

I don't realize I'm crying until an arm wraps around my waist and pulls me into the hard, warm flesh of a man's shirtless body. My body relaxes, still functioning nearly entirely on instinct. Scents mingle in the air, mine the strongest among them. I suck in a breath, trying to get my bearings in the room.

I freeze as the undiluted grapefruit scent overwhelms me.

"Ti sono vicina, Sirena."

Dominic's voice is low enough it rumbles through me, vibrating against my cheek. A flash of desire burns through my body, but I stiffen against it. The haze of the heat is gone, and the memory of his anger when we knotted in the kitchen floods me without my urging. His arm tightens on my waist as his hand trails up my spine.

"Non piangere. Andrà tutto bene," he murmurs.

I don't understand the words, the Italian phrases not ones I've heard him say before. His lips brush my temple as he sets soft kisses into my hair. Like he's worried about me. Like he wants to make sure I'm safe. Like he wants to protect me.

Confusion settles in my stomach.

The door opens with a near-silent click.

"Oh, sorry," Rylan says, exhaustion in his voice. "I didn't realize you were already in here."

The words float over my skin, adding to my confusion.

"She's all right?" he asks. "You've got her?"

Dominic murmurs a soft yes and then the door closes.

I have no idea what to say, what to ask, all the memories blurring together into a jumbled mess, making me hesitate to break the silence. Fear overlays most of them, a bone deep feeling of being unsafe, alone, with no one able to find me.

I sob, crossing my arms over my stomach. Fuck, I hate feeling helpless.

"What do you need, *Sirena*?" Dominic asks as a warm hand brushes away some of the tears. The thread of comfort through his words relaxes me, my body responding to the Alpha's desire to soothe. "Your scent is changed. Do you need food? Or a bath?"

I suck in a breath and force myself away from him. He doesn't want me. He doesn't even want to tolerate me being involved with Rylan or Jasper. He's not *safe*. Regardless of if he knotted me during my heat. Regardless of if he was angry at Eric for nearly forcing me at the hotel. It can't change anything. It *doesn't* change anything. The rage would have been normal, an expected reaction from the force of my induced heat.

He doesn't fight me as I wrap the blanket around me like it's the only armor I have. Which it is. I flinch at the thought.

The room is dim, the curtains pulled across the large windows overlooking the backyard. My chest shudders with my ragged breathing, the confusion giving way to the horrible need to be touched and held and comforted. It's always the worst immediately after a heat, as if the several days long sex-fest isn't already enough to satisfy the instincts. Maybe it is for other Omegas.

"Violet?" Dominic's voice breaks me out of my thoughts.

I drop my gaze to his and tighten the blanket around me, putting more distance between us before I throw myself at his feet and beg for intimacy he refuses to give. His eyes are dark and his gaze unreadable as he watches me move. A sheet haphazardly covers his hips and legs, and his hair is unruly with sleep. Hickeys cover his shoulders and neck, and my stomach clenches.

I refuse to be embarrassed. *Refuse*. But it's a near thing.

"What time is it?" It's a miracle my voice doesn't shake. "What day even is it?"

"It's Thursday," he says as he rolls and grabs his phone from the bedside table, glancing at the screen before setting it back down. The sheet drops low enough to put the hard, defined line of his Adonis belt on display. My core clenches, and my cheeks heat as my scent redoubles in the room. "And it's eleven in the morning."

I breathe through the shaking need for him, trying to focus on whatever will get me through this part of the surfacing. Thursday. Paperwork was due Wednesday. That means the annulment is final. I'm a matchless Omega.

The thought rings through me like a death knell.

I should take a shower and get dressed. I should call Faedra and see how her camping trip went. I should check with the Council about what happens now that I'm classified as matchless in their system. I should contact the universities and rescind my applications.

I should... I should...

"Breathe, *Sirena*." His voice is too warm, too much like safety when I know it isn't.

I shake my head, more tears falling. *Fuck*, I hate coming out of a heat. Everything feels so raw and hyperaware. Is this worse than normal? It feels like it. Maybe because it was forced. Is a nastier drop out of the heat also part of the risks of forcing a heat? I'm not sure. I never bothered looking up the side effects.

"I'll get out of your way," I mutter, twisting away from him. It doesn't matter that it's my nest and that really he should be the one leaving. I can't stand the idea of him getting angry with me again.

He sits up and shakes his head before I can manage more than a few inches toward the edge of the bed. The muscles of his stomach ripple with the movement, his hand held out toward me but not actually grabbing me. I ease away from him, keeping my hands tucked against my chest.

"We need to talk," he says, his accent thicker than normal.

Panic settles in my stomach like a stone. I swallow down bile and shake my head. I can't. Not right now. I can't hear him tell me he's happy I'm annulling the match, that he gets Jasper all to himself again without me being here. I can't hear him tear me down for things that I simply cannot control about my body and its responses to his.

"I need to check in with Jasper," I argue, trying to find an excuse that he'll believe enough to let me leave. I drop one leg over the side of the bed and clutch at the blanket to keep it from getting twisted up.

His jaw clenches, a muscle ticking along his neck.

"Take a shower first," he says, leaning back on an elbow. "He's out running."

I take the chance.

Why the fuck is he even still in here with me? Had he accidentally fallen asleep?

My pussy throbs with the memory of him fucking me, the muscles still sore from when he knotted me last. The sensations blur with those of Rylan until I can't quite manage to separate out the individual experiences. Except for one. I remember Jasper being part of one of them, his hands gentle in my hair and his lips insistent against mine.

Another wave of desire rushes through me, my scent growing stronger again. Dropping my head, I duck into the en suite and shut the door behind me.

This shower is nearly identical to the one in my room, so it's easy enough to figure out how to get it spitting out water despite not actually spending any time in the nest at all. I chance looking in the mirror and can't quite manage to hold back the flinch. Nearly every inch of my skin is covered in bruises and love bites.

One in particular along my shoulder seems the freshest, the crescent shape a deep, angry purple. Dread and pride twist together in my stomach until I can practically taste it.

The water is warm, the heat of it fogging up the mirror and shower doors and obscuring my reflection.

Thank fuck.

I force my mind to empty as I step under the spray and kick the sheet aside. Breathe through the nose and out through the mouth. I press a finger into a bruise until it hurts, using the pain to ground me as the panic rises in my chest. Time slips away from me, my eyes open but seeing nothing, that intrinsic *need* growing louder every second the men's scents wash away.

I'm not entirely sure how long I've been standing there, the water never growing any colder, when the door opens. I flinch, twisting toward the intrusion, and breathe out a half-sob when I see Jasper's messy blond hair and solemn blue eyes. He crosses the room and holds a hand out to me, not saying anything as I let him turn off the water and guide me out from under the comforting spray. He wraps one of the towels hanging on the wall around me before pulling me into his chest, his lips feathering across my temple.

That ache is back in my chest, that need for contact slicing through me as thoroughly as every nasty word my mother's said. My breath hitches, and his arms tighten.

"Let it out, love," he murmurs.

I shake my head and press my lips into his chest, keeping everything locked inside me. The moment I let it out, I won't be able to stop.

I can't risk that vulnerability. Not when I'm only hours away from having to walk away from him. It's so much worse knowing that he doesn't want to lose me, either. How can I possibly lose him a second time and still manage to get myself off the floor?

Maybe I can convince Dad to let me have access to my trust

despite my mom's anger. Maybe Faedra will let me stay with her for a bit while I try to figure out what to do. Maybe...

Fuck, but I don't want maybes. I want to stay here with Jasper and Rylan. And it's too fucking late for me to do that.

"Get dressed." His voice scrapes over me. He's quick to slide a dress over my head. I hadn't even realized he'd brought it in with him. "Do what you need to feel comfortable. Come out when you're ready. I'm going to get you some food."

Forty-Seven

VIOLET

You can do this, Violet.

I chant it to myself as I brush out my hair until the words seep into my bones. Whatever the Council makes me do, I can do it. I survived the awful heat in March. I survived the fallout. I survived my mother not just at the event but the last five years of being officially designated as Omega.

I'm strong enough to walk into that room and face Jasper for the last time.

I push away from the counter before I can actually lose my nerve.

And then stop dead in the threshold of the bathroom.

Dominic is still sitting on the far side of the bed, though the sheet's been replaced with a set of gray sweats. His eyes are closed, his head tilted back against the headboard, his hands resting on his stomach.

"Come sit, *Sirena*." His voice is a warm caress that has my body singing.

The need to be close still claws at me. That's the only reason I perch on the bed with a few scant feet between us. At least, that's what I tell myself.

The silence extends to the point of discomfort. I reach for something to say that will force this conversation to start so I can cry without him here. My mind catches on the nickname.

"What's that mean? What you called me?"

It's probably nothing good. Though how much worse could it be than your own mom calling you a whore? Her cutting voice in the bathroom twists in my gut, and I have to breathe through my nose to keep from crying again.

Dominic circles my wrist and urges me toward him.

For some bizarre reason I refuse to examine right now, I don't fight him. Instead, I let him urge me back across the bed until we're nearly touching. His brown eyes are dark and full of some emotion I can't manage to name, something I've only ever seen when he's looked at Jasper. Nerves claw up my throat, but I bite them back, forcing a swallow even as my mouth dries out entirely. I try to construct those walls that have kept me mostly insulated from my mother's jabs and barbs since that first time she laid into me about the nose piercing. I try, and I fail.

Maybe it's the fact I'm still in my nest, not even a few hours surfaced from a forced heat. Maybe it's the reality that despite me swearing I wouldn't let myself be vulnerable with this man, most of me wants to throw myself at him until he realizes I'll be whatever he needs, turn myself into whatever has him looking shell shocked when he doesn't think people are watching.

Yeah, like he'd want anything from me aside from my signature on that form so that he doesn't have to give up Jasper. And I've already given him that.

"It means siren," he says.

It takes me a minute to break out of my thoughts and catch up to what he's saying.

"That... doesn't feel like a compliment," I whisper.

The corner of his lip twitches, like he's trying not to smirk. "A beautiful woman luring in a man with her beautiful voice? Perhaps we have different definitions for compliments."

I purse my lips. "Sirens drown the men they lure. It's why they do it."

"*Che cavolo.*" His voice scrapes over me.

My gaze drops to his lips before I can help myself. Even after the heat, honeysuckle blooms from me, though not nearly as strong. He hums, his eyebrow rising in unspoken question, but I shake my head.

"I don't understand women," he mutters after a long silence. "I call you beautiful, and you take it as an insult. I use gentle touches, and you grow more skittish instead of less. Do I need to tie you to the bed so that you will actually listen to me?"

Heat flashes down my neck and onto my chest.

He laughs and shakes his head. "I am not even surprised you like the idea of being tied down."

The door clicks closed, and my heart races. The soft humor drains away from him as he sighs.

"*Cavolo*, I don't know how to do this."

I try to pull away from him. I don't want to hear this from him. Not ever, and especially not now, when I am still sore from where he's knotted me multiple times over the last several days.

"Violet, stop," he says, his voice gaining an edge of annoyance.

My body relaxes, the instincts responding without me willing them to. I glare at him and force my hand out of his grip. He doesn't seem angry. Instead, he twists and grabs a folder I hadn't noticed tucked on the table next to his phone. His gaze is intense as he hands it to me.

My stomach roils, those butterflies back in my throat, and I can't help the trembling of my hands as I take the folder, the rough, thick paper sitting like a lead weight between my fingers.

Was this instructions from the Council of what would be expected from me going forward? Did it contain my official classification as unmatched?

"It's only missing your signature," he says. "We were able to get a week's extension from the Council on the premise of you going into heat."

An extension? They didn't need to file an extension, not unless...

My throat closes.

There's a long silence. I don't move, don't even breathe. He keeps his eyes locked on mine.

"*Mi dispiace, Sirena*," he murmurs eventually. "I have spent my life resenting the designation, the instincts that are so deep they burrow in my bones even when I wish I could dig them out. I hate that I feel chained to them, that they are what controls my life and I am merely a passenger in my own life."

I knew how that felt, had raged against the universe for years when my blood work confirmed my worst fear.

"I am..." He trails off and mutters something in Italian. "I am not the only one who resents it, though, am I? What I am, what I have been forced to become because of my family."

My chest tightens.

I must give something away in my face because he nods once.

"Jasper explained it to me. How it happened for you. I... am ashamed I did not seek to know you better. That I assumed you were like the Omegas I encountered while taking the required learning from the Council." He circles my wrist again, the touch so hesitant I nearly laugh in shock. "I would like to learn, though. Your favorite color. Your favorite meal. How you enjoy your coffee in the mornings. They are intimacies I have enjoyed with

Jasper. I would like them with you, too, if you're able to forgive me for the way I've treated you."

It can't be that simple. There has to be some catch that he hasn't brought up yet. He's hated me from the day we matched, resented me for my designation and the assumptions of what that would bring to his relationship.

"You are welcome to deny it, of course," he says after another minute. "Your annulment is still filled out and could be filed instead." His eyes flash with anger before he runs his hands through his hair and leans against the headboard again. "I will understand if you'd rather not deal with me at all at this point. What I did to you would be considered unforgivable by many. I will not hold it against you if you find you are unwilling to trust me now."

"And if I stay?" I ask. My voice trembles, but there's nothing to help it at this point. "How long until you walk out on me again because you dislike something your body does in response to my own?"

There's a low grunt behind me, and I tense. I twist to see which guy it is, but Dominic stops me with a finger under my chin. He shakes his head.

"I'm done fighting it," he murmurs, even softer than before. "I thought Jasper would be enough. That between him and the rut suppressors, I would have enough meaning to ignore the ache the instincts cause. And perhaps if you were someone else..." He shrugs. "But you are not. You are too enthralling for me to ignore any longer. I don't want to."

The honesty rings through his words. His shoulders are relaxed, and a small smile tips his lips.

Something twists in my chest, and the truth falls from my mouth before I can bring it back.

"I don't want kids."

He cocks an eyebrow.

"I didn't even before I designated. I've... I've actually had two abortions."

Dominic drops his hand from my chin, running it down my arm until he presses it into my own. I'm not entirely sure why I lace our fingers together, but his skin is warm against mine, and some of the tension loosens. His gaze flicks to whoever is behind me. It's like the motion lets me notice them, their warm heat pressing closer to me as they step farther into the room. This time, Dominic doesn't stop me from looking over my shoulder.

Rylan holds Jasper's hand, his grip tight enough his knuckles are white, though Jasper doesn't show any discomfort. Rylan's eyes are intent on me, the green striking despite the dark circles that give away just how little sleep we've all gotten the last several days. His tattoo is marred with bruises. My chest flushes, and his lips tip up into a ghost of a smile.

They pause at the side of the bed. Jasper drops his free hand to Dominic's thigh.

"That's what happened after your heat in March?" Rylan asks after a moment. "That's what pushed you into choosing to be matched?"

I nod. "The Alpha didn't wear a condom. I didn't find out until afterward that he misread my information and thought I was on long-term birth control. I got my IUD as soon as they let me afterward."

Jasper's face hardens, anger stiffening his movements as he leans a hip against the bed. "Did you get him in trouble?"

"I never bothered to follow up with any of it after I reported it to the Haven." I shrug and trace the edge of the folder. "Anyway, I realized I'd rather risk the Council's wrath than put up with heats like that one."

Rylan nods and grabs my open hand, pressing a kiss to my palm before lacing our fingers together.

"Guess the Council really does know what they're doing

with the matches," Jasper jokes, his voice lighter than I've heard since surfacing. I tilt my head, scrunching my nose in confusion. He answers my unvoiced question. "Dominic doesn't want children, either. Rylan and I are more neutral about it. But you've known that about me for a long time."

I have. Since he took me to the clinic when we were dating. I hadn't even designated when it happened.

"Violet?" Rylan murmurs. "Do you want to file the annulment?"

I take a deep breath, looking at each of them, drinking them in, before focusing on the folder in my lap.

My voice is clear when I say, "No."

Forty-Eight

VIOLET

I can't help the moan that rips up my throat as Rylan sets an overflowing plate in front of me at the island. Jasper's the best cook I've ever met. If I hadn't heard how he plays the cello, I'd think his talents had been wasted. The grilled cheese is loaded with tomatoes and bacon, and the simple salad looks perfect, too.

Rylan chuckles as I dig in, a small smirk playing across his lips. My body flushes, my scent flooding the kitchen. He tips his head back and laughs in earnest, his Adam's apple moving in a way that has me wanting to crawl across the damn island to get to him.

Yeah, the crash from surfacing is definitely fading.

"It was practically impossible to feed you," Dominic murmurs from where he stands beside Jasper at the stove. He's leaning against the counter, his hands tucked in the pockets of his jeans.

I'm nearly positive I've never actually seen him in jeans.

Slacks, yes. Tuxedo, yes. Sweats, absolutely. But jeans? It feels almost... sacrilegious. He looks away from Jasper and catches me staring. My cheeks heat as he cocks an eyebrow.

I clear my throat and focus on the food again, my stomach rumbling now that I've realized just how hungry I am.

"Jasper was the only one who managed," Rylan agrees. "He's also the only one you'd let touch your hair. And by the third day, he was the only one who could convince you to use mouthwash, too. Came in clutch there, for sure."

He glances over at Jasper, a soft smile on his lips that lights up his whole face.

"And here he was thinking that first night that he wasn't going to be able to help. Felt so fucking guilty."

Jasper sighs and tips his head back. "Look, not my best moment, all right?"

Rylan nods, his face serious, but his voice is playful. "It's all right. Blowjobs have a way of putting everything into perspective."

My cheeks heat as the memory slams into me full force.

Jasper grins, looking over his shoulder at Rylan. "Practically a tradition at this point."

Curiosity races through me. I want to ask, but my stomach rumbles again, my body making itself very loud in its unhappiness following the intensity of my heat. I start in on the second sandwich.

"Definitely will need another one, *Tesoro*," Dominic murmurs, kissing Jasper's shoulder. He looks at me, his gaze intense. "And your apology gift will be here Saturday."

Something soft wells up in me. For the first time, I don't try to ignore it or force it away.

"I don't need one," I say, my voice hoarse.

"You're getting one regardless," he says.

I offer a small nod and focus on the food, trying to not panic over the fucking whiplash that has happened since waking up in my nest. My mind spins out a bit, trying to reorient myself without becoming a crying wreck. Not matchless. Not alone.

I... I have a match that *wants* me. They're not just tolerating me. Or waiting to wear me down into whatever they've imagined an Omega will be in their minds.

I chance a glance back toward Dominic, but he's texting someone. Rylan runs a hand down my back as he crosses the room, opening the door to the front study that's his music room. Jasper turns and grabs my plate, and his eyes soften as they meet mine. He dishes another sandwich onto the plate before turning off the burner and settling into the seat next to me.

He places the plate in front of me and sets my phone next to it.

"Faedra texted on Monday when she got back from her trip," he says, kissing my cheek. "I let her know you were in heat and you'd check in when you surfaced."

I ignore just how teary my eyes have gotten. I'm *not* a fucking crier. We'll blame the heat. Especially since it was forced.

Nerves claw up my throat at the memory of my mother at the event. I shove them down, swallowing around the lump, not wanting to ruin the mood with the reality of why I was in heat at all.

I send Faedra a quick update. Not even two minutes later, my phone flashes with her call.

I push away the last half of the sandwich, offering it to Jasper. He takes it with an easy smile. After wiping my hands on the towel Dominic tosses to me, I answer the phone.

"Oh my gosh, I'm so glad you're okay," Faedra says once I've offered a greeting. Her words are fast and nearly manic like her mother's often are. "We headed off for our trip on Saturday, and I had my phone off. The *panic* I felt when I got that text late on

Monday? For Jasper to then say you were in heat? Fuck, Vi, do not do that to me again."

"Sorry," I say, chuckling. "I'll make sure I don't accidentally end up in a forced heat while you're out of town next time."

Dominic's growl is loud enough that Rylan's soft guitar playing cuts off for a heartbeat. Faedra doesn't say anything, going so quiet that it's only the background noises of a crowd that tells me the call hasn't dropped.

"I'm sorry, say all of that again but slower," she says after a minute.

I repeat the sentence. Faedra chokes when I reiterate it being forced.

"Please tell me it wasn't by him," she says. "Oh my god, Vi. I will get on a plane right now. What the actual hell?"

Jasper kisses my shoulder again.

"It wasn't him. I..."

I glance at Dominic and then Jasper. We haven't actually talked about the whole my-mother-drugged-me thing yet. Do they know it was her? Are they waiting for me to bring it up?

Jasper whispers, "Authorities have it in hand."

I nod and let my lips brush over his cheek.

"It's still being sorted out. But I'm safe, so don't you dare have that guilty look I know is on your face right now," I say, firming my voice so she won't fight me. There's a loud cheer in the background. "Where even are you?"

"All right," she says, drawing out the syllables in her suspicion. "I'm at a baseball game. Logan's client is playing for the first time after being... Crap, I forgot the term. Called up? I think that's right. He got moved from a lower team to the big team."

Dominic rounds the counter, letting his hand brush along my shoulders before disappearing toward the bedrooms, his focus still on his phone. A minute later, the nearly silent sound of his shower filters down the hall.

"Does this mean he groveled enough that you're not submitting to be matchless?" Faedra asks when I don't say anything.

"It was a pretty impressive grovel," I say. Jasper tenses but kisses my shoulder again. "It helps he did it shirtless. And some parts of it were in Italian. Have you ever been given a pet name in another language? It's something *else*, Fae."

Faedra laughs. "Oh my gosh, Vi. You're wild." There's a short pause. "I wonder if Jude knows enough Latin," she says, trailing off.

I toss my head back and laugh.

"You didn't hear that," Faedra says, and I just *know* her cheeks are bright red right now.

"He also said he's getting me an apology present even though I said it's unnecessary," I offer, moving away from the topic.

"*Good*," she says, fire in her voice. "As he should. I can't even *imagine* how much that must have hurt. Just the thought of it has me freaking out."

I hold back my cringe. It's definitely not something I want to repeat ever.

"So now that the insanity of my week is resolved," I say dryly. "Let's move on to more fun topics. Like me flying out there for my birthday next month."

Jasper raises an eyebrow but doesn't immediately turn down the idea.

"Can the guys get enough time off?" she asks.

"Jasper and Rylan are on summer hiatus. And Dominic doesn't really need to request time off." I hold my breath, waiting to see if she'll ask about what job could possibly not need time off. When she doesn't, I say, "Besides, it'll keep my mind off of all these graduate program applications I have out that don't have special parameters for newly matched Omegas. I won't find out until *August* on some of them. You're so fucking lucky already knowing you've gotten into your top choices, girl."

She laughs, light and bright, and I smile at being able to smooth over her worries even from several thousand miles away. "Sounds like a plan. I'll chat with the guys and let you know, all right?"

She hums, and a man murmurs something too low for the phone's mic to pick up.

Probably for the better, anyway, since Faedra's breathless when she says, "We need to go. Send me pictures of his make-up present!"

"Of course," I say, smiling, letting her happiness embolden my own.

Jasper hums as I set down my phone. "How are you feeling?" he asks, his voice soft.

I breathe in the smell of his cologne, leaning my head against his shoulder. "Good. Tired. I'm typically tired coming out of a heat, though. Cautiously happy about signing the final paperwork later." He nods and wraps his arm around my waist. I swallow around the lump in my throat again. "Nervous to bring up the elephant in the room."

He hums and squeezes my waist. "Let's start with a nap. We can talk about Sienna's bullshit when you're not feeling so out of it."

Sienna's bullshit.

He knows. Do the others know, too? Jasper isn't one to keep secrets. I'm sure he told them as soon as he figured it out. I pull away from him, trying to gauge how he feels about all of it. His eyes are hard, his jaw tight enough that a muscle ticks in his cheek.

"Let's get you rested and feeling better, and then we'll talk about it," he says again, urging me to my feet. "It'll wait until this evening."

 Forty-Nine

JASPER

Violet's more nervous than when she ate lunch, though she's doing a really good job of hiding it. She twists a finger in the corner of her napkin and hums to the low music playing in the restaurant's speakers. Maybe it's because we took her out somewhere public, though the secluded table at Dominic's favorite restaurant is hardly the place to find wandering eyes. Maybe she's worried about talking about the fundraising event. Or maybe it's the unsigned match finalization that has her so anxious she won't even look at us.

I reach across the table and squeeze her hand.

"You good?" I ask her.

Her gaze snaps to me, her cheeks darkening with a blush. She nods and tucks a strand of hair behind her ear.

"I'm fine," she says.

Rylan leans into her, letting his shoulder brush hers as he palms her thigh. His throat is still covered in hickeys that he didn't even try to hide, but so is Dominic's where he sits beside me. Every single one she put on me is low enough I can hide it with ease. A flash of heat shoots down my spine at the memories of her putting them there over the last few days.

I force my mind away from the thought. We've had a six day sex-fest. There's absolutely no reason to be consumed with more right now. Besides, I only get to watch her sign this document once. I want to fucking enjoy it without a boner distracting me.

The waiter drops off our ordered drinks and appetizer before disappearing into the rest of the restaurant, sliding the frosted glass door closed behind him.

Violet blows out a breath.

"I know that you guys planned this so signing the finalization feels special," she says.

Rylan smirks even as Dominic raises an eyebrow.

"And the fact that you guys managed to thread the needle between public enough I feel special and private enough I don't feel like it's just a damn display is impressive." Her voice goes a bit ragged as she continues. My chest loosens at the compliment, and I take a quick sip of water. "But I can't sign it."

I choke. Dominic runs his hand down my spine as I try to calm my sore throat without making a giant scene. Rylan leans back, his eyes just as wide and shocked as I'm sure mine are. Before any of us can decide what to say to break the awkward as fuck silence, Violet grimaces, her nose scrunching.

"Shit, that came out wrong," she groans. She drops her head into her hands, rubbing at her eyes as she takes a deep breath. When she drops them back to her lap, she laces her hand with Rylan's and looks first at Dominic and then me. "I meant that I can't sign it until we talk about Saturday. I can't have my mom hanging over this memory."

Dominic clears his throat and leans forward, resting his elbows on the table and his chin on his clasped hands. I rest my hand on his thigh, and he hums, his purr kicking to life for the first time in days. More of the nerves fall away from me.

"All right," Rylan says. "We've figured out that she's the one who did it. And we're marginally sure as to *why* she thought something like that was excusable. What I don't understand is why she thought Fuckboy Extraordinaire was a better match for you than us." He smirks and brings her hand to his lips, kissing her wrist. "But I'm probably biased."

I laugh. "I mean... I'd let your dick cloud my judgment, too. Pretty sure you get to be biased."

Violet giggles, her nose scrunching again. The sound is lighter than it's been all day. I can't help but smile, and Dominic relaxes beside me.

"I imagine it's because on paper he's perfect," she says, wiping her eyes before her happy tears can smudge her makeup. "He's young, attractive, and apparently the heir to a sizable ship construction company here in LA. It would have reflected back on her really well. And I imagine she would have positioned herself so that Dad felt he had to try and acquire the company once we were—" She chokes on the word, coughing. "Once we were bonded. She'd probably even frame it as a way to get retribution for him overstepping."

"She's truly only concerned with her own image," Dominic says, disgust warring with anger in his voice.

Violet nods.

"I have to ask," I say. "Why the hell are you calling him Fuckboy Extraordinaire? Do you know him from somewhere?"

She grimaces. "He went to UCLA."

Rylan chuckles, but it's not a happy sound. "He forced her into a very loud public conversation the first time I took her out. It's what I named him after the fact."

Dominic grunts. "That explains why it looked like you'd been punched when you realized who he was on Saturday."

"Didn't expect him to be at something like that, to be honest," Rylan says, scratching at his tattoo. "Figured he was playing at being rich, not actually rich."

"What happens next is up to you, *Sirena*," Dominic murmurs. "Do you want to confront her about it?"

Violet purses her lips and messes with the Old Fashioned sitting untouched in front of her. "It won't be made public?" she asks.

"Unfortunately, it's not an option," I say. "The detective made it clear that the odds of her actually being convicted are extremely low."

She mutters a curse and sighs. "Then yes," she says, looking at each of us in turn. "I'm ready for her to be out of my life. I think confronting her is best. The sooner the better."

Dominic nods, then reaches into his suit jacket where it's draped over the back of his chair. Rylan turns, too, grabbing the folder containing the finalization paperwork. Blowing out a breath, I pull the small ring box from where I've had it stashed in the pocket of my slacks since getting ready this evening.

One thing I've still not adjusted to with having access to substantial wealth is the incredible speed at which expensive items and events can happen. A single call to the jeweler this afternoon, and the stacking rings were ready and delivered to Dominic before we ever left for dinner.

Violet's throat ripples with her swallow.

"You didn't have to get them," she says, her voice now shy and unsure, like when we realized Sienna had fucked us over in her dorm room. "It's not... I mean..."

She trails off as Rylan turns to her, twisting in his seat until his knees brush her thigh. He sets the form in front of her, a single pen resting on it, and then digs out the ring box from his pocket. With a flick of his wrist, he opens it and lays it on the paper, twisting it so the ring inside faces her.

"We know we didn't have to get them, pretty Omega," he says. Her cheeks darken, and he smirks. "Just let us spoil you. It's going to happen anyway, so you might as well get used to it."

She cocks an eyebrow, and I know she's about to say something sassy that has me wishing we were alone so I can fuck her. I cut in before she can really get going, opening my own ring box and setting it on the form beside Rylan's. Dominic's not nearly as flashy about it, sliding his beside mine and then taking my hand, running his thumb across my knuckles.

Violet stares at the rings and the paper, her eyes darting across all of them like she can't quite decide where to focus first. Tears flood her eyes, and she wipes one away as it falls over her lashes.

"Fuck, I'm not a damn *crier*," she mutters even as another tear slowly tracks down her cheek. "I just... I didn't think it would be this emotional."

She picks up my ring first, pulling it from the box and slipping it onto her finger. The light pink stones set around the gold band blaze against her skin. She pulls Rylan's next, his nearly identical to the one I chose, though the gemstone he picked made for a darker pink. Dominic's is entirely different, though it complements ours. She pulls it last, twisting it around in the dim light of our secluded table. The two gold bands intertwine, small white stones set between the curves. She adjusts how they sit on her finger, letting Dominic's sit between mine and Rylan's.

Before any us dare to break the silence, she signs the paperwork and moves it away from her still full drink.

"Thank you," she murmurs. "This is better than I imagined it could be when I filed for matching in March."

My heart soars. Because that? That's everything I've ever needed her to say about being with me for forever.

Fifty

RYLAN

Violet starts toward her bedroom, the simple black dress hugging her ass in a way that makes my dick stand up and take notice. It doesn't seem to care that we've just made it through the most extreme heat I've ever been a part of. She glances over her shoulder as I groan, low and mournful, my eyes still stuck on the way the fabric is moving over her body. She smirks, her eyes lighting with mischief, even as she starts pulling pins from her hair.

I hadn't realized she'd *put* pins in her hair. Where did she even hide them? Her hair had been down, for crying out loud. Jasper pauses beside me, his hands tucked into his pockets. Without saying anything, he eases something into my hand.

I glance down at the small black bottle before grinning.

"Really? You feeling up for it?" I ask.

"Are you?" He raises an eyebrow.

I palm the nape of his neck and pull him into me, his body a hard line against mine. His kiss is soft and curious tonight, a contentment about it that I haven't felt since we were matched a month ago. Happiness settles deep in my chest, and I pull him even closer to me, wrapping an arm around his waist and tucking my thumb into the waistband of his slacks. His cock lies hard and heavy against my hip, and I can't help but smile.

"Fuck, Jas," I mutter against his lips, and he laughs, the sound as light and free as I feel.

"*Sirena*." Dominic's voice is full of humor. "It looks like we might be left out of tonight's festivities. Seems wrong given you are why we are celebrating, but I've never claimed to understand Rylan."

Violet's laugh reverberates through the large room. Jasper smiles against my lips even as he works to get the buttons of my shirt undone. The third one down, he gets frustrated. With a grunt, he rips it the rest of the way and tosses it behind me.

"Hey," I mutter, "that's supposed to be my move."

"You got to do it last time. Figured it was my turn," he says, cupping my face and twisting his fingers into my hair.

Fair enough.

Dominic sighs as he strides past me.

"The living room rug isn't nearly as comfortable as it looks," he says, the same dry humor lighting his voice. "Didn't you learn that rugs are deceptive, Rylan?"

"Worth it," I mutter, tucking the bottle of lube into Jasper's back pocket so I can work his own shirt off. I run my hands up his stomach, smirking as his muscles clench from the touch.

Fuck, I love doing this with him.

"Maybe we can convince them to do it in my room," Violet says, just as snarky as Dominic. "At least then I'll get to watch and enjoy their scents after they fall asleep."

Dominic laughs. "You sure you're ready to watch one of us knot Jasper, *Sirena*?"

I can hear her choke on her breath over Jasper's groan as I

bite his collarbone, pulling the skin between my teeth to make sure it marks. Dominic laughs, and it skates over my skin, full of promise. A moment later, he crowds behind Jasper, tilting his head to the side and biting just behind his ear.

Jasper's surprised gasp has my dick twitching and a shiver racing down my spine.

"Except I'm pretty sure it's my turn, *Tesoro*, not his," Dominic murmurs.

Jasper's groaned words aren't really intelligible, his hands digging into my stomach.

I sigh and pull away from them. "You always argue that it's your turn."

Jasper grabs my waist, keeping me from stepping around them, grinding his hips into mine.

"Fuck me, at least let us get to a bed," I grunt.

Dominic wraps an arm around Jasper's waist and twists him around, urging his legs around his hips and walking deeper into the hall. Violet hums, and her eyes are wide, her pupils blown out, as I cross the room and take her hand.

"You're sure you're good?" I ask, running my lips across her jaw.

She rubs her legs together, her breath shuddering out of her. "Mm-hmm," she manages to say as I bite the sensitive spot below her ear. "Just watched the hottest fucking thing of my life. Totally fine."

Laughing, I pull her into my arms and follow the guys down the hall, kicking her door closed behind me to keep our scents from dissipating. She hums and runs her tongue along my throat, tracing the double snakes like it's her fucking job. My dick pulses again, my scent so strong it's suffocating in the space with her scent blockers still on.

Dominic already has Jasper naked and kneeling on the bed, his eyes glazed over and his shoulders red with love bites. The unassuming black bottle of lube is perched on one of Violet's nightstands. Jasper groans as Dominic starts to fuck him, his invasion slow and controlled just like everything else about him.

Violet whimpers, trembling where she stands in front of me.

"And here you gave me shit for starting without you," I mutter, shaking my head.

I kiss Violet's shoulder and ease the zipper of her dress down. The second the fabric is pooled at her feet, I'm easing off her bra and scent blockers, groaning as her honeysuckle floods the space like a fucking tsunami. The desperate, spicy edge is gone from it, the ultimate proof that her heat has really subsided.

I shove my slacks and underwear down before kneeling on the bed, just far enough away from Jasper that I can thread my fingers through his hair. He moans at the touch, twisting so he can bite my wrist.

Laughing, I hold my other hand out to Violet. She stands at the foot of the bed, her chest flushed and her nipples peaked, slick already starting to slide down her thighs. Her eyes are wide as she looks between the three of us.

"Come here, pretty Omega," I murmur.

She bites her lip, messing with the industrial piercing. I raise an eyebrow and wiggle my fingers.

She giggles and climbs onto the bed. "Where do I..." She trails off. "This is way wilder than anything I've ever done. I'm starting to understand how Faedra feels when I say something a bit scandalous."

Jasper laughs, though it's more than a little breathless. I guide her to me, kissing her until the nervous tension eases away from her and those little whimpers she makes are crawling up her throat nearly continuously.

"Don't overthink it," I murmur, and she nods. "And the first couple minutes are awkward. Always."

She giggles, and I nip at her lip, grinning when the laugh cuts off on a hard gasp. Her scent gets stronger, and it blends with Dominic's and mine so seamlessly, it's addictive. I pull away from her, turning her until her back presses up against my chest. Jasper doesn't hesitate, leaning forward and kissing her, cupping her face and twisting his hands into her hair.

I notch my cock into her entrance, holding her hips to keep her from moving, and then ease into her. The moment I'm sure she's adjusted and that I'm not hurting her, I ease her forward onto her elbows. She whines as Jasper releases her, and I laugh.

"Give him just a minute, pretty Omega," I murmur, my voice already haggard.

Dominic palms Jasper's throat, keeping him kneeling instead of following Violet to all fours as she opens her mouth and flattens her tongue in universal permission. Jasper groans with the first swipe of her tongue, his legs trembling from Dominic's movements already.

As promised, the first few minutes are awkward, trying to figure out the pace that accommodates us all. And then it suddenly clicks.

Violet's lips wrapped around Jasper are a fucking *sight*.

My body is wrung out from the last six days, my stamina nonexistent. My eyes unfocus as I work to hold out, focusing on the feel of Violet in front of and below me, her curves soft and molding to my hands as I trace down her spine and twist her hair around my fist.

"Love," Jasper grunts.

She hums. He nods, not pulling away as he curses under his breath and his body shakes with his release. The moment I know she's safe, I pull her up against me and circle her clit, focusing on her body falling apart against me as her release rockets through her. Her whines get louder, her scent so incredibly thick around us. She clenches around me, and I'm gone, my orgasm shooting down my spine and through my legs. My cock jerks inside her a second before my knot swells.

"Oh *fuck*," she gasps.

She collapses against me, her cheek against my shoulder, and I kiss her temple.

Dominic grunts, and then Jasper moans. He grabs my hand, lacing our fingers together, and I run my thumb over his knuckles. We're a mess of limbs as I guide Violet and me around to lay on our sides, managing to not move my knot so much that it hurts her. She hums as Jasper kisses her, his smile soft.

"Love you," he murmurs, and she smiles.

"Good," she whispers.

DOMINIC

I run my thumb over the seam of the ring box tucked into the pocket of my slacks as I lean against the threshold of Violet's open bedroom door. It's already lost the smells of our foursome from the other night, the sheets changed and one of the windows open on the far wall. The rest of the room is messier though, small items strewn about like she couldn't bring herself to put them away.

A small collection of porcelain elephants catches my attention where they rest on a simple bookshelf against the wall opposite her bed. They're white with painted designs, each elephant a different highlighting color. They're the exact opposite of Violet, and I almost laugh at the irony. She is anything but fragile and dainty.

I force myself to focus on why I'm actually standing in her door like some deranged lunatic.

She sits on the sofa, tucked into the corner, her legs crossed and her hair pulled back in a messy clip. A smattering of papers surround her as well as an unassuming though expensive laptop that's resting on the cushion in front of her, the screen turned away from my viewpoint at the door. The late afternoon sun reflects off the ocean, gilding her in light, making her seem ethereal.

She glances up as I tap my knuckles against the door, her eyebrows drawn low, her lips bracketed with tension.

"Everything all right?" I ask, my gift for her momentarily forgotten.

She nods, her gaze growing shy. "Just sorting through the last couple graduate applications. These ones are more involved because they offer accommodations for Omegas. I have to submit my blood work and confirmation from the Council as well as the match finalization."

"You have what you need?"

I haven't actually seen the finalization paperwork since signing it Wednesday while she was still in the depths of her heat. Not beyond watching her sign it Thursday night.

When she nods, I ask, "May I come in?"

She tilts her head. "What would you do if I said no?"

There's a bit of sass in her voice, and I raise an eyebrow.

"Suppose I'd try to lure you to my room with the promise of Kung Pao chicken," I murmur. "Though *Mamma* would be disappointed to learn that her own food would not be as alluring to you."

Her cheeks darken. "Where'd you learn I like Kung Pao?" she asks, her voice as soft and unsure as it had been when she'd realized we'd gotten her the customary stacking rings.

"Can I come in?" I raise an eyebrow.

She swallows hard and bites her lip for a moment before nodding.

"Will you tell me where you learned that now?" she asks as I cross the space.

She gathers the papers and sets them on top of her laptop, moving both to the floor on the other side of the sofa, leaning over the edge to manage the reach. Her shorts ride up, revealing the line where her thighs meet her ass, and fuck if my dick doesn't get hard at the sight.

I stretch my neck and breathe through my nose, reminding my body that we didn't come here to fuck her. Not that she'd even be interested, and I don't blame her. The ring box sits heavier in my pocket at the reminder of my own selfishness. Her lips are pursed as she resettles into the corner cushion, her expectation clear.

"I've been trying to make up for the last month," I say. "I'm not sure you want to actually know my information sources, though."

She tilts her head again before nodding once. "Yeah, I probably don't want to know just how easy it is to find out things like my preferred foods." Her eyes narrow. "Unless you have some in with the Council. Then that type of info would make sense."

I smirk. "Not me. Victor."

"That... makes a lot of sense, actually," she murmurs. She pulls the clip from her hair and runs her hands through it, frowning.

While she's distracted, I pull the ring box from my pocket and perch on the coffee table, letting my elbows rest on my knees as I lean toward her. Her hazel eyes are bright but guarded when she focuses on me again, her hands held limp in her lap and her legs crossed.

"I'm aware that this doesn't fix what I did to you, *Sirena*," I say, twisting the ring box around in my hands. "And I have no expectation that you'll actually choose to wear it. But in my family, you put your money where your mouth is. It's not often I am the one paying, but I'm willing to get used to it if it means I have a chance to build something with you."

Her heart flutters in her throat, but her breathing is steady.

I continue, not dropping my eyes from hers, making it as clear as possible just how serious I am about all of this. "I wasn't lying when I said I resent just how out of control my designation makes me. I often feel captive to desires that aren't wholly my own."

She nods. "I can understand that."

"I imagine you can."

A nearly-there smirk, and she messes with her industrial piercing.

"I won't get it right." Admitting the weakness tastes like ash, but I don't back down from the reality. "There will be more times when I offer you something like this. I'm sorry for those, too. For every time I will inevitably hurt you." She nods. I lay out the rest of my truth. "You are the only Omega I've ever wanted to figure this out between. No other has made me want to learn the balancing act between these instincts and my life as I would like to live it. I'm not expecting it to be easy. But I hope you will give me enough of a chance to build something that will weather whatever our lives throw at it."

A silence descends between the two of us, her eyes roving my face, like she's trying to see into the depths of me. I do my best to let her see it all, the vulnerability chafing. I'm ready to crawl out of my skin and lick my metaphorical wounds in my own room away from her searching gaze when she nods once.

She drops her legs, letting her feet settle onto the fluffy gray rug under the furniture.

"I'm approaching this pretty damn blind myself," she admits, her voice softer than I've heard before, the vulnerability weaving through it twisting my heart and settling that instinctive need to take care of her. "My parents' match is... Well, my dads only stayed because they didn't want to lose their kids. They love each other but tolerate my mother. And she does even less for them. I'm sure I will also need to apologize from time to time. I've just wanted the chance to try."

I offer my hand, and she presses her palm into mine, her fingers wrapping around my wrist. I run my thumb over her knuckles. The purr kicks to life nearly immediately. She tenses, her eyes widening in her sudden fear. My stomach clenches, and I tighten my hold on her even as I let the purr grow louder.

She swallows, and I watch the movement ripple through her throat. My scent explodes around us, stronger than I've grown accustomed to from the lack of suppressors.

"I've gone off the suppressors," I murmur.

Her eyebrow rises, and her hand flexes in my hold.

"Why?" she asks.

I shrug, and she purses her lips.

"Another place to put my money where my mouth is," I explain. "If I'm truly done fighting, then there's no reason for me to suppress the instincts."

"All right," she says.

I squeeze her hand and then open the ring box, twisting it so she can see the ring nestled between the black velvet.

"Holy shit," she breathes, and I can't help but smirk. "It's beautiful."

She takes the ring, adjusting the stacking set to her other hand and sliding the large emerald cut solitaire diamond onto her left hand like it's an engagement ring in truth. It's fucking perfect nestled against her golden skin, the yellow gold blending beautifully just like her other jewelry. Too much of me settles in the knowledge that there's such a clear mark that she's *mine* where everyone will see.

Her eyebrow cocks as she takes me in, her gaze seeing more than I'd honestly like.

"You like seeing me claimed?" she asks. There's no coy undertone, just open curiosity. When I nod, she hums. "Is it you that likes it or the instincts?"

I shrug and set the ring box behind me on the coffee table. "Both. *I* like it. A lot. In the same way I like making sure the world knows Jasper is mine. How much of that is me being a selfish asshole and how much is the instincts? I'm not sure they're all that separable at this point." She twists her hand, letting the diamond catch the light. "It's the same with wanting to bond."

She freezes, her gaze snapping to mine. I hold back my flinch. Didn't mean to actually bring up the thought I've had since fucking her in the back of the car on our way home from the fundraising event a week ago.

"I always assumed I wouldn't bond," she says. "Escape hatch and all that."

"Makes sense." I run my hands through my hair, closing my eyes to keep from making an even bigger fool of myself. I came in here to apologize, not ask for her to put out and then form an unbreakable link with me. "I always assumed the same. Don't worry about it."

Silence stretches between us until even I can't stand the awkward feel of it. When I focus on her, her head is tilted, a thoughtful furrow to her eyebrows, and her hands are twisting into the hem of her simple black shirt.

"I'm not so scared anymore," she whispers. "I had an escape hatch. I was ready to use it. I think... I don't think I need it anymore."

I don't dare breathe.

Cavolo, this is not what I planned on happening, but I can't find it in myself to be regretful.

She adjusts again, spreading her legs wider and leaning

toward me, letting one hand land on my knee. Her gentle tracing of my slacks' seam is nearly unnoticeable, it's so light.

I palm her cheeks and run my thumb over her cheekbone, breathing in her explosion of perfume around us.

"I don't want to hurt you again," I murmur. "I don't trust myself to not lose control."

I cringe away from the admission. I'm supposed to be the one that protects, that knows what I'm doing. But I've never fucked an Omega off the suppressors before. And fucking with possibly bonding? My cock aches, and I feel the haze of the rut fluttering around the edges of my mind.

Her eyes are wide as she nods.

"Let's just... see what happens," she whispers.

I press my lips to hers, keeping the kiss soft and exploratory until she shifts in her seat and whines in the back of her throat. Her voice washes over me, and that haze grows stronger.

"More."

VIOLET

Dominic's touch is so gentle, I'm halfway convinced it's someone else. Except his grapefruit scent entwining with my own denounces that possibility. His callouses catch on my skin as he moves to twist his hand into my hair, pulling me closer to him. I drop to my knees, wedging between his legs, and run my hands up his thighs.

His purr kicks up again, and I melt under the sound.

How can someone become so pivotal to your life in the span of days? It can't be the fact he helped me through a heat. Or at least not entirely. I've had other Alphas before, and I didn't crave them like this, didn't want them to mark me so permanently the way I do him.

His jaw clenches and his hands tremble.

"*Cavolo, Sirena,*" he mutters. "I'm going to fuck this up."

Maybe. But I might, too. And isn't that a wonderful thing to share? To understand your partner well enough to know that they'll forgive you if you're too abrasive with them?

I guide his hand down my body until he palms my breast.

"Touch me," I murmur. "I'm not fragile. You saw me through my heat. You know."

His eyes flutter shut as he swallows, his Adam's apple bobbing. He traces my nipple through the shirt, and I clench my thighs, my slick already soaking through my panties.

"Please, Dominic." The plea is desperate, practically a whine. My scent grows stronger, and I run my hands up his stomach, undoing buttons as I go. I push his shirt off his shoulders and lean forward, licking up his sternum.

His purr cuts off all at once, and there's a moment of blind panic, my body remembering what happened the last time. He palms the back of my neck and pulls me away from him, forcing my mouth wide as he kisses me with a desperation I've never felt from him before. Even our first time, there was an edge of irritation, of hatred to his movements. And the couplings during my heat were different entirely.

None of that is here now.

His hands are steady as he eases the shirt over my head. And then he groans, low and deep in his throat like he's dying.

His groan sets me aflame, and I scrabble at his belt.

"*Cazzo, non indossi il reggiseno,*" he breathes.

I pull away even as my chest shudders with my ragged breathing.

"What does that mean?" The question fades off into a moan because he traces one nipple and then the other, pinching each of them just hard enough that a flash of heat shoots through my core.

"You're not wearing a bra." His admission is just as low and tortured as the first time. My chest flushes, and he laughs, pinching my nipples again before pulling one into his mouth.

A rush of slick soaks my panties and coats my thighs. I whine, pulling away from where I'm undoing the button of his slacks to twist my hands into his hair, my eyes fluttering closed at the onslaught of sensation.

"Fuck, knot me please. Bond me." The words are ragged and desperate, a gasped plea between swipes of his tongue along my skin. My fingers clench in his hair as another bolt of pleasure works through my body. "I want to know what it feels like, what *you* feel like."

Whatever was holding him back breaks entirely. He pushes up from the table, grabbing me and lifting me until my legs can wrap around his waist.

Fuck, that will never *not* be the biggest fucking turn on of my life. How can he even just deadlift me?

His lips trace down my neck, his teeth scraping over the hollow of my throat in a wicked precursor to what we're about to do. I shiver. Holy fuck, I need him to move faster. He cradles me as he drops us to the bed, his arms taking the brunt of the hit and not jostling me at all. His fingers trace over my waist as he pulls away, pushing off his slacks and dropping them on the side of the bed, his bright brown eyes never leaving mine. His cock juts away from him, a bead of precum already dripping from the head, the ring of his knot just starting to expand. Another rush of slick coats my thighs as I push up onto my elbow and pull him toward me.

"Jasper is going to be angry I am first, *Sirena*," he murmurs, humor warming his voice, as he kneels between my legs and forces them wider, his palms like hot brands on my inner thighs.

I shake my head.

"He'll be excited it's happening," I say. My breath catches as he notches his cock in my entrance, teasing just the head of it with small thrusts, his stomach muscles clenching with each movement.

He hums. "Perhaps. He has wanted me to find a way to make it work so that he can have us all."

I nod and whine, tilting my hips, forcing him deeper. "Please, Dom," I beg.

His laugh is a low, sensual sound that skates over my skin as he pushes into me with one thrust, his hips nestling against mine as he pulls my legs around his waist. He murmurs something under his breath, the Italian too fast for me to have a hope of understanding, but my lack of response doesn't seem to bother him.

He runs his lips up my sternum, setting small bites as he goes, and holy *fuck* is this where Jasper learned that trick? If I thought he'd known how to straddle the line between pain and pleasure, Dominic's threading of that needle is fucking *perfection*. I arch into him, groaning, my whimpers growing closer together with each thrust of his hips. My body sings with pleasure, my skin sensitized and my nipples aching. Arousal shoots through me, so strong I can't help but fall into it and let it sweep me away.

Our scents mingle as he pushes the pace faster, his hands steady on my thighs and his hips never faltering.

"Where, *Sirena*?" He presses the question into the hollow of my throat, his teeth scraping hard enough that I moan and twist my hands into the sheets. "Do you want it visible for the world to see, like a good little traditional Omega? Or do you want it somewhere more scandalous? Somewhere that betrays the way I took you when I forged the bond?"

"Anywhere," I gasp. It borders on begging, but I can't find it in myself to apologize. "I just *need* you. Now."

His laugh skates over my skin. I whine again, arching into him, my body so fucking tight it feels like I'm going to combust.

"All right, *Sirena*, you can have me. Now. Tomorrow. For the rest of our lives."

The confession is like gasoline on a bonfire. He pushes into me, his fingers messing with my nipples, and I fall off the edge, my release pulsing through me. My mind empties as my legs fucking *shake*, my fingers tingling with the aftershocks.

His thrusts grow faster, harder, for a few minutes until the pattern stutters. He curses under his breath, his teeth parting over my collarbone.

The pressure of his knot forcing me into a second orgasm eclipses the sharp pain of his bite. My back bows as I scream, a sudden sensation of outright *pride* filling my chest with a foreign warmth. He kisses the bite as my body eases back down, my mind slowly piecing itself back together. His elbows bracket my head as he pulls away from my skin.

His eyes are bright and open, something very nearly like affection warming them. Nerves rocket through me before I can curb the reaction. His body tenses over mine.

"*Ti sono vicino,*" he whispers, kissing my neck and then across my jaw. "*Sei al sicuro.*"

I breathe deeply, relaxing under him, his affection singing through the bond now forged between us. His body releases its tension, his chest brushing mine as he lowers himself further, brushing his hands through my hair.

"*Sei bella,*" he murmurs.

I preen, and he chuckles. My lids grow heavy as his knot releases us, the rush of cum and slick almost enough to make me blush. Almost.

He pulls away, taking me with him, and then readjusts on the other side of the bed, turning me so that we face each other as he stretches out on his side. That same softness is in his gaze, and I can feel it roaring through the bond.

This time, I don't shy away from naming it.

"*Ti amo,*" he whispers.

Satisfaction sweeps through the link as I murmur it back.

Fifty-Three

VIOLET

Jasper leans his head against my knee, humming along to the song Rylan's picking on the acoustic guitar. I don't recognize it, but it's beautiful. Dominic leans against one of the large stacks of equipment scattered around the room despite Rylan glaring at him twice already.

Dominic's amusement weaves through my chest, and it takes all my control to not give away his humor at irritating the other Alpha. He leans over and runs a hand along my shoulders, tracing the shell of my ear, and I breathe slowly to keep from shivering.

It's not fucking fair, and he knows it.

At least I'm wearing scent blockers despite Rylan trying for five minutes to convince me they wouldn't be needed in the empty space.

His amusement grows stronger. I purse my lips and comb through Jasper's short hair, trying to ignore Dominic behind me. Not that it really works. Nothing has really worked since

Saturday evening. But I guess that's just part of the bonding experience. My stomach tightens at the thought of experiencing it with Rylan and Jasper, too. Since settling into the feeling of Dominic inside my chest—what a fucking wild thought that is— I've been dying to talk about it with Rylan and Jasper, too.

Not that we've had a chance to have more than five minutes together in the last several days, though. Rylan's been slammed with recording responsibilities pushed off due to my heat. By the time he's made it home the last few nights, I've already been asleep in Jasper or Dominic's bed. I really haven't even seen him since signing the paperwork Thursday.

Thus the four of us sitting in the studio together on a Tuesday afternoon.

You create time where you can. And listening to Rylan play is one of those small pleasures I'll appreciate even when we're old and gray.

Jasper's phone rings, and he digs it out of his pocket, keeping his head on my thigh. He taps on a message to read it but closes to his lock screen before I can snoop. He brushes his lips across my knee and then sits up.

It's like the others were waiting for him to move. Rylan cuts off in the middle of the song, standing up and packing away the guitar. He moves through his process with a steady easiness that should *not* be a turn on but that has my core heating anyway.

Dominic chuckles, low in his throat, and pushes off the metal rack, tucking his hand into his pocket before helping me out of the large rolling chair they'd pulled into the room for me.

"Where are we going?" I ask.

"Dinner," Dominic murmurs, leading me to the Alfa Romeo and easing me into the passenger seat.

"I'm not really dressed for a dinner out," I say, the statement very nearly a complaint.

I eye my shorts and fishnets. The types of places Dominic

always chooses are definitely *not* fishnet friendly. Dominic squeezes my hand and murmurs something in Italian. I glance at him, my eyebrow cocked, and he smiles.

Smiles. Not smirks.

It's like the sun fucking shines or something. I'm caught dumbstruck. He laughs at my speechlessness.

"*Sei bella, Sirena,*" he says just loud enough for me to hear.

I blush and duck my head, and he laughs again.

Rylan and Jasper load into the back, neither complaining of the seating arrangement, surprisingly quiet as Dominic puts the car in gear and leaves the studio's small parking lot.

I realize why once Dominic is navigating the rush hour traffic through downtown.

"Jealous I wasn't invited to make out in the back seat," I murmur, raising one eyebrow.

Jasper laughs, the breathless sound skating over my skin and making my nipples tighten.

Maybe we could just skip dinner and order something later. Orgasms sound way better than food right now.

"If they had invited you, *Sirena*, then we would not be on our way to dinner," Dominic murmurs. He reaches across the console and palms my thigh, running his thumb down the outside line of my shorts' seam. "Perhaps on the way home, though."

The restaurant isn't one I recognize, one of the newer pop-ups along the beach south of downtown. It's certainly not something Faedra and I would have ever tried before graduation. I'm sure a plate here costs as much as I made working at the Rowdy Seahorse.

Dominic hands off the keys to the valet while Rylan helps me from the car, tucking my hand into the crook of his elbow and kissing my temple. Jasper and Dominic walk behind us, a wall of heat that has my legs clenching and my breath catching.

Rylan chuckles. "And here I thought you being out of your heat would mean we'd be able to take you out places," he murmurs. "Going to need to start picking locations based off the bathroom situation it seems."

My chest flushes, but I manage to keep a straight face.

"Always so confident," I whisper. His laugh brushes over my skin, and I bask in the feeling of it.

It's a happy enough feeling that it takes me a minute to realize there's already people seated at our table in the back corner, another subtle frosted door partitioning the area from the rest of the dining space. Two men have their heads close together as they discuss something in low voices. Even with their faces turned away, I recognize them.

Tears well in my eyes, and I blink them away before they can mess up my makeup.

"You have turned me into a fucking *crier*," I mutter, elbowing Rylan hard enough in the side that he flinches.

Jasper laughs as he palms the small of my back. "You've always been one, love. You're just in denial."

Papa looks up, his eyes skating down me. Before he can say anything, Dad stands up and crosses the small space. He cups my cheeks, and I try desperately to not cry for real while reorienting myself to them both being here. His gaze is sharp but his touch gentle. After a long, unspoken moment, he pulls me into his chest and kisses the crown of my head.

"I'm so sorry, Violet," he says.

I shake my head. "Not your fault."

His hold tightens, and then Papa is pulling me into his chest, too, his beard scratching at my hair. Dad doesn't let go, though. I don't think I've ever appreciated their combined warmth and strength as much as I do in this moment.

"Darling," Papa murmurs. "I was so worried."

His voice breaks, and every piece of strength and resilience

I've had over the last several days crumbles at the sound. I lean harder into him, wrapping my arms around his waist, breathing through my nose to keep from crying. He hums and runs his hand up my spine. I vaguely hear the guys move around us and settle in at the table.

"We should probably sit down," I mutter into his chest.

His scent cocoons me, comforting me like it's done for the last five years. He makes that almost grunt of a hum, and I relax into him.

Dad kisses my hair again and tightens his hold on my shoulders.

"I've got you, sweetheart," he says. "We're going to fix it, all right?"

"You know?" I don't mean to ask the question.

Dad's hold tightens for a moment before they both nod.

Another bit of my worry and anxiety flows away from me realizing I won't have to relive that night, won't have to remember what Mom said and did to me in that bathroom. I take a deep breath, drawing on my dads' strength, leaning on the pillars they've both been my entire life. When I don't feel like I'm going to dissolve into tears at the drop of a hat again, I pull away and wipe at my eyes.

"She's coming?" I ask.

Papa nods as he laces his fingers with Dad's. He says, "Should be here any minute with Phillip."

They walk with me to the table, pulling out my chair and making sure I'm comfortably positioned between Rylan and Jasper. Dominic sits on the other side of Jasper, his arm thrown across the back of his seat, his fingers just brushing my shoulder.

I glance at him and frown. "You should have warned me."

It's Rylan that shakes his head and runs his thumb along my cheekbone.

"Absolutely not, pretty Omega," he says, his voice warm.

"You would have spent the entire day stressing out about this dinner when it would have changed nothing."

He's right. That doesn't stop me from pursing my lips, though. He smirks at me, grabbing my hand and kissing my palm before I can decide to do anything more extreme than pout. My mother's surprised voice cuts through the quiet.

"Oh."

Fifty-Four

VIOLET

I glance over my shoulder, Rylan's hold tightening around my wrist.

Mom stands just inside the frosted glass door, Father a step behind her. His gaze is tired and frustrated, his shoulders stiff and his lips twisted into a hard frown. It's the least like him I've ever seen. He's normally the happiest of my dads, the one that can always find a silver lining in the storm. His obvious dissatisfaction with Mom has the hairs on the back of my neck rising.

She's dressed to the nines tonight, a gold sequin dress hugging her body and a black velvet clutch tucked under her arm. Her makeup is done more subtly than typical, her eyes popping under the matte brown eyeshadow and heavy mascara. Between her perfect skin and her long black hair that's curled into effortless waves, we could pass as twins rather than mother and daughter.

My mom's small moment of surprise is quickly covered by

her flipping her hair over one shoulder and pinning Rylan and then Dominic with a dissecting once over. Her lips purse as she skips over Jasper entirely and focuses on me, her gaze catching almost immediately on the healed bond scar straddling my left collarbone.

"So happy to see you well," she says. "I wasn't aware you would be joining us. Such a lovely surprise."

The lie isn't even a decent one, falling as flat as her unsmiling eyes. When I don't say anything, she steps around the table and pulls the chair beside Dad.

Papa frowns but says nothing while Dad ignores her entirely. Father sits on the other side of Papa, across from Rylan—and the farthest away from Mom he can manage. I'm sure it's no accident that Dominic is the one nearest to her. It almost makes me feel bad. Almost.

"Oh shoot," I murmur. "Sorry, I forgot to introduce you. Papa, Father, this is Dominic." I grab his hand and squeeze his fingers. His humor is a soft whisper across the bond.

Wait. Humor? What about this does he find funny?

Papa smiles, mischief lighting his eyes. "We've met already, darling." He holds out his hand across the table, and Dominic takes it easily, dropping my grip to do so. "It's nice to see you again, though."

"You've already met?" I ask, my confusion so evident it must seem over the top. Dad nods, his cold gaze cutting toward Mom before focusing on me. "When?"

Father clears his throat while Papa pulls a folder from the bag stashed across his chair.

My eyebrows furrow with my growing confusion. What was going on?

"Dominic flew out to talk with us the day after your forced heat started," Father says, grabbing Papa's hand and lacing their fingers together. "He wanted to get to know us and update us on how you were doing."

Mom freezes for a heartbeat, her gaze flicking down the table, taking in each of my dads. Papa and Father both ignore her entirely, their focus on me. Dad, though, glares at her, not an ounce of softness anywhere in his body. For the first time in as long as I can remember, she suddenly seems unsure, her hands trembling.

"How lovely for him to give an update," she says, her typical chilly demeanor settling back into place. "I'm sorry I wasn't able to join."

Dad's jaw clenches.

"Whatever you need to say. Or nothing at all. It's your choice," Jasper whispers. I run my hand up his thigh in silent acknowledgement. He kisses my temple. "Whenever you're ready, love."

I take a deep breath, relaxing into the bergamot scent of Rylan beside me. He palms my knee as I lean toward him, his hand warm and grounding.

"I don't even need to know why you drugged me," I tell my mother, looking right at her. Her gaze snaps to mine, one eyebrow arching gracefully, her lips pushing into a reproving pout. "Eric found me easily enough once you ripped my scent blockers off. It's not hard to put the pieces together there." She doesn't react even as the rest of the table grows still and silent, like the moments before a tsunami strikes. "What I want you to know is that I'd already met him. He's spent the last year trying to fuck me, including cornering me at a bar last summer."

Rylan's growl is loud and swift, weaving a lethal and violent undercurrent to the already tense interaction.

Mom's eyes flash with surprise, her hand stilling on the stem of her water glass. "It seemed like you hadn't been introduced before," she says, poised and graceful like these types of conversations were normal.

"I don't fawn over every Alpha that I meet. I'm not a sycophant," I say, the words scathing. "Not like you."

Her eyes harden between one breath and the next as her lips pull back from her teeth. "You mind your mouth, woman. I control everything you have. You *will not* talk to me like that."

Papa clears his throat, but she doesn't even notice. Rylan's growl grows louder until Jasper reaches across me and grabs Rylan's wrist.

"What I do want you to know is that I know that you faked the breakup letter," I tell her, anger growing stronger in my gut. I'm almost positive it's wholly my own, but Dominic's stillness at the end of the table has me moderately worried. "I don't know what you told Papa, but I know that Jasper didn't drop by with a breakup note. And I know that because we compared the notes."

Mom pales, her tan skin losing all color even as her eyes widen with fear.

"You watched as I spent *months* thinking I was an absolute waste of space and time, told me there would be other people, that the Council would fix it, when you *knew* it had all been fake. But you know what wasn't fake? How much I fucking *loved* him, Mom. How much I still do. I was a complete wreck for a week when I found out the match the Council had made. It took all my courage to face him thinking he thought I was less than the dirt beneath my feet. But you know who actually thinks that of me?"

There's a long silence, only punctuated by my heavy breathing.

"You," I say, the word cold.

She scoffs and rolls her eyes. "Please, you are so immature. I've done nothing but give you the best chance of being successful."

Whatever else I had thought of telling to her, of saying in the hopes she'd come around and understand my side of everything, bleeds away at her complete disinterest in me.

"Successful like Scarlett?" I seethe, my anger breaking through the careful calm. Her lips purse even as she raises an eyebrow. "Scarlett who is currently filing dissolution paperwork after finding out one of the Alphas in her pack has been sleeping with her best friend for the last year and *got her pregnant*? She did everything you ever wanted of her. Took the diet pills, covered the bruises, wore the dresses that were too tight. And you know what she's gotten? Nothing but fucking *heartbreak*. If that's what success looks like to you, then I *don't fucking want it*."

She blinks, surprise flashing across her face before she can control it.

"How did she find out about Marcus?" she asks.

My mind spins.

Mom knew he'd been cheating on Scarlett? She's known and didn't tell her? Or confront Marcus about it?

She sees my dumbstruck expression and scoffs. "Please, of course I knew. It wasn't that hard to figure out. And Scarlett would have been willing to go along with it if not for you filling her with such ridiculous ideas of love matches and respect. Marcus comes from Old Money. She's set for life."

Anger roars through me, and I start to rise, the need to punch her so great it's overwhelming. Papa grabs my hand, squeezing my fingers. The forced pause helps me breathe through the anger, and I realize it's Dominic's as much as my own. I swallow and settle back in my chair.

Dad takes the folder from Father and sets it in front of Mom.

"We endured nearly thirty years of your bullshit to keep our children, Sienna," he says, his voice colder than I've ever heard. "And now you have just confirmed that you have harmed not one but *two* of them. We submitted proof of you drugging Violet to the Council."

Her mouth drops open, and she breathes, "No."

Dad nods. "Violet's testimony may not be enough for criminal court, but it's plenty for the Council. They've processed an emergency dissolution. You're allowed to keep what is currently in your own bank account. The rest you forfeit as of tonight at midnight. And before you think that you'll be able to move things around to your own benefit, know that you've been stripped of the only other account you have access to. The house will be listed as of tomorrow morning. You are expected to vacate by the end of June."

Mom's eyes are glassy. "But that's only a week."

Papa nods. "Perhaps your *next* pack will not care when you set up their children to be raped and forcefully bonded."

He stands, and Father joins him, their hands still intertwined. Dad stands, too, his eyes so cold my breath catches for a moment. Jasper eases me to my feet, and Rylan wraps his arm around my waist. Part of me fills with sympathy at seeing my mom look so small and broken in her seat. Her eyes are unfocused, her hands trembling where they rest on the folder. And then I remember Eric's awful floral scent and the bruises he left on my body.

"And Sienna," Father says. "Be grateful that Johnathan was concerned in leaving a legacy for our children. Because Kurt and I were ready to let Dominic burn everything you are to the ground. We don't need the wealth. We've never needed it. But you? You are *nothing* without it."

Dominic adjusts his cufflinks and joins Dad as he walks to the frosted door, never looking back at where Mom is still sitting at the table. Rylan and Jasper keep their touch on me, grounding me as I try to process everything even as we leave her behind, too. Papa and Father are a warm wall behind me, keeping me from glancing back.

Instead, Papa kisses the crown of my head. "Love you, darling."

Fifty-Five

VIOLET

"Victor," Dominic mutters into his phone, glancing over at me as he eases the Alfa Romeo into the garage. "*Cosa c'è che non va?*"

Rylan opens my door, so I'm not able to overhear what Victor's response might be. Not that I'd be able to understand it, since his Italian is even faster and lower than Dominic's. I don't understand at least half of what he says on a daily basis. Except for his nicknames. And telling me to go slower and look at him. A bolt of heat rushes through me, and my thighs clench.

My cheeks heat, and he glances at me, one eyebrow raised, his lips pulling into a smirk.

"I have already cleaned up a mess of Lorenzo's this month," Dominic says, his irritation evident. "This was supposed to be a rare occurrence, *fratello.*"

Rylan takes my hand and urges me from the car. Dominic sighs and puts the car back into gear.

"I'll be home late," he mutters. He drops his phone into the middle console, his lips tight and his eyes hard. His frustration is a palpable thing in my chest. I duck back into the car and kiss his cheek.

"Be safe," I say, trying to not sound clingy.

I am *not* clingy. That pit in my belly is just... a desire to be near him. All the time. With his scent covering me until it drowns out my own.

Shit, I might be clingy. Has it been too long since my heat to be able to blame it? I count back the days. Still less than a week. If anyone calls me on my stage five clinger antics, I'm blaming my heat. Or maybe the confrontation with Mom tonight. People are less likely to bitch when you bring up parent problems.

His growl of a response pulls me from my thoughts.

"Always, *Sirena*," he whispers, kissing me until I'm breathless and the car smells like grapefruit.

Yes. He runs his nose down my throat, feeling the need through the bond, and I relax further into him.

Jasper opens Dominic's door and crouches beside him, his eyes full of concern. I bite my lip to keep from whining as Dominic pulls away and focuses on the other member of our pack. Their murmurs are low, blending in with the dim light of the garage.

Rylan guides me into the house as they say their own goodbye, his palm like a hot brand on the small of my back and his bergamot scent surrounding me like one of my favorite blankets.

"I haven't had a moment with you all week," I mutter. It comes out damn near a petulant whine.

Rylan kisses my temple without saying anything. The garage door closes as he sets his things away, his wallet and keys and shoes. I toe off the simple black flats I wore today and cross the room, dropping onto the loveseat that looks out over the cliff.

The patio lights are off, so I can't see the ocean, the black expanse reflecting the room back at me instead.

Rylan's eyes are hot as he stands behind me, his hands propped on the back of the loveseat. He keeps our gazes locked in the pseudo-mirror as he leans over and kisses the top of my head. His purr vibrates through his chest. A rush of wet heat pulses through my core.

Purrs are supposed to be calming, not arousing, but I'm not about to complain about my body's crossed wires. The garage door closes again, louder than before, and then Jasper is kneeling in front of me, his body forcing my gaze away from Rylan.

The words fall from my lips before I can plan for them or make them alluring.

"What about bonding?" I ask in one quick rush of breath.

Jasper's eyebrow rises even as Rylan chuckles, low in his throat. My fucking toes curl. From a *laugh*.

I am so fucking screwed tonight. Or blessed. I suppose it depends on your perspective.

"I can't even make a joke about taking me to dinner first," Rylan says. He runs his hands down my neck and across my shoulders, his purr growing louder. I shiver, goosebumps rushing across my skin. His lips follow them a moment later. "But damn," his voice lowers, "I did not expect that to be what starts our night without Dominic."

"I guess I could have started with my other question," I say. Jasper palms my knees and forces them wide, inching forward until my legs bracket his waist.

The sight of him in the windows? Hottest thing of my life.

"What's that one?" Rylan asks, his voice filled with humor.

He bites the spot behind my ear, and I practically arch off the couch, tilting my head back on a gasp. Jasper slips his fingers under the hem of my shirt, the callouses catching, and I roll my hips even as I force a whine to stay in my throat.

"Your other question, love," Jasper says. "What was your other question? Before we get too distracted bonding you."

"Pretty Omega, I think we already have you too distracted," Rylan says as his lips brush over my ear.

Fuck. Me.

Wet heat pools in my core, and I can't help the small moan that slides up my throat this time. I know the moment one of them pulls away my scent blockers, slick is going to be dripping down my legs and my scent's going to be all over the room.

Someone needs to do it. Fast.

"I want you at the same time," I admit, my cheeks heating.

It's the wildest thing I've asked for aside from the foursome. And I hadn't technically asked for that.

Rylan laughs. "We should probably move to a bed, then."

"And deprive Violet of watching you knot her in front of a mirror?" Jasper shakes his head. "We'll make it work out here. It'll be my knees that pay the price anyway."

My breath catches.

Jasper pulls me to my feet, his lips soft but persistent against my own. There's a rustling of fabric behind us, and then Rylan settles onto the long sofa that faces away from the windows, his cock sitting long and heavy against his stomach, his knot just starting to inflate.

Jasper has me out of my clothes before I can even appreciate the sight that is Rylan right now. He tosses my shirt toward the kitchen, and then his hands are cupping my face and his tongue is delving into my mouth. I shimmy out of the scent blockers, letting them pool at my feet with my shorts and fishnets.

Honeysuckle explodes around us, nearly as strong as when I was in the depths of my heat.

Rylan groans. "Come here, pretty Omega," he says.

Jasper pulls away from me and urges me toward Rylan,

stripping out of his own shirt with one hand. That move is still *so fucking hot*.

Both men laugh as my scent redoubles and my cheeks grow darker.

Rylan's hand is soft as I straddle him. His eyes are bright, his cheeks flushed. I want to slam down on him, take him all at once, but I force myself to be patient. As Jasper digs through one of the side tables, I trace the lotus and vine tattoo that covers most of Rylan's chest.

"Why a lotus?" I ask.

He hums and palms my hips, urging me to rub against his dick, drenching it in my slick. Each small swipe against my clit has my legs shaking.

"They symbolize rebirth," he murmurs. He grabs the base of his cock and notches it into my entrance, tightening his hold on my hip to guide me down. I tilt my head back as I take him to the hilt and his hands trace up my sides until they circle my nipples. "I got it when Dom, Jas, and I moved in together."

"Does this mean I'll get a spot on your skin, too?" The question is breathless, my mind already halfway gone from the sensations of him fucking me.

"Of course, pretty Omega," he murmurs. "Now be a good little girl and tilt your hips back for Jasper."

The cool feel of lube pulls me from the building buzz of my pleasure. Jasper kisses the crook of my shoulder as he eases one finger in, waiting until I relax against him to add a second.

"You keep lube in the side table? How did I not notice that before?"

Rylan laughs. Jasper runs his lips up my neck.

"We keep lube everywhere. I'm not an Omega, remember? It's necessary."

He pulls his fingers away, and I cry out. Rylan palms the base of my throat and purrs.

"Easy, pretty Omega." He brushes his lips with mine. "He's coming right back. He's just making sure he doesn't hurt you. The only screaming we want tonight is when my knot locks us together and we bond with you."

My chest heaves with my pants, my palm pressed against Rylan's chest, as Jasper's heat presses against me again. His invasion is slow and controlled, his dick wedging inside even as my legs tremble and I groan from the overwhelming sensation. Rylan purrs again, the sound comforting to me, and traces my nipples, letting his hand fall away from my throat.

"Good job," Jasper murmurs. "Just relax into it. We'll do all the work."

I close my eyes, focusing on the feeling of them both so deep inside me. I feel so incredibly full, like I might burst from it.

"I haven't fucked anyone like this in a long time," Rylan mutters.

He runs his hands down my body until he grips my hips, his hold hard enough that it'll probably bruise. It only ratchets my arousal tighter, forces me higher onto the ledge.

"I don't remember it being this good." He groans as I sink even lower, my knees spreading a bit. It forces Jasper deeper, too, and my breath catches. "You good, Jas?"

Jasper's murmured affirmative is the only warning I get before Rylan is easing me higher onto my knees. They both slip out. Rylan lowers me back down, and they fill me again. It's somehow even more all-consuming than the first time, and I moan, dropping my head back onto Jasper's shoulder.

His hand spans my throat, keeping me still as they fuck me like they're one unit. That awkward moment Rylan warned me about last week is nowhere, their movements so incredibly in sync that I'm already halfway out of my mind.

Rylan's lips close around my nipple, his teeth scraping over the tight bud.

Nevermind. I'm *completely* out of my mind.

My climax roars through me, and I'm lost to the sensations. My pussy clenches, my legs shake, my toes curl. I can't manage to stop moaning, the sound both desperate and sated. Jasper's ragged groan cuts through the haze, and I feel his dick jerk where it's still so deep inside my ass.

"Jas," Rylan grunts.

"Ready," Jasper murmurs, breathless.

His hand is steady as he urges my head to the side, baring my throat. Lips press to the sensitive spot just under my ear. I clench around Rylan again.

"Shit, pretty Omega, here I come," he says.

He pulls me down as he thrusts up, forcing his knot completely inside. A second later, his teeth break my skin, and I scream. Jasper's hand flexes on my throat, forcing me to stillness when everything in me urges me to *move*, to rock against Rylan so I can feel his knot more acutely. The orgasm is so strong, I can't brace for it.

"Oh fuck, oh fuck," I whimper, mewling as everything in my body overloads.

Another set of teeth push into the same spot, and the pleasure grows impossibly stronger.

"Fuck, Jas, that's the hottest thing I've ever seen," Rylan says.

I can't manage words yet, still overwhelmed by the religious experience that is the two of them inside of me. In my chest. In my pussy. In my ass. They're literally everywhere. It should be claustrophobic but all I feel is pride and safety and... and contentment.

Shock rips through me at the realization, and Jasper stiffens behind me.

"You good, love?" he asks, tipping my head until it rests against his shoulder.

Rylan leans forward, running his lips over my jaw and then

the new bond mark still healing on my neck. Dominic's happiness interweaves with the others, and I bask in the sensation of feeling them all like this.

"Perfect," I mumble. "I'm so fucking perfect right now."

"I love you, pretty Omega," Rylan murmurs before kissing Jasper. "I love you both so fucking much."

I can't help but smile as Jasper whispers it back, his lips soft against my temple.

"Score one for the Council," I say, laughing. "Because I love you both, too."

Their laughs fill me, warmth spreading through my body, and I relax into it.

Because this? This is perfection. And I never thought I'd be able to have it.

Epilogue

FOUR YEARS LATER

JASPER

"Uncle Jas! Happy graduation!" The high-pitched voice carries over the din of everyone already mingling, our large main room overflowing with people. A small body slams into my leg before I can adequately brace for the impact, and I mutter a curse. "Uncle Jas! You're not allowed to say shit."

Rose's bright blue eyes stare up at me, her strawberry blonde hair done up in two twisted buns and her bangs sitting nearly perfect against her forehead. I need to ask Faedra what product she uses because *damn* it has some fucking holding power.

"It's fine, sweetheart," Logan says, his voice full of equal parts warmth and exasperation. "He was just surprised. And it's Violet's graduation."

"Oh. Sorry Uncle Jas. Happy *Violet* graduation." I laugh and run my thumb along her cheek. She purses her lips even as she taps on my leg. "I don't get to say shit."

"That's because you yell it in places that make Momma

blush, and not in the fun way." His voice is warm as he smirks, one eyebrow raised as I laugh. He scoops the toddler up onto his hip and kisses her cheek before turning toward me. "Hey, man, sorry we're late."

I shake my head as he hugs me and I kiss Rose's cheek. Her eyes narrow the exact same way Violet's do, and I can't help but laugh.

"How do you have Violet's expressions?"

"The video calls," Rose answers, grinning.

Another small person comes running through the front door, her unsmiling face focusing on me. She dodges around Kurt and Phillip as she crosses the room. I'm braced for her impact and manage to swing her into my arms before she can take out my knee like Rose.

"Hey, Iris," I say, kissing her cheek, too.

She leans into me, resting her head on my shoulder and running her hand over my collarbone.

"Uncle Jas," she murmurs, the cool, collected tone nearly identical to Jude's. How a three-year-old can manage that level of stoicism is beyond me. Genetics are wild. "Uncle Jas, Momma is tired. She cried."

I look at Logan, frowning. "You guys didn't need to come out here," I say. There's no reason to make Faedra more uncomfortable than absolutely necessary. I'm sure the graduation itself was hard enough for her to navigate right now. "We're more than happy seeing you guys tomorrow at lunch."

"I will miss one of Violet's milestones when I am dead," Faedra seethes as she crosses over the threshold and into our house, Carter a half step behind her. Her lips are tight in an unsmiling line, but there's a mischief in her eyes that betrays her humor. Jude closes the door with a soft touch, his unsmiling eyes softening as he focuses on her, pulling her bag from her shoulder and perching it on his own.

"And I will absolutely *not* be missing one as important as this for anything less than this baby coming three weeks too freaking early," she continues even as Jude threads his fingers through hers and kisses her temple.

The effect of her serious threat is lost with just how breathless she is. The simple green wrap dress looks beautiful on her. She runs her hand over her large belly, grimacing for a moment before breathing through her nose.

I take a step toward her, intent on helping her into a spot she can rest, when Carter wraps his arm around her waist, his gaze full of devotion as he takes her weight into his side. Her moan of relief is loud enough that it stops most of the party, everyone slowly looking toward where Pack Bennett congregates near the front door.

Faedra's blush is swift, and I chuckle.

Violet works her way out of the crowd, her eyes just as hard and intent as Faedra's. The moment the women lock eyes on each other, they squeal, and Violet runs the rest of the distance, wrapping Faedra into her arms the second she's within reach. Her joy moves in one great wave through the bond, and I can't help but smile.

Rylan stops beside me, taking my hand in his and kissing my cheek.

"You feel it, right?" he whispers, low enough that not even Logan pauses to look back at us.

When I nod, Iris lifts her head.

"Feel what?" she asks.

Rylan grins and touches the tip of her nose. "We can feel when Aunt Violet is happy or sad or angry."

Iris purses her lips and tilts her head to the side. "Does she have bites? Like Momma has bites? Momma says they let her feel Daddy and Dad and Papa."

Rose nods and looks over Logan's shoulder, her stoic gaze so intense I feel like I might be under examination. From a three-year-old.

Most terrifying examination of my life.

"But we can't have bites," she says. Her eyebrows draw together as she pouts. "It's not fair. I want to know when Papa is happy when he's at work, too."

I glance at Logan, trying to gauge the right way to approach this. He chuckles, his lips twisted into a smirk, but doesn't offer any kind of words of wisdom. When I turn to Rylan, he shrugs. Not really sure why he'd be helpful, to be honest. I clear my throat and smile at the little girl, trying to not look as awkward as I feel.

"Maybe one day you'll be able to decide to have something like that," I murmur. "But it wouldn't be with your dads. It'd be with someone else you love and care about."

Dominic comes up behind me, his body a wall of heat that has a bolt of arousal shooting down my spine. I just barely feel his amusement and desire through the hazy link. He palms my waist and pulls me into him, my back flush with his chest, and his purr kicks to life, the low sound vibrating through me.

Violet holds Faedra's hand as they walk toward us, Jude and Carter chatting with Kurt. Phillip and Johnathan join us, too, their smiles wide. Everyone hugs Faedra and kisses the twins' cheeks.

Happiness lights my chest, the link with Violet so bright it feels like it's visible to everyone around me. I squeeze her open hand and lean across Rylan to kiss her temple. His own contentment isn't as vivid, but I feel it just the same. He grabs me before I can straighten all the way up, palming my neck and kissing me. Iris giggles, and it kills the mood.

The benefit of being childfree is no little people interrupting us. Though I'm happy to endure for a weekend so Faedra can get a break.

I take a minute to survey the space again now that the excitement of Faedra's family joining has ebbed a bit.

Dominic's family is tucked away in the corner of their own choice, Alessia guarded by her lovers and Sarah tucked under Lorenzo's arm, her own belly just starting to swell. Her daughter clings to her legs, though her eyes are bright and curious as she focuses on Iris in my arms. Victor's hand is held tightly by his wife's, though that's as much contact as they maintain. The bond mark on her neck betrays their devotion, though. Her own belly is nearly as large as Faedra's, her due date only a week or so away.

Liz stands in the midst of her pack, her only child perched on her hip, his eyes the same green as Zach's. Huntley and Mason stand with them, as does Mark and Owen.

Our entire family and friends gathered to celebrate Violet's achievements. My own pride swells in my chest. Dominic hums in my ear before kissing the sensitive spot just below it.

"*Tesoro*, you are making me want to find a room," he murmurs.

"Can I find a room, too?" Iris asks. "Aunt Violet, can I play with your elephants?"

Rylan covers his laugh with a half-hearted cough.

Violet smiles but shakes her head. "They're taking a nap right now," she says, completely serious. "And they get cranky when they can't sleep. They get it from Dominic."

Iris giggles, the sound bright and happy over the din of the party. Dominic murmurs a string of curses under his breath, too fast for the toddler to have a hope of picking up on them. I, however, elbow him.

"Don't promise a good time when you know you can't deliver, Dom," I whisper, tilting my head back so that my lips are hidden.

He chuckles, the sound warm and inviting, and it skates over my skin. Before my dick can decide it wants to get involved, Johnathan holds up his champagne, and Bianca taps a knife against her glass, urging the room at large to silence.

"*Congratulazioni*, Violet," she says once the din of conversation quiets. "*Siamo così orgogliosi*."

Rylan groans. "Please, Bianca, for my sake, let's skip the part where you prove I still don't know any Italian."

Bianca smirks. Faedra laughs.

"Keep going, Bianca. It's my favorite part," she says with a grin. She turns to Violet. "*Ti amo*."

Rylan sighs, and both women laugh. Faedra grabs Violet's hands, her eyes glassy.

"Being assigned to your dorm as a freshman is the best stroke of luck I've ever had. You're the best friend any woman can hope for. I'm so proud of you graduating with your doctorate and starting your research. You're an inspiration for so many people, including me."

Violet wipes her eyes. "Damn it, I'm not a fucking *crier*," she mutters as she hugs Faedra again.

Johnathan smiles, and Kurt laughs.

"Keep telling yourself that, darling," Phillip says, humor in his voice. "Maybe one year it'll actually be true."

Rylan kisses Violet's temple and pulls her around so she's looking at the three of us.

"You're the best thing that's ever happened to us," he says, his Tennessee accent heavier than normal. Dominic hums his agreement, though I can feel it through the link, too. "We're so proud to have you be with us. And this is just the start of a legacy I know will follow you forever. Congratulations, pretty Omega. You fucking did it."

He pulls her into his chest, and I wrap my arm around her waist, kissing her hair to hide the fact that she's crying again.

Dominic's purr gets louder as he runs his hand down her cheek and traces our bond scar and then his own.

All of our friends clap, Liz handing off her one-year-old to Zach so that she can whistle. Huntley laughs but does the same. The raucous cheering grows as everyone converges on us, offering their own congratulations. Her dads are quieter with theirs, quick murmurs as they hug her again once Rylan releases her.

Contentment roars through me, my own mixed with that of my lovers. The four of us take a quick moment once the attention shifts to the food Bianca and Alessia made for the celebration and Faedra takes Iris from my hold.

"I love you," Violet murmurs, looking at each of us in turn. "Thank you for this life together."

"*Per sempre, Sirena*," Dominic murmurs.

"Until the end of time," I offer, squeezing her hand.

Joy sweeps through the bond, and I can't help but grin.

What a fucking life.

Content Warnings

ON PAGE

- Discussion of Abortion
- Toxic Parental Relationship
- Attempted Sexual Assault
- Nonconsensual Drugging
- Fatphobia
- Mild Violence

OFF PAGE

- Parental Death

Acknowledgments

You would think that each book I manage to get to this stage would make writing the acknowledgments easier. I've found it's actually the opposite.

So many people were influential to the creation of Knot Your Business. I'm sure I'll forget to mention some, and for that I'm so sorry. Know that you're still so important to me.

Thank you to Daniel for not being angry when I had to go full nest mode in May to get this sucker finished. Appreciate you. Love you. Always.

Thank you to my book chat girlies who have helped me through every single release. When the Imposter Syndrome is too loud, your hype always helps me keep the boat steady.

Thank you to my Beta readers who were so incredibly patient with me this time around. And whose comments have made for some truly excellent marketing. You're the real MVPs.

And thank you to every single reader that has taken a chance on me and has been patient in waiting for Violet's story. I hope I've done her justice.

About the Author

Jillian has been crafting stories since she was a young teen. She's always had a soft spot for heroines thrown into the deep end without any prior training. And while she, like most of Booktok, loves the dark-haired love interest, she secretly enjoys the blonde, Golden Retriever heroes. Other secret indulgences include the miscommunication trope, surprise or secret babies, and arranged marriages with age gaps.

Jillian enjoys soaking up the sun in Colorado. She can be found most days keeping the children and animals alive. During the summer, she enjoys testing the limits of her mental health by seeing how far into July she can remember to water the flowers and veggies in the garden. She spends most of the winter chasing after her snow loving children while silently cursing that she lives somewhere that actually gets cold.

Also by Jillian Rink

Serendipity Omegaverse

Ready or Knot

Beta

Amplifier Chronicles

Hidden

Haunted